Web of Desire

Jason studied the girl. Despite her shabby appearance, he sensed something untouched about her, some vulnerability that gave him an odd wrenching feeling deep in his gut. He frowned. It must be the brandy that caused him to imagine such things. She was just an uncommonly attractive whore, that was all, a delicious blend of angel and strumpet.

Mirella stared up at him with wide indigo eyes. When he caressed the silky skin of her cheek, her lashes fluttered shut and her lips parted slightly. It was the brandy, she tried to tell herself, but she knew it was not so. This man, her enemy, who was supposed to arouse revulsion in her was instead sending an unfamiliar fire surging through her veins. Her body was turning traitor under the influence of his touch.

His mouth came down on hers, gently but hungrily, as if he were starving for her. Her legs felt weak, and she leaned against him for support. He groaned deep in his throat and molded her even closer to his muscular frame.

Excitement bloomed deep within her. Her mind cried out that she was letting this seduction progress into a dangerous, unknown realm, but that warning was drowned out by the clamoring needs of her body. Somehow all she wanted was to get closer to him, to press her heated flesh against his. All thoughts of escape fled, leaving only a wild, insatiable yearning. . . .

DEFIANT EMBRACE

BARBARA DAWSON SMITH

ZEBRA BOOKS
KENSINGTON PUBLISHING CORP.

ZEBRA BOOKS

are published by

Kensington Publishing Corp.
475 Park Avenue South
New York, NY 10016

First printing: July 1985

Printed in the United States of America

*To my husband for his unfailing support,
and a special thanks to Melanie
for her many helpful comments*

Prologue

"Touch me again and you'll not live to see tomorrow!"

Her smoky-blue eyes blazed with hatred but secretly Mirella wondered what she would do to make good her threat if the man standing in front of her chose to call her bluff. She was a small woman, and though Sir Harry stood not more than two inches taller, he had the thick build and strength of a bull.

Mirella berated herself for being fooled by Sir Harry's pretext of a question about the household funds. Though she had caught him staring at her on several occasions over the past months, never before had he touched her. So tonight, without thinking, she had let him into her bedroom, unprepared for his subsequent attempt to seduce her.

Mirella shuddered in disgust, recalling how, just moments before, his hot lips had pressed down over hers and his hands had pawed at the bodice of her

7

gown in a caricature of a caress. She clutched the hard curve of the bedpost behind her with one hand while the other lay at her side tingling from the slap that still reddened one of Sir Harry's cheeks. The dark, feral eyes studying her reminded Mirella of a snake's sizing up its victim before the fatal strike.

Defiantly she assessed him in return, refusing to let him see her uneasiness. His clothing was always in the latest fashion but on his stocky figure the bright colors and frills of a dandy were somehow all wrong. The periwig he wore was thick with white powder, and, curled to fall below his shoulders, it gave him a top-heavy look. How he fancied himself to be attractive to her was beyond Mirella's comprehension.

"I'll overlook that foolish display of temper this time. When you are my wife, you'll be glad to have the attentions of a man of my social standing."

His egotistical tone amused Mirella. Sir Harry had always been pompous, imagining himself to be better than the rest of humanity. Did he forget that she was the daughter of a baronet? Or that not so long ago he had been a common tradesman? Though his present position might deem him a gentleman, his title did not automatically make him one in her eyes.

"I'll never marry you."

Sir Harry felt his temper flare at the haughtiness in Mirella's voice. Who the devil did the bitch think she was? He owned the Weston estate now and the baronetcy that went along with it. She should be on her knees thanking him for the opportunity he was offering her. After all, not many men would be willing to marry a penniless woman.

Besides, Sir Harry thought critically, she had little

sense of style. Mirella's comeliness would be improved greatly if she would powder that unfashionable ebony hair of hers so she fit in with the rest of society. Her grayish-blue eyes were extraordinary but all too often they expressed unladylike emotions—boldness, contempt, insolence. It was a shame, too, that the aristocratic line of her nose was marred by that slight uptilt. And though her skin was milky and smooth, its perfection was spoiled by the faint sprinkling of freckles across her high cheekbones.

Still, she had promise. Her petite body was rounded in all the right places, yet was slender enough for his hands to span her waist. Sir Harry's mouth curved into a self-satisfied smile. It would be a pleasure to teach her submissiveness. And once they married, he finally would have access to the dowry about which he was sure she knew nothing.

"We'll see about that, dear cousin. You should have learned by now that beggars can't be choosers." With a brief bow, he strolled out of the room.

Mirella clenched her fists in silent rage. It galled her to live here on Sir Harry's charity, especially when he threw it in her face. If she had only a fraction of the wealth the Westons had once possessed she would not be facing a bleak future, dependent on a man she despised.

Mirella walked to the window and looked out over the night-darkened grounds, remembering her childhood when sleek coaches had lined the curved drive in front of their country house here in Somerset, the brilliance of the thousand candles that lit the ballroom, the orchestra that played until dawn. Then, items which had been a central part of their everyday lives had begun to vanish mysteriously—the silver serving pieces, the fine bone china, the jewels, the extensive stable of horses.

In the eight years since her mother's death, Mirella had learned the truth behind the disappearances. Her father was an insatiable gambler whose losses had forced him to sell the familiar trappings of her childhood, squandering even the fortune her mother had brought to the marriage as a dowry. The discovery shocked Mirella to the core of her being. Sir Andrew Weston had been her knight in shining armor. But reality had dulled his luster with the tarnish of disillusionment. Though she would always love him, bitterness made Mirella shun the society that encouraged empty, pleasure-seeking pursuits.

In the end only their country house had survived the roll of Sir Andrew's dice. The small estate was entailed, to be passed on by law to her father's closest male relative. Sir Andrew's death six months ago had been a twofold tragedy; not only had she lost her father but his cousin, Harry Weston, had come into her life as heir to the estate and title.

Sir Harry had not bothered her at first but ever since her eighteenth birthday several weeks before, he had begun to press her about marriage. The thought of spending the rest of her life as his wife made her shudder, a feeling brought into sharp focus by tonight's episode. If that was the price she had to pay to remain in the home where she had grown up, it was not worth it.

Turning from the window, Mirella concluded there was nothing left here for her but childhood memories. Keeping that thought in mind, her decision to leave became almost painless.

By the light of a single candle, she moved about her bedchamber swiftly and surely as though her unconscious mind had been preparing for this for a long time. She changed into a worn but serviceable blue gown of linsey-woolsey which would keep her warm in the chill of the March night.

Looking through her few belongings, she took the cameo that was the only remaining piece from her mother's once-large collection of jewels. Though it was thick and heavy, on its finely carved onyx surface was a delicate silhouette of her mother. A jeweler might pay a fair amount for it, but to Mirella the cameo was priceless.

Her mother had shown it to her, Mirella recalled vaguely, when she had been perhaps eight or nine years old. But that happy memory was overshadowed by a more painful one. Only a few months after her daughter's tenth birthday, Caroline Weston had fallen from a horse and broken her neck.

Carefully Mirella pinned the cameo inside a pocket of her skirt. If only there were someone she could turn to for help, she wished fervently. But she had no close relation other than Sir Harry. Her mother had been an only child, and her father's two sisters were both dead, one in childbed and the other of a lung fever. She had only herself to depend on.

Mirella forced herself to wait a full hour after she heard Sir Harry close his bedchamber door. Then she threw a tattered mantle over her shoulders and tiptoed downstairs.

Sir Harry had a small private income, and she knew he kept some funds in his desk in the library.

Poking around by the faint flickering light of a candle, she pocketed a meager pile of silver coins. Sir Harry would doubtless accuse her of theft, Mirella thought derisively, but she felt no twinge of guilt. He had taken her home from her, and this was a miserly price for him to pay.

Then she saw the knife. As a woman alone, it would be comforting to have some means of defense. Wrapping the blade in her handkerchief, she slipped it inside her boot.

After one last look around, she extinguished the candle and crept out the unlocked kitchen door. In darkness lit only by the waning moon, she began the three-mile walk to the crossroads where at dawn a public coach left for the closest city, the seaport of Bristol.

Chapter One

Hunger pains made Mirella stop beneath a sign which creaked mournfully in the damp April breeze blowing in off the nearby ship channel. A tantalizing aroma of beef stew drifting from an alleyway that led to the rear of the tavern in front of her had attracted her attention. Though little remained of her stolen silver, her stomach for once spoke louder than her money-conscious mind.

After glancing up at the blistered sign illustrating the inn's name, The Crescent Moon, Mirella pulled open the heavy wooden door and stepped inside. She blinked as her eyes adjusted to the dimness within. The taproom had an air of decay about it from the soiled floor to the grimy windows. There were only a few people sitting at the rough-hewn tables, not surprising since it was midafternoon.

She took a seat against a wall which was streaked with black soot from the lanterns that were lit at night. A young serving maid brought the hot stew Mirella ordered, nervously fluttering about and nearly tipping the plate into Mirella's lap. At first Mirella thought she had unwittingly made the girl uneasy, but after observing her around the other customers, she concluded that the wench was merely high-strung.

Mirella turned her attention to her food and wondered, for the hundredth time, what she would do. For nearly a month she had tramped the filthy streets of Bristol looking for a job while her small supply of coins steadily dwindled. Though she was qualified to work as a governess or tutor, no one wanted to hire her without any letters of reference.

A prospect this morning, a sharp-faced woman who needed a nursemaid for her squalling twin sons, had said with blunt honesty that Mirella was far too pretty to have under the same roof with a husband whose eye had been known to rove. Mirella swallowed her pride and begged the woman to reconsider. Her answer was the door slamming in her face.

Despair drove her to wander the streets, barely noticing as the fashionable homes gradually gave way to squalid tenements near the docks. She walked until hunger made her stop at this rundown inn.

Now Mirella enjoyed every mouth-watering bit that warmed her body and revived her flagging spirits. If she lived frugally, she had enough money to last a few more days; certainly some sort of work would turn up in the meantime.

"Ye clumsy ox! Oi've 'ad enough o' ye! Git out o' 'ere and don't never come back!"

The thundering voice startled Mirella, and looking across the room to its source she forgot her own troubles. A customer was sponging a dark stain on his shirt, while cowering before another man, clearly the owner of this decaying establishment, was the same

14

girl who had served Mirella. Tears streamed down her dirt-streaked face.

"Nay, please!" she begged. "Don't send me away! Me mum'll kill me!"

But the innkeeper stood unrelenting, arms folded across a large belly that was no doubt the result of drinking too many tankards of his own ale.

"Out wi' ye!" he roared, pointing a beefy hand toward the door. "Now!"

The girl scuttled away, cringing from him as though she feared he would punctuate his words by striking her. With a loud bang, the door slammed behind her.

Poor thing, Mirella thought. Now she's out of work just like I am. But she really couldn't blame the innkeeper. Rough though he might have been with the girl, he could lose customers with someone as clumsy as her.

Then an idea struck Mirella. Why not apply to take the girl's place? She finished her plate of stew, considering the notion. A part of her cringed at the thought of working in such a filthy, low-class tavern, but still . . .

The wages would be far less than she had expected but wasn't it better than being forced to return to Sir Harry? She could always keep her eyes and ears open for a better position. It wouldn't hurt to give it a try.

Mirella stepped over to the bar, where the innkeeper was focusing his full attention on pouring a mug of ale from the spigot tapped into a large wooden cask. From close up, his corpulence was impressive. Bushy brows sprouted over dark eyes that seemed to disappear into the fleshy folds of his face. His body was massive, his arm as big around as one of her thighs.

"Excuse me, sir," Mirella said.

The innkeeper finished filling the mug, then raised it to his mouth and drank deeply. Wiping the foam off his lips with the hairy back of a hand, he turned to Mirella.

"Well, speak up, what d'ye want? Can Oi git ye somethin'?"

The man's gruff manner was daunting but Mirella reminded herself that he probably was still upset over losing an employee.

"You'll be needing someone to replace the serving girl you just dismissed. I could do her job."

The innkeeper stared at her, his gaze calculating as he studied her slender figure. "Ye don't look too strong. And ye don't look like ye've ever done a stroke o' work in yer life."

"Yes, I have," Mirella said, determined not to lose this opportunity. "I can work very hard. Try me out and you'll see."

The innkeeper scrutinized her from head to toe, his beady eyes making her strangely uneasy. Not for the first time since she'd left home, Mirella was thankful for the security of her knife. She might need it in a place like this.

"Mmm . . . Oi guess we can always use a good-lookin' wench around 'ere. 'Elps bring in the customers." He rubbed his large hands together and smiled, revealing a blackened set of teeth. "Me name's George Bates. What be yers?"

"Mirella."

"Git back in the kitchen, then,"—he motioned toward a dark passageway at the end of the room—

" 'til we be needin' yer 'elp out 'ere later." Bates pivoted to walk away.

"Wait, please," Mirella said. "I haven't anywhere to stay tonight. Would there be a place here I could sleep?"

The innkeeper chuckled, though she could see nothing amusing about her question. "Aye, wench. Don't ye worry, ol' Bates'll take care o' ye." He waddled off, his shoulders still shaking with mirth.

Mirella shrugged off his peculiar behavior and headed toward the kitchen. At least for one more night she had a roof over her head.

The job was backbreaking. Mirella was accustomed to hard labor since there had been few servants in her home these past lean years, but the constant lugging of heavy tankards of ale was wearing her out.

The taproom was crammed with sailors, its lanterns lit to chase away the darkness. As the evening grew later, the drunken crowd became boisterous, and more than once Mirella had to slap away a hand that sought to pinch her bottom or grab her breasts. She complained to Bates but he only leered at her and said that all the other wenches liked it.

When a man tried to haul her into his lap, she'd had enough. Mirella picked up his mug of ale and emptied the contents over his head. Luckily for him, there was barely an inch of liquid in it. The sailor shoved her away, hollering out, " 'Ey, Bates! 'Oo's the new wench? She ain't too friendly!"

With an angry frown, Bates lunged across the room to seize Mirella. The tray slipped from her hands, the tankards clattering to the floor. She was too stunned to

17

resist as the innkeeper dragged her over to the bar.

"Ye'll pay fer that, wench," he growled, his sour breath hissing against her hair. "Ye're goin' to do somethin' else to earn yer keep tonight."

His intentions bewildered Mirella but his malicious tone of voice sent raw fear pumping through her veins. "You animal!" she cried out. "Let me go or I'll scream the place down!"

"Nay, ye won't." Bates whipped her around so that her back was to his belly, slamming her against the bar with such force that the wind was knocked out of her. By the time she regained her breath, he had tied a filthy rag over her mouth.

Grabbing her flailing arms and wrenching them behind her back, he prodded Mirella toward the crowd. "Let's see 'ow much Oi can git fer yer pretty little body."

Horror washed over her in waves as she realized his motive. Bates was going to sell her to one of these drunken pigs as a whore! In a frantic attempt to escape, she strained against his grip as her heel moved backward to stomp on his instep.

"Ow!" he roared. His hands tightened cruelly, and he shoved her forward so that her feet could not touch him. "Stop it, wench, or Oi'll give ye cause to regret it!"

Pain shot up her arms when she tried to struggle. Knowing that his threat was no bluff, Mirella halted her useless wriggling. If he would but loosen his hold for a moment, she could reach her knife. That was her only hope.

" 'Ey, lads, lookie 'ere!" The innkeeper's gruff voice rang out above the din of the taproom. " 'Oo'll

18

give me a shillin' fer a night wi' this rare beauty?"

"Ain't no piece worth that kind o' money!" Loud laughter followed this remark.

"Think Oi'd rather 'ave ol' Fanny 'ere," shouted another sailor. "She'll do it fer free if ye treat 'er right."

Fanny, one of the other serving maids, playfully slapped at the man as, in an attempt to demonstrate the truth of his statement, he tumbled her into his lap for a lusty kiss. The other seamen cheered them on with catcalls and whistles.

As the throng focused its attention on the frolicking of Fanny and her sailor, Mirella feverishly hoped that Bates would relent and let her go. But her prayers were in vain.

"Lookie 'ere, lads, if ye're not convinced o' the prize Oi'm offerin' to the 'ighest bidder. See what fine tits this wench 'as!"

Releasing one of her arms, he reached around and ripped away the tight ribbon that held Mirella's bodice together. The gag muffled her startled gasp as her hand flew up in an attempt to cover herself.

A roar of approval rose from the ale-soused men as their attention returned to the front of the taproom. Taking full advantage of the moment, Bates roughly yanked her hand away from her bodice and again twisted it behind her back.

His action exposed her thin chemise, which was stretched taut over the creamy mounds of her breasts. The sheer wisp of material might well have been invisible for it did naught to conceal the dark blur at the tip of each breast or the fullness which strained to escape the garment's low décolletage.

19

She had no choice but to stand there, imprisoned by the innkeeper's meaty fists, as the throng of drunken seamen glimpsed what no man had ever seen before. Even her money-hungry captor licked his fat lips and wondered whether he should have saved this wench for his own bedtime pleasures.

Mirella choked back the bile that rose in her throat at the thought of lying beneath one of these rutting beasts while he used her body as a receptacle for his lust. But pride refused to let her show the fear and humiliation that gripped her soul. Defiantly she lifted her chin and glared with hatred at the ale-guzzling horde.

"Well, me laddies," Bates raised his voice above the whistles and cheers, " 'oo'll be the lucky one to pluck this lovely rose?"

His attention-getting ploy had worked well. Bids flew fast and furious for the privilege of sharing a bed with the petite, ebony-haired beauty whose bodice lay open to their leering eyes.

"Two shillin's," croaked a voice from the dimness at the rear of the crowded taproom.

"Two shillin's plus a tuppence besides." This offer came from a greasy-haired sailor with rotten teeth who was sprawled on a bench directly in front of them. Mirella was close enough to see a flea crawl in and out of his ragged beard, and felt her belly turn with revulsion.

" 'Ow's about a little sample o' the goods first so as Oi can see fer meself if the wench is worthy o' the price?" With these words, the man advanced on Mirella.

He grabbed at one breast, yanking it free of her lacy

20

chemise to subject her to a crude parody of a caress. She struggled feverishly to escape his repulsive grasp but the innkeeper's grip tightened until she feared her arms would be broken. Had she not been gagged, Mirella would have cursed them both with a vengeance that would have startled even these worldly-wise sailors.

"Come 'ere, me sweetie, 'ows about a little kiss to whet ol' Jack's appetite?"

Mirella recoiled in disgust as the seaman's foul breath hovered near her face. He was reaching around to undo the gag when help came from an unexpected source.

"Pay up first, Jack, or ye'll git no more." The innkeeper struck him away but not before Mirella instinctively thrust her knee upward to join in the attack. Jack howled in pain as she made firm contact, swiftly retreating with both hands clutching his groin.

"Oi'm dyin'! Oi'm dyin'! Oooh, that witch maimed me fer life!"

The crowd roared with laughter at poor Jack's plight, not to mention the contradiction in his words. Feeling the innkeeper's grip slacken as he joined in the mirth, Mirella slipped one hand free and quickly tugged her chemise back into place. Then she reached down surreptitiously for her knife.

But before she could snatch the weapon from its hiding place, Bates grabbed for her with a lightning swiftness that belied the ponderous appearance of his massive body. Slapping her head with one beefy palm, he jerked Mirella back so that she slammed against his paunch, both of her hands firmly entrapped. When he spoke, his voice was a low hiss meant only for her ears.

"Ye lost me a good-payin' customer, ye bloody bitch! Pull another stunt like that one and Oi'll be lettin' 'em all mount ye right 'ere, the 'ole lot o' 'em. Think on it good, wench, fer ol' Bates'd enjoy seein' 'em pumpin' into ye, ye wi' yer fine ladylike airs."

Mirella twisted in a vain attempt to escape the stench of his breath. Her fingers itched for her knife. One thrust between the innkeeper's fleshy ribs would wipe away the leer she was certain he had on his face. It took all of her willpower to force herself to calm down and use her wits. Even if she could reach her knife, against this crowd of burly sailors and other assorted riffraff, one lone woman with a small, though lethal, weapon could have little chance of success.

Her only real choice, then, was to bide her time. If she could convince these drunkards that she'd been cowed into submission, she just might be able to turn the situation to her advantage. That meant enduring this humiliation with false meekness, awaiting an opportunity to escape later when the odds were much improved—when she was alone with the man who had made the highest bid for her services this night.

Abruptly Mirella stilled her struggling and fell limp against the innkeeper's potbelly. Bates gave a chuckle of satisfaction.

"Aye, lass. Now that be more like it. Ye're gonna earn ol' George Bates a pretty penny tonight."

Raising his voice above the raucous din, he again addressed the throng of customers. " 'Ey, lads! Now that ol' Jack's out o' commission, 'oo'll be takin' 'is place wi' this comely wench?"

* * *

Jason Fletcher sat alone at a table in a corner of the taproom at The Crescent Moon, his back to the tipsy sailors who were celebrating their brief shore leave. Peering morosely into his glass of brandy, he cursed the luck that had brought him to this squalid inn which lacked a private dining chamber where he might consume his spirits in relative peace. The Crescent Moon had no such nicety. Its regular customers preferred to save their hard-earned silver for ale and whores.

Jason's ship had arrived this day from London and what with the unloading of hogsheads of tobacco, there had been no time to seek out finer quarters. Of course, he could have remained aboard for the night but he had grown tired of the sea. It felt good to have solid earth beneath his feet once more.

He polished off the contents of his glass, then poured another measure from the half-empty bottle which sat on the rough wooden table before him. It was irritating, Jason mused, that his business in England had taken over three months already. Had it not been for the problem he'd had with his factor in London, his captain could have handled this journey alone, as usual. But now, if all went well, in a few days he'd have filled the hold of his merchant ship with British goods and would be on his way back to the wide-open spaces of his tobacco plantation in Virginia.

By damn, he'd be glad to get home again! Neither London nor Bristol, Jason reflected, held the glamor they'd had for him when he'd first seen them, so long ago, through the eyes of a boy approaching manhood. How his interests had changed in these past ten years!

Now he'd just as soon drink by himself in this crowded taproom as sip tea in some fine aristocratic mansion while the daughter of the house flirted shamelessly with him when her parents discreetly turned their backs.

Stretching his long, muscular legs, Jason smiled cynically into his glass. At one time he had been flattered by the interest of the nobility. But maturity had made him see their hypocrisy. The attention they paid him stemmed only from the desire for an alliance with the wealthy owner of tens of thousands of acres of prime colonial farmland.

Unfortunately, he had learned his lesson the hard way.

What a fool he had been to believe that Lady Elizabeth Stirling really loved him! Daughter of an earl, beautiful as an angel—and with all the heart of a serpent. But by the time he had realized her true nature, it had been too late, for they'd already married.

Jason still felt the crushing pain of disillusionment, though a decade had cushioned the blow. He had traveled to London on business at the impressionable age of eighteen, while mourning the recent death of his parents. There, he'd met Elizabeth, and had been so besotted that he'd proposed to her within a few days. On their wedding night, he'd received his first shock—his wife was no virgin. In response to his angry questioning, she'd taunted him, freely admitting numerous sexual encounters. Fearing a scandal, her father had ordered her to choose a husband quickly before he selected one for her.

When Jason had threatened to have the marriage

annulled, Elizabeth had relented, employing all of her wiles to convince him that her mistakes would never be repeated. Though hurt and devastated, he'd trusted her. Then, several months after they'd arrived in Virginia, he'd come home early one afternoon and discovered her in bed with another man.

That had ruined whatever was left of their marriage.

Some weeks later, Elizabeth had learned to her disgust that she was pregnant. Not knowing whether or not the baby was a bastard, Jason had resolved to raise the child as his own. Elizabeth had hated the way her condition distorted her figure, and had made life miserable for everyone around her. When at long last the infant had finally been born, he had lived only a few hours, and Elizabeth had succumbed to a fever within a few days.

Jason poured himself another brandy, downing it in one burning gulp. That experience had all but destroyed his belief in love; yet he couldn't help remembering the happy relationship his parents had shared. Though theirs had been that rare treasure—a blissful union—it had colored his expectations nonetheless.

But never again would he endure the hell of giving his heart, he vowed grimly. Women were fickle creatures who cared only for themselves. Besides, the most important relationship between male and female took place in bed, and a man didn't need the shackles of wedlock to have that.

Samantha Hyatt was a prime example. She was so greedy to get her hands on his money that she willingly gave him her body in an attempt to entice him to the altar. Little did she know he'd sooner trust

25

a rattlesnake. Samantha was but a convenient mistress. For some years now, he had taken what she offered, avoiding any permanent entanglements.

Experience had taught him that an unmarried female was either a giggling girl or a scheming woman. Yet both shared a common goal—to put a collar around a man's neck and then lead him around like a dog.

Few women did not fit either of these types. There was Pandora, of course, but Jason supposed his sister didn't count since she was only fourteen years old. For a moment his expression lost its pessimism, and he smiled. God help the man who eventually married that little hoyden! After the death of their parents, Pandora had been raised by a succession of servants, none of whom could control her rebellious temper. Without the proper feminine guidance, she had turned into a hellion who could spit farther and climb a tree faster than any boy for miles around.

Jason sighed and ran restless fingers through thick hair the burnished gold-and-brown color of cured tobacco. By damn, it was all his fault for not knowing how to raise a girl. Long ago he probably should have married again, to some sweet, compliant miss who might have set a good example for his sister.

Was there a woman somewhere who might fulfill his fantasies of love and assuage the loneliness which flared in him more and more often of late?

Toying with his empty glass, he shoved it away in disgust. He was getting soft and sentimental. The truth of the matter was that he was waiting for a dream, an illusion—an ideal woman who existed only in his mind. All he needed at the moment was a whore

26

to provide a release for his pent-up frustrations.

And one thing was certain. If he continued imbibing at this rate, he'd soon be as soused as the throng of seamen surrounding him. Unfortunately, the liquor that turned most men into fun-loving rowdies tended to make him brood. He had done enough of that for one night.

As Jason picked up the bottle of brandy to seek out his bedchamber, he became aware of the whoops and the bellows of merriment that filled the taproom. Though he was accustomed to the noise of taverns, this was louder than normal. Curiosity made him twist around on the wooden bench.

"Three shillin's!" piped a squeaky voice from the middle of the room. The skinny lad who had spoken looked to be barely out of his midteens. His companions hooted with laughter at his words.

"Aw, come on, Johnnie!" one of them said. "Ye ain't got the equipment to pleasure a fine female like that one. Leave 'er to me—a man 'oo's got the proper experience!"

Johnnie jumped up, puny fists ready to do battle with his burly adversary. "Oi've bedded many a wench, that Oi 'ave! And they been mighty well pleased wi' me, too!"

But this speech only brought him another round of hearty laughter. The hapless youth stammered a few more words in his own defense, then finally gave up and slumped back down onto the bench, muttering to himself.

Watching the exchange, Jason grinned. He might have guessed the louder-than-usual camaraderie involved haggling over a whore.

27

Peering through the dim, smoke-filled room, he spied the source of their attention. It appeared that the innkeeper was auctioning off a small, dark-haired harlot to the highest bidder. It was not uncommon in a place like this for a serving girl to earn some extra silver by selling her body. Jason remembered seeing this girl earlier. His gaze had been drawn to her attractiveness.

He was puzzled, though, by the need for the filthy cloth which covered her mouth, for the wench had a meek, submissive air about her. Why bind her like that if she were willing? One look at the innkeeper's greedy face gave Jason his answer. Most likely, the bastard was demanding more than his fair share of her price. The gag would serve to stifle any protest she might have.

His intent to retire for the night was momentarily forgotten as Jason decided to have a closer look. He shouldered his way through the horde of sailors, his tall frame almost causing his head to brush against the wooden rafters supporting the low ceiling. He chose a vantage point near the front of the taproom and leaned against a wall to watch the action.

By damn, she was a beauty! Jason felt his loins tighten in a familiar response as he studied the whore. Long, soot-black curls outlined the delicate features of her face, and sable lashes shuttered eyes which looked meekly downward, shielding their color from his view. The bodice of her tattered gown was undone, and the gossamer fabric of her chemise revealed the lushness of her breasts. From far away, her petite stature had made her appear girlish, but now that he was nearer, he saw that her shapely curves were those of a woman.

28

His fingers tingled for the feel of her softness responding to his caresses. Almost as though she felt his eyes stroking her body, the girl looked up, directly at him.

The noise of the room faded. With one glance into the depths of her gaze Jason knew he was lost, drowning in the twin seas of those haunting, dusky-blue eyes that held at the same time defiance and fear, that were bold yet beseeching. For one brief moment their souls touched and entwined, then the girl dropped her gaze to the floor.

With a ragged sigh, Jason let out the breath he hadn't realized he had been holding. The image of those expressive eyes remained before him as he sought to calm his quickened pulse. He had to remind himself that she was a harlot, a common woman of the streets who sold her body to any available man.

But he couldn't deny the strange feeling that possessed him. It was something beyond simple lust, of that he was certain. Perhaps the brandy was mellowing him, for to feel this surge of protectiveness toward a whore was not within his realm of experience. Without further thought, Jason knew he had to have her.

"Five pounds."

The quietly drawled words held a ring of command which caused Mirella's head to swing upward in surprise, toward the tall man leaning casually against the wall. An uproar of disbelief at the high bid rose from the sailors; then slowly the room became still, only an occasional drunken mutter puncturing the shocked silence.

Instinctively, Mirella had known who had spoken. She had noticed the man, just moments earlier, staring

29

intently at her. Why she had been so drawn to him she could not guess. But she was struck now as she had been then by his aura of virility.

Through the dimness of the lamp-lit chamber, his hair and eyes appeared to be the color of strong tea. His clothing was simple—a plain white linen shirt open at the neck, dark breeches, and black knee-high boots. The foppish elegance of Sir Harry paled when compared to the potent masculinity evident in this man's square jaw; in his brooding, restless eyes; and in the rugged line of his cheekbones. Though not as rough looking as the other sailors present, his lean, muscled physique would doubtless make him the winner of a match with any man here.

But why he had bid such a foolishly high price when he could have had her for much less, she could not guess. Mirella did not puzzle long on the strangeness of this; all that really mattered was that he had purchased her, and her hatred, which had been directed toward the lusting crowd, now could be centered on this one man.

Briefly, Mirella tilted her chin defiantly before she remembered the façade of humility that might earn her a chance at freedom. Dropping her head slightly in what she hoped would be interpreted as meekness, she continued to meet his gaze unblinkingly.

After a moment, he walked toward her, a bottle of brandy in one hand. His action broke the silence. The buzz of conversation began to fill the room again as the seamen recovered their tongues. Knowing they had lost the comely harlot, they turned their attention back to serious drinking, and calls for more ale and rum kept the serving wenches busy.

Stopping in front of Mirella, the man reached into a pocket of the breeches that seemed molded to his powerful thighs.

"Your share," he drawled, tossing the innkeeper a handful of coins.

Bates caught them greedily. Dropping one in his eagerness, he waddled quickly after the rolling piece of silver. Mirella's gag stifled the half-hysterical giggle that bubbled up into her throat at the sight of the fat man scrabbling around on the filth-strewn floor like a rutting pig.

" 'Tisn't enough! Ye've cheated me!" the innkeeper grunted, counting the coins that lay in his pudgy palm.

"The rest of the money belongs to the lady."

Either the echo of authority in the man's voice or his menacing frown conveyed the message well, for Bates stilled his protests. Grudgingly, he prodded Mirella toward her buyer.

" 'Ere. She's all yers."

Mirella stumbled and would have fallen had not the man reached out a strong arm to steady her and draw her against his warmth. His touch startled her. She stiffened, her mind registering the lean, hard feel of his body as her fear of what lay ahead returned in full force.

When he made a move toward the narrow staircase that led to the bedchambers above, Mirella's legs refused to follow his lead. Her body seemed paralyzed, rendered powerless by the thought of what she had to do—and what would happen to her were she unsuccessful.

The man glanced back at her, puzzlement on his face, then a devilish grin brightened his brooding features.

"So you're the sort who likes to play games. Well, never let it be said that Jason Fletcher was unwilling to join in the fun."

He dropped his bottle of brandy on a nearby table and, before she realized what he was about, he bent and hoisted her up, slinging her over his shoulder like a sack of flour. Picking up his bottle, he placed it in the hand that securely held her legs so that it lay cold against her warm skin. Then he started again for the stairway.

Momentarily stunned, Mirella hung there, his hard shoulder cutting into her belly, her posterior ungracefully pointed toward the ceiling. Anger gushed through her, and she kicked her legs in a futile attempt to achieve her release. Against the gag, the protests that automatically rose in her throat came out as incomprehensible mumbling.

Her captor laughed and swatted her bottom none too gently, tightening his grip on her legs. Brandy sloshed from the bottle he carried. Cold and sticky, it ran down the warm interior of her boot. A roar of approval rose from the sailors, who clearly appreciated this mastery of man over woman.

Tears of fury and humiliation stung Mirella's eyelids, but she refused to let them fall. She forced herself to cease her useless struggles. Cunning and clear thinking were necessary to make good her escape. She must play her role of whore well.

Then, when she had her chance, by God, she would pay this Jason Fletcher back in full!

Chapter Two

Carrying his prize easily atop his wide shoulder, Jason smiled as he opened the door to his bedchamber. He might have paid a ridiculous sum for this lovely harlot but he had a strong feeling that she would be well worth every pence.

Kicking the door shut behind him, he strode into the cramped room that was the best the inn had to offer. Moonbeams drifted in the uncurtained window to paint the dingy furnishings with a soft glow.

After placing his bottle of brandy on the dressing table, he eased his captive off his shoulder and let her slide to the floor, keeping his hands on her waist to guide her descent. Gently grasping her chin, he tipped it upward so that the silvery light fell full on her face.

Jason studied the girl, trying to reconcile his contrasting impressions of her. Despite her shabby appearance, he sensed something untouched about her, some vulnerability which gave him an odd wrenching feeling deep in his gut. She seemed like a shy little thing, yet downstairs he could have sworn he had seen defiance in those dusky-blue eyes.

He frowned. It must be the effect of consuming half a bottle of brandy that caused him to imagine these traits in her. She was just an uncommonly attractive whore, that was all.

Suddenly wanting to see her lips, he reached around to untie the filthy rag that hid them from his view. The knot was tangled in her silky black hair, and she flinched at his efforts. Tears sprang to her eyes, making them luminous.

"Sorry, love," he murmured, trying to be more careful.

The knot finally gave way. Jason felt heat mount in his loins as she lightly ran her tongue over lips which were reddened from the tightness of the gag. Were she not a doxy, he would have thought it an unconscious gesture lacking any intentional overtones of sensuality. Indeed, he was becoming more and more aware that this was a rare woman, one who could deliberately inflame his desires and, at the same time, appear to be without the slightest hint of guile.

Yet so taken in was he by concern for her comfort that he found himself pouring a measure of brandy into a pewter tumbler.

"Here, drink this down," he said, handing her the brandy. " 'Twill ease your thirst."

The girl hesitated, then took the goblet and swallowed its contents. Immediately she coughed, raising a hand to her heaving bosom. Jason couldn't help but grin, for the liquor must have burned her throat.

He took the vessel from her and deposited it on a nearby table. Pillowing her head against his chest, he rubbed her back soothingly until the fit passed. Then he began to pluck out the wooden pins holding her chignon in place, letting them drop to the floor one by one. His hands slid into the whisper-soft mass that rippled down to her waist. Burying his face in the thick black curls, he breathed in her feminine fragrance. His pulse quickened as he felt her hands tentatively move upward to encircle his neck.

Easing his head back, Jason again looked down at her. She stared up at him, the color of her eyes as deep as the smoky-blue dye extracted from the indigo he grew on a portion of his Virginia plantation. When he touched the silky skin of her cheek, her lashes fluttered shut and her lips parted slightly. He had to resist a strong desire to bed her right then and there, for he wanted to prolong their pleasures.

Continuing his exploration, he let his hand drift downward, his fingers tracing the line of her small jaw, then caressing her slender neck and the ivory skin above the torn décolletage of her gown. She gave a tiny gasp as his caress delved intimately inside her chemise.

Brushing away the sheer garment, Jason freed her breasts from their binding. The soft mounds had the delicate, creamy white texture of magnolia blossoms. He stroked them gently; the sensitive honey-brown tips tightening in response.

She seemed like something out of a dream, he thought, puzzled, for she was too perfect to be real. He was suddenly filled with the desire to know everything about her, who she was, where she was from, why she sold herself in this filthy tavern when she could so easily live in comfort as the mistress of some wealthy lord.

"What's your name?"

The girl's lashes flew open in response to the question, confusion briefly dancing across her face. "Mirella," she whispered.

There was a hesitation in the way she spoke which seemed strangely out of place for a seasoned harlot. His tastes of late had run to more fiery women, yet this sweet mite of a girl fascinated him. She was, Jason mused, a delicious blend of angel and strumpet. A bewitching whore in a squalid dockside inn— the contrast continued to perplex him but he did not dwell long on it. He decided that his other questions could wait. Mirella was enchanting him, and he was eager to sample her body further. His eyes drifted to the ripe invitation of her lips as he savored the anticipation of their kiss.

Mirella looked up at Jason, trying to stop her head from spinning. It was the brandy, she tried to tell herself, but his hands gliding slowly, hypnotically over her body bespoke a bewildering truth. This man, her enemy, was supposed to arouse revulsion in her but instead his nearness sent an unfamiliar fire surging through her veins.

She had expected his touch to arouse the intense loathing she'd felt when Sir Harry had attempted to seduce her. But to her surprise—and fright—her body was turning traitor under the influence of this man's caresses, making her want to both kiss him and kill him at the same time. Desperately she prayed that he would move away so that she would have a chance to make her escape.

Instead he was bending toward her, and she knew he sought her lips. She forced her confused thoughts into a semblance of calm. At this moment, with his strong arms holding her captive, she could not reach for her knife without awakening his suspicions. Her plan would have to be postponed until the right opportunity arose. Meanwhile, the best—the *only*—course of action was to continue her meek acceptance of his advances.

As his head descended toward hers, Mirella noted fleetingly that his tallness pleased her, though she knew not why. Had he but another inch of height, she would have been forced to stand on tiptoe to meet his lips.

She closed her eyes automatically as his mouth came down on hers, gently but hungrily as if he were starving for her. She let him lead the way, for she had little knowledge of what pleasured a man. His hands cradled her cheeks, his thumbs stroking the feathery tendrils at her hairline.

As his tongue probed her lips, she froze with surprise. Was this the way a man kissed a woman? Remembering her role of whore, she parted her lips to him. The unexpected intimacy as his tongue explored the interior of her mouth caused strange shivers to course through her. He tasted of warm, sweet brandy. Shyly, Mirella imitated his action. He groaned deep in his throat and molded her even closer to his muscular body. His instant response gave a peculiar feeling of delight, awakening her to the power a woman could have over a man.

Reminding herself that she needed to induce him to let down his guard, Mirella ran her hands up the strong column of his neck and into the rough silk of his hair, then back down again to spread her palms against the hard contours of his chest. The strength of him was intoxicating. She slid her fingers inside the open neck of his shirt and over his bare skin. Her legs seemed oddly weak, causing her to lean against him for support.

His mouth left hers to wander down to the wild pulse in her throat. She caught her breath, feeling his lips close around the tip of one breast, his tongue laving the taut crest. Her fingers clung to his shoulders, digging into the firm muscles.

Excitement bloomed deep within her. Her mind cried out that she was letting this seduction progress into a dangerous, unknown realm, but that warning was drowned by the clamoring needs of her body. Somehow all she wanted was to get closer to him, to press her hot flesh against his. Instinct made her reach for his shirt buttons but her trembling fingers had trouble undoing them.

Fletcher raised his head and gave a soft chuckle. "Eager for me, are you, my sweet Mirella? Let us undress, then. We've the entire night to enjoy our pleasures." He left her, turning his back to brace a hand on the bedpost as he tugged off his boots.

His words were like a splash of cold water on Mirella's overwrought senses. With the removal of his hands and lips, the sensual languor that possessed her limbs slowly ebbed. In its wake, white-hot fury gushed through her veins. How dare this Jason Fletcher have the nerve to act as though it were *she* who wanted *his* services!

She glared fiercely at his back, the desire to punish him blocking out all else. Then her breath quickened as she realized that this was the opportunity she had been awaiting.

Her eyes watchfully on him, Mirella lifted the hem of her gown and drew the small knife from its hiding place inside her short boot. The handle was sticky from the brandy that had trickled down over it when he had carried her upstairs. She weighed it in her hand for an instant, planning feverishly. The blade was dull, so to be effective she must strike decisively and without delay, for Fletcher was unbuttoning his shirt and would soon turn to her.

She stepped forward on silent feet, heart pounding, weapon raised to attack. Fleetingly, her hand wavered as she stared at her target, the broad back covered by an expanse of white linen. Never before had she injured—let alone killed—anyone.

Yet Jason Fletcher sought to bed her as though she were a common whore. He might be more refined and handsome than the rowdy sailors downstairs, but he was still a lusting man. This was her sole chance at freedom.

Outrage gripped her soul once more, and she swung the blade toward him. But her slight hesitation had betrayed her.

He must have caught sight of the weapon from the corner of his eye for even as Mirella made her thrust, he swiftly flung back his shirt. Her arm tangled in the soft folds of fabric, spoiling her aim. The blade glanced off his shoulder, leaving an angry red trail.

As he spun toward her she lost her balance and tumbled onto the bed. The knife slipped from her fingers, to hit the floor with a muted thud. With a strangled cry, she tried to leap up, but Fletcher hurled his shirt aside and pinned her to the mattress, crushing her naked breasts intimately to the mat of dark hair on his chest.

"You deceiving little bitch! What the devil do you think you're doing?"

Mirella fought frantically to escape his iron grip. "You beast!" she panted, wriggling beneath him in helpless fury. "Let me go!"

"What's the matter?" he taunted. "Am I not paying you well enough for your services? Do you dare conspire to rob me of the rest of my money, too?"

A belated fear froze her as he made a leisurely survey of her body. Moonlight gleamed over the male planes of his face, a face that bore a hint of menace. He looked like some demon king who had cornered his quarry.

"Foolish girl," he sneered. "Do you not see that stealing would reap you only a paltry sum? But if you please me well, I might consider making you my mistress, and you would have more wealth than you could ever spend. Would that satisfy your greedy heart?"

"Nay! You do not understand!" Panicked, Mirella jerked against his powerful hold. But her agitated movements only served to return his attention to her naked breasts.

"You're right . . . I don't understand." His husky voice bore a note of angry bafflement. "You have the speech and mannerisms of a fine lady, and yet you are but a common dockside whore, selling your body to me for the night. Damn you for bewitching me so."

His lips came down on hers in a crushing kiss unlike the gentle one they had shared earlier. This was unleashed passion, the result of a man being pushed to the brink, then denied the object of his desire. With feverish intensity, his tongue sought hers until Mirella gasped for breath. He shifted, one hand imprisoning her wrists. His fingers slid around the firm swell of her breast, caressing and stroking.

An unexpected warmth raced over her skin, and her belly flamed with need. Wildly she fought the sensation, jerking her head from his kiss. Fletcher only chuckled and applied his lips to her breast. His tongue traced a tantalizing track over the soft skin before his mouth captured the tip with a gentle suckling. Her perceptions were suddenly heightened. She drew in his male scent, heard the pounding of blood in her ears, felt the burning flow of desire between her thighs. Instead of fighting, she found herself melting beneath him, spreading her palms over the muscles of his bare back. She wanted more. . . .

Her eyelids fluttered open as his weight lifted from her. He rolled lightly to his feet to stand alongside the bed, fumbling with the buttons of his breeches. Her breath caught in her throat as passion changed to panic. Dear God, what was she doing? This stranger intended to take her innocence!

"No!" she gasped in frantic fear. Swiftly she rolled to the opposite side of the bed in a blind attempt to flee. But her gown entangled her feet, and Fletcher caught her easily. Writhing beneath him, she heard the rumble of a chuckle deep in his chest.

"My lovely would-be thief, does this coy game amuse you? Indeed, if it inflames your passion all the more, I'll gladly play along."

" 'Tis no game!" she panted, terror bubbling in-

41

side of her. She thrust against his naked chest, kicking and scratching as he again reached down to unfasten his breeches.

He frowned, flinging his leg over her thighs to imprison them and capturing her wrists in one strong hand. He bent and tugged off her boots, tossing them to the floor with a thud.

"My love, you carry this sport too far," he said, half teasingly, half sternly. "Would you seek to injure that part of me which will give you such pleasure?"

"I seek only to be free of you!"

He shook his head impatiently. "Nay, Mirella. Do you so quickly forget you sold yourself to me? I wish only to sample what I have rightfully purchased."

His fingers played with the taut nipple of her breast, wreaking havoc with her senses. "But you cannot!" Desperate to convince him, she blurted urgently, "I'm no doxy—I've never been with a man before!"

"An innocent employed here at The Crescent Moon?" Fletcher scoffed in cynical amusement, though he stilled his mesmerizing hand. "You cannot expect me to believe that."

" 'Tis the truth, I swear it on my mother's grave! Please, please do not force yourself upon me." Her voice halted as her throat went taut, hot moisture stinging her eyes.

He stared at her, skeptical. "Only a simpleton would swallow such a tale." Yet there was gentleness in his touch as he traced the track of a tear that slipped down her cheek. After a moment he gave an odd laugh. "But by damn," he uttered softly, "I find myself believing you."

Abruptly his expression hardened, and he thrust himself from the bed, springing to his feet with the litheness of a panther. Hands on hips, he towered over her, glaring down with an expression that made her shiver.

"So help me God, if I find you've played me for a fool . . ."

The menace in his voice made her swallow hard. Mirella could think of nothing but escaping before Jason Fletcher changed his mind. Clutching together her torn bodice, she slid across the mattress and swung her stockinged feet over the edge. "I . . . I'll be going—"

"You'll do nothing of the kind!" he snarled. Seizing her shoulders, he pressed her back against the pillows, his features dark and resentful in the silvery moonlight. "I paid dearly for you this night, and here you'll stay."

"But . . . but you said you believed me."

"Do not fret," he ground out. "I've little stomach for bedding an unwilling virgin. Or does your eagerness to flee my company arise from a desire to return below so that Bates can sell your body to another?"

Mirella could only shake her head in numb denial, cowering beneath his cold eyes.

Spinning sharply, he snatched a tinderbox from the bedside table and strode to the fireplace, kneeling to light the logs lying in the hearth. Then he dragged an ancient wingback chair across the tiny chamber and positioned it in front of the door, barring her escape. He yanked on his linen shirt before sinking into the chair, stretching his long legs out before him, and covering his eyes with a hand.

43

Mirella watched him apprehensively, her body taut with tension, until his deep, steady breathing told her he was asleep. Careful not to make a sound, she crawled beneath the ragged quilt without removing her ripped gown.

She promised herself that she would remain awake, lest her captor rescind his word and rape her in the darkness of the night. But as the warmth of the snapping fire invaded the chilly air, she slowly relaxed, slipping into the world of dreams.

In the gray light of dawn Jason awoke, his head aching. Groaning, he recalled the excessive amount of brandy he had consumed the previous night. Then he realized that his large frame was crammed uncomfortably into a chair, and the bed across the room was occupied by a small, feminine shape. The memory of his frustrating encounter with Mirella came rushing back to him.

Jason sprang up and strode over to study the sleeping girl. She was curled up on her side facing him, lashes lining her closed eyelids like a thick, even scattering of cinders. The quilt and sheets lay in tangles around her shapely legs, the tatters of her clothing baring much of her body to his appreciative gaze. Her hair streamed over the pillow and onto her breasts like an ebony river. Last night he hadn't noticed the gentle tilt to the end of her nose or the faint sprinkling of freckles across her cheekbones that gave her an angelic look. She was both innocent and womanly at the same time, he mused, recalling her initial passionate response to his love-making.

Had he been gullible to believe her claim to virginity?

Jason frowned, remembering her seesaw behavior, all meekness at first, then her attack with the knife, and her frenzied fighting. He had been angered and confused by her actions. At first he had thought her to be trying to rob him, then to be playing some game to enhance their mutual enjoyment.

But clearly she must have had second thoughts about selling herself. How like a woman to change her mind at the very last moment! Though Mirella might appear to be different from Elizabeth and Samantha, last night only confirmed his belief that all females were schemers, concerned only with themselves.

Jason sighed, kneading his aching forehead with a sun-bronzed hand. He had been a fool not to have seen from the start that she lacked the experience of a seasoned whore. He should have recognized her background from her speech and the softness of her hands. Who was she? An impoverished gentlewoman who had encountered circumstances so desperate that she had been driven to auctioning off her virginity to the highest bidder?

In a brandy-induced stupor he had almost forced her to yield, until her tears had broken through the haze that had dulled his perceptions. He was not a man to take a woman against her will. So why then had he kept her here with him?

The question nagged at him. Even now, his fingers hovered near her face wanting to awaken her with his caresses. He knew he could arouse that same passion he had glimpsed in her last night. How tempting was the prospect of making her yield!

But the tug of an equally strong and primitive

emotion stayed his hand. Mirella might lack his superior physical strength but it was that very fragility which stirred in him an unfamiliar feeling of fierce protectiveness.

Lost in thought, Jason continued to stare down at her, noticing how she smiled in her sleep. Last night he had purchased her, believing they would be together for only a few sweet hours. But now he knew he could not let her go. Despite her virginity, he still wanted her with an intensity that would not be quenched until he made love to her.

Moving quietly so as not to disturb her slumber, Jason walked over to the chipped pitcher which sat on the dressing table. The cold water he splashed on his face and body was invigorating, washing away the grogginess that was an aftereffect of the brandy.

With a scrap of cloth, he rinsed the dried crust of blood off his injured shoulder. Thank God he had caught sight of the faint glimmer of moonlight on the knife blade before she had struck him! The wound caused only a slight twinge of discomfort. Doubtless it would heal soon.

Donning his clothes, Jason turned his thoughts to the day ahead. He had sold most of his cargo of tobacco in London, and now the hold of his ship was half filled for the return trip. To make this voyage more profitable, he planned to carry back a full load of the highest quality English goods, all much in demand in the fine plantation homes of tidewater Virginia. He must visit several merchants this morning in order to be ready to depart within the week.

As he walked across the chamber to pull on his boots, his foot struck a small object and sent it skidding across the floor. Reaching down, he picked up Mirella's knife.

A small smile touched his mouth as Jason thought again of her valiant attempt to preserve her innocence. No, he would not let her go. Whether it was frustrated desire or a sense of protectiveness, he was not sure, but he was compelled to keep this enchanting girl-woman for himself. There was no denying the bond which had been forged between them by his fateful purchase of her.

He thought of the plan that was slowly taking shape in his mind. Here in Bristol, she would be forced to survive by selling herself to a succession of strange men who might abuse her. It would be far better for her to accompany him to Virginia where she would have a home with him. He would have to come up with a plausible excuse to convince her to agree to the scheme.

Given time, he knew he could persuade her to overcome her maidenly shyness. The prospect sent fire pulsing through his veins. Judging by her reluctance last night, it would take some wooing but he was confident that he would be successful.

In a gesture of unexpected tenderness, Jason reached down and drew up the quilt to shield Mirella against the cool morning air. With her gentle upbringing and passionate nature, she would make an ideal mistress. But his pride demanded that when he finally made love to her, he would do it with her full acquiescence. Until then, and as long as he desired her thereafter, he would allow no other man to touch her.

Jason considered the weapon he held in his palm. It

was no larger than a penknife, the blade barely the length of his thumb. Though it offered scant protection, he would feel better knowing she had some means of defense in his absence.

Placing the knife on the bedside table, he pulled on his boots and hoisted the chair back over beside the now-cold fireplace. Then he quietly let himself out of the chamber.

Chapter Three

Shame swept through Mirella's body, hot as the midmorning sun streaming in the uncurtained window. Just moments before, she had awakened, smiling from some pleasant dream which still lingered on the edge of her consciousness. Eyes closed, she had stretched like a cat in the narrow bed, feeling more rested than she had in days.

But on opening her eyes to the strange room, the memory of the previous night had washed over her like a floodtide. She had nearly lost her innocence to a stranger. And worst of all, she had enjoyed his caresses!

Now her mind tormented her, calling forth images of her wanton behavior. She remembered moaning in pleasure when he had touched her naked breasts. Indeed, though she had been successful in preventing him from raping her, her body had yearned for his. How could she have felt such a shocking desire for a man about whom she knew nothing but his name?

" 'Tisn't true," she whispered aloud, wishing her denial could magically turn what had happened into an illusion concocted by her imagination. But the silence of the empty room seemed to mock her.

Groaning, Mirella sat up and put her head in her hands. She had allowed, nay, *encouraged* Jason Fletcher's attentions. There had been no need to let him go on caressing her so intimately. And suppose the real reason she had hesitated, knife held high in the air, was because she had hoped he would stop her? Perhaps in her heart she *was* the whore he had believed her to be.

Stop it! Mirella ordered herself firmly. It did little good to berate herself. The truth of the matter was that she had experienced for the first time the natural response of a woman to a handsome man. Though it was something she had expected to feel only within the bonds of holy matrimony, she could not allow this experience to make her feel any less a lady than she had before.

Besides, ultimately she had resisted him. A wave of self-righteous rage swept over her. Come to think of it, Jason Fletcher was far more at fault than she. The fact that he had purchased her in the first place bespoke a low moral character. Though more attractive physically, he was no better than Sir Harry or the sailors downstairs. God, how she despised men! All they wanted was to satisfy their bodily lusts.

Mirella concluded that, at the moment, only one course of action was prudent—she must get as far away from Jason Fletcher as possible. Draping a sheet over her bare breasts, she stepped quickly to the door. The knob rattled uselessly in her hand. He had locked her in!

In angry frustration, she pounded on the thick

wood with both fists, calling for help. But when she paused to listen, the hall outside was silent. Either no one had heard her or Jason had paid them well to ignore her.

The window was the only other possible avenue of escape. Eagerly she ran over to peer out into the late April sunshine. Her hopes were dashed when she saw the straight two-story drop to the busy street below. The innkeeper and another man she vaguely recognized as having been in the crowd last night stood down there talking. She toyed with the idea of enlisting their help, but common sense told her she might be better off staying put. It would do no good to exchange one aggressive male for two.

Besides, where could she go without the proper clothing? The bodice of her gown was ruined beyond repair. Having unsuccessfully attempted to pull together the torn edges, she wrapped the threadbare sheet around her more securely so that her naked flesh was hidden from view.

Then she paced the small chamber, learning every inch of the rough-planked floor. Why had Jason imprisoned her? His motivation was puzzling. Did he plan to hold her captive until she yielded her innocence in return for her freedom? No, she could not, *would not*, lie beneath him, allowing him complete mastery over her. She would die first!

Yet suppose he turned her back over to the innkeeper. That might be an even worse fate. If only she had some means of defense . . .

Suddenly remembering the knife, Mirella flung herself to the floor, her fingers scrabbling through the dust balls under the bed. When her quest proved

51

fruitless, she knelt, head resting against the rumpled bed in despair. Jason must have taken the weapon with him.

Then she spied it sitting on the bedside table and, with a cry of delight, snatched it up. But, immediately, her brow puckered in bewilderment. The knife had fallen to the floor last night, she was certain of it. That could only mean that Jason had deliberately left it on the table for her. A foolish move on his part—she sniffed—but she was thankful to him for this small gesture of trust.

Feeling somewhat more secure, Mirella dragged the battered wingchair into the warm sunlight. She settled herself in it to await Jason's return, tucking her stockinged feet beneath her and placing the knife beside her within easy reach. The longer she sat, the angrier she grew. And it didn't help her temperament any that her stomach was rumbling from lack of nourishment.

How dare this Jason Fletcher lock her up as if he owned her! Perhaps he felt he had not yet gotten his money's worth. But that was his problem, not hers. If he refused to let her go, she'd find some way to escape him, that was certain!

After a while, the combination of the sun's warmth and boredom made her drowsy. Snuggling more comfortably into the chair, she leaned her head to one side and slept.

Something was tickling her nose. Sleepily, Mirella brushed it away, but it soon returned to plague her. Wrinkling her face in annoyance, she reluctantly opened her eyes to see Jason bending over her, a devilish grin brightening his rugged features. Still groggy from her unaccustomed nap, she found herself studying him, noting the pleasing contrast of his white, even teeth against his sun-burnished skin. In the daylight, his hair was not entirely dark brown but contained an abundance of honey-colored streaks similar in shade to the buckskin breeches that hugged his muscular thighs. His eyes, too, seemed lighter, more like molten gold than the plain brown they had appeared to be the previous night.

Holding a strand of her ebony hair, Jason leaned over and again tickled her nose. "Do you like what you see?" he teased.

Mirella stiffened, appalled at herself for her unconscious admiration of him. Thrusting past him, she scrambled out of the wingback chair, nearly tripping before his amused eyes as she stepped on the end of the sheet wrapped around her.

" 'Tis time you returned! I was beginning to think I would be locked in here forever!"

Jason ignored her outburst, smiling indulgently as if she were a child having a temper tantrum. What Mirella did not know, he mused, was that his mood was better than it had been since before he'd left Virginia. For once on this trip, the morning's business had not been fraught with problems. Returning here to this pretty woman had raised his spirits all the more.

"I brought you a gown to replace the one that was ruined." He gestured to a large box which lay on the wrinkled bed. "Much as I approve of that makeshift garment, I'm sure you would prefer something a little less . . . revealing."

Mirella gasped, realizing that the sheet was gaping open, baring her breasts to his gaze. She jerked the edges of the fabric together, flushing from head to toe. Her pulses were beating madly, but she assured herself that it was outrage that heated her blood. How dare he look at her as if she were an object designed for his amusement!

"You've no right to lock me in there," she hissed. "I demand that you release me at once!"

"Clad like that?" Jason asked drily.

"I meant after I've changed." Clothed the way she was, she felt at a decided disadvantage, yet she managed to summon a haughty poise. "Now if you would be so kind as to leave, I'll dress and then be on my way."

His smile faded. "You're not going anywhere without my say-so," he stated flatly. "I'm taking you back home with me—to Virginia."

Mirella stared in shock. A colonial! That explained his peculiar drawl, so different from the precise speech of her own upbringing. Anger whipped through her. Who was he to think he could force her to accompany him to some strange and savage land?

"You must be mad to think you can drag me off to some godforsaken wilderness as if I've no choice in the matter!"

Jason laughed. "Virginia is not as uncivilized as you think. Believe me, you'll be far safer there with me than you could ever be here at The Crescent Moon."

"Your concern is touching," she mocked. "However, where I live is a decision that will be made by *me*, Mr. Fletcher, not by some stranger I hadn't even

54

met at this time yesterday."

"Call me Jason. And we're not exactly strangers anymore, are we?"

The tone of his voice had deepened, and his eyes had narrowed slightly, lending a sensual cast to his golden gaze. With a sharp intake of breath, Mirella realized Jason was referring to his intimate knowledge of her body. The thought made her burn . . . with anger, she assured herself. The fool acted as if he owned her!

"We're strangers in all things that truly matter, *Mr. Fletcher*," she said, stating his name with cold emphasis. "I fear you'd best resign yourself to traveling to Virginia without me."

His lips tightened in stubborn determination. "You're coming with me, like it or not. I'll not leave you here at the mercy of the men who frequent this tavern. I intend to keep you under my protection."

"Your protection!" Mirella gave a bitter laugh. "You wish to use me for your own amusement."

"You're wrong. I only want to help you." But inside Jason knew there was an element of truth to her words. He hid his uneasiness from her. It was never good to let a woman see any weakness in you because she would only use it to her advantage.

"And you expect me to believe that?" She shook her head, her stockinged feet angrily pacing the wood-planked floor. "Nay, you're no different from other men."

"Another man would have ignored your protests last night," he pointed out.

"What difference if you force me now or postpone the taking until later? 'Twould still be rape!"

55

His good humor was rapidly dissolving under the persistence of her attack. Indeed, Jason was now on the brink of exasperation. He strode to the bed and leaned against the post while he calmed himself. He hadn't thought it would be so difficult to convince her to come to Virginia. Most women would have been eager to escape a hellhole like The Crescent Moon.

"Mirella, there's one important point you're overlooking. How can you blame me for what almost happened when 'twas you who sold yourself to me in the first place?"

"But I didn't!"

Jason's upraised brows illustrated his disbelief, making Mirella seethe with wrath. So he still thought she had the morals of a whore despite the way she had fought him off. That explained why he was insisting she stay with him. Hadn't he said last night that if she pleased him, he would set her up as his mistress? No doubt the pompous ass believed she would jump at the chance.

A budding shiver of longing pricked at her nerve endings. Shocked, Mirella realized that at some deep, primitive level she was tempted by the thought of being his woman. She quickly crushed that momentary madness. Her mind clamored for escape from this arrogant man who sought to steal her independence. She had to persuade him to release her. Clearly the first step toward that goal was to convince him she was not what he believed her to be.

"Perhaps you'll understand better when I explain what happened," Mirella said coolly. "Yesterday I was hired here as a serving girl, but at the time I had no idea that Bates and I had differing ideas about what my duties were to be. When he enlightened me, I resisted, so he gagged me. There was naught I could do in my own defense. Do you have any idea what it feels like to be one woman against a crowd of drunken, lecherous men?"

She paused, enjoying the expression of startled understanding dawning on Jason Fletcher's face. "So I waited until I was alone with you, pretending to be agreeable until I had an opportunity to use my knife. The rest I'm sure you can work out for yourself."

To Jason, her words shed new light on what had happened. He had not even considered the possibility that she might have been an unwilling participant from the start. But her story fit, he reflected, remembering the defiance he had glimpsed in her indigo eyes long before she had ever drawn her knife. So the conclusion he had come to early this morning was wrong. Mirella's reluctance had not stemmed from her having had second thoughts about selling herself. Her purpose had been firm from the very beginning.

He sighed and strode to the window to stare pensively through the dirty glass at the sun-lit scene outside. Lost in thought, he absently noticed, over the rooftops, the tall masts that pierced the blue sky, indicating where ships, including his, were anchored in the nearby channel. He realized that Mirella sought to use her tale to goad him into releasing her. Instead it had strengthened his resolve to whisk her away from Bristol before she got herself entangled in even worse trouble.

There was only one point still nagging at him. Pivoting to face her, Jason asked, "How did you come to be at The Crescent Moon to begin with?"

Mirella opened her mouth to answer, then closed it. He had caught her off guard with that sympathetic look and, for a split second, she had been tempted to spill out the story of Sir Harry. But common sense told her he would be less likely to free her if he knew her desperate straits. And in any case, she reminded herself, men were not to be trusted, least of all one who had exhibited so little regard for her wishes.

"I needed the money," she hedged, giving a shrug which she hoped conveyed the impression that his question was immaterial.

But Jason persisted. "I'm no fool, Mirella. You don't belong here. You should be in a drawing room of some elegant home entertaining suitors and drinking tea from fine porcelain cups. So what brought you to this squalid inn?"

"My past is none of your concern."

Her obstinate expression warned him not to probe any further. Most likely, then, she was running away from someone or something. But despite her proud bearing, she had an innate innocence that aroused in him a curious urge to draw her into his arms and to protect her from the evils of the world. If she was reluctant to reveal her past, then so be it.

He stepped to where Mirella stood near the fireplace, reaching out to tangle a gentle hand in the black silk of her hair. She stiffened at his touch, and her smoky-blue eyes flashed as cold as sapphires. Jason suddenly longed to see her gaze warmed by desire as it had been so briefly the previous night. Would their caresses be as sweet now without brandy and moonlight to heighten their senses?

Reluctantly he tamped down the fire that flared in

him. When he finally bedded her, he reminded himself, she would be a willing partner. And judging by her present temperament, that would require him to engage in a goodly amount of courting.

"I don't really care where you're from," he said quietly. "In truth, if you'll stop to think about it, I'm willing to take you far away from whatever it is you're fleeing."

Mirella started at his perception. How had Jason Fletcher known that she was running from someone? She reassured herself that it was only a shrewd guess on his part. Still, she could not help but admire the way he had used it to his advantage. Accompanying him to Virginia *would* be a way to make certain Sir Harry would never find her. She was suspicious of Jason's motives but decided to find out more—cautiously.

"Why would you want to help me?"

His eyes glinted like gold coins in response to her first tiny step toward possible capitulation. But when he spoke, neither his words nor his tone betrayed any evidence of the small sense of victory she was sure he felt.

"We would be helping each other. I've a fourteen-year-old sister who, I fear, hasn't been disciplined well since my parents' death some ten years ago. I thought to hire you to give her the feminine guidance she needs."

"You have no wife then?"

"Nay." Abruptly his eyes narrowed. "And lest you have any ambitions in that direction, let me tell you now that I have no intention to wed anytime soon."

Mirella gave a derisive laugh. The conceit of the

man to assume she would plot to trap him into marriage! "Let me tell *you*," she retorted, "that even were I in the market for a husband, your name would be at the bottom of my list of prospects!"

Jason's lips curved into a disarming smile. "Then we're finally in agreement on one matter. Perhaps now we can agree on what your duties would be as my employee."

"I suppose warming your bed would be one of them." Despite his explanation of why he proposed to take her to Virginia, Mirella was certain that he wanted someone conveniently located in his own home to satisfy his lusts.

"Mirella, I promise I will never force you to do anything against your will," Jason swore, his face as solemn as the vow that left his lips.

His persuasive tone caused her mind to waver from its resolve. Perhaps he did mean what he said. . . . But just then, she caught his admiring gaze sliding down her body.

Her lips tightened in response to a returning storm of wrath. Doubtless, he was trying to lull her into a false sense of security with his tale of a sister. Then, once he had her safely away from England, he would waste no time seducing her. She would be no doxy even if it meant starving to death in Bristol! Never again would she be fooled by a man!

Mirella whirled around, presenting her back to him as she adjusted the sheet which was slipping precariously before his interested eyes.

"I refuse your offer," she threw over her shoulder, not bothering to hide her contempt. "Now, I've work to do, so I'll thank you to—"

Her words were cut short as a pair of large hands clamped over her upper arms. Jason whipped her around to face him.

"Let us get one point clear, Mirella!" he sneered. " 'Tis not an offer I'm giving you, but an order! I know your type. Now that you've had a brief taste of the secret pleasures of the bedchamber, you'll be downstairs peddling your wares to any man with a purseful of gold!"

"That's a lie!" Mirella recoiled in shock at his crude accusation. Vainly, she tried to extract herself from his viselike grip. "I never want to be touched by another man so long as I live! Why else do you think I stopped you last night?"

"Then just what kind of work were you referring to?" His tone was suspicious, his features still fierce with fury.

"Not what you think! Now, let me go—you're hurting my arms!"

For a moment, Jason stared blankly at her, the strength of his sudden emotion seeping out of him. His blind rage had surprised him as much as it had her. Frowning, he loosened his hold on her. What the devil had gotten into him to accuse an innocent like her of being a common whore?

As if in apology, his hand stroked the spot it had just released, his touch light as a feather. Then he let his fingers gently glide down her arm. When he reached her bare wrist, he firmly encircled its fragile curve. He was startled to see her wince. Looking down in puzzlement, his eyes widened as he saw the purplish bruises that marred the milky hue of her skin.

"By damn, did I do that?" His voice was incredulous, his face stunned. Swiftly he drew up her other wrist for comparison.

"I swear by all that is holy, I do not remember harming you like this last night." His thumbs softly traced the twin discolored shapes. "But how else could you have come by these bruises?"

Mirella was tempted to lie and say it was indeed his fault. But his stricken expression softened her. " 'Twas the innkeeper, I'm sure, who caused them when he twisted my arms behind my back."

"That bloody bastard!" Jason exploded. "I'd like to wring his fat neck!" Then a contrite look flashed over his features. "Though I fear I very nearly did you far more damage last night than he."

Lightly he ran a finger along the satiny skin above her breasts. The breath caught in her throat as a burst of sensation tightened her belly. It was the height of madness to let him touch her but her limbs seemed to have turned liquid, rendering her incapable of action.

"Believe me, I would never knowingly harm you," he drawled softly. "I'm sorry I accused you like that a moment ago. 'Tis only that last night I caught a glimpse of your passionate nature. Can you blame me for not wanting any other man to see that in you?"

Mirella could think of no reply. His voice was low and seductive; his molten gold eyes mesmerized her, holding within their brilliant depths an invitation to draw nearer. Yet already she was close enough to catch his male scent, as intoxicating as brandy. Her flesh was weakening in denial of the mistrust that her intellect knew he deserved.

"Come with me," he murmured, "and I vow I'll never make love to you against your will."

"Nay, you're lying!" she moaned, struggling to halt her instinctive response. "I won't be your mistress." Yet she didn't move away.

"Sweet Mirella." His hand wandered over to cup the curve of her breast, its taut peak betrayed by the thinness of the sheet covering it. "Can you truthfully say you don't want me to touch you ever again?"

Mirella wrenched herself from the caress that sent chills shivering over her spine. It was time he understood that he did not own her.

"Get out of here," she hissed through gritted teeth.

To her surprise, Jason smiled and strolled obediently toward the door. Hand on the knob, he pivoted toward her, masculine assurance etched in every lean muscle of his body.

"Think about what I've said, Mirella. And remember this, if I catch you trying to escape, you'll have to bear the consequences." His bold eyes swept over her curves, leaving her little doubt as to the form that punishment would take.

"I'll never go with you to Virginia, do you hear me? I'll fight you any way I can!"

But the door slammed shut in the middle of her tirade, and she heard the rattle of the key in the lock.

So he thought he had her under his thumb, did he? In frustrated rage, Mirella looked about wildly. When she saw her knife, which lay forgotten on the chair, she snatched it up and hurled it against the closed door.

It fell harmlessly to the floor with a thud.

Chapter Four

Mirella paced the tiny bedchamber until the heat of her anger abated and a cold, calculating resolve took shape in her mind. One thing was certain, she vowed silently, no way in heaven or on earth would she willingly abandon the country of her birth and accompany that . . . that colonial *oaf* to some wilderness clear across the ocean!

She wracked her brain for a way out of her dilemma. It was unnerving to feel so helpless. But with the door locked, she was Jason Fletcher's prisoner, and there was no one she could turn to for aid. At the moment her only recourse was to be prepared just in case an opportunity did arise in which she could slip out of his clutches.

First and foremost, it would be foolhardy to go out into this dockside neighborhood clad in ripped garments which gaped open to any lusting eyes. She must doff her ruined clothing and don the new gown Jason had brought her.

She unwound the threadbare sheet and threw it onto the rumpled bed alongside the large wooden box.

Lifting the lid of the box, she caught her breath at the beauty of the deep rose silk within. Her fingers stroked the soft, rich fabric. Not since she was a young girl, before her father had gambled away the family fortune, had she possessed a gown of such stunning elegance. How had Jason managed to obtain it on such short notice?

That question was swiftly forgotten as Mirella pulled the garment out of its resting place. The deep rose, she discovered, was an overskirt which parted in front to reveal a triangular panel of blush pink silk, its peak touching the tiny waist and its fullest glory spread across the ruffled hem. Tiers of Brussels lace cascaded from the three-quarter-length sleeves, while ribbons of the purest white satin adorned the bodice.

After shaking out the wrinkles, she carefully laid the gown on the bed. Then she looked into the box again to find undergarments, shoes, and stockings, all fashioned of the finest quality materials. There was even a minuscule vial of perfume from which emanated the delicate scent of violets.

This was raiment designed for a lady of wealth and leisure. With an eagerness she hadn't felt in years, Mirella stripped the tattered blue wool off her body. She was about to toss it aside when she remembered her mother's cameo. Reaching into the pocket of the ruined gown, she unpinned the piece of jewelry and withdrew it. Lovingly, she ran a finger over the finely carved onyx silhouette. At least, Mirella reflected sadly, she could be thankful that her mother had not lived to see her daughter reduced to fleeing home and being held against her will.

Finding a deep pocket in the rose-and-pink silk

gown, she refastened the cameo out of sight of prying eyes. Since it was all she had left of her mother, she didn't want anyone to steal this, her most precious possession. Her sole possession, Mirella revised with a wry smile. Oh, if only it were possible to regain the innocent happiness of her childhood . . .

But now was no time for foolish daydreams, she reminded herself. She had best don her new attire and await an opportunity to escape. Her ragged undergarments joined the pile of blue linsey-woolsey on the floor as she stripped down to bare flesh, shivering in the slight chill of the air.

She was reaching into the box for a chemise of frothy lace and satin when the key suddenly rattled in the lock. Jason Fletcher! Panicked, she grabbed a sheet off the bed and quickly wound it around her naked body. The shortness of the material forced her to leave her shoulders uncovered in exchange for concealing more of her shapely thighs.

The door swung open. Mirella parted her lips to hurl a caustic invective at Jason for his rudeness in failing to knock first. But it was not her captor who entered.

It was Fanny, one of the other serving maids, who sauntered into the bedchamber, balancing a tray in her hands.

" 'Ello there," Fanny said cheerfully. "Oi brung yer some vittles." She swiftly dumped the tray onto the dressing table, and then turned and locked the door, dropping the key into the low bodice of her dirt-streaked white blouse.

Taken by surprise, Mirella realized only belatedly that she had missed a prime opportunity to escape out the door. Yet now her mind churned with fresh hope. If she could trick Fanny into freeing her . . .

"The gen'man said Oi was to stay 'ere wi' ye while ye ate." Fanny waved a hand at the steaming plate of food.

"Thank you, but that won't be necessary," Mirella said in her most regal tone. "If you'll just leave the door unlocked, when I'm through, I'll place the tray out in the hall."

Fanny gave a determined shake of her carrot-colored hair, folding her arms across an overflowing bosom. "Oi can't do that, mum."

"Whyever not?" Mirella countered impatiently.

"The gen'man said ye'd try to escape. And 'e said Oi wouldn't git no money if'n Oi didn't keep the door locked."

Damn that conniving colonial! Mirella fumed. It was plain that he had secured Fanny's undying loyalty by enticing her with the clink of coins. What recourse did that leave? Did she dare hope that an appeal to the serving maid's sympathy might work? It was worth a try.

"Fanny, the man purchased my services for one night, and one night only. Now he seeks to hold me here without further payment. 'Tisn't fair!" In agitation, Mirella began to pace back and forth in front of the bed. "Don't you see? He cares not for my feelings! Because he is stronger than I, he believes it his right to demand that I remain with him, though it be against my free will."

She looked at the serving wench to assess the impact of the impassioned speech. But Fanny's wide-eyed attention was captured by what lay on the

68

rumpled sheets.

"Oooh, my . . ." she breathed, a hand rising to her buxom breasts. As if in a trance, she brushed past Mirella to finger the exquisite rose silk of the gown Jason had brought. "Oi never seen anythin' so fine."

"Yes, yes," Mirella agreed impatiently. "But Fanny, you haven't given me an answer. You must help me get away from here, please!"

"Why would ye want to flee from a man 'oo'd give ye such a pretty present?"

Mirella pursed her lips at Fanny's uncomprehending look. "Because he seeks to take me off to Virginia with him, and I don't wish to go!"

"A lover's tiff, eh?" the serving girl returned with an expression of sly understanding. " 'E's a 'andsome buck, that 'e is. Oi see 'e must 'ave kept ye up all night since the sun's 'igh in the sky, and ye're still not dressed yet."

Mirella flushed scarlet, fastening the sheet tighter over herself. Spine erect, she pushed away the disturbing memories of her intimate encounter with Jason. "I . . . I merely slept late," she replied stiffly.

"Aw, come on now," the buxom redhead wheedled, her eyes avid with curiosity. "Ye can tell ol' Fanny. Oi'll wager 'e's a lusty one betwixt the sheets, ain't 'e?"

" 'Tis none of your concern!" Mirella snapped, her tolerance wearing thin. "Now will you help me or won't you?"

"Won't. The gen'man said 'e wouldn't pay me if'n ye got away from me."

Mirella gave an exasperated sigh, her bare shoulders slumping in defeat against the bedpost. It was obvious that she was wasting her breath in trying to appeal to the other woman's good nature. If only she had something with which to bargain . . .

Suddenly she straightened up. "Fanny, if you unlock that door, I'll give you this gown," she said, waving a hand toward the frothy concoction of silk and lace lying on the bed. "You could . . . you could sell it, couldn't you? And you'd get far more money, I'm sure, than the pittance Jason Fletcher is offering you."

Fanny's hazel eyes gleamed with greed as she leaned over to touch the fine fabric longingly. Then abruptly she shook her head. " 'E said if ye was to try and bribe me, why just to tell 'im, and 'e'd double yer offer."

"Damn him!" Mirella burst out, as her last hope was dashed to pieces. Taking a deep breath, she went on, "Please, Fanny, I beg you. As a woman, can you not see my plight and take pity on me?"

"Sorry, mum," the serving wench said, with a stubborn shrug of her shoulders. "Oi'll just set meself down right 'ere while ye eat." She perched her ample behind onto the mattress, alongside the rose silk gown. "And the gen'man said, too, that Oi was to 'elp ye dress if ye asked. Oooh, ye're so lucky to have such a fine man 'oo'll give ye such fine things." She sighed enviously, eying the richness of the gown.

With angry frustration, Mirella saw that there was no reasoning with Fanny. She would have to think of another means of escape. For want of anything better to do, she stepped over to the dressing table to pick up the wooden tray. Though her stomach was churning with tension, the savory odors rising from the tin

70

plates of food made her realize that she was ravenous.

She settled into the wingback chair, balancing the tray on her lap. There was a meat pie, along with stewed cabbage and an apple pudding. Using her three-tined fork to dip into the fare, Mirella pondered her dilemma. It appeared she'd have to be more cunning. As she ate, a plan slowly formed in her mind. She sipped on a tumbler of cheap red wine, considering the idea. Perhaps she could create a situation in which she could catch Fanny by surprise.

"Fanny?"

"Aye, mum?" The serving girl's eyes bobbed up from their awed admiration of the silk gown.

Mirella pasted a gracious smile on her face in an effort to convince Fanny that she had resigned herself to the situation. "Before I dress, I would appreciate it very much if you would bring me water for a bath."

"But the gen'man said Oi was to stay 'ere wi' ye until ye was through."

"I'm finished."

"Well, all right, then." Obediently, the carrot-haired girl slid her plump body off the edge of the bed, and took the tray. Plucking the key from her bodice, she unlocked the door and slammed it shut behind her, a rattling sound in the keyhole telling Mirella that the serving wench would not be careless in her role of gaoler.

Jason Fletcher must be paying Fanny well for her to be so eager to please, Mirella decided in disgust. Blast that aggravating man! It was time to put the rest of her escape plan into action.

She marched over on bare feet to pick up her knife, which still lay where she had thrown it earlier, on the

71

floor near the door. Staring down at the blade resting in her palm, she wrestled with her conscience. It was one thing to use the weapon on Jason, when he had been about to rape her, and quite another to contemplate stabbing Fanny. The serving girl was no true villainess for desiring to make a little extra money on the side.

Cursing her soft heart, Mirella tossed the little knife onto the bed and instead picked up a chipped pitcher from the dressing table. A good smack on the head would knock Fanny out but not injure her permanently. She took up a position behind the door to await her victim.

The minutes ticked by with agonizing slowness. Just when she thought she could not stand the tension one moment longer, the key clattered in the lock.

Hands trembling, Mirella raised the pitcher, ready to strike. The door swung open.

She froze in surprise to see an unfamiliar serving girl totter into the room, hefting two large steaming pails of water. Right on the first girl's heels was Fanny, carting a similar load, and behind her, still another wench carrying a small wooden tub.

Mirella lowered the makeshift weapon in frustration. How could she fight three at once? Why, she railed at herself, hadn't she anticipated this turn of events?

Fanny deposited her buckets on the floor and closed the door. "Did ye want somethin'?" she asked, eying the pitcher curiously.

"Uh, yes," Mirella stumbled, searching for an explanation. "The wine I had with my meal wasn't sufficient to quench my thirst. I wondered if you'd mind fetching me some more." She thrust the vessel at Fanny.

"Oi don't need no pitcher fer that. Oi'll jist bring ye up the 'ole bottle." With one last look of puzzlement, she shrugged and began to direct the other wenches in the positioning and filling of the bathtub.

At least Fanny seemed content with the excuse, Mirella decided in relief, as she watched one of the girls light a fire in the hearth. It was vitally important not to be robbed of the element of surprise should another opportunity arise.

"Ye can git yerself settled into yer bath, then, while Rosie 'ere'll be bringin' ye some more 'ot water," Fanny advised. "An' Oi'll be back wi' 'er in a twinklin' to bring yer wine." Shooing her giggling helpers out the door, she locked it behind her.

Mirella slammed the pitcher back down on the dressing table, letting out an irritated sigh. Now what was she to do? It was useless to contemplate escape with the two of them trooping back in a few moments. She might as well take advantage of the bathtub. There was always the possibility that she could lure Fanny back alone later on the pretext of needing help in donning her gown.

Unwinding the sheet, she threw it onto the bed. On impulse, she took the vial of perfume Jason had given her and tipped a few drops from it into the low tub, which was situated near the merrily burning fireplace. Then she eased her naked body into the heated liquid, not minding at all that the cramped basin required her to sit with her knees scrunched up almost to her chin. It was a marvelous luxury to cleanse herself like this when, for the past month, she had been forced to

73

content herself with sponge baths.

Misty tendrils of steam rose from the water, and the subtle scent of violets filled the air. Mirella dunked her hair and scrubbed it clean using the cake of soap Fanny had left her.

Then, sighing with contentment, she arched her head back on the edge of the tub as her limbs relaxed under the influence of the gently lapping warmth. The chamber was silent but for the soft snap of the fire. Her eyelids drifted shut, her long ebony locks floating like seaweed in the enveloping water.

When the doorknob rattled again, she paid little heed, too lazy to even lift her head to greet Fanny and the other serving girl. Two sets of footsteps walked across the wooden floor, one light and pattering, the other heavier, thudding. Odd, that one pair sounded more male than female. . . .

Mirella's eyelids flew open as she jerked upright in the tub. Jason Fletcher! He was standing a scant foot away, staring at her, a goblet in one hand, wine bottle in the other. Following the direction of his admiring golden gaze, she realized to her horror that her breasts were well above the water level, their creamy mounds exposed in full glory.

She gasped and slid back down into the half-filled basin, concealing as much of her nakedness as possible. A flush that had nothing at all to do with the heat of the surrounding liquid suffused her entire body.

"What are you doing here?" she squeaked.

"Why, I brought you your wine," Jason said, grinning as she crossed her arms in a somewhat futile attempt to cover herself. "Fanny said you were most insistent about wanting it, didn't you, Fanny?" He sent a smile in the serving wench's direction.

"Aye, sir." Fanny batted her eyelashes at him, blatantly flirting. A pail of water occupied one of her hands, but with the other, she patted the frizzy carrot mop atop her head and then adjusted the revealing bodice of her blouse so that it dipped even lower still.

Silly, simpering female! Mirella thought derisively. Was Jason bedding that hussy? "Fanny, come over here," she commanded, surprising herself with the sharpness of her tone. "Please pour the rest of that water in here at once."

"Aye, mum." She brushed past Jason to tip the bucket into the tub.

Mirella felt only slightly better as the rising level covered a few more inches of her bare, rosy skin. Her mind was a muddle of anger and acute embarrassment. If only she had her knife handy she would gladly plunge it into Jason Fletcher's arrogant hide!

"That'll be all, Fanny," Jason said, flipping her a coin.

"As ye wish, sir." She caught the piece of silver with an agility that was surprising for her plumpness, then bobbed a quick curtsey to him. With one last envious look at Mirella, she sashayed out the door, banging it shut behind her.

"Do you want that wine now?" Jason asked, placing the goblet on the dressing table and pouring from the bottle.

"All I want," Mirella hissed, "is to see your backside heading out of this bedchamber!"

He chuckled. "Now, is that any way to address the man responsible for preserving your virtue last night?"

" 'Twould seem your concern for my virtue has vanished with the light of day," she retorted, trying to hide her mortification behind a shield of rage. "If you had but a scrap of decency, you'd leave here at once."

Jason strolled to the hearth, his lean body towering over the bathtub. "Ah, but 'tis too enjoyable an experience to end so swiftly." He held out a pewter goblet to her. "Here, my sweet, drink this down and you'll soon overcome your maidenly shyness."

"I don't want it. Take it away!"

"Then 'twould seem, fair lady, that you force me to drink the wine myself . . . and in my own fashion."

Jason knelt alongside the tub, and before she realized what he was about, he tipped the goblet so that a thin stream of burgundy liquid trickled onto her bare shoulder and slid down to hover enticingly above the swell of breast concealed by its shield of tightly folded arms.

Mirella gasped as the cold sensation hit her warm flesh. She was still reeling from the shock of his boldness when Jason bent his tawny gold head, putting his mouth to the droplets of sweet liquid that clung to her skin. The sensual touch of his tongue and lips sent shivers coursing over her body. It suddenly became difficult for her to catch her breath.

"Don't, please. . . ." she moaned.

When Jason lifted his head, she thought it was to heed her plea. But, wide-eyed, she watched him pour more wine, this time christening her other shoulder and breast. The blood pounded through her veins as he kissed away all traces of the nectar. His nearness seemed more intoxicating than any brew, more potent than any drug.

Then he looked deeply into her indigo eyes, his fingers wandering over her flushed cheeks. " 'Tis a far more pleasant way to drink, is it not?" he murmured.

"Nay," Mirella whispered, fighting the languor that swamped her senses. "Please, leave me be."

She slipped down as far as possible into the steaming water, feeling the blush on her face grow hotter. She had to tighten her arms around herself to resist a mad impulse to reach up and stroke his bronzed skin and tawny hair. What was he doing to her? He had even managed to steal the weapon of anger from her with his honeyed words and seductive touch.

Jason continued to caress her cheek. "Your body yearns for me, Mirella. If you would but yield to its demands, our coming voyage to Virginia would be so much the richer."

The reminder that she was his prisoner cut through the film of desire that bedeviled her brain. She took refuge in the rage that again bubbled up inside of her. Did he expect her to be grateful for the chance to be his mistress? She was no Fanny, who would grovel at his feet in adoration merely because he had graced her with a smile.

" 'Twill be a cold day in hell when I yield to you!" Mirella snapped.

His golden eyes mocked her. "So the warm woman vanishes, and the shrewish maid returns," he teased. "What is the cause of this magical transformation?"

"Look no farther than yourself for the answer, you cloddish knave!" She tossed up her chin, her wet ebony hair tumbling around her face in riotous disarray. "Now get out, and let me conclude my bath in peace."

"Allow me to offer my services," he said with a devilish smile. "Surely you'll require my aid in scrubbing your back." He made a move toward her.

"Don't touch me!" Eyes wide with fear, Mirella shrank away, tightening her arms over her naked breasts.

As he gazed at her, she was seized by the realization that she was completely within his power. What could she do to fend off his superior strength should he choose to force himself upon her?

Some inkling of her distress must have reached him, for there was a slight softening of his rugged features. "A compromise, then. I'll stand over by the window and wait for you to finish."

"Nay, leave!"

" 'Tis my only concession," he cautioned, his voice stubborn. "Do not try my patience any more than you already have."

Mirella frowned. His offer was better than nothing. "Then at least be gentleman enough to turn your eyes from me," she ground out in frustration.

"Agreed. But don't dally too long, else I'll consider the bargain void." Jason rose to his feet and strode over to the window.

As soon as his back was to her, Mirella reached for the cake of soap. The quickness of her movements was due to both Jason's warning and the growing coolness of the water. Lathering her skin, she pondered her dilemma, her thoughts coming fast and furious.

There must be a way to escape him! An idea struck her, and she wracked her memory. All was not lost! The cocksure bastard hadn't locked the door when Fanny left, had he? And since he was at the opposite

78

end of the room, with the tub between him and the door, that just might give her the advantage she sought.

With burgeoning hope, she stood up, water rolling down her naked body as she grabbed the scrap of linen towel Fanny had draped on the wingback chair.

Jason heard the splash of liquid as she stepped out onto the floor. Hot blood surged to his loins. In his mind, he pictured her womanly figure, all rosy and glowing from her bath, looking like Venus rising from the pink pearlescence of a seashell. The male fingers resting on the window frame tightened. This was a temptation that would sorely try the willpower of a saint. He longed to turn and drag her into his arms, making love to her until she was pliant and passionate, begging for his caresses.

But he reminded himself that she was a virgin, and if he hoped to convince her to be his mistress, he would have to exercise patience. Gritting his teeth, he stared fiercely out the dirt-streaked glass, concentrating on the forest of ship masts rising from the nearby channel.

Why did he torture himself like this? Why hadn't he simply complied with her request and left her in peace?

Because he was bewitched, he admitted. It was that same fascination which had induced him to return to this chamber, when his better judgment had urged him to grant Mirella time to ponder his decision to take her to Virginia.

Behind him, Jason heard the slither and rustle of fabric. Mirella would be donning the chemise he had given her which, along with the pink gown, he had purchased in London for his sister Pandora, in hopes of persuading the young girl to give up her tomboyish ways.

He imagined how Mirella would look in the undergarment, her creamy breasts pressing against the frothy lace. His mind again formed the beguiling image he had seen on first walking into the bedchamber. She had been lying there in the bathtub, her ebony hair dripping like a mermaid surfacing from the ocean depths. Her throat was arched, her eyes closed, as if she were dreaming of her lover's touch. And her skin had smelled like violets when he had licked the sweet wine from it. How he wanted to kiss her soft flesh again. . . .

"Are you clothed yet?" he demanded impatiently.

"Nay . . . only a few moments more, please!"

Mirella hurried, her fingers trembling over the white satin ribbons lacing the bodice of the rose-and-pink silk gown. The garment clearly had been sewn according to another woman's measurements, for the hem was several inches too long, and the fabric was a wee bit tight over her full breasts. Given time and a needle and thread, she could correct these minor faults, but now they were the least of her worries.

Judging by the restless way Jason was tapping on the window frame, it was plain that he wouldn't hold to his promise much longer. And she had to be out of here before he turned around.

Foregoing shoes, Mirella tiptoed to the door on bare feet, trying to keep her gown from rustling. The knob rotated easily in her fingers. It was unlocked! Slowly she eased the door open.

"Mirella, you've had time enough—"

She caught just a quick glimpse of Jason's startled, angry face as she darted out into the dim hall. Hiking up her hem to avoid tripping, she scurried toward the stairs, her damp hair streaming behind her. The thud of his boots close on her trail made her feet fly down the narrow, wooden steps.

Heart pounding, Mirella emerged into the taproom. For a split second, she hesitated, glancing about wildly. Only a few customers occupied the rough tables, and Bates was nowhere to be seen.

Deciding that Jason would expect her to head straight for the front portal, she pivoted sharply and sped down the dark passageway leading to the back of the inn. She released her hem to shove open the door to the kitchen.

The smell of food struck her as a swift glance revealed Bates chastising the cook, a stout woman with a mutinous expression on her broad face. The two serving girls who had brought up the bathwater earlier were cowering behind the cook. All eyes swung to Mirella.

"Say, what's goin' on 'ere?" Bates growled.

The sound of hurrying male footsteps in the corridor behind her made Mirella's heart leap. She whirled toward a door at the rear of the kitchen—and ran smack into Fanny. The stack of linen in Fanny's arms scattered over the floor.

" 'Ey, watch where yer—" Fanny's eyes widened as she identified Mirella. "Yer not supposed to be 'ere!"

Ignoring the serving girl, Mirella dashed over the snowstorm of sheets and towels, her gaze trained on the door that led to freedom.

She would have made it, too, she assured herself

81

later, had she not tripped on the dragging hem of her gown.

She tumbled onto her knees in a flurry of rose silk and white linen. Her brain had scarcely registered the shock of the fall when two male hands came from behind to clamp onto her arms and hoist her to her feet. Stunned and limp, she was twisted around to face the furious gold eyes of her captor.

Breathing hard, Mirella tossed back her wild, damp hair and stared at Jason defiantly, drawing herself up to the fullest extent of her petite height. Her pride refused to let him see her despair at the defeat she had suffered.

"You sneaking little witch," he snarled, shaking her by the shoulders none too gently. "Did you truly think you could escape?"

"Unhand me!" Mirella's eyes flashed sparks of blue fire. "Pray recall that you do not own me."

"You are under my protection, like it or not!" he retorted, his voice harsh and grating on her ears.

She gave a derisive laugh. "Your protection! You expect me to meekly lie down and satisfy your lusts."

"I expect you to obey me!"

"I am not your slave to order about as you please!"

They glared at each other. Mirella was determined to stand her ground no matter what threats or demands he doled out. If he were to rape her in retaliation, at least he would first feel the lash of her anger.

" 'Ere now, take yer squabblin' elsewhere," Bates broke in gruffly. "Yer disrupting me kitchen."

"All right, all right," Jason snapped, flipping the brawny innkeeper a piece of silver. "Here's something for your trouble. Indeed, I, too, am of a mind to carry this quarrel to more private quarters." With a grim expression, he swooped Mirella up into his strong arms before she could protest.

"Release me, you swaggering bully!" She kicked her legs and beat on his wide chest with her fists in a wild attempt to free herself.

"I'll put you down when I'm good and ready."

His grip tightened around her, seeking to pin her flailing arms, until she could scarcely draw a breath. Panting, Mirella wriggled and struggled to no avail. She caught a quick glimpse of the serving maids staring in awed fascination, then Jason shouldered his way out the kitchen door and mounted the narrow staircase leading to the upper story.

Inside their bedchamber, he kicked the door shut behind him and strode across the wooden floor, dumping her without ceremony onto the rumpled bed. He stood over her, his fists perched on his lean hips, a forbidding expression on his face. Glaring up at him in mutiny, Mirella fiercely assured herself that the frenzied thumping of her heart had naught to do with the memory of that hard body pressed to hers or the masculine scent that still teased her senses. She hated this arrogant brute!

Rising slightly, she propped her hands behind her on the mattress. "And now what?" she taunted bravely. "Do you seek to rape me to prove the superiority of your strength?"

"You would try the patience of a saint," he growled, raking a hand through his golden brown hair. "Why can you not simply accept the fact that you are accompanying me to Virginia?"

"Because I won't go! I vow I'll escape you if 'tis the last thing I ever do!"

Jason's eyes gleamed, roving over her tangled damp hair and tumbled skirts. " 'Tis time, then, to mete out your punishment. Mayhap you will change your mind when I show you what the penalty is for thwarting my wishes."

Mirella gasped as he lowered himself to pin her to the soft sheets. Whimpering in sudden fear, she tried to twist away but his larger bulk had her snared like a baby rabbit in a trap. Frowning with determination, Jason imprisoned her hands with one of his to prevent her from striking him. Then he bent his head to take her lips.

She jerked her face aside but he seized her chin with his free hand and drew it back firmly. With all of her willpower, Mirella resisted the seductive play of his mouth. She told herself that his kiss was repulsive, but slowly her body deemed her a liar. Her senses careened wildly, responding to his masterful, demanding touch until she felt that she was swooning. She found her lips parting to the temptation of his tongue. Dimly she was aware of Jason releasing her hands, and then somehow her arms were winding around his neck, her fingers dipping into the thick silk of his hair. His hard chest pressed into her soft breasts, and she could feel the heavy thud of his heart matching the frantic pace of her own.

Abruptly his lips lifted, and she opened her dazed eyes. Her whole body was flushed and trembling. For a moment, Jason's warm, quickened breath caressed her face as he gazed down at her, an odd expression on his rugged features. Then he reached out to frame her delicate jawline in one large hand.

"Such is your punishment," he pronounced unsteadily, "that you should now be plagued with the memory of how easily I can melt your protests."

He thrust himself from her and strode to the door. In stunned awareness of his words, Mirella stared after him, her insides still quivering with passion.

Paralyzed with shame, she heard the clatter of the key in the lock, then the sound of his footsteps disappearing down the hall.

Chapter Five

Jason strolled along the cobbled pavement, idly eyeing the congested quay, where merchant ships from abroad were moored. The waterfront of Bristol was typical of other ports he had visited. Dilapidated buildings lined the wharves, and a stomach-curdling stench rose from the overflowing gutters to mingle with the damp smell of the sea and the fragrance of tropical spices.

The street was crammed with people watching the ocean-going vessels discharge their goods. Some of the milling crowd were there with legitimate purpose; others were pickpockets or prostitutes hoping for an easy mark. The air was filled with the raucous shouts of tradesmen and the clatter of carts and carriages.

From experience, Jason knew that bribes alone secured the prompt unloading of the heavily laden ships. Even then, cargo sat in a custom house until being cleared by excise officials who became miraculously swifter in their work once they were slipped a fistful of silver.

But thankfully, that tedious task was behind him

now and with luck, in a day or two he would set sail for Virginia. The prospect gave Jason's spirits a boost, momentarily driving from his mind the bodily frustrations that had tormented him of late.

He stepped aside to avoid a ragged workman who was rolling a wooden barrel along the uneven cobblestoned surface. The distant tolling of a church bell made Jason quicken his pace, betraying his eagerness to return to The Crescent Moon. The hours this afternoon had dragged, but now that dusk was beginning to darken the sky, the minutes seemed to fly by on winged feet.

A brooding expression crossed his face. Deep down, he acknowledged that his sudden impatience was due to the enticing woman who occupied his bedchamber at the inn. Three days had passed since Mirella had tried to escape . . . three days since that devastating kiss he had intended as a reminder of his dominance over her. But who had he ended up punishing more, Mirella or himself?

He had vowed to woo her slowly, but what he hadn't banked on was the intensity of his hunger for her. Only a willpower forged of steel had kept him from her bed. Each evening, he stayed away from their chamber as long as he could, lingering in the taproom over a bottle of brandy. And the drink also served a second purpose, mellowing him so that the sharp bite of her tongue seemed less important. Why did he put up with her shrewish ways when there were scores of other females who would welcome his attentions?

Because Mirella had bewitched him, Jason admitted silently. He so longed to feel her writhing beneath him in the throes of passion that he could think of little else. She was like a wild mare, he mused, saddle-shy and ripe for mastery. His loins stirred with heat at the thought of caressing her delectable curves. Introducing her to the pleasures of the flesh would be well worth the wait.

A straw-haired trollop suddenly latched onto his arm, promising the heavenly delight of her body in exchange for a single coin. With scarcely a glance, he shook the wench's dirt-begrimed claw off the sleeve of his chocolate brown frockcoat. Ah, if only a certain lady with ebony tresses were so eager to share a bed with him . . .

Jason frowned. But Mirella was as adamant as ever about escaping. Though he had made certain that she had had no further opportunity, her ceaseless hostility aggravated him. She had even managed to make him feel guilty for imprisoning her when he was only acting in her behalf!

His mouth tightened in frustration. Why did Mirella continue to flout him so? How could she fail to see that he was promising her a far better life than she could ever lead here in Bristol?

He hurried down the crowded street, the heels of his boots ringing purposefully on the stone pavement. All the while, his mind traveled a well-worn path, putting forth arguments until he felt completely justified in his actions.

Yes, he assured himself, Mirella would fare far better as his pampered mistress than as a whore in a dockside inn. He would give her a life of luxury in which her every whim would be fulfilled. And when he finally tired of her, he would settle a modest income on her that would keep her in comfort for the rest of her days.

Perhaps his disquiet would ease once he had her safely aboard his ship. It had occurred to him to ensconce her there immediately, but he had swiftly rejected the notion. He had a strong suspicion she would try to convince his sailors to free her. And despite any orders he would give to the contrary, he was afraid that by using her feminine charm she just might succeed in swaying one of the crusty seamen who manned his vessel.

The inn loomed ahead through the waning light. Jason's attention was briefly captured by the sight of a scrawny, tow-headed lad awkwardly hammering an oblong sheet of paper on the door as he struggled to maintain his hold on the stack of handbills tucked under his arm. Peering over the boy's shoulder at the fluttering scrap of white was Bates, fists perched on his massive hips.

Jason halted his quick footsteps to let a horse-drawn dray rattle past, then he crossed the narrow street. As he drew nearer, he absently noticed the youth scuttle around a corner leading to an alleyway.

Were he not so preoccupied, the scene in front of the inn would have amused Jason. Bates was engrossed in reading the handbill, his fleshy face screwed up in concentration as if the task were sorely straining the limits of his literacy. His fat lips moved in unison with the stubby finger that slowly underscored each word on the flyer.

"Bates." Jason gave the oversized man a perfunctory nod as he reached for the handle of the door leading to the taproom. His thoughts were centered on Mirella, and he had little curiosity for news tidings or advertisements.

" 'Ey, wait jist a minute 'ere."

Jason paused at the innkeeper's statement, pivoting with barely concealed irritation. "Yes, what is it?"

"Oi think ye'll want to read this 'ere notice what was jist posted."

Jason afforded the piece of paper only half a glance. "I'm not interested."

"Then maybe that hoity-toity miss yer keepin' upstairs might want to take a gander at it."

"What are you talking about?"

"Jist lookie 'ere." Bates waved a meaty hand at the flyer.

Swallowing his impatience, Jason took a step closer and scrutinized the bit of paper. With indifferent concern, he perused the top line of smeared black print, which read, "WANTED for thievery."

But it was what followed that abruptly shook him out of his apathy: "A runaway female by the name of Mirella Weston."

His gaze whipped down to scan a detailed description of her. At the bottom of the page, it said to contact Sir Harry Weston at an address in a posh section of Bristol to lay claim to a reward of ten pounds for information leading to her whereabouts.

Stunned, Jason continued to stare at the notice, oblivious to the din of the street and the raspy creak of the peeling inn sign overhead. So he had been right about Mirella fleeing from someone! Perhaps this was precisely the leverage he needed to persuade her to go with him to Virginia.

"Now, ain't that a pretty kettle of fish yer in," crowed the innkeeper. " 'Is lordship is offerin' ten 'ole quid jist fer 'anding over that wench yer beddin'."

"Well, he won't be getting her." Jason ripped the handbill from the wall, folding it and tucking it into a pocket of his coat.

"An' why not?" Bates asked, his beady eyes gleaming with greed. "Oi'm of a mind to collect that reward meself."

Rage exploded in Jason like red-hot lava, and he seized the innkeeper by the crude leather vest covering the heavy man's dirty shirt. Hauling Bates's chunky bulk close, he gave him a rough shake.

"You do and you won't live long enough to spend it!"

" 'Ere, now," Bates sputtered bravely. "Oi've got me rights! Ye can't be threatenin' me."

Jason tightened his grip, so overcome by fury that he scarcely noticed the innkeeper's stench. "Your rights be damned!" he snarled. "If you so much as breathe a word of this to anyone, I'll rip your fat flesh from your bones."

"But what about me ten quid?"

Jason glared at the innkeeper's piggish, wheezing face, then abruptly thrust him away. Why had he reacted with such violence? He should have anticipated Bates's greed, and dealt with it calmly.

"If the reward is all you're interested in, then here, take this." He reached into a pocket of his breeches and tossed Bates the bribe money.

The burly man deftly caught the silver pieces. With an expression of glee, he bit into one with his blackened teeth to verify the authenticity of the metal.

Jason eyed him, plagued by doubts. Would the currency secure the innkeeper's silence? The thought of losing Mirella made his heart beat with a fear he had never before felt. He could only hope that the prospect of reprisal would prevent Bates from betraying her.

"I trust you'll keep your fat lips sealed about this."

"Aye," Bates said, still engrossed in counting the coins nestled in his pudgy paw.

"Mind that you do, then, else I'll be forced to tear you limb from limb." Jason turned on his heel and strode through the door.

Bates watched him leave, his expression darkening as soon as the customer disappeared inside. Who the hell did that bloody colonial think he was, threatening the owner of The Crescent Moon?

"Nobody kin push ol' Bates around," he muttered.

His attention returned to the money he held in his palm. A covetous gleam shone in his eyes as he closed his chunky fingers around the coins. What kind of ruddy fool did that Jason Fletcher take him for? Gold and silver, not men, were the only masters he obeyed.

An idea began to take shape in his head. Why not collect double the profits in this matter of the wench? He already had the colonial's ten quid, and who'd be the wiser if he claimed the same from this Sir Harry Weston?

Chuckling, Bates waddled into the inn. Yes, the sum at stake certainly made it well worth his while to risk the wrath of one man.

Mirella sprang up from the wingback chair in disgust, throwing the slim volume of poetry onto the threadbare seat. The endless references to love in

Shakespeare's sonnets only brought to mind a certain masculine image. And that was preposterous! Jason Fletcher sought only to bed her. It would be a happy day indeed when she saw the last of him.

She strolled to the window, aware of a restlessness deep within her. Not in the three days that had passed since that disturbing kiss had she been able to put it from her mind. She was tormented by the memory of how easily he had overcome her resistance. Her nights were spent tossing and turning, her body aching in a strange way that she could only attribute to the tension of her imprisonment.

The enforced idleness grated on her nerves. Upon ascertaining that she could read, Jason had been thoughtful enough to give her a few books with which to while away the hours, yet the prospect of escaping still occupied much of her time. But none of her plotting had borne fruit. Fanny no longer attended to her without someone else present, and Jason continued to sleep in the wingback chair, guarding the door to the bedchamber. He even took the precaution of robbing her of her knife during the hours he was there with her.

At least he had not forced himself on her, Mirella's conscience made her admit, albeit grudgingly. But if he didn't intend to rape her, then why did he not let her go free?

Turning troubled eyes to the grimy window glass, she peered out into the deep blue dusk. A wave of warmth washed over her when she spied Jason standing in the crowded street below, engaged in earnest conversation with the innkeeper. Stiffening her spine, Mirella denied the sudden leap of her heart. It was simply surprise at seeing Jason, that was all.

Deliberately, she shifted her attention to the other side of the cobbled road. Through a break in the people streaming past, she caught sight of a drunken sailor lolling against a ramshackle building, a bottle of gin in his lap.

Men! she ranted to herself. Was there nothing they thought of other than drinking, lusting, and gambling? Experience had taught her that all males were selfish creatures, concerned only with satisfying their own desires.

Her thoughts continued their wearying course. She simply had to get away from Jason. In a short time, his ship would be departing for the colonies, and she had no wish to be on it. Her only hope was that when Jason took her from this room to his vessel, some means of escape would present itself.

Without conscious intent, her smoky-blue eyes strayed back to the spot just below the window. Both Jason and the innkeeper had vanished. By now she knew well her captor's schedule. He likely had gone into the taproom to indulge in his daily tot of brandy.

But the familiar heavy thud of his boots in the hall outside her bedchamber belied that notion.

At the sound of the key in the lock, Mirella whirled to face the door, the deep rose and pink of her skirt swishing about her slim legs. The chamber had grown dim with the swift fall of twilight but she could easily discern Jason's tall form as he entered.

"Greetings, my lady." He sketched her a sardonic bow.

"Good evening," she forced out, in her most haughty tone.

Her gaze absorbed his male figure as he strolled to the small table beside the bed to light two candles, using the tinderbox provided. She had been asleep when he'd taken his leave this morning, and thus hadn't had the chance to note his attire for the day. With reluctant admiration, her eyes traversed his masculine physique. How well his chocolate brown frockcoat fit his muscled body. The pure white of his ruffled shirt heightened the deep bronze hue of his complexion. His thick, tawny gold hair was tied neatly at his nape with a leather ribbon.

Mirella suddenly was aware of an unexpected feeling of pleasure. It was only due to this change in what had been a most boring day, she assured herself.

She watched as Jason left one taper on the table, placing the other on the fireplace mantel. The soft glow of candlelight banished the murkiness of night, throwing flickering shadows into the corners of the room.

He turned to face her, hands resting on his lean hips as he studied her with that familiar warm gleam in his eyes. A delicate flush stained her cheeks, yet she stood unflinching. Abruptly his deep voice broke the silence.

"So, Mirella Weston, how went your day?"

Mirella opened her mouth to speak, but the sarcastic retort died on her lips. She had never told him her full name, she was certain of it!

For a long, dismaying moment she stared at Jason. Finally in a faint tone that was worlds away from her usual acerbity, she asked, "How did you discover who I am?"

Without saying a word, he dug into the pocket of

his coat and held out a piece of paper. A premonition of disaster made her hands tremble as she stepped forward to take the sheet. Aided by the light of the candle on the mantel, her eyes focused on the bold black print.

"Oh, no!" Mirella couldn't contain a horrified gasp as she read the flyer. Sir Harry had finally guessed that she had fled to Bristol!

Her gaze was wide with worry when she raised it to Jason's face. "Where did you come by this?"

" 'Twas posted near the front door of the inn."

"Did anyone else see it?"

Jason gave a negligent shrug of his wide shoulders. "Only Bates."

"Only Bates!" The handbill fluttered to the floor as her shaking fingers flew to her cheeks. "He'll tell Sir Harry of my whereabouts! I must be away from here, and quickly!"

Mirella darted past him, her only thought to escape before Sir Harry showed up. But she hadn't taken two steps toward the door when Jason latched onto her shoulders, bringing her to an enforced halt. He gently hauled her back around to face him.

"Slow down, Mirella. There's no need for you to flee."

"No need!" she repeated, her mouth agape. "I won't go back to Sir Harry. I'd rather die first!"

She twisted within his grasp, pushing at his hard chest in an effort to wrench herself free. But her exertions were to no avail. Panting, she tossed back her mane of ebony hair and glared up at him.

"Calm yourself," Jason ordered. "I've taken care of everything."

A horrifying possibility occurred to Mirella. "You despicable cur! Did you inform Sir Harry yourself?" With a strength born of fury, she renewed her struggling. "Let me go! I'll not let you return me to that monster!"

"Hush up, little minx," Jason growled, giving her shoulders an impatient shake. "If you would but listen to me, you'd learn the truth. What I've done is to bribe Bates so that he'll keep his lips sealed. I paid him the ten-pound reward, and that appeared to satisfy his greedy heart."

Mirella went still. "You did, truly?"

"Truly," he assured her. "Now, please sit down and explain to me your relation to Sir Harry, and why he's searching for you." He guided her to the wingback chair and gently pressed her into it.

"I'm not obliged to tell you anything," Mirella stalled, unsure if she should trust him.

"Of course not." Jason propped an elbow on the mantelpiece and sent her a mocking smile. "I merely thought you might desire to, considering the sum I spent protecting your lovely hide."

The candle beside him caused harsh shadows to dance across his rugged features. Yet somehow she felt safer here with him than she ever had with Sir Harry.

She wrestled with her conscience. Regardless of her suspicions of his motivation, by bribing Bates Jason had done her a favor. Doubtless, he wanted to keep her with him for his own lustful purposes. Yet perhaps she did owe him something for foiling Sir Harry's plan. And at this point what harm could it do to tell him her tale?

Mirella cleared her throat and spoke. "Sir Harry is my father's cousin."

In a halting voice, she went on to describe the events that had led to her running away, including her mother's death, Sir Andrew Weston's gambling, and the chance of birth that had brought Sir Harry into her life after her father had died the previous autumn.

"Sir Harry tried to convince me to marry him." A shudder of revulsion ran through her, and she stopped, unable to speak of that final episode when he had pawed at her body like a beast of prey. She frowned down into her lap, her hands plucking at the soft folds of her skirt.

Footsteps sounded on the wooden floor; then long fingers grasped her chin and firmly raised her face. "Mirella, tell me the rest," Jason commanded softly. "What happened that finally forced you to flee?"

"He . . . he kissed me and touched me. . . ." Her voice trailed off, and she bit down hard on her lip.

"The bloody bastard!" Jason exploded, his tone harsh and grating. He let loose of her chin to slap his hand against his muscular thigh. "And the thievery of which he accused you? Was that a lie?"

"Nay, but the pittance I took was naught in comparison to what he stole from me." Mirella felt anger begin to course hotly through her veins. She sprang up from her chair to pace the small chamber. "He seized the only home I've ever known, and drove me away with his lusting ways. It seemed only fair that I take a few paltry pieces of silver to help me make good my escape. 'Twas but a tiny portion of what was owed to me!"

"Yet 'tis doubtful that the law would view it that

way," Jason pointed out.

"That is precisely why I must avoid being caught by Sir Harry."

Jason frowned. "Surely he is not evil enough to have you tossed into gaol?"

"Not immediately, though he likely would threaten to unless I succumb to his desires." She gave a despairing laugh. "I do not know which fate would be the worse, to live in misery as that villain's wife, or to spend the rest of my days rotting in some dark, rat-infested cell."

"Then you must let me help you." Jason strode over to her, placing gentle hands on her shoulders. "Come to Virginia with me, Mirella, where you'll be far away from Sir Harry. He'll never find you there."

She gazed at him, buffeted by a desire to throw herself into his strong embrace and accept his offer of protection. His golden eyes, gilded by candlelight, mesmerized her. She was conscious of the tantalizing scent that was his alone, a mixture of brandy and sweat and maleness. The memory of his kiss flashed through her mind, and longing made her blood throb faster. If she agreed to his plan, she would have the chance to taste his lips once more. . . .

She started to sway toward him, then caught herself in time. What was she thinking of? Jason Fletcher lusted after her in the same way as Sir Harry. And at least Sir Harry would bed her within the bonds of holy matrimony, in contrast to Jason's desire to turn her into his doxy.

"I'm staying here in England."

His face darkened, and his hands tightened on her shoulders. "And if Sir Harry finds you? What recourse will you have then?"

" 'Tis my problem, not yours."

"Nay, I cannot accept that," he warned. "If you refuse to go freely, I shall have to take you aboard my ship by force. Do not put the both of us into such a disagreeable position."

"You would not dare do such a despicable thing," Mirella hissed in a pained whisper.

"I would," Jason stated flatly. His stern look faded, and he touched her soft cheek with his calloused fingertips. "Though 'twould not be the manner in which I'd hoped to begin our voyage together."

She turned her head from his disturbing caress. "Prepare yourself then, for your hopes are doomed to be dashed. Under no circumstances will I set foot on your vessel of my own free choice."

"And is there no means of persuading you otherwise?" he asked, his voice low and enticing.

"My mind is quite firm on the matter." But the warmth of his breath on her hair sent a disquieting shiver coursing over her skin.

Mirella felt caught in a dream as Jason ran his fingers down the tender flesh of her throat, continuing his seduction of her senses. Brushing aside an ebony curl that had slipped onto her breast, he traced the path of creamy skin just above the décolletage of her gown.

"But I seek only to help you, my sweet," he murmured. "Why is that so hard for you to accept?"

"Because you lie!" she cried out. "You seek only to make me your mistress!" It required all of her willpower to wrench herself from him. Even then, she had to clutch at the bedpost to support her jellied knees.

"Please, Jason, leave me be," she begged. "I am weary, and do not desire to speak of this anymore."

His face, illuminated by fluttering candlelight, was suddenly blank. "As you wish, then, though pray don't think the subject closed for good. I shall fetch you your supper now, that you may retire early."

With a mocking nod, he ushered himself out of the chamber, locking the door behind him.

The instant his footsteps had disappeared down the hall, Mirella chastised herself for her weakness. Why did her resolve crumble at his touch? she railed silently. His caress was like the heel of Achilles, an alarming vulnerability that could destroy her life.

Yet what could she do? Flee from Jason only to end up in the clutches of Sir Harry? A shudder scurried over her skin as she thought again of her cousin's grasping hands and hot lips.

She felt so sickened by the memory that she could scarce work up an appetite for the meal which Jason delivered to her a short while later. But pride caused her to conceal her worries from him. She managed to control her churning stomach only through strength of will.

While she forced herself to eat, Jason built a fire in the hearth to chase away the evening chill. Once he had left again with her empty tray, Mirella swiftly doffed her gown and petticoats. She blew out both candles, then slid beneath the cool sheets of the bed, clad only in her thin chemise.

Despite the radiating warmth of the flames, she found herself shivering. She wondered whether Jason had been a fool to trust Bates. The man had no loyalty, save to silver. Look at the way he had tricked

102

her! Accepting a bribe was no sure sign that the innkeeper would keep silent.

And even if Bates held his tongue, without a doubt Sir Harry had seen to it that handbills were posted elsewhere. Supposing someone saw one and identified her? The reward of ten pounds was a temptation which few of the ragged sailors inhabiting this waterfront area would be able to resist.

Hearing the rattle of the key in the lock, Mirella pulled the quilt up to her neck and rolled over on her side, pretending slumber. For the first time, the muffled sounds as Jason readied himself to sleep in the chair by the door failed to anger her. It soothed her mind to know that he was there.

But even that measure of security wasn't enough. Her thoughts sped onward, building upon her fears. She opened worried eyes to study the eerie shadows that dipped and swayed on the dingy walls. The only noises were the crackling of the fire and the muted din of merriment from the taproom downstairs.

Plagued by restlessness, Mirella tossed and turned, imagining the disgusting feel of Sir Harry's hands fondling her in their marriage bed, until exhaustion finally thrust her into the depths of slumber.

She was hurrying along the deserted, fog-shrouded docks. The dampness of the air invaded her clothing, sending violent chills over her body. It was night, though oddly, she could see well enough to pick her way through the gloom. That fact puzzled her, for even if there were a full moon, the fog was too dense to allow any light to penetrate.

Her slippers flew over the pavement, carrying her

on some errand the purpose of which she was not sure. Still, she obeyed the compelling urge within that kept her moving.

The air was silent, except for the steady tap-tap of her feet and lap of water against the quay. Then suddenly, an alien sound came from behind. She whirled toward it, heart pounding as she strained to peer through the swirling mist.

Alarm bubbled up inside of her. What was the source of that noise? The scrape of a boot? Was that the reason for her haste? Because someone was hunting her?

She stood frozen in the clutches of fear. A gust of chill wind bit through the fog, sending vaporous clouds billowing around her. Abruptly the sound came again, and this time it was closer. Without a doubt, it was a man's footstep.

Panic choked her as she tore down the empty wharfside street with little regard for direction. All she was conscious of was a driving need to get away.

The clatter behind her grew louder, as if her pursuer had also increased his pace. Her cloak flapped around her like the wings of a frightened bird. Gasping for breath, she kept running and running down the never-ending roadway—until her foot slipped on the damp cobblestones.

She tumbled down onto the hard pavement. The jarring impact shot through her body, dazing her.

The world spun giddily as she tried to rise. Groaning, she fell to her knees, too shaken to save herself.

The sound of his boots rang on the cobblestones. Dread squeezed her chest like a malignant growth. Her pursuer was getting closer!

Suddenly his grotesque visage burst through the clouds of mist. He looked familiar—it was Sir Harry!

As he uttered a spine-tingling chuckle, his ugly face loomed nearer, his dark, taloned claws ripping aside her cloak to clamp onto her tender breasts.

A scream of pure horror tore from her throat. The monster meant to rape her! She fought with all her might, sobbing and panting with effort. But he was the stronger, for her limbs were steadily weakening.

His hot body pressed against her, and his voice muttered strange incantations. Gradually, the meaning of his words penetrated her terror.

"Mirella, wake up! 'Tis only a dream!"

She opened her eyes to Jason's face. He was half-lying atop her, holding her flailing body. A muted glow from the dying fire in the hearth softened the angles of his familiar features.

Mirella ceased struggling, though her heart beat fast with the remnants of fear. Shivers wracked her body at the memory of the chilling dread that had gripped her soul. Her brain felt sticky, confused, as if she were still caught in the tentacles of that grisly creature.

" 'Twas only a nightmare," Jason reassured her as he gently stroked a lock of hair off her damp forehead. "Everything will be all right now."

"Yes . . . I . . ." But it was difficult for her to speak with her teeth chattering the way they were.

Jason frowned in concern, placing his hand on the bare skin of her arm. "By damn, you're freezing!"

In the throes of her dream, she had kicked off the

105

quilt, and her slender form, clad only in a sheer chemise, felt like ice. It took just an instant of debating for him to make up his mind. Her comfort was far more important than any sexual frustration he would be forced to endure.

The bed dipped beneath his weight as Jason slid in beside her, pulling the coverlet over them. Wrapping her in his embrace, he hugged Mirella close to his warmth. He drew in his breath when she trustingly slipped an arm around him. At least his shirt and breeches provided somewhat of a barrier between their bodies, for the enticing softness of her womanly figure was almost more than he could endure.

"I . . . I was so frightened," she whispered, gazing up at him, vulnerability lurking in her big, smoky-blue eyes. "It seemed so real."

"I know," he soothed. "But you're safe now. I'm here with you."

Mirella tucked her face into the crook of his neck, listening to his gentle murmuring as he stroked his fingers over her hair. His strong arms were like a haven. She was afraid to move away lest the demons of darkness return. Gradually, her shivering abated as his warmth seeped into her body. The terror of the nightmare waned, and she felt herself being lulled into a sense of security.

Her limbs grew languid, and her mind drifted lazily, though strangely, she was not the least bit sleepy. Beneath her ear, she could hear the steady, reassuring beat of Jason's heart. It seemed a trifle fast, but she was feeling too tranquil to wonder why. She was safe within his embrace, and that was all that mattered.

Yet gradually a new tumult was invading her body. It took a moment for the source of it to sink into her torpid brain. The focus of Jason's attentions had shifted. The mouth that had been whispering in her ear was now dropping tiny kisses over her forehead, and the hand that had been stroking her hair had drifted to the soft curve of her bottom.

A deep, pulsing heat began to throb in her loins. It seemed only natural when he pressed her back against the sheets. He stared down at her, their faces almost touching, their warm breaths mingling. Her heart skipped a beat at the desire in his dark gold eyes. Then, ever so slowly, he bent toward her, closing the gap between them.

Stop him, her mind screamed. He seeks only to seduce you to make you his mistress! 'Tis the chance he has been awaiting, to break through your defenses and use you to satisfy his lusts.

Yet one kiss could do no real damage to her virtue, she reasoned. Intuition told her that he would stop if she but said the word. And if he didn't, there was always her knife, lying on the nightstand, which she could see out of the corner of her eye.

The temptation was overpowering. Mirella opened her lips to the familiar, thrilling taste of him. His kiss was tentative, as if he were afraid she would pull away. Yet the tender, cherishing way he touched her ignited greater flames inside her than a more domineering technique would have done. In rash abandonment, she curled her fingers around his shoulders as he tasted the inner secrets of her mouth with leisurely enjoyment.

They drew apart reluctantly. In the same unhurried, gentle way he'd kissed her, Jason's hand tarried over the creamy skin just above her breasts. Mesmerized, Mirella caught her breath, well aware that only a cobweb of lace hid the soft swells from his view.

His eyes intent on hers, he reached for the satin strap concealing one shoulder, easing down the fabric. Then he did the same to her other side. Dallying over the task, he peeled away the bodice of her chemise inch by slow inch until she was bare to the waist. The brush of his fingers against her naked skin caused an ever-spreading quiver of pure pleasure to throb through her body.

When he finally bent to put his mouth to one honey-brown tip, Mirella couldn't repress a sigh of delight at the delicious sensation. A portion of her mind was appalled at the liberties she was granting him, but her power of resistance seemed to have vanished like a will-o'-the-wisp.

His hand moved to the curve of her hip as he continued to pour hot kisses over her breasts. Mirella wove her fingers into his tawny gold hair, aware of a yearning deep inside of her that intensified with each passing moment. How was it possible that her body could so rejoice in this man's touch?

Jason's fingers strayed to the hem of her chemise, seeking the secrets that lay beneath. His wandering hand trailed up her thigh until he found what he sought. She tensed at the intimacy, then desire rushed through her, a pleasure unlike anything she had ever before felt. Gently he stroked her, plunging her into a sea of sensation that was beyond the realm of her experience. Her world tilted dizzily, until she was writhing and moaning with passion.

No protest formed on her lips when he tugged at the satiny undergarment pooled at her waist. Indeed, she lifted her hips to aid in its swift removal. Dazed, driven by a need she couldn't define, she reached for Jason, knowing only that she wanted his dominant strength to cover her nakedness.

But instead he rolled off the bed and onto his feet. She whimpered a protest, thinking he meant to desert her.

"Patience, my sweet," he murmured, smiling crookedly at her. " 'Twould be difficult to make love to you properly with all my clothes on."

In a haze of desire, Mirella lay back and watched as he doffed his shirt and breeches. Her eyes widened as she caught her first glimpse of a naked man. The pale glow from the dying embers in the hearth gilded his bronze skin. His physique was that of a Greek god, broad shouldered and narrow waisted.

But it was the evidence of his full male arousal that made a sliver of reality penetrate her drugged mind. The realization of what was about to happen drove the languor from her body, and she sat up straight, her hand flying to her mouth in dawning horror.

"Nay . . . you must not do this!" She yanked the sheet over herself as she scooted to the side of the bed, frantic to escape.

Jason was on top of her in an instant, pressing her back against the soft mattress. His eyes searched her face with urgent intensity.

"Mirella, God help me, I want you," he groaned, his breathing harsh and ragged. "Don't deny me!"

"But . . . 'tis wrong!"

"Not if we satisfy a mutual desire. Can you truly say you feel nothing?"

He bent his head to kiss her breast. She tried to twist away from the temptation of his caress, but his strong body held her snared.

His hand sought the center of her womanhood, igniting the fire in her loins until it again flared to a full, raging conflagration that drove all thought from her mind. Her entire being focused on the wonders he was evoking.

When she was moaning with need, he stilled his fingers. "Do you now wish me to cease?" he rasped, his chest heaving with the effort of his enforced restraint.

"Nay . . . please . . ." In some distant corner of her brain, Mirella was appalled by her begging. Yet she couldn't keep from arching her hips, craving the thrill of his touch.

He slipped between her thighs, and she froze at the sudden piercing pain as he penetrated the softness deep within her. Murmuring gentle, soothing words, he held her quietly in his embrace until the sharp sensation faded. Mirella buried her face in the moist warmth of his neck, hearing the swift, heavy thud of his heart beneath her ear, feeling the hardness of his muscles against her breasts.

Slowly he began to move again, taking care not to hurt her. An overpowering need held her captive. She felt alive in a way she had never before been, as if she were drowning and soaring at the same time.

At long last, when she thought she could bear the sweet torment no longer, an all-consuming pleasure burst upon her. In the midst of her release, she was dimly aware of Jason crying out her name in ecstasy.

In the warm afterglow, she drifted into a deep sleep, her mind drugged with languor, and her naked body shamelessly entwined with his.

Chapter Six

Impatiently, Mirella jiggled the doorknob as if by some magical force it might have unlocked itself. But the door refused to open. She was a prisoner still!

Crossing her arms over her breasts, she let her restless, slippered feet carry her over the floorboards. Her pacing took her back and forth across the small chamber, following the same path she had trod since an hour past dawn.

Upon awakening alone in her bed that morning, she had hoped for one heart-stopping moment that the events of the previous night had been but a dream. Then her horrified eyes had encountered the evidence of her lost maidenhead staining the sheets.

Now, with the late afternoon sun dipping low in the gray clouded sky, her mind continued to turn over and over the agonizing thoughts that had occupied her all day.

A hot flush of shame colored her cheeks as Mirella recalled for the umpteenth time her wanton response to Jason's love-making. And what was worse, even now the mere memory of their impassioned coupling made her loins throb with longing, wanting to experience again that wild ecstasy.

She groaned aloud, digging her nails into the silk and lace covering her arms. Why did Jason Fletcher have the power to make her forget her principles? Yesterday she had been unsullied, a woman of virtue; today she was little better than a harlot. How could you have behaved so rashly? she railed at herself. Oh, if only there were a way to undo that disgraceful deed!

Her eyes caught sight of a bit of paper half hidden beneath the wingback chair, and her fingers swooped down to pick it up. It was the handbill that had begun the previous day's distressing chain of events. Perusing it again, Mirella recalled the nightmare in which that hideous creature bearing the features of Sir Harry had attempted to molest her. Yet in truth it had not been he who had stolen her purity. It had been Jason, the man who claimed to be her protector.

Accursed knave! she accused silently. He had pretended to comfort her while she had been in the grips of that horrifying dream. And she had been fool enough to trust him!

Her thoughts boiled onward as she paced the room. Jason had taken advantage of her in a moment of weakness, playing on her vulnerabilities with sweet words and soothing caresses. Then, when he had lulled her into security, he had commenced his seduction.

The swaggering ass! she fumed. It would be just like him to think that one display of his masculine virility would transform her into a meek doxy who would eagerly spread her legs whenever he snapped his fingers. Little did he know that her resolve to escape him had only been strengthened by what had happened. She would sooner take her chances at being caught by Sir Harry then let Jason bed her again.

When her eyes lighted on the knife lying on the bedside table, angry footsteps carried her across the chamber. Mirella snatched up the small weapon, wishing with passionate fervency that she had used it last evening when she'd had the opportunity. Never should she ever have allowed Jason to touch her in the first place!

But that deed was done, she reminded herself, and no good would come of continuing to chastise herself. All she could do was to plan for the future.

Taking great care, Mirella thrust the bare blade into the depths of her skirt pocket, where it would be within easy reach. If Jason dared come near her again, she vowed, she would not hesitate to use the weapon.

Her heart gave an involuntary leap as Mirella realized that it was nearly time for him to return for the day. Stepping to the window, she peered out into the blue dusk. As usual, the street was teeming with people who scurried about their tasks before darkness drove them indoors.

The key suddenly rattled in the lock, and she whirled around, expecting Jason. But it was Fanny who sauntered into the bedchamber, with a timid serving maid dogging her heels.

" 'Ere's yer supper, mum," Fanny announced, giving a grand sweep of her hand at the other girl, who tiptoed forward to thrust a tray at Mirella.

Automatically, Mirella reached out and took the

food. "Isn't it a trifle early for this?" she asked, frowning.

"Aye, mum, but the gen'man said you was to eat up since ye was goin' onto 'is ship tonight."

"Tonight?" Shock made Mirella collapse weakly onto the wingback chair, nearly spilling the heavy tray in her hands."Are you certain of that?"

"Oi'm jist a-tellin' ye what 'e said." Fanny settled her ample behind on the bed, then turned her attention to the other serving wench. " 'Ey, Rosie, don't jist stand there, light the lady some candles so's she don't 'ave to eat in the dark." The girl scurried over to the nightstand to do Fanny's bidding.

Mirella assumed a casual pose, picking up her fork to spear a piece of meat, though inside she was a bundle of nerves. "Did he say what time we were to leave?"

"Soon's 'e gits back."

"Back?" Mirella jumped on the word. "Is he gone, then? Where did he go?"

Fanny shrugged. "Oi dunno, 'e jist said fer ye to be ready when 'e got back 'ere." She gave Mirella a look of undisguised envy. "Blimey, ain't ye the lucky one! Ye'll never 'ave to do another lick o' work in yer life. 'E's the type 'oo's loose wi' 'is pursestrings—'e already paid me, and more than 'e'd promised. Said Oi'd done a good job." She patted her carroty hair with pride.

"I suppose that all depends on one's point of view."

Mirella's dry comment went right over Fanny's head as the serving wench continued to rattle on about Jason's virtues. "Oh, and 'e's such a 'andsome buck! What Oi wouldn't give to slip me 'and into 'is—

116

Oops, sorry, mum, Oi didn't mean Oi'd really try to swipe your man."

Mirella repressed a half-hysterical laugh as she ate her food without tasting a single morsel. If Fanny only comprehended the truth! For all Mirella cared, the serving girl could have Jason on a silver platter if she wanted him.

Mirella swallowed hard as an idea occurred to her. If Fanny wanted him, she could certainly have him. . .

The fork clattered to her tray. "Fanny, do you suppose you and I could talk—alone?"

"Oi'm sorry, mum, but the gen'man said—"

"It'd only take a minute," Mirella pleaded. "He'll never find out. And anyway, you said he'd already paid you, so what have you to lose?"

"Oi dunno. . . ."

Seeing the serving girl weakening, Mirella threw out the bait. "It might earn you a lot of money."

Fanny hesitated, then gave an impatient wave at the other wench. " 'Ey, Rosie, git on out o' 'ere. Mind that ye wait right outside, though."

As the girl scuttled out, Fanny wiggled off the mattress and locked the door. Then she reseated herself on the bed. Mirella rose and placed her half-finished dinner on the dressing table. Lacing her fingers in front of her to hide their trembling, she turned to face the serving girl.

"Have you ever thought of leaving here, Fanny?"

"Why would Oi want to do somethin' like that, mum? Oi ain't got nowhere else to go."

"What if you were offered a great deal of money to say, move to the colonies? Would you do it?"

117

Fanny cocked her head in doubt. "Oi dunno, mum. One o' the sailors told me there was wild Indians a-roamin' the woods over there jist awaitin' to murder people."

"Oh, but he was pulling your leg, Fanny! Why, Jason assures me that Virginia is every bit as civilized as England itself." Jason *had* told her that, Mirella rationalized. He could be telling the truth, though privately she didn't believe a word he said.

"But why would Oi wants to go there anyways when Oi gots me a good job right 'ere?"

Mirella nervously smoothed the ebony hair that was piled in a lustrous swirl atop her head. It was so important that she be convincing. She took a deep breath before speaking.

"You've said that you envy my position, so what would you think if I suggested you go with Jason to the colonies in my place?"

"Instead of ye, mum?" Fanny gave a puzzled shake of her frizzled mop of hair. "Oi don' understan'."

"What I'm trying to say is, I have a number of reasons why I'd prefer to stay here in England, and since Jason merely wants someone to, ah, warm his bed, there's no reason why you couldn't go in my stead, is there?"

Fanny looked doubtful. "Oi don' think the gen-'man'd go fer that, mum. 'E seems pretty bent on takin' ye wi' 'im."

"But any woman would do!" Mirella began to pace the small chamber, conscious of precious time slipping by. She had to persuade the serving girl before Jason returned and discovered what she was up to.

"Think on it, Fanny. Jason Fletcher is a very

wealthy man. He lives in a huge mansion with a fleet of servants who would be at your beck and call." Mirella knew she spoke a pack of lies, but noticing the way the serving wench was leaning forward in avid interest, she embroidered the fantasy.

"You'd never lift a finger again, Fanny. And you'd be gowned in the finest silks from China and laces from Belgium . . . why, you could probably even have your very own French dressmaker. And all you have to do is let me go, then when Jason returns you can offer your services in my place."

Fanny's eyes were round. "Cor, d'ye really think 'e's that rich?"

"You've seen the fatness of his purse. Isn't that evidence enough?"

"And ye really don't want to go?" The wench clearly thought Mirella was daft.

"Positive."

"But . . . d'ye think 'e'd really take *me*?"

"Whyever not? You would not mind . . . ah . . . fulfilling his demands in exchange for living like a princess, would you?"

Fanny's carrot curls bobbed back and forth in eagerness as she shook her head. "Oh, nay, mum!"

Mirella stifled an odd ache deep inside of her at the thought of Jason lying in intimacy with another woman. "Then you've naught to lose in the trying," she said crisply. "But you've first got to release me."

"But what'd Oi tell 'im 'appened to ye?"

Mirella shrugged. "You'll have to make up a tale of how I escaped. I'm sure you can manage that, can't you?"

A calculating expression appeared on Fanny's face.

"Aye, mum, that Oi can."

With amazing agility, she bounded off the bed and to her feet, making for the door. Unlocking it, she poked her head out into the hall. Mirella heard the buzz of her voice as she spoke to the waiting serving girl.

Then Fanny closed the door and turned around, plump fingers digging into her dirty apron. "Oi jist sent Rosie to fetch ye some more wine. Now all's Oi 'as to do is say ye knocked me o'er the 'ead while she was gone." She quickly scanned the chamber, then grabbed the empty water pitcher from the dressing table and threw it to the floor, where it smashed into pieces.

"When Oi 'ear Rosie a-comin' Oi'll do this." Fanny collapsed into a plump heap next to the shards of crockery, holding her head as she let out a series of loud, pitiful groans.

Mirella couldn't help smiling. "Brilliant performance. If this does not work, you might consider making your living on the stage."

Fanny grinned her appreciation, then gave an urgent wave, apparently anxious lest her sudden prospect of wealth should vanish. "Well, go on wi' ye, afore someone catches us!"

Mirella darted to the door on winged feet, awash in a feeling of relief. She was free at last! On impulse, she turned back toward Fanny, who squatted on the floor in preparation for her coming bit of playacting.

"Thank you ever so much, Fanny. And good luck to you!"

"'Tis Oi 'oo should be thankin' ye, mum!"

Mirella stifled a twinge of guilt at the way she was

120

tricking the serving girl. Jason could not be near as rich as she'd made him out to be, yet what did that really matter? She had a suspicion he'd be so angry at her escape that he'd pay scant attention to anything else. Poor Fanny would never make it to her fantasy mansion in the colonies, yet no harm would come to her.

Mirella put a hand into her pocket to feel the delicate oval of her mother's cameo, and then the reassuring blade of her knife. She had all she needed to make good her flight.

Turning the knob, she checked to be certain no one else was around, then crept out into the dark hall, closing the door behind her. She forced herself to ignore an urge to run out as fast as she could. The danger was far from over. After all, Jason could stride into the inn at any moment, and she would not be safe until she was as far as possible from his reach. Then once he left for America, she could focus her attention on eluding Sir Harry's clutches.

Tiptoing down the narrow stairway, Mirella stopped just short of the taproom. As it was early evening, the large room was filling with patrons. She poked her head around the corner, taking the utmost care to stay within her shadowed alcove.

Her eyes scanned the crowd. Several serving wenches threaded through the ragged seamen, busily taking orders. She thanked the stars above that Jason was nowhere to be seen in the throng.

To her left, she spotted Bates's corpulent bulk standing behind the bar, his back to her as he poured a tankard of ale from the spigot attached to a large wooden cask. Rosie, the timid serving wench, was at his heels, apparently waiting for the innkeeper to fill Mirella's flagon of wine.

Trying to make herself as inconspicuous as possible, Mirella slipped around to her right, heading toward the rear of the inn. At the end of the dim passageway, she opened the kitchen door a crack and peeked inside.

The cook was bending her stout figure over the massive fireplace, basting a side of beef as a little boy who could be no more than five years old slowly rotated the spit. There was but one other person occupying the room, a woman with her back to the door who was engrossed in paring a mountain of potatoes.

Mirella took a deep breath to calm her galloping pulse. Creeping inside, she moved stealthily past the trio of inn employees at the other end of the wide room. Only the tiny lad noticed her, his tired eyes following her progress with a glimmer of interest. Despite her predicament, Mirella couldn't help but smile at him. She placed a finger over her lips to indicate secrecy, praying he would hold his tongue.

The boy glanced over at the cook, who was still busily pouring juices over the meat. Then he looked back at Mirella, and he winked, an impish grin on his grimy face.

Mirella tiptoed to the door which she knew led to the rear of the inn. Opening it as quietly as possible, she gave the lad a little wave of thanks before slipping outside. Heart pounding, she leaned against the inn wall as relief washed over her. She drew in deep gulps of air, not caring that the light breeze was laced with the odors of horse droppings and rotting garbage. She had escaped!

Well, almost, she reminded herself. There was still a faint chance that Jason might return suddenly and stumble upon her. That was why she needed to get as far away from here as possible. Mirella took stock of her surroundings. The darkness was pierced only by the wavering light of a lantern hanging just inside the stable doorway ahead of her. Thankfully, though, no one seemed to be about.

For want of a better plan, she decided to head toward the center of Bristol, away from the waterfront. It would be best if she kept off the main street at least until she was a safe distance from where Jason might spot her.

Hugging the wall of the inn, she began to carefully pick her way through the bits of rubbish scattering the gloomy mews. She had just reached the corner of the structure, and was about to venture past an alleyway separating the inn and its neighboring building, when a scraping noise came from behind. It sounded oddly like a footstep.

Her heart leaped to her throat, and she whirled around, searching the shadows.

Slender fingers gripped the lace and satin at her bodice as Mirella stood perfectly still, listening. In the distance, a dog barked and a door slammed. For one brief, horrifying moment, she thought she detected the sound of a man's heavy breathing. Then the sudden hoot of merriment from inside the tavern made her realize that what she had been hearing was the distant rise and fall of voices.

The breath came out of her in a relieved sigh. She took a step into the alleyway and stopped again, unsure of why she still felt a strange prickling of uneasiness.

A shiver coursed over her skin. It was merely the damp chill of the night breeze, Mirella assured herself. Rubbing her hands over the thin silk covering her arms, she indulged in an instant's longing for a thick, warm cloak.

Looking toward the front of the inn, she saw that the dim light from the lanterns in the taproom spilled out of the windows and into the narrow lane, casting an eerie illumination over the low fog which rolled in from the nearby harbor to carpet the cobbled pavement in pewter puffs. The mist swirled no higher than her knees, yet soon, she judged, it would cover the area with a soupy mass that would work to her advantage in making good her escape.

Mirella inched her slippered feet forward, intending to continue down the darkened mews. But suddenly another noise came from behind, this time closer and louder than before.

With a gasp, Mirella spun around, heart hammering. A flash of déjà vu made her dizzy with fear. Wasn't that the same sound she'd heard in her nightmare, the scrape of a boot on pavement?

Yet no matter how hard she strained her eyes, she could detect no one lurking in the charcoal shadows.

Your mind is playing tricks on you, she told herself firmly. 'Twas just a horse in the stables beyond striking the side of his stall with his hoof.

Mirella squared her shoulders and swung back around. She hurried past the dimly lit alleyway, heading for the murky darkness behind the neighboring building. She was a mere step shy of the enveloping blackness when there was a sudden burst of activity behind her.

Heavy male footsteps clattered over the cobblestones. Startled, Mirella froze in her tracks as terror gushed through her veins. A quick glance over her shoulder revealed a shadowed human form barreling straight toward her.

She bit back a scream of fright. Her legs recovered from their momentary paralysis to carry her on a helter-skelter path from her pursuer. Fog billowed about her waist as she tore blindly down the alleyway, heading for the main street.

But she was not swift enough.

Halfway to her destination, rough hands seized her from behind. Her skirts tangled about her legs, and she plummeted to the hard pavement. A jarring pain shot through her body. Gasping for breath, she whipped her head around to confront the face of her hunter.

But the world was all swirling gray.

Cruel fingers wrapped around her arms and jerked her upward, out of the damp shroud of fog. Mirella's heart cringed in horror as she recognized her attacker's bulbous nose and feral eyes.

It was Sir Harry!

"Thought you'd escaped me, eh, Mirella?" he grunted, the stocky chest inside his canary yellow frockcoat heaving from the exertion of the chase. "When you first emerged from the inn, I was not certain 'twas you. How gracious of you to walk right out and into my hands."

"Let go of me this instant, or I'll scream!"

He gave a snort of laughter. "Scream away. Judging

by the caliber of men in there"—he jerked his peri-wigged head toward the noisy taproom—"they would likely be eager to join in the fun I'm planning to have with you."

"You wouldn't dare do anything to me," Mirella challenged, though inside she felt a twist of raw fear. A swift glance around told her that the alleyway was deserted. She had only her knife with which to defend herself, but with Sir Harry grasping her arms, she could not reach into her pocket.

"I'll dare whatsoever I please." A crafty smile creased his fleshy cheeks. "Don't forget, dear cousin, if you fail to do as I wish, I can always turn you in to the authorities for stealing. Would you like that, Mirella? To spend the rest of your days in some moldy cell?"

" 'Twould be better than marrying you!" she spat back.

His hands bit brutally into her tender skin as he yanked her to him, so close that she could feel his hot breath on her face.

"Hear me now, bitch, and hear me good. We will post our banns the instant we return to my estate, then wed before the month is out. You have no choice in the matter." Sir Harry let go of one of her arms to fasten his hand to the gentle curve of her breast. His fingers roughly pinched her flesh as his eyes darkened with lust. "How long I've waited to feel your ripe little body writhing beneath me in passion!"

" 'Twill never happen!" Mirella tried to wrench herself out of his wolfish grasp, but his grip was too tight. Revulsion twisted her stomach at the thought of intimacy with this rutting pig. She wracked her brain

126

for a way to dissuade him.

"I . . . I'm no longer untouched," she cried out in desperation. "Surely you would not want another man's leavings."

Sir Harry merely gave a cackle of laughter. "So, the mare has been broken to the saddle, has she? All the better, for perhaps you've learned some tricks of the trade, eh?"

"You are disgusting!"

"How many men did you lie with, Mirella?" He pressed his groin against her soft thigh, so that she felt his hard arousal. "As your future husband, I demand that you tell me every detail."

For a moment she was taken aback by his repulsive command. Then loathing sent a spurt of adrenaline flooding her veins. Catching him unawares, she gave a swift twist of her body and jerked herself from him.

"Damn you, bitch!" he roared, lunging at her.

But Mirella ducked and eluded him. Recklessly, she sped back toward the rear of the inn, in the faint hope of losing herself in the shadowy mews. Close on her heels, she heard the heavy thud of Sir Harry's boots on the cobblestones.

Clouds of fog boiled up all around her, and her hands clutched her skirts high to keep from tripping. But the mad race was to no avail.

Catching up to her, Sir Harry slammed her against the inn wall, knocking the wind out of her. With vicious strength, his thick fingers clamped around her shoulders.

"Any more tricks like that, wench, and I vow I'll break your neck!"

"You bastard!" Panting with effort, Mirella struggled against his oxlike body.

Sir Harry let out an evil chuckle that sent a chill down her spine. "That's no way to address your future husband, my dearest cousin."

"I'll never marry you!" In desperation, she opened her mouth wide and screamed for help as loudly as she could.

Sir Harry's palm cracked across her cheek. "Bitch!" he grunted. "I'll teach you not to defy me!"

His hands suddenly circled her neck, and he pressed his thumbs into the tender skin of her throat until she gasped for breath.

He meant to kill her! Fear washed over her like a floodtide. In a frenzy, Mirella yanked at his stocky arms and kicked at his shins, but Sir Harry only gave a satanic laugh, continuing to squeeze tighter and tighter.

Specks of darkness danced before her eyes. Then the dim memory of her knife hit her.

Thrusting a hand into her skirt pocket, she scrabbled frantically for the weapon.

Chapter Seven

A gray mist surged around the tops of Jason's boots as he strode down the night-darkened quay. The lantern he carried enabled him to see his way through the surrounding murk. He frowned, realizing that the fog would likely thicken over the next few hours, blanketing the harbor and complicating navigation. Yet he wasn't about to let a spot of inclement weather alter his plans to depart on the early morning tide.

Behind him, he could still detect the cacophony of loudly barked orders, thumping footsteps, and grunts of effort as a swarm of workers scurried about by torchlight to load his cargo. Other men clambered up the rigging, doing last-minute repairs to the masts and sails. Now that his captain had rounded up the remainder of the crew, nearly all was in readiness. That is, Jason corrected silently, all but the collecting of one final passenger.

He quickened his pace toward The Crescent Moon, his mind drifting to the woman who had occupied his thoughts all day. The memory of her wild, abandoned response to his love-making even now sent heat rushing to his loins.

An image burned into his brain . . . Mirella reclining on the tangled sheets, watching him discard his clothing. She had all the beauty and innocence of a naiad, yet the seductiveness and sensuality of a siren. Her skin glowed like rich cream in the firelight, while her hair tumbled around her face like black silk. Her deep indigo eyes were warm and welcoming, her lips ripe and moist from his kisses. Then suddenly something had made her fight him like a wildcat.

Jason took in several deep breaths of chilly night air in an attempt to cool his hot blood. He had sworn not to make love to her until she was willing. But when he had gathered her in his arms to comfort her after that nightmare, the feel of her soft body clinging to his had been more than he could bear. Did Mirella hate him all the more for introducing her to the pleasures of the flesh? Or had the experience softened her, so that she would agree eagerly to accompany him to Virginia? Likely, it was the former, though he could not be certain.

Tendrils of mist writhed around his lean thighs as Jason raised the lantern and frowned into the gloom ahead. His inability to predict Mirella's response was frustrating. At any rate, he reassured himself, it did little good to wallow in guilt over the deed. Strictly speaking he had not forced her; it had been her own physical desires that had overwhelmed her. And why torture himself over what had been inevitable? He couldn't honestly say he regretted having made love to her.

A wave of tenderness washed over him as he recalled the sight of her delicate face, peaceful in slumber, reposing on the pillows early that morning. There was no way in heaven or hell that he would leave her to fend for herself in this seedy wharfside neighborhood. It was strange, Jason mused. He had never been so obsessed with a woman before. His brief taste of the bewitching sweetness of her body appeared only to have fanned the flames of his passion.

Yet surely all it would take to break the spell she had woven around him would be to spend a few months in her company. Her attraction would soon begin to pall as she became demanding and petulant, like Elizabeth and Samantha and so many other females he had known.

A mangy mutt materialized out of the darkness, his stringy black body seeming to float atop a cloud of fog as he slunk by, growling and barking. Jason's boots rang purposefully on the cobbled pavement as he hurried toward the portal leading into the tavern. Pushing open the heavy wooden door, he let it slam behind him as he entered the dim, smoky taproom. The tables were crammed with sailors, and the air was ripe with ribald stories and loud laughter. Bates was behind the bar busily filling tankards of ale and rum.

Without removing the mist-dampened cloak draped carelessly over his shoulders, Jason wended his way through the throng, heading for the rear of the room. The lantern he held cast a flickering light over the narrow staircase as his long, impatient strides ate up two steps at a time.

Anticipation swelled inside him as he reached the second floor. It was a feeling to which he was growing accustomed, he admitted with a wry twist of his lips. Mirella aroused an eagerness in him that he had never

131

before felt.

Walking down the deserted passageway, he suddenly saw that the door to their bedchamber was cracked open.

His muscles tensed and his good mood vanished as suddenly as if a fist had been slammed into his gut. Foreboding gripped him. Had Mirella escaped? Muttering a curse under his breath, he thrust the door back all the way.

A lone candle fluttered on the mantelpiece. Beneath its pale light, a serving girl knelt, gathering up the shards of pottery that scattered the rough-planked floor in front of her. Just behind her, Fanny was leaning against the bedpost, arms crossed over her buxom bosom, a complacent smile on her round face.

As Jason strode into the room, both looked up. With an expression of horror, the girl on the floor dropped the pieces of crockery with a loud crash. Simultaneously, Fanny put both hands to her carrot-topped head and tottered toward him, moaning.

"Oi'm so glad to see yer! The most awfulest thing's 'appened 'ere." Fanny gave an artful stumble and fell against Jason, clutching at his damp, dark cloak.

He dumped his lantern on the dressing table, fear pumping through his veins as he grabbed the wench by her chubby arms. "Where is Mirella?" he demanded.

"Oi dunno where she be. The last thing Oi remembers, she 'it me o'er the 'ead wi' that there pitcher." Fanny gestured weakly at the mess the other girl was cowering near. "Oh, me poor achin' skull! If ye'll jist 'elp me git into bed—"

"You little fool!" Jason snarled, giving her a none-too-gentle shake. "How could you have let Mirella get past the both of you?"

" 'Twarn't nothin' Oi could do about it," Fanny whined. "Rosie 'ere went down to fetch some more wine. And whilst she was gone, the lady 'it me from behind." She gave another moan and swayed against him.

"I warned you not to stay here alone with Mirella, so if you're hurt 'tis your own bloody fault."

Jason pushed Fanny aside. Pivoting sharply, he strode to the door, grabbing his lantern on the way.

" 'Ey, wait!" Fanny scurried after him and latched onto his cloak. "What's yer 'urry?"

"I should think that's obvious," Jason said coldly. "I'm going to find Mirella if it takes me all night."

"Why not jist ferget the lady? Oi knows all about 'ow to keep a man 'appy. And Oi'd be more'n willin' to go on yer ship wi' ye, if'n ye gits me meanin'." The serving wench batted her stubby, carrot-colored lashes.

A sudden suspicion occurred to Jason as he recalled what he'd seen when he'd first entered the chamber. Fanny hadn't looked injured in the least. And now she was clinging to him like a limpet, practically begging him to take her with him. Was it possible that she and Mirella had concocted this whole scheme together?

He seized the wench by one shoulder. "Did you let Mirella go on purpose?"

"Oh, nay, sir! Whyever would ye think a thing like that?" But the way she evaded his gaze told him the truth.

"You're lying." He tightened his grip on her, giving her a rough shake. "Now tell me, where did she go?"

A glimmer of fear leaped into Fanny's eyes. "Oi don' know nothin', Oi swear it!"

"By damn, if I find out you're hiding something from me, you'll wish you'd never been born!"

Jason thrust her cringing body from him. He was furious, though in truth, he felt a twinge of regret at frightening Fanny so. He was sure Mirella had talked her into this foolish plan, and there could be no purpose in wreaking vengeance upon someone who had been only a pawn.

With nary a backward glance, he sprinted out the door and down the stairs, the lantern he carried casting eerie, swaying shadows over the walls. Entering the noisy taproom, Jason hesitated and glanced over at Bates, then decided it would be a waste of time to confront him. The innkeeper would likely yield no useful information regarding Mirella's whereabouts. He would be better off trying his luck elsewhere.

Judging by her other escape attempt, Jason suspected that Mirella would have slipped out the back. Besides, the odds were that he'd have seen her on his way in if she'd gone out the front. He strode down the passageway to his right and pushed open the kitchen door.

There were three employees occupying the large, smoky room, but only a small lad who slowly rotated a roasting haunch over the fireplace flames looked up at the sound of Jason's heavy, hurrying footsteps. Jason was opening his mouth to ask the cook and her helpers if they had seen Mirella when he heard a distant, distinctly female scream.

For an instant, he stood frozen. The desperate cry had come not from the taproom but from the rear of the inn.

Jason leaped into action, his long strides carrying him to the back of the kitchen. The door flew open under one quick thrust of his hand. Raising his lantern to illuminate the dark, foggy path in front of him, he ran straight for the stables.

But on hearing a muffled scuffling noise off to the right, he veered sharply in that direction.

Jason's blood ran cold as he saw Mirella struggling with a man at the far end of the inn. Her white-wigged assailant was of stocky build, and wore the bright colored clothing of a dandy. His thick hands were wrapped around Mirella's slender ivory throat. He was choking her!

Both fury and fear surged inside Jason, propelling him forward with a speed that sent the fog billowing about his body and the lantern careening wildly in his hand.

From a few feet away, he lunged toward them, dropping the lamp. Even as it fell, its flickering flame flashed onto something metallic as Mirella's hand arced through the night air. Her attacker gave a loud, strangled cry, and his broad fingers released her neck. At the same instant, Jason seized him from behind, roughly jerking him away from her.

But the man paid Jason no attention. He was staring down, wide-eyed with horror, at the hilt protruding from his chest. A teardrop of red seeped from the wound to stain the front of his canary yellow frockcoat.

Then, without uttering another sound, he went limp, his bull-like body sagging.

Jason tightened his grip, his jaw tightly clenched at

135

the frustration of being cheated of the chance to throttle Mirella's assailant. Unvented rage burned like a fire within him. With a violent curse, he shoved the man away so that he slumped to the ground to lean crookedly against the side of the inn, only his head and shoulders visible above the swirling mist. His face was as pasty white as the powdered wig that sat, askew, on his head.

A small sound made Jason whirl toward Mirella. She stood huddled against the wall, hands at her reddened throat as she struggled to draw in shallow, rasping breaths. His hot fury was drowned in a sudden flood of concern.

Closing the distance between them with one long stride, he gently gathered her into his arms. "Mirella, are you all right?"

She gave a jerky nod and clung to him, her soft body trembling. Her subtle feminine fragrance enveloped him. Lifting a hand to the silken strands that had escaped her chignon, Jason felt a surge of fierce protectiveness. He swore a silent vow to watch over her more closely from this moment forward. No man but he would ever touch her again. Nestling her within the warm folds of his cloak, he held her tightly until her heartbeat slowed its frantic pace and her breathing returned to normal.

"Feel better now?" he asked finally.

Jason's quiet question penetrated the shock that blanketed Mirella's brain, and the horror of what had happened washed over her once more. Shifting in his arms, she turned to stare at Sir Harry's lifeless form lolling against the inn wall. A new kind of fear twisted her insides. As she raised panicked eyes to Jason, her hand went to her throat, which still ached from the brutal attack.

"Oh, dear God," she whispered. "I . . . I've killed him, haven't I?"

"Does it matter?" Jason growled. "If the villain is dead, 'tis a fate he well deserves."

"But what am I to do? I'll be hanged for murder!"

"There is naught to worry about, my love." He touched her cheek with gentle fingers. "No one will think to seek you in the colonies, not even Sir Harry."

She gave a half-hysterical laugh. "Of course my cousin is no threat. How could he harm me when he lies before us dead? Nay, 'tis the long arm of the law I fear . . ."

Mirella stopped short, sensing a sudden tension in Jason as his narrowed eyes darted to where Sir Harry lay. Her stomach lurched in sickening awareness. How could she have been so blind? Of course Jason hadn't known her attacker's identity! And now she had given him a handy tool which he undoubtedly would use to blackmail her into becoming his mistress.

A thrill feathered over her spine as she became conscious of the warm, hard chest she was leaning against. His embrace was comforting, deceptively secure. Belatedly, she recalled that Jason was as much her enemy as Sir Harry. Last night, the large hands that now held her so gently had plundered her body's most intimate secrets. Regaining control of her senses, Mirella wrenched out of his arms, taking several steps backward on shaky legs.

"This is Sir Harry Weston, then?" Jason demanded.

She gave a reluctant nod, nervously rubbing the silk covering her arms.

"How did he manage to track you here?"

"He . . . he didn't say."

"I smell the stench of Bates in this," Jason ground out, slamming his fist into his palm. "I should never have trusted that conniving bastard."

Mirella bit her lip anxiously, feeling as though the jaws of some huge trap were closing about her. She couldn't decide which was the worse, her fear of being hanged for murder or her need to escape the man standing before her.

"Jason, I . . . I must get away from here. And quickly, before anyone finds me with Sir Harry."

But as she turned to plunge into the gloomy shadows, Jason's hand shot out to detain her. "Wait, Mirella," he said gently. "Before you act hastily, perhaps we should first determine if Sir Harry is indeed dead."

Jason released her to bend over a bright spot of fog. After a moment's search, he drew forth a ship's lantern, its flame casting an erratic yellow light over the surging mist. Mirella realized that Jason must have dropped the lamp before grabbing Sir Harry. The narrow bands of brass encircling its chimney had prevented the glass from shattering.

"Pray, hold this for a moment." Jason thrust the lantern at her.

Automatically, her clammy fingers closed over the cold metal handle. As he knelt before Sir Harry's limp form, she passed her hand over her forehead in confusion. Maybe Jason was right . . . it wouldn't hurt to at least find out if her cousin were dead or alive.

She watched in horrified fascination as Jason examined Sir Harry. The fog was steadily growing thicker; it seemed as though they were suspended in a tiny, glowing island apart from the rest of the world. Only the muffled roar of laughter from inside the taproom penetrated their little bubble.

But safety was only an illusion, Mirella reminded herself. She shivered, not knowing if it was due to the damp, chilly air or an encroaching fear. If Sir Harry were dead, where could she hide to escape the hangman's clutches? Was there anywhere in England she would be safe?

". . . so he must only have passed out."

"Pardon?" She was suddenly aware that Jason was standing again, speaking to her.

"I said, I can detect a faint heartbeat. He's alive."

Mirella felt a burst of relief. "Are you certain?"

"Without a doubt."

"Oh, thank God above. I do not need to flee the country."

"I would not be too hasty in that decision."

Her forehead wrinkled. "But if he is not dead, then I am no murderess!"

"Yet Sir Harry may live only long enough to name you as his slayer. The law would then hunt you down as easily as a wounded hare. Where will you go, Mirella, that no one will find you?" Jason paused, then added softly, "Where but to Virginia, with me?"

"Nay."

But even as she whispered the denial, Mirella knew she was beaten. Given the choice of the hangman's noose, or exile to the wilderness with a man who sought to make her his whore, she would take her chances on the latter. After all, couldn't she deflect his seduction attempts for the duration of the voyage? Then, once they'd reached Virginia, surely there would be a chance to escape him.

Jason took a step nearer. "Mirella, I warn you, if you don't go willingly, I shall have to resort to force. Is that what you prefer, to be dragged kicking and screaming through the streets?"

"No, I . . ." She drew in a deep breath. His masculine scent wafted through the damp night air, causing a sudden shiver to course over her skin. A memory flashed into her mind, of her face buried in the fragrant crook of his neck as his hands roamed her naked flesh . . .

"You're chilled, Mirella! Here, let me give you this." Jason slipped off his cloak and draped it around her shoulders.

"That isn't necessary," she protested weakly. She didn't want to wear the cloak because it carried Jason's smell and body warmth. The sensation was too dangerously close to being held in his embrace. But she couldn't think of how to refuse the garment without him guessing the true source of her trembling.

"I insist you wear it," he said crisply. He relieved her of the lantern, holding it up so that the flame bathed his rugged features in soft, golden light. Despite his fussing over her, his expression was stern and relentless. "Well, then, Mirella, I await your answer."

Her fingers tightened on the cloak. She had but one choice, she reminded herself bitterly. "All right,

140

Jason, you win. I'll go with you."

He looked a trifle startled at her meek yielding. Then a small smile touched his lips. "Let us be away, then; we have tarried here long enough."

Placing a hand at the back of her waist, Jason guided her forward, around the corner and down the narrow alley that led to the front of the inn. They had advanced but halfway to the main street when he stopped short. "One moment, Mirella."

Leaving her alone in the shadows, he spun around and strode back from whence they came. Puzzled, Mirella watched his lantern disappear into the thickening fog. The mist curled in damp ribbons around her hair, touching her face like cold fingers. She clutched the voluminous folds of his cloak more closely about her slender form, grateful now for its warmth.

Jason offered not a word of explanation on his return a few moments later, and it was not until they reached the docks that she discovered the reason for his abrupt absence.

Phantom ships loomed through the fog, water lapping against their invisible hulls. The smell of the sea was stronger here. Far ahead on the quay, Mirella could hear the distant din of cursing voices, along with thumping and banging noises that she guessed were due to the loading or unloading of some vessel.

She followed Jason as he stepped cautiously to the edge of a deserted pier, holding the lantern high to light their path through the swirling gray haze.

The arc of his hand was so swift that she very nearly missed seeing what it was he pitched into the harbor. On recognizing the small object, Mirella gasped. An instant later, she heard a muted kersplash as it vanished into the dark, briny waters.

It had been her knife, with a bloody handkerchief wrapped around the blade.

"No sense in leaving any positive proof that 'twas you who stabbed Sir Harry, is there?" Jason said calmly.

Mirella could only shake her head in numb acquiescence. She felt the subtle pressure of his palm between her shoulderblades as he urged her down the waterfront. The warmth that radiated from his hand through the layers of her clothing was somehow comforting.

Carefully picking their way through the mist, they headed for the other end of the docks, the sounds of bustling motion steadily growing louder. Suddenly the quay became a beehive of activity as objects began to take shape through the haze. Mirella could see figures scurrying about by the light of torches and lanterns. Fog draped the area in gauzy tendrils, creating an ethereal scene that contrasted sharply with the ribald curses filling the air.

Clasping Jason's strong hand, Mirella trailed him through a maze of crates and barrels. They paused to let a dockworker roll a keg of rum past, then advanced toward the three-masted ship berthed alongside the wharf. As they drew nearer, she could just barely make out the bold white lettering on the bow that proclaimed the vessel's name, the *Argo*.

Mirella couldn't help the tiny smile that rose to her lips. Jason had christened his ship for the craft which had carried the mythological hero on his quest for the golden fleece.

Just ahead, a cow gave a mournful moo, its hooves clip-clopping slowly on the gangplank as a sailor tugged on its rope to coax the animal on board. Mirella and Jason followed the unlikely pair up the swaying wooden ramp. Nodding a greeting to several passing seamen, he led her through a chaos of cartons on deck. By the light of his lantern, they descended a short companionway, turned a corner, then stopped in front of a narrow door.

With a sardonic flourish, Jason twisted the knob and waved her inside. "Your quarters, m'lady."

Mirella walked into the cabin, which was lit by the soft glow of a brass lamp hanging from the ceiling in the corner. The space was small yet was far more luxurious than she had anticipated. A compact walnut armoire occupied the space beside the door, and a Turkish carpet covered part of the wood-planked deck. There was a minuscule desk against one wall with a shelf of books above it. A narrow strip of oak held the row of leather-bound volumes in place. Just in front of her, below the porthole, rested a quilt-covered bunk. All the furniture was bolted down to prevent it from shifting in rough seas.

"I trust the accommodations are satisfactory," Jason said.

" 'Tis finer than I had expected," Mirella admitted. "Indeed, I am surprised that a merchant ship would provide its passengers with such elegant furnishings."

"I regret to disappoint you, my love, but none of the other passengers will spend the coming weeks in such comfort." Jason closed the door and placed his

143

lantern on the desk. When he raised his gaze to hers, his expression reminded her somehow of a beast of prey.

"You see, Mirella," he added slowly, "this is my cabin."

Chapter Eight

Mirella stared at Jason, lips parted in shock. His cabin! She had assumed that aboard the ship, she would at least have the safety of her own quarters to which she could escape if the need arose. How foolish she had been to underestimate his intentions!

His dark gold eyes gleamed in the lamplight as they roamed with lazy interest over her cloaked figure. The walls seemed to shrink, imprisoning her in a gilded cage with this tall, virile man who was essentially a stranger to her. Whether she was willing or not, he meant to take her to his bed and touch her as he had last night, again and again and again. . . .

The thought made her insides flutter with a yearning that appalled her. Crushing the sensation, Mirella sought refuge in anger. She would not tolerate the helpless position into which he had maneuvered her! He might own this ship but that fact didn't grant him the right to possess her, too. She would not humiliate herself by meekly surrendering to his lust.

"I must find somewhere else to stay, then."

Chin tilted high, Mirella marched past him to the

door. But when she tried to yank it open it refused to budge. A glance upward revealed why. Jason's large hand was splayed over the wood, pressing it shut with effortless strength. The sound of his low chuckle vibrated in her ears.

She spun around in a fury, to find the white ruffled shirt covering his broad chest only a scant inch away. His arms straddled her, his scent and body heat engulfing her. Though the cabin was cool, she felt a sudden shortness of breath, as if she were stifling. The half-smile on his handsome face made her temper seethe. The situation amused him, as if he were a cat playing with a cornered mouse!

"I demand that you let me out of here this instant!"

"Whyever would you want to leave? There are no finer accommodations anywhere on this vessel."

"I care naught for luxury if the price of it is sharing your bed."

"You didn't seem to mind last night." His calloused fingertips traced the faint sprinkling of freckles across the soft skin of her cheekbones.

Mirella felt her face flush. Why did he have to remind her of that? Jerking her head aside, she tried to elude his disturbing caress. "You despicable cad," she choked out.

Jason chuckled again, and the throaty, sensual sound threw her senses into a turmoil. "Do I detect censure in your voice, Mirella? And here I was under the impression that you had enjoyed our love-making."

"You took advantage of me," she retorted, awash in a sea of anger and arousal and acute embarrassment.

"Now that I know how unscrupulous you are, it will never, ever happen again!"

"Never is a long time," he murmured. "Are you truly certain you can live up to such a stringent vow?"

Without warning, his arms slid inside her cloak and tightened around her back, crushing her breasts to the hard wall of his chest. Instinctively, Mirella's hands came up to push him away, but her efforts were to no avail. He was far stronger than she.

"Jason, don't," she pleaded, as his relentless face swooped nearer. Then his lips captured hers in a kiss that was masterful and tender, hungry and intoxicating.

Erotic longing pulsed through her. But Mirella held herself rigid, her mouth clamped shut against the expert teasing of his tongue. So he expected her to respond with all the eagerness of a bitch in heat, did he? He would soon learn that she meant every word she said!

Remaining passive was no easy task. There was an aura of total possession about his technique that plunged her into a torrent of need. His overwhelming presence swamped her senses, his scent, his taste, the warm feel of his body. She was all too aware of his hands moving in mesmerizing patterns over the thin silk covering her back. Her fingers dug into the fine material of his shirt as a treacherous weakening gripped her limbs. But though it taxed the limits of her willpower, she managed to resist his coaxing seduction.

Mirella focused defiant eyes on Jason as he finally raised his head. Bracing herself to deal with an outraged, frustrated male, she was startled when he merely flashed her a mocking smile. Somehow that angered her all the more.

"How dare you!" she ground out.

"You should know by now that I would dare almost anything."

A helpless fury surged within her. "I hate you!"

He shook his head in a combination of amusement and exasperation. "Ah, Mirella, why do you continue to fight it?"

"Fight what?"

"You know well and good what I mean. There is a feeling between us that cannot be denied, no matter how hard you try."

"Feeling!" she scoffed. "This has naught to do with any emotion. You lust after me, and there is naught more to it."

"Aye, but there is," he avowed, his voice low and husky. "Are you forgetting that you desire me, too?" His hands slipped around from behind to brush the sides of her breasts.

Mirella caught her breath at the arrow of heat that shot through her body. Wrenching herself away, she stepped to the center of the small chamber and swung to face him.

"Jason, I mean what I say! I will not share this cabin with you."

He leaned against the door, a hint of humor on his face. "Ah, Mirella, is the prospect of my companionship truly so distasteful?"

"Yes!" she hissed. "Now, if you'll kindly move out of my way, I'll find somewhere else to stay."

"And where would that be?" Jason mused. "The only other passenger cabin is occupied by a newlywed couple, and as they undoubtedly value their privacy at this early stage of their relationship, I'm sure they would not welcome an intruder." His hand stroked his strong jaw in reflection. "Then again, you could always bunk with the crew in their common quarters below decks. Perhaps you might even learn to enjoy being passed from man to man. There is, after all, something to be said for variety."

"I'll take my chances." Mirella refused to be daunted by the grim picture he painted. Surely there was some private cubbyhole she could use. "Now, I demand that you move aside."

Jason crossed his arms and settled more comfortably against the door, a maddening grin on his face. "Give me one good reason why I should let you go."

"Because I asked you to!"

"Not good enough."

She let out her breath in angry frustration. "What else do you expect me to say then?"

"Hmmm." Jason rubbed his jaw, considering her. "You could try making your request in a more agreeable manner, perhaps by saying 'please.' "

Mirella gritted her teeth. What did he hope to gain by this cat-and-mouse game? Yet, desperate as she was, she had little choice but to play along. "Please, will you move aside," she forced out.

"Ah, now that wasn't so difficult, was it? In truth, since you ask so nicely, I shall make the noble sacrifice of vacating the premises in your behalf." Jason picked up one lantern and turned to open the door. "Sleep well, my love."

She blinked in astonishment. "Where are you going?"

"I'm bunking in the first mate's cabin." He paused, then added with a wicked grin, " 'Tis where I'd planned on staying all along."

As the door closed quietly behind him, Mirella felt rooted to the plush rug beneath her feet. Jason had deliberately led her to believe he meant to make love to her when all the while he had intended to quarter himself elsewhere!

She tried to summon up righteous anger, but somehow she only felt a curious sense of deflation. How could she despise him when he had been gracious enough to give up his own cabin for her? Wasn't that what she really wanted anyway?

The events of the evening suddenly made her weary. Removing Jason's cloak, Mirella readied herself for bed, then doused the lantern and slid between the cool sheets. Not even the distant noises as cargo was loaded into the hold could prevent her from slipping into the sanctuary of slumber.

The first sensation that lured Mirella from the depths of her dreams was the awareness of muted light against her closed eyelids. Gradually she became conscious of an unfamiliar dip and roll beneath her and, on hearing a muffled splashing sound, the memory of the previous night came rushing back at her.

She scrambled up to peer out the small porthole above the bunk. Through patches of early morning mist, she caught a glimpse of the coastline of England sliding by in the distance. The ship was underway! Hurriedly, she donned her gown, wound her hair into a hasty topknot, and headed out the door.

Climbing to the deck, she surveyed the scene with interest. The rigging above was swarming with men who were busily unfurling the great, white canvas sails. A few yards from her, a ruddy-faced man barked rapid, unintelligible orders, and baggy-breeched sailors scurried about to perform their bidden tasks. She didn't see Jason anywhere.

Feeling somewhat bewildered by the strange cries and actions around her, Mirella cautiously wended her way over to the railing, to a quiet corner out of the path of activity. There, she leaned into the brisk breeze, breathing in the strong scent of salt in the air.

Her thoughts leaped to the previous night. Remembering her encounter with Sir Harry, she shuddered with horror. Was that villain still alive? Perhaps at this very moment, the law was searching high and low for her. Unless . . . What if Jason had returned to the scene of the crime to make certain of Sir Harry's death? Mirella searched her conscience for remorse, but found none. If Jason had slit Sir Harry's throat, she owed him a debt of gratitude, for it meant that perhaps there was a faint possibility that no one would think of connecting her with the slaying.

She clung to the rail, oblivious to the slowly rising sun that burned away the lingering fingers of fog. Her brow wrinkled in confusion at the memory of what had occurred later, in Jason's cabin. Why hadn't he forced himself upon her last night? She had been at his mercy. If he had wanted to, he could have easily overpowered her.

Reluctantly, Mirella acknowledged that Jason wasn't crude enough to use brute strength to take a woman. His seduction of her would be more subtle.

151

Did he bide his time, then, waiting for her to beg for his caresses? The question made her lips tighten. He would rot in hell before that happened!

Yet she was trapped on this ship with him for the coming weeks, and she had little doubt that Jason would again try to seduce her. The unbidden image of their naked bodies entwined in passion made her tremble with a yearning she immediately stifled.

Mirella couldn't help a shiver of apprehension as she wondered about the future. What would happen on reaching America? Would Jason ever accept the fact that she did not welcome his attentions? Would he pursue her if she tried to flee from him, or would he eventually let her go, bored with her continued refusals?

The screeching of sea gulls filled the air. Leaning against the wooden rail, she let the chilly breeze wash over her. Deliberately, she thrust aside her fears and misgivings, deciding there was time aplenty for worry. Besides, she was underestimating her own strength. She would control her own destiny.

The realization gave her strength, and a feeling of exhilaration began to flow through her veins. The slap of water against the bow was like music to her ears. Even the thought that she was departing her homeland failed to daunt her lifted spirits. There was something immensely appealing in starting a new life, leaving at least some of her troubles behind.

" 'Tis a breathtaking sight, is it not?"

She swiveled at the sound of a female voice. The young woman standing rather hesitantly behind her reminded Mirella of a sparrow. Her slight figure was clad in a sober, dun-colored gown and dark mantle.

She was someone who might have faded into the woodwork were it not for the sparkle of intelligence in her topaz eyes and the delicate bone structure that gave her a certain elfin beauty. The wind had loosened a few tendrils of brown hair from the severe knot at her neck and had spread a pink flush of health over her cheeks.

Mirella studied her in curiosity. This must be half of the married couple Jason had mentioned the previous night. "Yes, it *is* lovely," she agreed. After a quick glance at the distant scenery, she looked at her unexpected companion. "I'm Mirella Weston."

"My name is Emma Colby," the girl said with a shy smile. "I hope you don't think I'm intruding on your privacy, but I was so glad to see another woman aboard."

Mirella smiled back. "Then I hope we'll become good friends, Mrs. Colby."

"Oh, please call me Emma. I'm not quite used to being Mrs. Colby, and anyway it makes me feel so old." She wrinkled her nose in mock distaste.

Mirella laughed. "All right, but only if you too dispense with formalities. So, you are newly wed, Emma? Is your husband about?"

Emma waved a hand in the vague direction of the companionway. "He's down below helping some men rearrange the cargo. It seems Mr. Fletcher was in such haste to depart this morning that not everything was put in its proper place. Lucas—he's my husband—and I wondered what the hurry was. Would you by chance know?"

"Um, I'm afraid not." Swiftly, Mirella searched for another topic of conversation. "Tell me, Emma, why

153

are you traveling to Virginia?"

A sober expression stole over the other woman's face. " 'Tis a long tale, one which I'd not wish to bore you with."

"Oh, but 'twould interest me greatly," Mirella assured her.

" 'Tis best then to tell it to you from the beginning." Emma leaned against the rail, staring out over the misty waters. "Lucas and I grew up in a small village outside of Bristol, so we have known each other nearly all our lives. My parents frowned upon our friendship. You see, my father was rector of the church, while Lucas was merely a penniless orphan apprenticed by the blacksmith. And unfortunately, Lucas has always been rather a misfit because he is a trifle slow witted. Ever since I can remember, the other children in town used to tease him and call him names."

Emma's lips pursed at the memory, then she laid a hand on Mirella's arm, gazing at her anxiously. "You must not be unduly alarmed on meeting Lucas. He's a large, hulking sort of man, and many people are afraid of him at first." Her topaz eyes grew dreamy. "But he has the kindest, gentlest soul of anyone I have ever known. 'Tis why I fell in love with him."

Mirella felt a stab of envy at the strong emotion that shone in the woman's eyes. Would that she herself could find such happiness!

"Lucas and I have had a secret understanding ever since we were children," Emma continued. "When we had saved enough for him to open his own shop in a neighboring village, we planned to marry." Her face hardened. "But one evening without my knowledge a group of local men enticed Lucas into a game of cards. Despite the way people have treated him, he's quite gullible and trusting. Before the night was over, he had lost every pence of our savings." Her small fist slammed down on the railing. "I cannot blame my husband, for he has the innocence of a babe. But I should have kept a closer watch on him. Why, oh, why didn't I?"

Mirella gave the other woman a quick hug of sympathy, aware of a feeling of helpless anger. Men were such fools when it came to the lure of gambling!

"You must not torture yourself so, Emma. 'Tis over and done with, and berating yourself will accomplish little."

"I know." Emma managed a wan smile. "And at least things have turned out reasonably well. Against my parents' wishes, Lucas and I ran off to Bristol and got married, hoping to find employment there. By a sheer stroke of luck, we met Mr. Fletcher, and he offered to take us to the colonies as his indentured servants."

"Indentured?" Mirella was only vaguely familiar with the term. "Does that mean you'll have to work off the cost of your passage?"

Emma nodded. "Lucas has his blacksmith skills, and I know a little of seamstressing. In five years' time, we shall be cleared of our debt."

"Five years!" Mirella was appalled. "Jason would force you to labor so long merely to cover the cost of your fare?"

"Oh, nay!" Emma hastened to explain. "I've heard tales of unscrupulous men who pay only passage, but Mr. Fletcher has promised us twice the fifty acres due each servant at the end of his indenture. We are ever so grateful to him. Though we hated to leave England, at least now we can look forward to someday having a farm of our very own."

"I see."

Against her will, Mirella felt her animosity toward Jason soften a little. Though she was certain he had the ulterior motive of gaining two hard workers in Emma and Lucas, she grudgingly admitted that it was decent of him not to try to take advantage of the Colbys.

"And what of you, Mirella? Might I ask why you are traveling to Virginia?"

Mirella froze at Emma's innocently asked question. What was she to reply? She certainly couldn't mention Sir Harry, or reveal that Jason wanted her to be his mistress. All she could come up with was Jason's lame excuse about a sister who needed feminine guidance. Emma might accept the tale now, but what would happen later, when she saw the attentions he paid to the woman he had hired to be his sister's companion?

"Good morning, ladies."

The deep timbre of Jason's voice saved Mirella from answering. Welcoming the intrusion, she turned to see him standing on the deck behind them.

"Good morning, Mr. Fletcher," Emma answered shyly.

As Jason and the other woman exchanged pleasantries, Mirella studied him. His windblown hair glinted like gold in the morning sunlight. Today he was dressed as plainly as any seaman, yet the fine tailoring of his clothing contrasted with the ill-fitting attire of the ordinary sailor. A white linen shirt hugged his broad shoulders, while snug fawn breeches emphasized the muscles in his thighs. But more than his garb set him apart from the other men aboard, she mused. There was also a quiet air of command about him which seemed an innate part of his character.

"I do hope I didn't interrupt anything," Jason was saying.

"Not at all," Emma replied. "Mirella and I were just getting to know one another."

"As a matter of fact," Mirella added on sudden inspiration, "Emma was asking me why I was going to the colonies. Perhaps you might want to explain the reason to her." There, she thought with glee, let him be the one to come with a plausible excuse!

"My pleasure." He flashed her a sardonic smile before looking at the other woman. "You see, Mrs. Colby, by accident Mirella and I met one another in Bristol. During the course of conversation, we discovered that we are distantly related. We were quite surprised to learn of the connection, were we not, Mirella?" There was a trace of laughter in the deep gold eyes he turned on her.

"Oh, quite surprised, indeed," she agreed dryly. Trust a liar like him to dream up such a wild tale. Yet she had to admire the logic of his explanation. Emma would think it only natural that he would endeavor to spend time with a blood relation.

"When I learned that Mirella's parents had died and left her penniless," Jason continued, "I suggested she accompany me to Virginia to act as a companion to my younger sister, Pandora."

"How very kind of you, Mr. Fletcher," Emma

gushed, gazing at him as though he were a saint.

Jason gave a modest shrug. " 'Twas the least I could do for my dear, long-lost cousin. I've made it my personal responsibility to look out for her happiness."

He lifted an arm and settled it lightly across Mirella's shoulders in what she knew would appear to Emma as a gesture of cousinly affection. What the other woman couldn't see, though, was that Jason's fingers were playing with the fine hairs at Mirella's nape. The arousing sensation sent an involuntary shiver down her spine.

"Are you cold, Mirella?" Jason looked at her solicitously, though his eyes were teasing. "Shall I fetch the cloak I lent you last night? I'm sure you must have goose bumps all over from this brisk wind."

Mirella saw his gaze flit down to her breasts, and realized to her consternation that the puckered tips were visible through the thin silk of her gown. Longing to slap the appreciation off his face, she forced herself to calmly step away from his disturbing caress.

"Aye, 'tis a bit chilly out here. If you two will excuse me, I believe I'll go below in search of some breakfast."

"Why, I'd be happy to escort you since I haven't eaten yet, either," Jason said, taking her elbow in a firm grip. "How about you, Mrs. Colby? Would you care to accompany us?"

" 'Tis kind of you to include me," Emma replied, her cheeks dimpling prettily as she smiled back at him.

"The pleasure is all mine," he avowed, offering her his other arm.

158

Not wanting to make a scene, Mirella had little choice but to stroll across the crowded deck at his side. She chafed inwardly at the smooth manner in which he had orchestrated the situation. Blast that aggravating man! Couldn't he see that she loathed his company?

Jason guided them to a small dining cabin below deck, which he explained was for use of the ship's officers and passengers. The chamber's only occupant was a plump balding man, who sat at a narrow table finishing a plate of biscuits and sausages. He rose on seeing them.

Jason performed the introductions. "Ladies, this is Captain Zeke Lassiter. Captain, may I present Miss Mirella Weston and Mrs. Emma Colby?"

The captain sketched them a gallant bow. "Welcome aboard. 'Tis rare indeed that I have the pleasure of sailing such loveliness across the high seas."

"You'll have to be careful of old Zeke," Jason warned them. "There's naught he loves better than to flirt with a pretty woman. Why, 'tis a proven fact that he's left broken hearts in ports all over the world."

The captain's leathery face creased into a merry smile. "Hogwash! Don't you ladies listen to a word he says. That lad is far more guilty of being a skirt chaser than I."

The two men good-naturedly argued the topic back and forth before the conversation drifted to other subjects. Learning that neither of the two women had been to sea before, the captain patiently answered their questions.

"If we are going west," Emma asked, "then why can we still see the coastline of England?"

159

Zeke Lassiter smiled. "My dear, I fear we are not yet out of the Bristol Channel. Once we are, we shall head down to the Azores to pick up the prevailing trade winds that will carry us across the Atlantic. Now, if there is anything else you need to know, I'm sure Jason would be happy to oblige you. I, regretfully, must return to my duties."

After the captain left the cabin, Jason directed the two women to a sideboard which was bolted to the wall. The ship rolled beneath their feet as they filled their plates with food, and Mirella had to be careful to avoid losing her balance.

She was surprised at the fine porcelain and silver provided for their use. It appeared that Jason was accustomed to life's luxuries, despite the rustic setting she was sure he had grown up in.

As they sat at the narrow table eating their breakfast, he regaled them with stories about Zeke Lassiter, who had captained the *Argo* for many years. Emma hung onto Jason's every word, Mirella noted with disgust. Not that she could blame the poor woman. Jason was at his most charming today, and Emma had no inkling of his true character. Wouldn't she be shocked, Mirella thought, to hear how he had imprisoned her and plotted to make her his mistress!

Even now, he was continuing his subtle seduction. He sat beside Mirella, his long leg brushing against hers. Surreptitiously she tried to inch away, but the table was small. If she moved any farther, she would slide off the wooden bench they shared.

The topic of conversation returned to the voyage. "How long will it take to reach Virginia?" Emma asked Jason.

"Anywhere from five to eight weeks." His calm voice gave no hint of the battle being waged beneath the table, where his hard thigh pressed firmly against Mirella's softer one, causing an unbidden thrill to course through her.

"Why is it not possible to pinpoint our arrival date?" inquired Emma, innocent of the undercurrents between her companions.

"So much depends upon favorable weather conditions. A severe storm could blow us off course, or a lack of wind might slow us down."

Mirella put down her teacup. "And what of provisions?" she asked with a sweetness that belied the annoyance she felt. "If the crossing takes longer than expected, would there be enough to feed everyone aboard?"

As she spoke, she brought the heel of her shoe down hard on Jason's instep, and was pleased to see a muscle jump in his jaw. There, that ought to make the cocksure knave keep his distance! But her gloating was short-lived. Jason jerked his foot free, and before she could guess his intentions, he had angled his leg in front of hers, effectively trapping her in place. She couldn't twist away without causing a scene.

"Rest assured, dearest cousin, you will not starve," he replied, placing a large hand over hers. "Remember that I have vowed to take care of you under all circumstances."

His husky tone made plain the lengths he would go to watch over her. If he had his way, the gleam in those gold eyes told Mirella, the fulfillment of his attentions would extend far into each night!

Despite her antagonism, his nearness haunted her

161

senses. His warm body pressed against her side. Without conscious intent, her gaze drifted to his mouth, and she recalled the taste and feel of his lips. Instinctively she swayed toward him. *Madness!* her mind screamed. She stopped herself with a jerk.

"Excuse me . . ." she faltered.

Aware only of a driving need to get away, Mirella yanked her hand out from beneath his. But when she tried to stand, she forgot that Jason's leg still confined her. At that very moment, fate decreed that the vessel dip from the effect of a large swell.

She lost her balance and, in catching at the table to steady herself, she knocked over the porcelain cup in front of her just as she plopped back onto the hard bench.

"Oh, no!" she cried in dismay as lukewarm tea spilled down her bodice and into her lap.

"Allow me." Grabbing a damask napkin, Jason wiped at the brown liquid soaking into the blush pink silk. The gentle stroking of his hand just beneath her breasts made her whole body tingle.

"I can do it myself." Beyond caring if she sounded cross, Mirella snatched the square of cloth out of his fingers, dabbing at the blemish herself.

"Oh, Mirella, is it badly stained?" Emma asked in concern, standing up to peer across the table.

" 'Twould appear that way," Mirella replied, gazing dolefully at the darkened spot.

"You should return to your cabin immediately," the other woman urged. "Whilst you change into another gown, I can try to wash this one out for you."

"I thank you, Emma, but I'm afraid 'tis my only gown," Mirella admitted ruefully. "I have no other."

162

"No other?" Emma repeated, gazing at her curiously. "But this one is so fine, I thought surely Mr. Fletcher must have provided you with . . ." She blushed suddenly. "Forgive me, 'tis none of my concern."

"But you are absolutely right, Mrs. Colby," Jason said. "Unfortunately, this was the only gown I had to give to Mirella, since I had purchased it in London for my sister. 'Tis scarcely adequate to fill her needs, though. If I may, I shall arrange to have several bolts of cloth taken from the hold for her use. Would you object to helping her sew whatever garments she needs?"

"Object?" Emma exclaimed. "Why, I would be happy to!"

Jason turned to Mirella. "And you, dear cousin? Do you have any opposition to the arrangement?"

Mirella was of half a mind to tell Jason precisely what he could do with his fabric. She didn't want to accept any handouts that might make her beholden to him. But despite her reservations, practicality won out. The prospect of spending the long weeks ahead clad in the same gown held little appeal.

"Indeed, *dear cousin*," she replied, placing a pointed stress on the last two words, "I am grateful that you are so very thoughtful."

"There is no need for thanks betwixt relatives. Rest assured, I take great enjoyment in giving you pleasure." There was a touch of wickedness in his expression as he leisurely perused her slender, full-breasted figure. The precise nature of the pleasure to which he referred was evident in his bold, blatant eyes.

Mirella tightened her lips and stood up, feeling a

flush warm her cheeks. As she and Emma strolled out of the dining chamber, she could feel Jason's hot gaze stripping her naked. The disturbing sensation lingered as they walked to Mirella's cabin. Not even Emma's chatter as she sponged out the tea stain could help Mirella shake the flustered feeling she felt deep inside of her.

Chapter Nine

Mirella stood in the center of her cabin, biting her lip in concentration, her arms stretched behind her as she struggled to fasten the silk loops over the tiny pearl buttons that marched down the back of her gown. With a sigh of relief, she secured the last one. She wore no stays; not only because her slender figure needed no such artifice, but because it would have been well nigh impossible to lace the undergarment by herself. Of course, Emma had offered her services as a ladies' maid but Mirella had been reluctant to agree, aware of the debt of gratitude she already owed the brown-haired woman.

In the two weeks that had passed since their first meeting, she and Emma had become fast friends. Emma was an accomplished seamstress, and was largely responsible for fashioning the six new gowns which now hung in the small walnut armoire. Mirella had aided her as much as she could, doing the tedious seam stitching while Emma designed the patterns, cut the fabric, and sewed the exquisitely detailed finishing work.

Mirella smoothed a hand over the elegant material cascading over her, a gown which they had completed just that afternoon. It was made of a midnight blue silk shot through with silver threads, with an underskirt of the purest white satin. The elbow-length sleeves were edged with Valenciennes lace. And the garment required only one item to complement its beauty.

Opening the armoire, she found the rose-and-pink gown Jason had given her. Her fingers lingered on the lovely fabric for a moment as she recalled that Jason had purchased it in London for his sister. No matter what his other shortcomings, she couldn't fault his generosity. He had given her bolt after bolt of the finest taffetas and brocades, cambrics and muslins. Not wanting to be obligated to him, Mirella had been determined to select only the most sober and inexpensive cloths but Emma had stubbornly outvoted her.

Remembering her purpose, Mirella dug inside the pocket of the gown and unpinned her mother's cameo. Then she fastened the piece to her lacy bodice, between her breasts.

She assessed her appearance in the small mirror on the wall. The delicate cameo added precisely the touch for which she was striving. Her lustrous ebony curls were arranged in a chignon. The deep blue color of her gown enhanced her indigo eyes, making them seem darker and more mysterious in the waning light of evening. Would Jason find her attractive when she saw him at supper tonight?

Annoyed, Mirella stifled the thought. Why was it that nary an hour slid by that she did not think of him? Even at night he invaded her dreams, and she would waken to find her body aching for his. Was she so weak willed that she could not put him from her mind?

Of course, Emma didn't help matters. The needle-woman never missed an opportunity to sing his praises. Apparently she had decided that Jason and Mirella would make a perfect pair, for she was forever scheming in none-too-subtle ways to throw the two of them together. If they were eating their noon meal with Emma and Lucas, Emma suddenly would complain of seasickness and ask her husband to escort her back to their cabin, leaving Jason and Mirella alone. If she and Mirella were sewing, she would ask Mirella to fetch another spool of thread from the hold, knowing full well that Jason was busy at some task down there.

Jason took a wicked delight in Emma's matchmaking efforts. Though Mirella had gone to great lengths to try to avoid him, there was not a day that passed in which he had failed to make her aware of his virile presence. No matter where she went on the small vessel, he always seemed to be there.

Despite her antipathy, she had to admit a certain, reluctant admiration for Jason. He was never idle, forever willing to lend a hand where needed even if it meant scrambling up into the rigging to help alter the sails. Her heart nearly stopped each time she caught sight of him balancing on the footropes high above the deck.

It was simply an automatic fear she would feel for any human being, Mirella convinced herself. In truth, she wouldn't care a whit if something happened to that aggravating man! Despite the conniving of everyone around her, hadn't she proven time and time again that she could resist him? She was no spineless weakling who would melt like butter at the touch of his hands!

Tilting her jaw in determination, Mirella left the cabin to join the others for supper. By now she was used to the rolling of the ship, and could maneuver about as easily as the best sailor. Luckily, the weather thus far had been good, so she had experienced little queasiness.

She stepped into the small dining cabin to find everyone else already there. Jason stood, a glass of brandy in his hand, with Captain Lassiter and the first mate, Norris Podswill. Politely, she greeted them before joining Emma and Lucas.

Gowned in dove gray dimity, Emma looked like a dainty doll beside her husband. Lucas Colby was a big bear of a man, dark and fearsome looking, with bulging muscles. In sharp contrast to his appearance, though, Mirella had seen that he possessed a quiet, gentle nature. When a cask of rum had accidentally rolled over the leg of the ship's cat, she had seen Lucas soothe the mewling creature and set the injured limb in a splint. And the adoration he felt for his wife was evident in the protective arm he had draped around her waist.

Mirella had spoken but a few words to them when she suddenly felt strong male fingers lift her wrist, then a cool silver mug was pressed into her palm. Startled, she glanced up to see Jason standing beside her.

"I thought you might like some wine," he murmured.

His fingers lingered over hers a moment longer than necessary, and Mirella felt an irresistible thrill race over her skin. Judging by the glint in his golden eyes, she fumed, that was precisely the effect he had intended.

"Thank you," she forced out with false politeness. Conscious of his warm gaze, she took a sip of the sweet Madeira, wishing he would heed her hints and leave her alone.

" 'Tis a pretty cameo you wear," Emma commented. "I've not seen it before, have I?"

"Nay," Mirella replied, glad for the diversion. "I've never worn it aboard the ship before tonight. 'Tis all I have left of my mother's jewelry."

"The figure is carved of onyx, is it not?" Jason queried.

He was staring pointedly at her bosom, where the piece was pinned. She shifted in embarrassment, sure that he was looking not at the cameo, but at the milky swells of her breasts. Why, oh why, had Emma cut such a daring décolletage for this gown?

"Yes," she said curtly.

"Lucas," Emma addressed her husband, "let us go sit down at the table. I fear I am quite weary of standing."

Lucas gave them a shy smile as he led his wife away.

"I believe I shall accompany them," Mirella said, seeing through Emma's ploy to leave her alone with Jason. "If you will excuse me."

"As m'lady wishes," he drawled, giving a mocking bow.

But, to her annoyance, Jason trailed right along behind her, seating himself on the bench next to her

169

before she could protest. The captain and the first mate joined them, sitting as was their custom at either end of the table. A cabin boy brought a side of beef, boiled potatoes, carrots, and biscuits.

"Enjoy the fresh meat while it lasts," Captain Lassiter told them. "We had space for only a limited number of animals aboard, and soon we will be forced to rely on salted pork and beef and whatever fish we can catch."

Though Jason made no further attempt to touch her, Mirella was acutely aware throughout the meal of his presence beside her. Afterward, when Emma suggested the four of them take a turn around the deck, Mirella came very near to refusing. But the prospect of spending the remainder of the evening cooped up in her cabin lacked appeal. She reasoned she would be safe enough if she stuck close to the Colbys.

She left the others for a moment to stop at her cabin and don a mantle. Though it was May, the night air was cool. But when she made her way onto the deck, she found only Jason waiting in the moonlight.

"Where are Emma and Lucas?" she demanded.

Jason shrugged, though his eyes held a devilish twinkle. "I'm afraid Mrs. Colby changed her mind. She was feeling a bit weary, so she and husband retired for the night."

"I should have guessed." Chastising herself for being so gullible, Mirella spun around, intending to go back to her cabin.

But before she had taken two steps, Jason's hands clamped onto her shoulders. "Wait, Mirella," he said, twisting her back toward him. "I thought you wanted some fresh air."

"I can get all the fresh air I need by opening my porthole."

"And what of exercise?"

She let out an irritated sigh. "Jason, you can't possibly believe I'd be fool enough to stay out here with just you."

"Afraid of me, hmm?"

Mirella refused to respond to his baiting question. "I merely wish to return to my cabin."

"Why? What would be the harm in spending a few short moments in my company? We have spoken so little these past two weeks."

"Because there is naught I have to say to you."

"Ah, but I can think of much to discuss on such a fine night." His grip gentled, and his fingers began to massage her shoulders through her mantle. "I would speak to you of the beauty of this vessel rushing into the wind with its sails unfurled,"—his voice grew low and soothing—"the influence of the stars on our fate,"—his sensual stroking made her limbs go liquid, banishing her irritation in favor of a headier feeling—"the way the shimmering moon hangs low in the black velvet sky."

He paused, and a tiny smile lifted the corners of her lips. "I had no idea you were a poet, Jason."

" 'Tis merely the effect of your lovely presence."

The statement was such a blatant display of flattery that she couldn't help laughing. "Sir, I assure you I am impervious to your compliments."

"Then it shouldn't matter if you spend a few minutes out here with me," Jason countered smoothly. He loosed her shoulders to extend an elbow to her.

171

"Come, let us take a stroll around the deck."

Mirella hesitated. He did have a point. Though she could not claim to be totally immune to his attraction, she *was* capable of resisting him. And the lure of the fresh sea breeze far outweighed the prospect of spending a boring evening alone in her cabin. Taking a deep breath, she curled her fingers around his proffered arm. His flesh was hard and warm beneath her hand, and his masculine scent mingled with the salty smell of the air.

They walked without speaking for a while, Jason apparently as content as she was to enjoy the beauty of the night. Slowly Mirella felt a sensation of peace steal over her. The only sounds were water splashing against the hull, the snap of sails in the wind, and the creak and sigh of boards buffeted by the waves.

As they passed the fo'c's'le, she caught a glimpse of several small specks glowing in the darkness. "What are those lights, Jason?"

"The sailors often gather there when they are off duty. 'Tis the only place onboard where they are allowed to smoke their pipes."

"Why only there?" Straining her eyes, Mirella could just barely make out the shapes of men in the shadows. The faint aroma of burning tobacco drifted to her nose.

"Because of the threat of fire. Remember, this vessel is built mainly of wood. An ember dropped in the hold might cause the entire ship to go up in flames."

"It seems strange to worry of such things when we are surrounded by so much water," she mused.

"Yet 'tis a danger that cannot be ignored."

172

Making the circuit of the bow, they turned and strolled toward the stern. When they reached the rear of the vessel, Mirella released Jason's elbow. The deck tilted slightly from the effect of the waves, and she clung to the railing for support, heedless of the occasional droplet of cold spray that touched her cheeks.

"We have had such fine weather these past few weeks," she remarked. "I am beginning to understand why men devote their lives to the sea."

Jason chuckled. "Enjoy the easy sailing while it lasts. I've not been on a voyage yet where there was not at least one terrible storm."

"Sir, do you endeavor to frighten me?" she asked lightly.

He leaned against the railing beside her, so close that she could feel the heat of his body. When he spoke, his voice was soft and husky. "If 'twould impel you to seek the protection of my arms, then the answer is aye."

Mirella felt an erotic stirring deep inside of her, then was angry at herself for her weakness. "Jason, I will not be seduced again."

"Yet can it hurt for me to try?" he bantered.

"Yes!" she hissed. "If you continue to plague me with these unwanted attentions, someone will eventually guess your true intentions toward me. I have little wish to be branded a woman of loose virtue."

"Ah, but I have been most discreet, have I not? And who would think to question me? 'Tis only right and decent that I should take my long-lost cousin into my own household."

"You dare speak to me of decency? Every time we

are alone together, you ignore all propriety. Why, you are such a liar, I doubt that your sister even requires a companion as you claim she does."

The teasing light faded from his eyes. "What I said of Pandora is true. She is quite the tomboy, and I confess I'm at my wit's end. I know not how to deal with her."

In spite of herself, Mirella found her anger fading at the the flash of vulnerability on his face. "Perhaps 'tis time you told me about her, then."

Jason hesitated, then gave a brief nod. "The problem began over ten years ago when my parents died within days of each other, both from typhus. Pandora was but a child of four at the time. Since I knew naught of raising a young girl, I left her in the care of servants. Everyone felt sorry for her because she had no mother, so they indulged her desire to run wild. That was a grave error. Having grown up a hellion, is it any wonder that she now refuses to have anything to do with more feminine pursuits?" He rubbed his forehead. "I must take full blame for her hoydenish ways. I was so wrapped up in my plantation that I paid her scant attention."

"Have you have tried to discipline her at all?"

Jason lifted his shoulders in a helpless shrug. "I'm afraid no one, not even me, seems to be able to control her for long. And punishment only serves to estrange the two of us, which makes matters worse."

"It sounds like she's spoiled."

"Perhaps, but not in the sense that she's petulant and demanding. She merely wishes to spend her time fishing and climbing trees, rather than conducting herself with ladylike decorum."

"Surely there's someone she could look to as a model. Another sister, perhaps, or an aunt?"

"Only my younger brother, Troy, and I fear he's been no more successful than I."

"Jason, Pandora, and Troy." Mirella couldn't help smiling. "Your parents appear to have had an affinity for Greek legend."

He grinned back, and the shadows shifted, gilding his features with moonlight. " 'Twas my mother. She was a bit of a dreamer. Whenever she wasn't hard at work, she had her nose buried in a book of mythology." His expression grew wistful. "How happy are those youthful memories. I thank God that at least I still have Troy and Pandora with me."

Mirella felt a lump form in her throat. Jason spoke so warmly of his family that it made her wish she'd had a brother and sister of her own.

"Have you ever thought of starting a family yourself?" She was appalled at the question that popped out of her mouth. Why should it matter to her what he chose to do with his life? Yet she could picture his children, miniature versions of himself with laughing gold eyes and honey-brown hair.

His gaze narrowed. "I've little wish to be saddled with a wife," he said sharply. "And why should I be, when with the right woman I can reap all the benefits of marriage without having any of the encumbrances?"

His bitter attitude intrigued her. "I find it difficult to believe you would feel that way, Jason, considering your happy upbringing."

"I have my reasons. When the time comes to sire an heir, I will do my duty and take a wife. But until

175

then, why should I relinquish my freedom?"

Mirella shivered. "You make it sound so cold and logical."

"Marriage should be approached that way." Jason's voice grew husky and low as he added, "But a love affair, now that is altogether different. There are no considerations save that the man and woman feel a burning desire for each other."

His hand lifted from the railing to her hair, and he tangled his fingers in the soft strands which the wind had tugged free of her chignon. The light caress sent a thrill down her spine. There was a deep and dangerous vulnerability inside her that made her feel as defenseless as a lamb being pursued by a wolf.

"Jason, don't start this again," she pleaded.

"But 'tis impossible to keep from touching you," he murmured. "You are so very lovely. . . ."

He captured her cheeks in his palms, his thumbs stroking her silken skin tenderly. There was a latent strength in his hands, yet he held her with infinite gentleness. For a long, eloquent moment they stared into each other's eyes. Against her breasts, she felt the power and warmth of his chest, and behind her, the firm rail pressing into her back. She tried to tell herself that it was madness to be here with him like this, but she could no more move away than she could touch the stars sprinkling the inky sky above.

"Mirella," he whispered as he bent over his head nearer. His hard mouth covered hers, lingering persuasively over her lips like a honeybee sipping at the nectar of a flower.

Silently branding herself a fool, Mirella stood unresisting within his embrace. Slowly her willpower crumbled beneath the mesmerizing lure of his caresses. Though they were shrouded in shadows, she reasoned that Jason could dare only so much in so open a place. What harm could it do to indulge her longing with one kiss?

A moan trembled in her throat as her lips parted to let his tongue plunder the depths of her mouth. He tasted faintly of the sweet wine they had drunk at supper, and the scent and feel of him made the blood course hotly through her veins. In wanton yearning, she pressed herself against his muscled frame. Her fingers dug into his shirt as she clung to him for support.

His lips increased their demand, and his hands moved over her mantle, following the curve of her back down to her derriere. Curling his fingers into her pliant flesh, Jason lifted her, arching her to him so that she felt his hard male need. Desire pulsed warmly between her thighs. The sounds of the surging sea and the snapping sails receded until she heard only the harshness of his breathing and her own soft sighs of delight.

He trailed a path of kisses across her cheek and down to her throat. Reveling in the hungry heat of his mouth, Mirella leaned her head back. She felt his fingers pluck at the fastening to her mantle, then the garment fell open and his lips burned over the soft swells exposed by the low décolletage of her gown. In a moment he would slide a calloused fingertip into her bodice and stroke the sensitive peak of her breast. . . .

"Sail ahoy!"

The distant cry from the lookout perched in the rigging above penetrated the sensual haze surrounding Mirella. She stiffened as the realization of where they were came flooding back.

Uttering a muffled curse, Jason dragged her tightly against him so that his heart thudded heavily beneath her ear. Then he released her to draw the edges of her mantle over her breasts.

Mirella leaned against the hard railing to support her weakened knees. Looking toward the bow, she saw the ship's officers emerge from below. The deck was filled with concerned sailors, for pirates were an ever-present danger on the high seas.

Captain Lassiter strode to the side and raised a spyglass to his eye. Automatically, Mirella turned to peer over the moon-glazed waters, though in her distracted state of mind she found it hard to concentrate.

White canvas sails glimmered in the distance. As they slowly approached, the captain called out a reassurance to the crew, identifying the vessel as a fellow merchantman bound for England.

While Jason's attention was diverted, Mirella slipped through the crowd to her cabin, wracked by a deep, bitter shame. Had it not been for the fortuitous interruption, he might have taken her right there on the shadowed deck.

And not one word of protest would have left her lips.

Chapter Ten

In the clear blue days that followed, life settled into a humdrum routine. Mirella spent long hours berating herself in the isolation of her cabin, enduring the stifling warmth as May slowly became June. How could she have come so close to yielding to Jason again? Hadn't she learned her lesson? And with the wanton way she had behaved, it was no wonder he wished to make her his mistress. He likely thought her a cheap woman with no morals. She took greater care than ever to avoid being alone with him, though he continued his relentless attentions whenever the chance arose.

The weather remained fair, until one morning when Mirella awoke to feel the ship pitching beneath her with greater force than usual. She peered out the porthole at the gray clouded sky. Stumbling slightly as the vessel listed from side to side, she managed to dress in a cool, aquamarine gown of tabby silk, pinning her ebony hair into a loose coil at the back of her head.

Then she went to breakfast, only to find the dining

cabin empty but for Norris Podswill, the first mate. In response to her questioning, the taciturn little man mumbled that Emma was confined to her bed, suffering from seasickness. Hurriedly, Mirella drank a cup of tea and ate a biscuit, wrinkling her nose at the platter of salted beef. The fare had become dreary of late, and she could work up little appetite for the meat.

When she was through, she walked to the Colbys' cabin. Lucas opened the door to her knock.

"Mornin', ma'am."

Mirella had given up on trying to convince Lucas to call her by her Christian name. No matter what she said, he stubbornly clung to the notion that she was his better, and thus ought to be addressed with the proper respect.

"Good morning, Lucas. I came to see Emma. How is she?"

His brow puckered with worry. "Feelin' poorly, I fear."

He stepped aside to let her in. The cabin was tiny in comparison to Mirella's, with no rug to cover the rough-planked floor. The furnishings consisted of two narrow cots, with a trunk belonging to the Colbys pushed against one wall. Lucas made the space seem even smaller with his towering size.

Mirella stepped to Emma's bunk and bent over her. "How are you doing?" she asked gently.

Emma opened weary topaz eyes, her face a greenish hue. "Oh, I've felt better," she joked weakly.

"Can I get you anything? Some tea, perhaps, to settle your stomach?"

"No . . . no, the very thought makes me feel

180

worse," she moaned.

"I been a-wipin' her forehead with this here cloth," Lucas said, holding forth a strip of tattered linen as he hovered over them with an anxious expression.

"Lucas has been ever so helpful," Emma said, managing an affectionate smile as she lifted her arm to him. Her husband grasped her frail hand in his huge paw and stroked it tenderly.

"Perhaps I could sit with you for a while, then," Mirella offered. "Lucas, I'm sure you're ready for a break."

"Oh, ma'am, I couldn't leave Emma—"

"I insist. You look tired, and you're probably hungry. Now, go on with you." Against his protests, she shooed the big man out the door.

Mirella knelt beside Emma, occasionally bathing her friend's brow with cool seawater from a nearby basin. The air was stifling. Only an occasional humid breeze drifting in the open porthole brought a measure of relief, and even that would soon be over, she thought. Before the storm hit, all portholes would have to be closed tightly to prevent water from rushing inside.

Lucas returned a short time later, and Mirella left with a promise to check back with them in a few hours. Then she stopped at her own cabin to fetch her mantle before going up on deck.

Carefully making her way to the railing, she looked out at the approaching storm. Heavy black clouds roiled to the west of them. The sea was dark and choppy, the waves capped with white foam. In the distance, she could see an occasional flash of lightning illuminate the darkness, though it was yet too far off for her to hear the accompanying peals of thunder.

Men were already swarming aloft to reef some of the sails. The air was filled with the loud bark of orders, the tramping of feet, the creak and groan of timbers, not to mention the growing fury of the gale.

Glancing toward the helm, Mirella saw Jason's tall, wind-whipped figure at the wheel. She had often seen him take his two-hour turn at the helm, along with the other trusted sailors. In these rough waters, she imagined it took a great deal of skill and watchfulness to steer the craft.

An odd feeling of exhilaration swept over her as she leaned onto the railing, holding tightly as the ship canted beneath her feet. A fine, cool mist struck her cheeks. There was something exciting in the turbulent air, as if this were the reward for the tedium of the past weeks.

"We're in for a big blow, that we are," said Captain Lassiter, coming up alongside her.

"When do you think it will hit?"

He squinted into the wind. "Oh, sometime in the early afternoon, I'd judge. You'd best get below to your cabin. I'd not want to see such a pretty lady as yourself get washed overboard."

"Will it really be that severe?"

"Like as not, worse," the captain pronounced calmly. "Now run along with you."

Walking cautiously over the lurching deck, her cloak flapping in the gusting wind, Mirella obeyed his command and headed below. The cabin was hot and stuffy after the coolness outside. She hung up her mantle, then went to the open porthole to catch a breath of fresh air. Soon, though, Norris Podswill knocked on her door and entered to shut the round opening.

"Cap'n's orders, ma'am," was all he mumbled before scuttling back out.

The tilting of the ship steadily worsened. A violent rainfall began to drum on the decks above, and the darkness grew thicker. The heavy rumbling of thunder joined the cacophony of wailing wind and crashing waves.

Mirella went to check on Emma's condition, but found that there was little she could do for her ailing friend. Since Lucas seemed to have the situation in hand, she returned to her own cabin. Lying down on the bunk, she tried to nap, but the turmoil outside kept her awake.

Idly, she wondered where Jason was. Still at the helm, or was his shift over? If the latter were true, knowing him, he would be busy at some other task. Perhaps he had shinnied up the ropes to help reef the sails.

Unbidden, her brain conjured up an image of him slipping from the rigging. In slow motion, she saw his flailing body plunge helplessly into the churning black waters. She told herself that it was a fate he well deserved, yet found herself sitting straight up in bed, her hands fidgeting restlessly. The longer she replayed the fantasy in her mind, the more real it became.

Mirella rose and paced the floor, no easy task with the way the ship was heaving. Finally, convincing herself that all she needed was to escape the stuffiness of her cabin for a moment, she threw her mantle over her shoulders and stumbled out. It wouldn't hurt to take a quick peek on deck, would it? She dismissed

Captain Lassiter's warning, assuring herself that she would take the utmost care.

The hatch leading outside was tightly secured, but she managed to loosen the fastening. Salt water dripped through the cracks and trickled onto her head. As she inched the wooden cover open, cold spray shot into the narrow opening to hit her face, blinding her. Utilizing all her strength, she threw back the heavy door, then scrambled up on deck, her skirts tangling in her feet so that she nearly tripped.

Mirella hugged the slick wall of the fo'c's'le, her fingers seeking purchase as she struggled to maintain her balance on the drunkenly tilting vessel. The chilly rain beat against her skin like a thousand tiny hammers, and the wind howled like a lost soul. She began to shiver as her clothing became drenched.

Straining her eyes against the unnatural midday darkness, she peered upward at the masts. She could detect shadowy human forms clinging to the rigging, completing the partial furling of the sails to lessen the impact of the gale. As she watched, one of the shapes detached himself from the others and began shinnying down the wet ropes.

He was halfway down when she realized it was Jason. Her heart clogged her throat. At any moment, Mirella expected her dream to become reality. He would plunge into the savage sea, his body never to be found. . . .

She felt an enormous relief wash over her when his feet hit the deck. He looked at her and lifted a hand in an impatient gesture, a frown furrowing his brow. She saw his mouth form her name, but the wind whipped away the sound before it could reach her ears.

Was he angry at her for coming out here? Let him be, Mirella thought sourly. Couldn't she take care of herself?

Suddenly Jason lunged across the short distance separating them. She had but an instant to wonder at his horrified expression before the wave hit.

As the ship heeled, a great wall of water poured over the decks. Mirella lost her balance under the force of it. Even as she fell, she felt Jason's fingers dig into her icy flesh to cling with brutal strength.

Then they both slid helplessly along the deck, careening wildly into unknown objects. Somehow, his arms were around her, shielding her from the worst of it. She swallowed a gulp of cold, briny liquid as panic overwhelmed her. They were being washed overboard!

But abruptly they came to a halt, and the suffocating wave was gone. Gasping for breath, Mirella opened her stinging eyes to see that she and Jason rested against the rail of the ship.

She was still reeling with shock when he stood up, hoisting her against him. He half-carried, half-dragged her over to the open hatch. She felt his hard arms tighten around her, then they were down the dim passageway and inside her cabin. Kicking the door shut behind them, he dumped her onto the bunk.

Jason towered over her like a vengeful god, hands astride his hips. Despite the lurching of the vessel, he appeared to have no trouble keeping his feet firmly planted on the floor. His wet clothing was plastered to his body so that every muscled contour was displayed in blatant splendor. The water had darkened his golden hair, and his face flashed with fury.

"What in holy hell were you doing out there?" he

demanded harshly.

Mirella could only stare up at him mutely, her arms quivering as they supported her in a half-sitting position. As if from a great distance, she heard the groaning of the ship and the wild lament of the wind. It struck her that she had lost her mantle somewhere. Her hair had come undone, and the wet strands dripped down the back of her sodden gown.

"Answer me!"

"I . . ." She swallowed, unable to form a coherent thought beyond the realization of how close they had come to drowning. Violent shivers wracked her body, and the taste of salt trickled into her mouth.

"You bloody fool!" Jason stormed on. "You could have killed the both of us! Don't you have any—" He stopped, and his voice changed. "My God . . . you're weeping!" Abruptly he sat down on the bunk and pulled her against him.

Feeling weak and oddly ashamed, Mirella pressed her face into his warm shoulder, holding onto him as if he were a lifeline. She hadn't known at first that the hot moisture coursing down her cheeks was tears. Trembling uncontrollably, she felt the heat of Jason's breath on her forehead.

"Hush, love," he crooned softly. "It's all over. I'm sorry I lashed out like that, but when I looked down and saw you standing there on deck, it frightened me out of my wits. I could have lost you." His arms tightened convulsively as he repeated, his tone fierce, "I could have lost you!"

His lips sought hers in sudden frenzy. He thrust her down on the mattress, his tongue pillaging the interior of her mouth. His kiss was bruising, searing, consum-

186

ing, and it inflamed Mirella to the core of her being. Desire scorched her veins like a ball of fire. Her hands cupped his damp hair as she welcomed the blissful urgency of his mouth. It was as if all the fears and frustrations of the past weeks broke forth in a fury. She felt that she was drowning, being swept away by a tidal wave that was more powerful than any generated by the raging seas outside. Desperately, she clung to him as her anchor in the storm.

Abruptly he sat up and dragged her up against him in a half-sitting position. His arms encircled her, and Mirella felt his fingers tearing savagely at the tight, sodden loops that circled her buttons. Mindless with need, she buried her face in the warm crook of his neck, kissing and nibbling the saltiness of his skin.

With a groan of frustration, Jason gave up the impossible task. He pressed her back against the bunk, reaching for the hem of her drenched gown and shoving it up to her waist. Then he stripped off her undergarments and unbuttoned his breeches. Without further preliminaries, he parted her thighs to plunge into her delicate softness.

Writhing and arching beneath him, Mirella was caught in a chaos of sensation. She was past thought, beyond awareness of anything but a driving, desperate desire. Her low moans mingled with the sound of his harsh breathing. The heat of him deep within her roused her to a pulsating passion that exceeded the fury of the tempest outside, until it finally culminated in a cataclysm of rapturous release.

Sanity returned in slow stages. Mirella became aware of the heavy weight of his body, the pitching of the ship beneath them, the clammy heat of her clothing. A staccato burst of raindrops hit the port-hole above them, and the wind keened, as if sympathizing with her for the wretched distress that was creeping into her soul.

How could she have succumbed to him again?

A seed of rage took root amidst her despair. Jason had deliberately taken advantage of her in a vulnerable moment. The moment he had seen the tears running down her face, he had made his move. He was no better than a viper hiding in a pile of brush awaiting its unsuspecting victim.

The more Mirella thought about it, the angrier she grew until her insides burned like wildfire. When Jason lifted his head, his face relaxed with lazy satisfaction, she glared at him, her eyes narrowed with loathing.

"Get off of me," she snarled through gritted teeth.

His brow furrowed in perplexity. "What?"

"I said, remove yourself this instant!"

Jason rolled away, his expression contrite. "Did I hurt you in some way? If I did, pray accept my deepest apologies, for I never intended to take you in such haste." Reaching out, he gently stroked her bare thigh.

"You unprincipled cad! Take your hands off me!" Mirella jerked away from the disturbing caress, scrambling to the edge of the bed to tug her soggy gown over her nakedness. "How dare you push yourself upon me when you know how I despise your attentions!"

"Push?" He gave a laugh of scornful disbelief. "Why, your need for me was as great as mine for you."

"You took advantage of me in a moment of weakness, just as you did before. Only a scoundrel like you would prey on the emotions of a weeping woman!"

His face darkened. "If that is true, what of the night I kissed you up on deck? What excuse can you offer for your wanton behavior then?"

"Your conceit astounds me." Angrily, Mirella whipped back a strand of wet hair that had fallen to her cheek. "But let us not stray from the vital issue— that you pressed your suit knowing full well how I felt about you!"

"You've a fine way of showing your disgust for my lovemaking," Jason sneered. He leaped to his feet, savagely refastening his breeches. " 'Tis a shame we were interrupted that night, Mirella. You were so hot and eager for me, I'd wager you'd have let me take you right there on deck for any prying eyes to see!"

Mirella's mouth dropped open. How could he have the gall to bring that up? Refusing to admit any truth in his words, she felt her blood boil. He was no gentleman to speak so crudely to her!

She sent him a cold glare. "You're naught but a . . . a bragging peacock! No woman in her right mind would ever stoop so low as to be your mistress."

"Then tell that to the other women I've bedded. You're the only one from whom I've heard any complaints. And I wonder just how truthful you're being." Deliberately, Jason reached down and ran his finger over her breast. The tip contracted to a hard bud that was clearly visible through the wet material.

Mirella struck his hand away. "I loathe you," she hissed. "Don't you ever touch me again!"

"As you wish," he stated, his voice frigid. He turned on his heel and strode to the door, pivoting to face her.

189

"Just think on this, lady. The next time you want me in your bed, you'll have to come begging!"

"Hell will freeze over before that happens!"

The only reply she received was the slam of the door, and the mournful shriek of the wind.

Jason emerged on deck, pausing for a moment to let the chilly, driving rain pelt his upturned face. The fierce gale was no match for the turmoil of emotions raging within him.

The image of Mirella's hate-filled expression burned into his brain. By damn, she despised him! The knowledge twisted painfully in his gut like salt rubbed into a raw wound. Even Elizabeth's treachery had never made him suffer so.

No, he wasn't hurting! he denied violently. It was just that he was so damn infuriated by Mirella's vacillation. First she was blazing hot for him, then suddenly she went stone-cold. How like a woman to be so inconsistent, so indecisive!

By God, he'd love nothing better than to return to her cabin and relieve his frustrations by sinking into her silky flesh over and over again—not to mention prove to her just how much she really needed him. What the devil was wrong with her that she could not admit the simple fact of her desire for him?

The memory of her feminine body arching beneath him in passion sent hot blood surging to his loins. Why was it that she roused him like no other woman? He certainly had bedded others of equal beauty. Was it the very fact that she claimed she didn't want him that had him so intrigued? Or was he fascinated by the aura of innocence that lingered about her despite the loss of her maidenhood?

Perhaps she was right. Perhaps he should never have taken her virginity.

Jason swiftly stifled his twinge of guilt. By damn, wasn't he promising her a far better life than the one she'd have had in Bristol?

Women! Would he ever understand them? Mirella might appear to be different than Elizabeth and Samantha but were there not some essential similarities? All any female wanted was money. She was selfish, incapable of any real affection for anyone except herself.

Likely, the reason Mirella loathed his attentions was that she failed to realize the extent of his wealth. Perhaps once she saw that his vast plantation holdings made him a prince in the hierarchy of Virginia society, she would reveal her true colors. She would seek him out, humbly offering to be his mistress.

This fantasy brought a satisfied smile to Jason's water-drenched face. Balancing himself as the ship lurched from side to side, he put a protective hand over his eyes and peered upward through the drumming rain. Most of the crew members were gone from the rigging, their task of reefing the sails complete. Since he wasn't needed up there, he might as well head below to ride out the storm in relatively dry quarters.

As he carefully secured the hatch behind him, Jason realized that his hot fury had abated, and in its place was a cold resolve. By damn, if it killed him, he would keep his hands off Mirella! When next they made love—and he was certain they would—she would have to come crawling to him first.

Chapter Eleven

"Lord have mercy!" Emma exclaimed. " 'Tis a wild-looking place, is it not?" She and Mirella stood at the rail, watching as the *Argo* maneuvered up the James River into the tidewater region of Virginia.

Mirella nodded, torn between apprehension and excitement. The shores were half forest and half marsh, with an untamed splendor that was unlike anything she had seen in England. What sort of life lay ahead for her here?

"Oh, look," she breathed, pointing toward the embankment. A deer stood quietly amongst the thick maze of trees, appearing to stare at the passing vessel. Enthralled, she and Emma observed the animal until it bounded off into the woods.

For the first time since the storm had ended over a week earlier, the sun sparkled in a cloudless, sapphire sky. The combination of vibrant blue and verdant green seemed to reach out and touch Mirella's very soul. Was it possible to fall in love at first sight with such a rustic place as this?

Every now and then, there were signs of encroaching civilization. In between stretches of virgin wilderness, she saw wagons traversing the dirt road that hugged the bank, a small settlement nestled in a clearing, or a magnificent mansion perched far back from the water's edge. The wide, winding river was teeming with vessels of all sizes, from large ocean-going ships to tiny one-man crafts fashioned from what looked like hollowed out tree trunks.

It was a strange yet lovely land. Gazing at it, Mirella felt a shiver of foreboding. Up until today, Virginia had been merely a name, a tiny dot on a map, but now it had become a reality. Even if she were to escape Jason, how would she find her way about this unfamiliar and undoubtedly treacherous territory?

"See that, ladies?" Zeke Lassiter's voice came from behind, and they looked in the direction he was pointing. A marshy outcrop of land lay ahead on the right. Scattered over it, Mirella could just barely discern a few ruined buildings nearly overrun by creeping vegetation.

" 'Tis Jamestown," the captain informed them. " 'Twas the site of the first English settlement in America."

"What happened to all the people?" Emma asked, her eyes wide. "Were they massacred by savages?"

Captain Lassiter smiled. "Oh, no. Jamestown did suffer its share of Indian attacks, but I'm afraid there's a far less dramatic reason for why 'tis now deserted. You see, about fifty or so years ago, the capital was moved to Williamsburg, a short distance inland. Burwell's Landing there, 'tis where cargo bound for the city is unloaded."

He pointed toward a clearing they were passing, where a track led off into the tangled woods. There was a wharf crowded with vessels and men were loading goods into horse-drawn drays, preparing to haul them into nearby Williamsburg.

"We carry merchandise in our hold which is bound for the capital, but Jason didn't wish to stop," the captain said. "Impatient to get home, I'll wager. So I'll have to be heading back this way come tomorrow. Another few hours and I reckon we'll have you ladies in your new home."

He excused himself with a bow. Mirella leaned on the railing beside Emma, mesmerized by the passing scenery. The James widened and narrowed, twisted and turned as they slowly snaked their way deeper and deeper into the wilderness, aided by the thrust of the incoming tide.

They were rounding a bend in the river when she espied a tall, slim lad standing on the embankment to the left, half-hidden in the swaying tendrils of a weeping willow tree. He was clad in dark, tattered breeches and a loose white shirt, with a straw hat covering his head. With one hand, he balanced a fishing pole on his shoulder, while with the other he shielded his eyes from the bright sunlight as he peered at the passing ship.

Mirella turned to Emma, intending to point out this rustic settler, but just then Lucas came up from behind them to engage his wife in conversation. When Mirella looked back, the boy had vanished.

As the ship fully rounded the curve in the river, the deck and rigging bustled with increased activity. Up ahead, a long wharf stretched out into the water. The air was filled with the loud bark of the captain's orders and the shouts of men ashore grabbing the towline as the vessel carefully maneuvered alongside the pier.

Mirella looked at the large warehouse that stood at the end of the dock, then her eyes lifted to the expanse of lush green lawn sloping upward from the embankment. Here, the forest had been pushed back, though a few scattered trees still provided a cooling shade. She caught her breath in surprise as she spotted the structure at the top of the hill.

Dominating the knoll was the most stately mansion she had yet seen along the James. It was three stories tall and built of red brick. White pillars supported the porch and the balcony that ran the length of its front. There were twin chimneys at either end of the roof, though no smoke rose from them on this balmy June day.

This was Jason's home? She had expected something far less imposing, more like the rough log cabins they had passed alongside the river!

Mirella followed Emma and Lucas to the gangplank, eager to have her feet on firm soil again. On feeling someone's fingers grasp her elbow, she looked up, startled, into Jason's unsmiling face. Her heart gave an involuntary leap. Today, he was disturbingly handsome in a fawn frockcoat with waistcoat and breeches of coffee brown. The white ruffled shirt he wore might have made some men look effeminate, but on him it only served to emphasize his virile masculinity.

"If I may assist you," he said politely.

Without waiting for her acquiescence, he escorted

her down the swaying ramp. Mirella raised her chin a fraction, determined not to let him see how his presence affected her. Ever since their argument the day of the storm, he had treated her in this stiff and formal manner. Were she not so certain of his insensitivity, she would almost have thought he was hurt. But far more likely, she told herself, it was his pride that suffered. He wasn't accustomed to a woman refusing the dubious honor of becoming his mistress.

Dark-skinned children raced down the hill to cluster in a small, well-behaved group at the edge of the grass. Mirella couldn't help staring, enchanted by their fuzzy hair and brown flesh. She had heard of the Negro slaves kept by the colonists, but this was the first time she had seen any.

Jason greeted several of the children by name, teasing and joking with them. His golden eyes were alive with warmth when he turned back to the Colbys. But when his gaze fell on Mirella, his expression reverted to a distant chill. It was as if that brief moment of softness had never existed.

"Welcome to Elysian Fields," he said. Pivoting, he strode up the sloping lawn.

How inappropriate a name for his home, Mirella scoffed to herself as she and the Colbys trailed him up the gentle incline. So long as Jason was around, this could never be a place of ideal happiness, at least not for her.

As they neared the house, the door burst open, and a plump black woman waddled out onto the porch. However, it was the young woman dogging her heels who captured Mirella's attention. Tall and willowy, she was dressed in an apricot gown that complemented the golden tan of her skin, but the effect of her fashionable attire was spoiled by the bare feet that peeped out beneath her hem, and the dirt that smeared one of her cheeks. Her hair was a rich blond, no two strands seeming to be of precisely the same hue. But it had clearly been hastily arranged, for a honeyed piece trickled down her back, and unruly wisps framed her excited face.

Jason had stopped at the base of the porch, and he broke into a smile when he saw the girl. She bounded down the steps with coltish grace and came to a halt in front of him, hanging back awkwardly as if she wanted to hug him but wasn't quite certain if he would welcome such a display. His features grew stern as he studied her appearance.

"Look at you, Pandora!" he chastised. "You should be ashamed of yourself! Your hair is a mess, and your face is filthy. And where in God's name are your shoes?"

The happiness drained out of his sister's expression. "I hate shoes," she muttered belligerently.

"Nevertheless, you shall wear them, and cease behaving like such a hoyden!"

Mirella saw hurt flare into Pandora's silver-green eyes as Jason turned toward Emma and Lucas to introduce them to his sister. Her heart went out to the unhappy girl. Why, Jason hadn't even spoken a word of greeting to Pandora before he'd lashed out at her! Though he did have a point about her untidiness, he could have handled the situation with gentleness and tact. If this was his usual method of dealing with her, it was no wonder she rebelled!

Mirella observed Pandora more closely. She had the

oddest prickling sensation that she had met the girl somewhere before. But it must be simply that Pandora shared some of her brother's features—the high cheekbones, the aristocratic nose, and the tall stature which even at age fourteen made her top Mirella by a good four or five inches.

"This is Mirella Weston," Jason told Pandora. "She's a distant relation on Mother's side of the family. She's to be your companion."

"Hello, Pandora." Mirella smiled warmly, but the girl merely regarded her with hostile silver-green eyes.

"Can you not be at least polite enough to return her greeting?" Jason said sharply. "She's traveled all the way from England for your benefit, to teach you how to be a lady."

"I don't want to be a lady!" his sister burst out. "I don't need a companion . . . I don't need any of you!" Lifting her skirts to her bare knees, Pandora took off like a shot, running toward a tangle of trees.

"Pandora!" he roared. "Come back here this instant!"

He made a move, as if to follow her, but Mirella wrapped her fingers around his forearm. "Let her go, Jason."

His furious gold eyes frowned down at her. "I won't have her insulting people so! I've a good mind to tan her hide for her behavior!"

"Give her a little time to grow accustomed to the idea of my being here," Mirella argued gently. "You'll not help matters by punishing her as though she were still a child."

He continued to glare at her but she felt his tension relax somewhat and removed her hand from his arm.

"Miss Mirella be right," put in the black woman standing in the background, hands perched on her ample hips. "How can you holler so at that poor motherless child?"

"What I say to my sister is none of your business, Ophelia," Jason said testily.

"It sure is my business," Ophelia huffed. "Ah raised that child like she was my very own. An' you talk about her havin' no manners! Why, Ah didn't even hear you say no howdy-do afore you lit into her like that!"

"That's enough, Ophelia." Dismissing her, Jason turned and gestured to the Colbys, who were standing quietly outside the group. "Come along with me, and I'll show to your quarters." Emma tossed Mirella a wide-eyed look before hurrying after Jason and her husband.

"Well, Ah guesses the massah be wantin' you to have one of the upstairs bedrooms," Ophelia said. "Ah'll just fix you up if'n you'll follow me."

"Thank you, Ophelia." Mirella trailed the ponderous black woman up the steps to the wide porch.

"This here be the drawin' room," Ophelia gravely informed her as they entered a spacious chamber paneled in white. The furnishings were as elegant and tasteful as any she had seen in England. Only the edges of the polished floor were visible; the center was covered by a soft Turkish carpet on which brocaded chairs and chaises were arranged. A young black girl was busily dusting some porcelain figurines on the fireplace mantel.

"Hey, gal, don't you forget to shine them candlesticks over there." Ophelia pointed to a silver pair on a nearby table, and the girl leaped to do her bidding.

Ophelia sashayed out the door, waving a plump hand to her left. "An' over there be the dinin' room." As Mirella hurried after the black woman, she caught a glimpse of a chamber with a pale green Chinese wallpaper above the wainscoting.

They entered a great hall with a graceful staircase curving upward three stories. This, Ophelia explained, was the front of the house while the river side was the rear. There were several portraits adorning the white walls. Mirella strolled past them, guessing that the dreamy-eyed older woman in one was Jason's mother.

Another gilt-framed painting caught her eye. She stopped before it, staring up in strange fascination at the young woman immortalized on the canvas. That the subject was a lady was evident in the aristocratic lines of her face and in the softness of the hands which clasped a single, perfect rose. Her lustrous golden hair floated over a bare shoulder. Clad in a gown of pale orchid purple which enhanced her slender form, she had the ethereal look of an angel.

"Who is that?" Mirella asked.

"That be Missus 'Lizabeth, the massah's wife," Ophelia replied. "She was some rich earl's daughter he met in London. They wasn't married more'n a year when she died of a fever after birthin' his son."

Mirella stared at the black woman. "Jason has a son?"

Ophelia shook her head mournfully. "Naw, the poor child only lived a few hours."

"When did all this happen?"

"Lemme see now—'bout nine years ago."

Briskly, Ophelia turned away, apparently unwilling to discuss the matter further. Mirella swallowed the rest of her questions as she tried to absorb the startling revelation. Jason had had a wife and a child! Why did that arouse in her a disquieting stab of something that felt almost like jealousy? With an effort, she focused her attention on what the housekeeper was saying.

"Over thataway be the library, and there"—Ophelia nodded her mobcapped head to the right—"be the massah's chamber."

Through the opened door, Mirella saw a wide, four-postered bed. "Are not all the bedchambers upstairs?"

"The massah and missus at most all the plantations hereabouts sleeps on the first floor."

With an arrogant sniff, Ophelia began to ascend the stairs, grasping the carved walnut balustrade with one hand and lifting her aproned skirt with the other. Mirella followed, inwardly amused by the woman's haughty air. It was plain that Ophelia was a devoted servant, proud of her position with the almighty Fletcher clan.

And though it appeared that she ruled the household with an iron hand, Ophelia clearly had a soft spot in her heart for Pandora. Perhaps she might be more inclined to answering questions about the girl than she had been about Jason's dead wife and child.

"Ophelia, perhaps I'm being presumptuous, but is Jason always so hard on his sister?"

The housekeeper stopped just short of the second floor, huffing from the exercise. "The massah, he sure do love that gal, but he just don't know how to handle her wildness no more. Them two, they both so hard-headed they won't neither of 'em give an inch or admit when they's wrong." She pursed her lips. "Lawdy me, but the massah sure gits mad at that poor child sometimes. Ah just can't bear to see my baby hurtin'. One o' these days he gonna holler at her an' she gonna run off an' never come back."

"You don't think she'll do that today, do you?" Mirella asked, startled.

"Naw, she probably just sulkin' a spell. She be back afore it gits dark. Leastways, Ah hopes so."

Muttering under her breath, Ophelia mounted the remaining steps. There were three bedchambers on either side of the spacious hall, and as they headed down the passageway, the black woman jabbed her finger first at one door, then at another.

"This here be my honey child's chamber, and this one be Massah Troy's whenever he comes a-visitin'."

"He doesn't live here?"

"Massah Troy, he gots his own plantation," Ophelia said proudly.

"Is he married, then?" Mirella asked, unable to quench the curiosity that burned within her. She wasn't sure why, but she wanted to learn everything there was to know about Jason's family.

Ophelia chuckled. "Naw, but that boy sure is a devil with the ladies. Y'all be careful round him, you hear?"

So philandering runs in the family, Mirella thought as she trailed the servant to a door at the rear of the hall. Dear Lord, if she had another like Jason to contend with . . .

The subdued beauty of the room they entered drove

203

all else from Mirella's mind. The walls were a delicate cream, and a rich Eastern rug in shades of rose, ivory, and cobalt covered the floor. There was a fourposter with draperies of pale blue silk damask edged with lace, and a rosewood dressing table stood beside the pair of French doors which afforded a view of the winding river.

"Ophelia, 'tis lovely!"

The black woman beamed at the compliment. "You just git yourself settled in now, an' Ah'll send up a gal with some bathwater." She waddled out the door, shutting it behind her.

Mirella walked onto the balcony, letting the fresh breeze caress her face. Leaning on the railing, she idly watched as the *Argo* was unloaded in the distance. She had never dreamed that Jason lived in such elegant surroundings.

A sad smile crossed her face. The trappings of the bedchamber reminded her of the luxuries of her childhood, before her father had squandered the family fortune.

Reaching into the pocket of her lavender gown, she pulled out her mother's cameo, running a light finger over its surface as she had a hundred times before. Would she ever regain the happiness of her youth? Despite her father's addiction to gambling, at least he had always made her feel loved. If only she could find a man who would cherish her . . .

Her mind veered to the portrait of Jason's dead wife. Was he still in love with her? That was the only plausible reason she could think of to explain why he had left the painting hanging in the entrance hall for all these nine years, where he would see it whenever he walked into the house.

The thought made her heart twist oddly. Why was it that a rogue like him could fascinate her so? Why did her knees go weak whenever he so much as looked at her? Why did even their most violent confrontations make her feel so alive? It was ridiculous to have any respect or liking for him when all he wanted to do was use her.

No matter how her body might long for his, Mirella knew she must resist him, for there could be grave consequences to lying with him. Her lips tightened. She would not bear his bastard! A typical man, Jason lost no sleep worrying of such matters. He took his pleasure, then went on his merry way, with no thought to the seed he might have implanted in her belly. Thus far, she had been lucky—her monthly flux had arrived on schedule a few days past. But if she were to let Jason bed her again, who could say what might be the result?

There was a knock on the door, and Mirella went to admit a small army of servants. One of them set down a tub in front of the fireplace, while the others filled it with buckets of steaming water. Another placed a silver tea service on a table beside the hearth. Then they all scurried out, though one young woman of about her own age lingered behind.

"Ophelia says Ah was to help you, ma'am," she said, shyly bobbing her curly black hair.

Mirella gave her a warm smile. "Well, then, perhaps you could be so kind as to unfasten my gown."

The woman nimbly performed the task, then waited expectantly for further instructions.

"Thank you, but I can manage the rest," Mirella

205

said. "Why don't you come back in half an hour or so to help me dress?"

"Yes'm."

"What's your name?" she asked as the woman left.

"Clea, ma'am."

The door closed quietly. Mirella hurriedly doffed her clothing, torn between her longing for some tea and her need for a bath. She solved her dilemma by moving a small table beside the tub, then setting her cup upon it.

Immersing her naked body in the steamy, violet-scented water, she let out a sigh of pure delight. Aboard the ship, she had been forced to rely on sponge baths for cleanliness. This was a bliss she hadn't experienced since they had departed England. She reached for her porcelain teacup, savoring the hot liquid that slid down her throat. Outside, she could hear the drone of a bee, and the far-off rumble of voices as the servants went about their tasks. It was so peaceful here. . . .

It occurred to her that she could sneak aboard the *Argo* tonight, before the vessel left for Williamsburg on the morrow. But the prospect of being cast adrift in this strange and wild land was daunting. And she couldn't return to England, for fear she might be sought in Sir Harry's murder. Wouldn't it be best if she stayed here in Jason's home until she learned her way about the colonies?

Then, when the chance arose, she could escape his clutches once and for all. Her nerves quivered strangely at the thought. It was simply the anticipation of leaving this island of civilization to face the dangers of a savage country, she convinced herself, but she must make sure that the cold manner in which Jason had been treating her of late would last until she fled.

Putting aside her teacup, Mirella dipped her hair in the bath water. With a bar of soap, she lathered away the salt that still clung to the ebony strands from her dunking the day of the storm. After washing the rest of her body, she stepped out of the tub and rubbed herself dry with a large linen towel.

Mirella wrapped the cloth around her wet hair. Just as she was slipping on her undergarments, there was a soft knock on the door.

"Who is it?" she called through the wood.

"Clea, ma'am."

Mirella opened the door, and the black woman entered, carrying a fresh gown of mauve lustring silk.

"Soon's you git yourself dressed, ma'am, Ah'll bring up your other belongin's from the ship."

Mirella stepped into the gown, letting the servant fasten the back. Then she sat at the dressing table, enjoying the luxury as Clea brushed her long, dark hair until it was dry and shining, and deftly wound it into an attractive chignon.

"The massah say you is to come down for dinner at seven," she said, bobbing a quick curtsey as she left.

After the tub was hauled away, Mirella paced the floor restlessly, aware that she had more than an hour to wait before the meal hour. Perhaps she could fill in the stretch of time by looking for Pandora. Her heart had been touched by the unhappiness she had glimpsed in the girl, and she sensed Pandora might be less hostile if they spoke when her older brother wasn't around.

The door to Pandora's bedchamber was slightly ajar,

and Mirella knocked softly. "Pandora? Are you there?"

When there was no reply, she pushed the door all the way open. Walking inside, she gazed at the furnishings with interest. The walls were paneled in a light oak, and a rug in ruby reds and creams stretched over the floor. The draperies were a rich wine hue, parted to let in the late afternoon sunlight. The most feminine touch was the lace coverlet on the fourposter.

The décor had a certain distinction, a bold drama that was unlike the subdued elegance of her own chamber. Yet this room was every bit as appealing. It was not what one would expect from a fourteen-year-old girl, Mirella mused, but from a more mature woman who had the courage to follow her own sense of style.

She was about to turn and seek Pandora elsewhere when she saw something sticking out from beneath the bed. Curious, Mirella pulled forth a wad of clothing. Smoothing them out on the coverlet, she frowned in puzzlement. White shirt, dark breeches. They were similar to the garments she had seen on the slave children who had greeted the ship, but what were they doing here?

Taking another peek under the bed, she hauled out a straw hat and placed it on top of the rest of the costume. There was something oddly familiar about that hat. . . .

Mirella's mouth dropped open. It couldn't be. . . .

In her mind, she saw a clear image of a lad standing on the embankment watching the *Argo* round the bend in the river. He was tall, and wore a baggy white shirt and dark breeches. He had a straw hat on his head and a fishing pole over his shoulder. That had been Pandora!

No wonder Pandora had looked so disheveled, as if

she had thrown on her gown in great haste! She must have raced back to the house and changed clothing so that Jason wouldn't catch her roaming the countryside dressed as a boy! It also explained why she'd had the vague feeling she'd seen Pandora somewhere before.

"What are you doing in here?"

The antagonistic female voice made Mirella whirl, surprised to see Jason's sister standing in the doorway.

Pandora marched into the room, an angry light in her silver-green eyes. "You have no right to sneak into my chamber and—"

Her voice faltered as she saw what lay on the coverlet behind Mirella. She ran and snatched up the garments. "How did these get there?" she squeaked.

"I found them under your bed," Mirella said calmly. "Would you like to tell me what they were doing there?"

Pandora's fingers tightened convulsively around the clothing. "I . . . I don't know. I . . . I guess Ophelia must have dropped them or something. I'll go ask her." She spun toward the doorway.

"I saw you wearing those things, Pandora."

The girl stopped dead in her tracks, then turned slowly toward Mirella. "What are you talking about?" she demanded, her chin lifted in defiance.

"When the ship was rounding the bend, I saw a boy standing on the river bank, watching us. But that wasn't a boy, that was you, wasn't it?"

Pandora's belligerent expression crumpled, and her eyes became as vulnerable as a child's. She sank into a chair, staring at the floor, tangled strands of blond hair cascading about her shoulders.

"You're going to tell my brother, aren't you?" she asked tonelessly.

Mirella's heart twisted. She had a feeling that it was not the prospect of Jason's wrath that made Pandora so unhappy, but the thought of disappointing him. Though the girl loved him, she stubbornly clung to her tomboyish ways. Perhaps what Pandora needed right now was a friend with whom she could share her troubled adolescent emotions, rather than another harsh taskmaster like her brother.

"Nay, I'll not tell Jason."

Pandora lifted her head, eyeing Mirella with suspicion. "Why? There's no reason for you to protect me."

"Of course there is. Since we're going to be spending a great deal of time together, 'tis best that we be friends rather than enemies."

Pandora jumped up, throwing the bundle of clothing aside, her hostile look returning. "I don't need any companion! No one's going to turn me into some . . . some simpering female!"

"Like it or not, Pandora, you are becoming a woman," Mirella said gently. " 'Tis time you accepted that fact."

"Not if it means I have to stop going fishing just to sit and embroider some silly old sampler! I'd sooner die than spend all day moldering indoors!"

"I see no reason why you should spend time sewing if you despise the task."

" 'Tis more than just that! Why am I forbidden to do what I enjoy? You are all so unfair!"

Her stony expression told Mirella that it would accomplish little to argue further. Yet Pandora had to learn that it was time to curb the wild habits of her youth. If there were only a way to convince her that becoming a woman was not so distasteful . . .

"A compromise," she said slowly, musing aloud. "What?"

Mirella hesitated, pondering the idea that was taking shape in her mind. "I know little of the activities you love so dearly. What if, in exchange for you practicing the ways of a lady here in this house, I were to go fishing with you?"

Pandora stared. "But Jason would never allow it."

That was the truth. If he were ever to discover what was going on, Mirella shuddered to think of the consequences. Hiding her inner misgivings, she gave a casual shrug.

"He cannot forbid what he knows nothing of, can he? 'Twill be our little secret."

"You . . . you would do this for me?" The vulnerable tone in Pandora's voice assured Mirella that she was doing the right thing.

She flashed the girl an impish grin. "To be truthful, it sounds like fun. But I warn you, I know naught of the sport of angling! I shall probably scare away all the fish for miles around."

A slow smile transformed Pandora's face. "I would be more than happy to teach you all I know."

"Then we have a bargain."

Mirella held out her hand, and Pandora took it eagerly, both of them pleased with their new-found friendship.

Chapter Twelve

The trilling of a bird outside her chamber woke Mirella the next morning.

She lay in bed listening until the sweet notes faded. The linen sheets were soft against her skin, but that, she knew, was not what made her feel so good. It was the absence of motion after six weeks of continual rocking aboard ship. With a rueful smile, she acknowledged that she would never wish to lead the life of a sailor. She far preferred to have solid earth beneath her feet.

A gentle breeze wafted in one of the open windows, and the cool sensation beckoned to her. Mirella slipped out of bed and padded to the balcony doors, throwing them open wide. Leaning against the doorframe, she gazed out over the tree-dotted lawn to the wide river twisting lazily in the distance. Something was different about the scene, and it took a moment to realize what it was. The *Argo* was gone. Captain Lassiter must have departed as planned on the early tide.

Below her, she heard a door slam, then heavy

footsteps descended the porch stairs. Idly curious, yet not wishing to be seen on the balcony in her night-dress, she drifted to one of a pair of windows facing the side of the house. Perching a knee on the cushioned windowseat, she looked down.

Jason strode into view, and all of her nerves leaped to life. Mirella studied his handsome profile as he headed along an angled path bordered by ornamental shrubs which led to a small brick building just visible through the trees. He wore the plain white shirt and snug fawn breeches which she was beginning to recognize as his working attire. Knee-high leather boots hugged his muscular legs.

As she watched, a big black man walked up to him. Jason stopped, and though she could not make out the words they exchanged, the rise and fall of their voices floated to her ears. Then Jason clapped the man on the shoulder in a friendly fashion, and they both continued down the path, disappearing into the building.

Mirella remained motionless, her senses keenly alert. She was aware of the rich texture of the cushion on which she knelt, the sweet smell of some vine flower drifting from outside, the soft drone of a bee as it flitted by in search of nectar.

Abruptly she stepped away from the window, annoyed at the way her blood stirred at the mere sight of Jason. Was she some weak ninny who had no control over her own mind and body?

Pursing her lips, Mirella turned her thoughts to Pandora. She smiled, recalling Jason's surprise and pleasure last evening when his sister had appeared for dinner, her face scrubbed clean, her hair and gown tidy. After the meal, while they sat in the drawing room, Pandora had entertained her brother with tales of their friends and neighbors during the time he had been away. Granted, when Jason turned his back to pour himself a brandy, the girl slipped off her shoes surreptitiously and gazed longingly into the darkness outside the opened windows. But at least it was a start, Mirella told herself.

She would have to be very careful that Jason never discovered the impetus behind his sister's startling transformation. She must make certain not to be caught living up to her end of the bargain.

The clock softly ticking on the white-painted mantelpiece told Mirella that it was already nine o'clock. Her bare feet sank into the plush rug as she walked to the armoire and opened it. As she slipped on a simple gown of lilac muslin, there was a quiet knock on the door. Clea entered, carrying a breakfast tray. Mirella pulled a chair upholstered in shell pink over to a small table, and began to eat the ham, biscuits, and fresh fruit served on a delicate porcelain dish. The black servant bustled about, tidying the chamber.

"Clea, you don't need to do that," Mirella protested, as the slave woman straightened the rumpled bedsheets.

"Ma'am?" Clea's head was tilted in puzzlement.

"I'll make my own bed as soon as I finish eating," Mirella explained.

Clea looked horrified. "Oh, no, ma'am! The massah, he say Ah was to be your maid. Why, you be his long-lost cousin, he says, an' Ah'm to make sure you ain't wantin' for nothin'."

"I see."

Mirella frowned, absently nibbling on a juicy strawberry. Long-lost cousin, indeed! Jason intended to continue the charade about their relationship, obviously believing that if he kept her around long enough, she would come begging for a chance to share his bed.

What a surprise he was in for! Yet if he wanted to give her the royal treatment, then so be it. Why should she not enjoy having a personal servant for a short while? After all, there would be no such luxuries when she fled this plantation.

Finishing her breakfast, Mirella descended the wide, curving staircase to find Pandora in the drawing room, running idle fingers over the harpsichord keys. The tinkling tune which filled the air revealed a certain amount of talent and training, but when she saw Mirella, the girl slammed the lid shut and surged eagerly to her feet. The apple green gown she wore accentuated her pretty features, and her honey blond hair was arranged with relative neatness.

"Cousin Mirella! I've been waiting for you ever so long."

Mirella laughed. " 'Twould seem, then, that you should have awakened me. I'm not in the habit of sleeping so late."

"Jason said I wasn't to disturb you." She glanced out the window, her silver-green eyes alive with a restless yearning. "Would you like me to show you the woods today? Oh, 'tis so lovely out there in the summertime!"

Mirella hated to disappoint the girl, but knew that what she proposed was too risky. "I fear we dare not venture there so long as your brother is nearby."

"I knew you'd say that." Pandora slumped back down on the stool in disgust. "I don't know why Jason won't let me do anything fun."

Tactfully, Mirella overlooked the girl's complaint. "Tell me, does he stay close to the house as a rule? Or can we expect him to be gone part of the time?"

"He quite often spends the entire day riding over the plantation." Pandora gave a heavy sigh. "I suppose 'tis best if we wait until he's away. But, oh, I believe I shall stifle if I stay another moment in this house!"

"I see no need for us to spend such a fine morning indoors. Why don't we take a stroll, and you can show me the grounds?"

Mirella smiled as Pandora jumped up, bubbling over with impatience. No doubt it would tire her out to keep up with the young girl, but she had a suspicion she would enjoy the stimulation of Pandora's company. Already, she felt a stirring of affection for her, as if Pandora were the sister she had never had.

They left the house through the wide oak doors in the entrance hall. Pandora skipped down the path in a manner more befitting a child of half her fourteen years. She pointed out the plantation office, which Mirella had seen Jason enter earlier, then the coach-house, the stables, the icehouse, and in the distance a cluster of small, neat cabins which she explained were the slave quarters. Mirella's shoes crunched on the crushed oyster shells covering the walkway as she struggled to keep up with her guide.

"Whoa, slow down!" she teased. "This is supposed to be a quiet stroll, not a race."

217

Pandora slackened her pace, her expression abashed. "Oh . . . sorry."

At a more subdued rate of speed, they continued their tour. Remembering her misconceptions about Jason's home, Mirella felt a rush of shame. She had automatically assumed that conditions here would be primitive at best. Like some snooty aristocrat, she had looked down her nose at him because he came from a place outside England. But this self-contained community was every bit as civilized as her homeland. And to be master of all this, it was obvious that Jason was far wealthier than she had ever imagined.

Neatly trimmed boxwood hedges enclosed the formal gardens. As they meandered through them, Pandora rattled off the names of those plants which were foreign to Mirella. Others Mirella identified as vegetation which also grew in England. The delicate aroma of flowers filled the air. Larkspur bloomed alongside tawny day lilies and hollyhocks. But the patch of fragrant roses, Mirella noticed with a frown, was in sad need of pruning.

A short distance from the main house, on the other side of the path, was the kitchen. Behind that was another garden nearly an acre in size, surrounded by a low brick wall. Strawberries and grape vines grew within, in addition to a variety of herbs. In one corner there were several beehives. Beyond the wall was a field of corn and other vegetables; and there was an orchard of apple, cherry, fig, plum, and apricot trees.

As they strolled through the kitchen garden, Mirella was appalled at the weeds choking the tender plants. Overseeing this was the responsibility of the mistress of the manor, and young though she might be, that was Pandora's role. Though not wishing to weigh the girl down with work on their first day together, Mirella resolved to instruct her in her duties as soon as possible.

As they toured the dairy and poultry yard, there was again some evidence of neglect. Despite the bevy of black women working industriously, the butter churns wanted scouring, and fresh straw was needed in the milking stalls. Mirella viewed the scene thoughtfully. All that was lacking here was the supervision of the lady of the house.

In the brick building where the plantation's laundry was done a room had been set aside for spinning and weaving. It was there that they came across Emma standing over a table and snipping into a bolt of blue cotton. The fresh scent of newly washed clothing permeated the air.

"Good morning!" She laid down her shears and came forward to greet them.

"Good morning to you, too," Mirella responded warmly. "I wanted to see if there was anything I could do to help you settle in."

Emma patted Mirella's arm. "Oh, 'tis kind of you to offer, but Lucas and I are quite comfortably settled into our own cozy cabin." She glanced at Pandora, who had wandered restlessly to the open window to gaze outside. "And what of you?" she asked in a lowered voice. "Yesterday, Mr. Fletcher was so angry with his sister. I'm relieved to see that today she's more tidy and well mannered. How did you manage such a miracle?"

Mirella sighed. "It took some doing. 'Twould appear that I'll have my hands full keeping brother and

219

sister at peace with one another."

They chatted for a few minutes, then Emma said regretfully that she needed to return to her tasks. Promising her friend that they'd talk more later, Mirella followed Pandora out into the warm sunshine.

With a pensive smile, she watched Pandora skip toward the house, carefree and exuberant. It was a shame that children had to grow up, she mused. She could sympathize with the confusion Pandora was experiencing, that of being not quite an adult yet no longer a child. She herself at a tender age had been forced to assume the responsibilities of the household after her mother had died, and though Pandora might rebel, there was no halting the womanly curves blossoming on her youthful body. Most girls her age were already preparing for marriage by learning the duties entailed in running a home.

Pandora didn't realize how very lucky she was. Oh, to have the chance to be mistress of a home like this. . . .

As she trailed the honey-haired adolescent around the house and toward the river, Mirella recalled the fantasies that had colored her own girlish expectations. How many times had she longed for a knight in shining armor to carry her off in his arms? She had yearned to bear his children, to love him, to make a home for him.

Her lips curled in bitter disillusionment. In retrospect, she could see how foolish she had been. No man would wed a penniless woman unless like Sir Harry he lusted after her body. And Jason, she reflected with contempt, hadn't even offered the sanction of marriage before he had taken what he'd wanted. Like most men, he considered a woman alone to be easy prey.

She was so lost in thought that she nearly bumped into Pandora. The girl was standing on the lawn near the back porch steps, shading her eyes with her hand as she peered down toward the river.

"Look who's here!" she cried out, her face glowing with pleasure.

A small boat was gliding alongside the dock, its one sail fluttering in the warm breeze. The lone man aboard hopped onto the pier in one lithe stride. Mirella's heart skipped a beat as she thought for a brief instant that it was Jason. But that was impossible. Jason was working in the plantation office this morning.

After securing the skiff, the man straightened to his full height. As he turned toward them, she realized that he bore more than a vague resemblance to Jason. His shoulders were broad beneath the white shirt he wore, and his legs were long and muscular. A grin crossed his tanned face as he raised a hand to them in greeting. As he started up the slope, Pandora raced down to meet him halfway. Mirella followed at a more sedate pace.

"Oh, Troy, I'm so glad to see you!" Pandora squealed, throwing herself in the man's arms.

"Pannie, you're getting to be far too old for this nonsense." But he laughed and swung her in a circle before letting her feet slide back into the grass.

So this was Jason's brother, Mirella thought, studying him more closely. The likeness was evident in his square jaw, strong cheekbones, and in the tawny brown hair drawn back neatly into a queue at his neck.

The brothers shared that same aura of male virility. Yet in Troy she sensed a carefree, teasing nature, whereas Jason tended to be serious and brooding.

Eyes of a deeper green than his sister's focused on Mirella. With frank admiration, Troy perused her from head to toe before his gaze returned to her face.

"And who have we here?" he asked, his voice deep and drawling. "Pray forgive me if I stare, for I'd no idea a new beauty had moved into this neighborhood."

"This is Mirella Weston," Pandora said. "She's our cousin. Jason met her in England and brought her over here to live with us."

Troy stepped forward to take Mirella's hand. "Cousin, you say? I am most pleased to make your acquaintance."

The slight raising of his eyebrows combined with the amused twitching of his lips told her that he questioned the tale his sister had swallowed so readily. And why not? Mirella thought in annoyance. Hadn't Ophelia warned her that Troy was a womanizer just like his brother? Naturally he would guess Jason's true purpose in bringing her here.

She forced a gracious smile onto her face, hating the need to lie, yet unwilling to humiliate herself by acknowledging even a hint of the base manner in which Jason wished to use her.

"Yes, we're related on your mother's side of the family," she said sweetly. "The connection is so distant and complex that I fear you would be quite bored were I to explain it to you."

"You, dear cousin, could never bore me." Troy bent and brushed his lips over the back of her hand.

222

Without releasing her fingers, he straightened and smiled into her eyes. "Such a vision! Indeed, had I known England held such loveliness, I'd surely have insisted on accompanying my brother there."

Mirella couldn't help laughing. "Sir, 'tis too early in the morning for me to digest such outrageous flattery. Perhaps you should save your charm for a more gullible ear."

"You doubt my sincerity?" His tone was wounded, though his green eyes twinkled. "Why, I speak only—"

"Hello, Troy. Good morning, ladies."

Mirella whipped her head around at the familiar voice. Jason stood on the lawn a few steps behind them, hands on his lean hips. Guiltily she tugged her fingers out of Troy's grasp, then scolded herself for acting with such haste. She hadn't done anything wrong. Lifting her chin, she met Jason's cold gaze unblinking. It would be no business of his even if she had been kissing his brother!

She glanced back at Troy only to see him avidly studying the two of them. She realized that from where he stood, Troy couldn't have missed seeing his brother's approach. That meant he had deliberately flirted with her, probably to see if his suspicions about her relationship with Jason were correct!

Troy stepped forward to give his brother a quick embrace. "Jase! 'Tis good to see you again after so many months. When you sent word you'd arrived home, I hurried over as quickly as I could."

" 'Tis good to see you, too." Jason's harsh expression relaxed somewhat, then he turned his golden eyes on his sister. "Pandora, I've been looking for you.

Your music master has arrived. He's in the drawing room, awaiting you."

"Do I have to have a lesson today?" she protested. "Surely you cannot expect me to practice that dreary old harpsichord when we have visitors."

"No excuses," her brother commanded. "Now, be off with you."

Defiantly, Pandora stuck out her tongue at him. "You're mean," she cried out, then picked up her skirts and ran up the grassy slope leading to the house.

"For your insolence, you can go to your chamber afterward and spend the rest of the day there," Jason shouted after her.

"Jase, you know it wouldn't hurt to let the poor girl off for one day," Troy chided.

"She's too wild as it is," his brother said curtly. "She'll never learn a damn thing if everyone continues to indulge her whims."

Troy shook his head without saying more on the matter. Mirella sensed that this was an argument they'd had before. In a way, both of them were right, though Jason was too stern and Troy too lax. She had to bite back the urge to speak her mind. It would be best for everyone, Pandora included, if she handled things subtly.

"So did you get the problem straightened out with your agent in London?" Troy asked his brother.

"Yes, I was forced to fire him. That thief had been lining his pockets with my gold for nigh onto three years."

" 'Twas a profitable journey, then. I trust you were able to bring back a full cargo of goods?"

Deep in conversation, Jason and Troy started walking up the gentle hill, heading toward the plantation office. Mirella followed, intending to find some task with which to occupy herself while Pandora was at her lesson. Perhaps in one of the barns she could get a trowel and begin weeding the flower beds.

But as they approached the front of the house, the two men stopped. Mirella halted alongside Jason as they gazed down the poplar-lined drive to an approaching carriage.

"It seems we have a visitor," he said.

"Well, well," Troy drawled. "News of your return travels swiftly, Jase."

There was a cynical note to his voice that made Mirella look at him in surprise. A few moments later the carriage pulled up, and the black driver jumped down to hold the horses while the passenger stepped out.

Mirella stared at her. The woman possessed an exotic beauty, accented by the vivid red hair swirled artfully atop her head. Her almond-shaped ice-blue eyes were set above aristocratic cheekbones, and her complexion was clear and creamy. Her willowy figure was accentuated by a gown with a voluminous hooped skirt of thin scarlet and white stripes. A scandalously low neckline revealed all but the tips of her small breasts. She was like a hothouse flower, delicate yet incredibly sensual.

In her simple gown of lilac muslin, Mirella suddenly felt like a wilted bloom. Not that it mattered, she thought in disgust. Both sets of male eyes were glued to the new arrival as she sashayed over to Jason. Amidst a waft of heavy perfume, the woman threw her arms around his muscled torso.

"Jason, darling, I've missed you so!"

Standing on tiptoe, she pressed her pink lips against his. He made no attempt to avoid the kiss; in fact, his hands were splayed over her back to hold her close. Mirella caught a glimpse of the woman's tongue lashing out like a viper's to enter his mouth. And Jason, damn him, appeared to be enjoying the way she wound her fingers into his hair and rubbed her body against his.

She was obviously one of his mistresses.

Mirella was seized with an urge to tear those flaming curls out by their roots. With great effort, she reminded herself that she cared not a whit if he took other women to his bed. What she was feeling was indignation that he would carry on so in broad daylight!

She knew Troy was gazing at her, but she refused to look at him, concentrating with all her might on the tinkling notes of the harpsichord which drifted from the drawing-room windows. When Jason finally lifted his head, he stared straight at her, as if searching for a jealous reaction. But Mirella was able to meet his gaze with an expression of cool indifference.

"Samantha, I'd like you to meet my cousin from England, Mirella Weston," he said. "Mirella, this is Samantha Hyatt. Her father's plantation adjoins mine."

"I'm pleased to make your acquaintance," Mirella said politely.

Samantha afforded her only a brief nod before turning her attention back to Jason. "Oh, darling, I came over the moment I heard you'd returned. It's been so very dull without you around."

"And I've missed being here." Jason flashed the woman a sensuous smile that made Mirella clench her teeth.

"Then won't you go for a drive with me?" Samantha wheedled, touching his strong jaw with a well-manicured finger. "There's so much we have to catch up on." Her sultry tone made it plain that she meant more than mere conversation.

" 'Tis a very tempting offer, but I'm rather busy today," Jason said regretfully. He looked at Troy. "That reminds me. I was just going over the ledgers with Noah before you arrived."

"I'm sure you'll find everything in fine shape," his brother replied. "I made a point of stopping here once a week to keep an eye on things. Noah seemed to be doing a satisfactory job."

"You entrust your books to a darky?" Samantha asked, giving a delicate shiver.

Mirella realized that they were talking about the black man she had seen with Jason earlier that morning.

"And what, may I ask, is wrong with that?" he demanded.

Samantha blithely ignored the dangerous edge to his voice. "Why, Noah couldn't possibly have the intelligence to do the accounts. And even if he did, he'd rob you blind."

"Noah is more honest than many a white man I've known. I'd sooner pay someone I know I can trust."

"Pay!" Samantha's eyes widened in indignation. "But he's a slave. He belongs to you!"

The tension emanating from Jason was almost

tangible. "Samantha," he snapped, "may I remind you that how I choose to run my plantation is none of your damn business."

Seeing his anger, she hung her head in girlish apology. "There's no need to curse at me, darling," she sniffed. "I guess I just don't know much about these dry old business matters."

"I'm glad you realize that," Jason growled.

"I was only thinking of your welfare. Why, you know how much I care for you." Samantha looked up at him and blinked. Incredibly, a tiny crystal teardrop clung to the end of her eyelashes.

"Now, don't get all upset," Jason soothed. "'Tis naught for you to worry your pretty little head over."

In a moment I'm going to be sick, Mirella thought in disgust, watching him lap up the redhead's attention. How could any woman fawn so over a man?

"I'm beginning to think you didn't miss me even one little ol' bit," Samantha pouted, rubbing her body against his. "Why, you won't even go for a carriage ride with me when we haven't seen one another in months."

"Say, that might not be a bad idea," Troy broke in. "Why don't Mirella and I go along with you two? 'Tis too fine a day to waste indoors."

Jason glanced over at Mirella, and his gaze hardened. "Unfortunately, I've no time to spare for pleasure rides," he refused brusquely. "If you ladies will excuse me."

He turned as if to stride away, but Troy caught his arm. "Whoa, Jase. You'll be wanting to check out the fields anyway, and while we ride, I can fill you in on all the news." He released his brother and slid an arm

228

around Mirella's slender waist. "Besides, if you don't go, I'll just have to escort the ladies all by myself. I'll wager our lovely cousin has never even seen a tobacco plant, have you, Mirella?"

Troy lightly stroked her cheek with his knuckles, and gazed deeply into her blue-grey eyes. Startled by the unexpected caress, Mirella stood, unresisting, within his embrace. She glanced over at Jason to see him watching them with a peculiar intentness.

"All right, then," Jason growled, as if the words were being wrenched out of him. "Prepare to depart in fifteen minutes."

Wheeling around, he strode toward his office.

A short while later, with a picnic lunch prepared by Ophelia lashed securely to the back of the carriage, the Negro driver directed the four-horse team down the poplar-lined road. Mirella sat beside Troy, with Jason and Samantha opposite them. The seating arrangements were not Mirella's doing; after helping the ladies into the carriage, Troy had settled next to her, casually placing a muscled arm along the leather cushion behind her back. More and more, she suspected he was deliberately trying to rile his brother, for every time he brushed against her or bent his head to whisper some comment in her ear, he would glance over at Jason as if to assess his reaction.

But if Troy were attempting to make his brother jealous, Mirella thought, he had failed miserably. Feeling a strange pang inside her, she observed the attention Jason was paying to Samantha. They laughed and whispered to one another, their words often too muffled for her to understand. If he bothered looking over at her at all, the amusement would drain out of his face, and his eyes would become dark and brooding.

It was almost as if he hated her.

Well, let him, she told herself. What difference did it make?

Her lips forming a determined smile, Mirella cast off the odd depression seeping into her soul. She forced herself to concentrate on Troy's teasing comments. After a while, it became less difficult to feign enjoyment. Jason's brother was easy to talk to, and more than willing to lavish his carefree charm on her. She felt a warm affection grow inside of her, for though he flirted freely, she sensed that his true interest in her was simply that of a friend.

They passed field after field thick with waist-high tobacco plants. The lush green foliage reminded Mirella of the patch of sweet corn she had seen growing behind the kitchen. Black men worked between the rows, hoeing weeds.

Once, Jason stopped the carriage and got out to speak to an overseer. Her gaze followed him as he walked away from the vehicle, male grace evident in every long stride. The sun made his hair gleam with gold highlights. She needn't use her imagination to know what his body looked like minus those form-fitting clothes. He was all bronze skin and powerful muscles, with the physique of a Roman gladiator.

Flushing, Mirella jerked her attention back to Troy.

The air grew hotter and moister as morning slid into afternoon. It was far warmer than she had been accustomed to in England, and she felt a tiny rivulet of perspiration trickle between her breasts. It irked her that the heat didn't seem to affect Samantha's cool beauty. Yet she was oddly satisfied that the strong sunlight revealed small wrinkles around the other woman's eyes. Samantha, she judged, must be nearly ten years older than herself.

It was early afternoon by the time they halted for lunch. Troy set their picnic basket in a stand of pine trees alongside a stream, amidst a profusion of black-eyed Susans and Queen Anne's lace.

Mirella spread a white linen cloth on the grass. As if such a menial task were beneath her, Samantha stood by idly, chatting to the men while Mirella laid out the feast Ophelia had prepared. There were slices of ham and beef, fried chicken, cheese, bread, several bottles of wine, and a jug of apple cider.

"Do these woods mark the border of your plantation?" Mirella asked Jason as they sat down to eat.

He flashed her a mocking smile. "Hardly. We could ride for the remainder of the afternoon and not leave my land."

"Jase owns some thirty thousand acres around here," Troy said casually.

Mirella put down the biscuit she was nibbling, and stared at Jason. "And do you grow tobacco on all of it?"

"No," he replied, a bit brusquely. "The farther south and west you go, the more stands of timber you'll see. Growing tobacco leaches the richness out of the soil, which makes it necessary to clear new land on a regular basis."

"One resource the colonies have in abundance is fertile land," Troy said. "A couple of years ago, Jase and I both purchased about fifty thousand additional

231

acres in the wilderness northwest of here." He sighed. "Ah, Albemarle County and the Shenandoah Valley. Such magnificent country. I'd love to settle there someday."

Mirella was intrigued. "But wouldn't it be dangerous to live there because of the Indians?"

Troy laughed, waving a leg of fried chicken. "Where's your sense of adventure, cousin?" His green eyes danced with excitement. "Why, you couldn't help but fall in love with the mountains. From a distance they appear to be covered in a soft blue haze. Maybe I'll have the chance to show them to you someday."

At the husky deepening of Troy's voice, Mirella thought she saw a muscle tighten in Jason's jaw. But the fleeting impression vanished as Samantha snuggled up to him, apparently annoyed that no one was paying her any attention.

"My daddy's got some wooded property in the next county that you'd dearly love to have, doesn't he?" she cooed to him. "I just hope it hasn't slipped your mind that I'm his only heir."

Jason's eyes strayed to Samantha's near-naked breasts as the woman leaned into him. "I haven't forgotten," he murmured lazily, smiling down at her.

Mirella was unprepared for the strong emotion that slashed through her. Was Jason contemplating marrying that . . . that flame-haired hussy? It made sense, for Samantha owned land that would serve as a dowry.

Mirella drank from her silver goblet, scarcely tasting the fine Madeira. Perhaps his plan was to take Samantha for his wife, while keeping herself for his mistress. Well, he could think again! she fumed. She would be long gone before he could even attempt to make that scheme a reality.

Troy cleared his throat. "Jase, did you know that Governor Gooch has retired?"

Jason turned to his brother. "Nay, when did this come about?"

"He made his farewell speech to the General Assembly back in May. John Robinson has taken over as acting governor."

They discussed politics for a while, then their conversation switched to business matters—the number of foals born to Jason's mares that spring, whether or not the wheat was ready to be reaped, one of the overseers whom Troy had been forced to dismiss due to the man's continual drunkenness.

Mirella was fascinated by this glimpse into the running of the large plantation, but apparently Samantha felt differently, for she threw down the piece of cheese she had been daintily nibbling, and let out a deep sigh.

"Oh, must you two go on so about such dreary matters?" she pouted. "I vow I'm bored to the point of tears."

"Well, now, we can't have you reddening those lovely blue eyes, can we?" Jason murmured, lightly stroking Samantha's cheek. "Why don't we continue on our tour?" Leaping up, he gallantly assisted the woman as she rose.

Mirella clenched her teeth and gathered up the remains of the picnic, getting no help from Samantha. As if she were a slave to do that bitch's bidding! she seethed.

She threw the last item into the basket and

slammed the lid shut, assuring herself that the churning sensation in her stomach was due to the embarrassment of having to watch Samantha hang all over Jason. Why, it was disgusting the way that trollop acted as if he were her personal property! And he appeared to enjoy her crass coquetry!

Samantha continued to cling to Jason until the party returned to the house late that afternoon. Everyone seemed to take it for granted that she and Troy would stay for supper. By that time, she was grating so badly on Mirella's nerves that Mirella was counting the minutes until the redhead left.

As she entered the dining room on Troy's arm, Mirella had a chance to hiss, "Is Samantha never going to leave?"

"Oh, I expect she plans on spending the night here, as do I." He paused, then added with a grin, "Why? Is there some reason you would object to her staying here?"

"Of course not," Mirella said stiffly, realizing belatedly that she sounded almost jealous. And she certainly wasn't *that*!

To make her denial convincing, she spent the meal flirting with Troy and talking to Pandora while ignoring the other couple. But after several more hours of forced gaiety, her face hurt from smiling. The headache she used as an excuse to escape from the drawing room after dinner was in fact no lie.

After undressing with Clea's aid, Mirella lay in her darkened room, listening to the soft tick of the clock on the mantel and the rasp of crickets outside. Though she longed for peaceful oblivion, slumber was a will-o'-the-wisp which slipped from her grasp when she yearned for it most.

She studied the shifting shadows shed by moonlight shining through the branches of a tree outside her opened window. Sounds of laughter and conversation drifted from the first floor, then gradually the warm night air grew quiet. The dual click of doors in the hall outside told her when Troy and Samantha finally retired to their chambers.

And still, sleep eluded Mirella.

Finally, with a sigh of frustration, she slid off the bed and fumbled on a nearby table for a flint. Lighting a single taper, she found a sheer silk robe and pulled it over her nightdress. Then, her path lit by a wavering candle flame, she headed into the hall and down the stairs, intending to get a book from the library in the hopes that reading would lull her to sleep.

She stopped on the bottom step as she became aware of the low murmur of voices—a husky tone that could only belong to a man, and then a woman's high-pitched giggle.

Mirella froze, her eyes glued to the faint light beneath Jason's bedchamber door. He had Samantha in there with him!

A feminine moan of pleasure floated into the dark, empty hall. The sound broke the spell that had pinned Mirella's bare feet to the step. Whipping around, her long ebony hair braid streaming behind her, she fled back up the stairs as though the hounds of hell were nipping at her heels.

Safe within her chamber, she snuffed out the candle, barely noticing the subtle odor of myrtle berries which rose from the softened wax. She flung herself

235

onto the rumpled sheets, staring up at the lace canopy overhead and seeing a mirage of two naked bodies entwined in a bed.

Jason and Samantha. It was one thing to suspect an illicit relationship, but quite another to discover the proof of it.

Abruptly Mirella rolled over and punched a fist into her pillow. Samantha might wear the trappings of a lady, but she was a common strumpet underneath. She was indecent, improper, indecorous, indelicate, and if Jason lusted after her, then he had neither discretion nor taste! And to think he had once desired *her*! It was humiliating to be placed in the same category as that vulgar, low-class tart!

But once her wild rage abated, Mirella moaned. Digging her fingernails into the tender flesh of her palms, she forced herself to face the mortifying truth. She was jealous! *She* wanted to be the woman in Jason's bed.

It was wicked to desire him so, but she couldn't seem to help herself. The question was, what was she to do about it?

Chapter Thirteen

Twin tapers perched on either end of the mantel-piece cast a pale, flickering glow over the walnut furnishings of Jason's bedchamber. The corners of the room were shrouded in deep shadow. Eerie shapes swayed on the richly paneled walls, but no one saw their strange dance, for the occupants of the wide, four-postered bed were otherwise engaged.

Samantha's alabaster body gleamed in the candle-light as she lay half-draped over Jason, stroking and caressing his naked flesh. Her skill was based on many years of practice, Jason thought, watching with cynical gold eyes as she nibbled a moist path down his chest. His blood warmed in automatic response, yet he felt an odd distaste which kept him from joining in the love play with the same enthusiasm as his partner.

When Samantha had stolen into his bedchamber, uninvited, the ill temper that had been building within him all day had almost caused him to toss her back out in a most ungentlemanly manner. But she had cajoled and teased until he had permitted her to stay. Though he knew Samantha schemed to lure him to the altar, her attentions were a balm to his battered pride. And there was nothing wrong with enjoying her freely offered favors, he reasoned grimly. So why was he feeling so dissatisfied?

Jason clenched his teeth in frustrated rage. After spending the entire day watching Mirella flirt with his brother, he felt like wringing someone's neck, rather than making love. Oh, God, if only it had been Mirella who had walked through his bedchamber door tonight!

Closing his eyes, he saw a vision of Mirella standing beside his bed, slowly peeling away her clothing until her lovely body lay bare and tempting to his hungry eyes. With a provocative smile, she leaned over him, her long ebony hair swinging forward to entice his waiting skin. Slowly, seductively, she straddled him, kissing and caressing him until his blood burned like red-hot lava. . . .

A feminine tongue licked his hard erection.

Jason groaned as a lightning bolt of desire seared his body. *Oh, my sweet Mirella!* His hands reached out blindly to touch the woman bending over him. In the fantasy enveloping him, the hair spilling over his fingers was not red, but black as night. The breasts that brushed his heated flesh were not small and pointed, but lush and full. The scent wafting to his nose was not cloying and heavy, but delicate and feminine.

Driven by a frenzy of passion, he hauled her up to press her against the sheets as he plunged his throbbing shaft inside of her. Their tongues tangled in a steamy kiss. *Mirella, my lovely Mirella . . .* The rake of her nails down his back and her lusty moans of pleasure heightened his fever. His thrusts grew deeper and swifter until release burst upon him in a pulsating explosion of ecstasy.

Spent, he hovered in a hazy realm of delicious exhaustion, vaguely aware of a reluctance to return to reality. There was some knowledge he shied away from remembering. . . .

The woman in his arms stirred sensually, uttering a sultry sound of satisfaction. "I knew you'd missed me, darling," she purred triumphantly.

Jason opened his eyes to stare blankly at the red-haired woman lying beneath him. Her strong perfume choked his senses, and he felt a sudden sickness deep in his gut.

By damn, he had been fantasizing about making love to Mirella! He rolled off Samantha to sit on the edge of the mattress, his head cradled in his hands. Mirella had him so bewitched that he now dreamed of her even as he lay with another woman! Was there no escaping her spell? It was growing increasingly difficult to remember a time when he hadn't been haunted by her alluring body. For weeks now, he had hidden his desire behind a façade of ice, leashing his passion only by the strength of his willpower. Why the devil couldn't he purge her image from his brain?

Jason felt Samantha's arms snake around him from behind. Her fingers fondled the hair on his chest as she rubbed her naked breasts against his back.

"That was sensational," she cooed into his ear. "I vow you're the most exciting lover in all of Virginia."

He surged to his feet and pivoted to face her, unsure if he was more disgusted with Samantha or himself. "I thank you," he mocked. "Coming from a woman of

239

your experience, that's quite a compliment."

Samantha preened. "Why, Jason, there's no need for you to be jealous. You're the only man I really want."

Jason eyed her contemptuously. That tumbled red hair and pale skin bathed in candlelight failed to excite him. The almond-shaped eyes which he had once thought exotic now seemed feral and calculating. What had he ever seen in her? If he weren't so bored with the conversation, he might correct her mistaken notion that he was jealous. Now, were he to learn that Mirella had slept with another man, *that* would transform him into a green-eyed monster breathing fire and lusting to kill. . . .

He snatched the heap of her clothing from the floor, and flung the garments at her. "Get dressed, and then get the hell out of here!"

"Why, darling, we have the whole night before us." She held out her arms, wiggling her small breasts coquettishly. "Come back to bed, and I'll show you a new position I thought up while you were away."

"Samantha, if you're not gone in exactly two minutes, I shall be forced to help you leave in a manner I'm sure you won't enjoy."

The message in his clipped, icy tone must have gotten through to the woman, for she slid off the bed and began pulling on her undergarments.

"I know you're angry about those other men," Samantha pouted, "but 'tis no reason to threaten me. Why, if you'd wanted to keep me all to yourself, you shouldn't have gone away for so long."

Jason stood, hands on his bare hips, watching dispassionately as she donned her gown. He felt not a flicker of desire for her. Today she had been a useful tool in soothing his frustrations, but that was the extent of it.

Now fully clothed, Samantha threw her arms around him and kissed him full on the mouth. "You'll get over your jealousy, darling, once you realize how much you need me. I'll be waiting to hear from you." With a confident smile, she sailed out of the chamber, her long red hair hanging down her back.

Jason strode to the fireplace and leaned a shoulder against the mantelpiece, staring moodily into the empty hearth. Women were users, all of them. Samantha couldn't wait to get her greedy hands on his riches, just like the shallow aristocratic ladies he had dallied with in London. Elizabeth had been typical of that breed.

And Mirella? He let out a bitter bark of laughter. For days, he had been banking on the fact that when she discovered the extent of his wealth, she would come crawling to him, begging for the chance to be his mistress. Instead, she had focused her wiles on his brother!

Suddenly he was consumed by a violent resentment of Troy. But as swiftly as the emotion struck, Jason stifled it. He slammed his fist onto the mantel, welcoming the jolt of pain as his flesh hit the hard wood. By damn, he would never allow that enchantress to destroy the love and respect he felt for his brother!

Though Mirella might be in his blood, he would rot in hell before he would be any woman's slave! Somehow, he would find a way to drive her from his system once and for all.

* * *

"Here's what you do, Mirella." Pandora deftly secured the wiggling worm onto the hook at the end of her fishing line. "See? Now, you try to bait yours."

The girl dug into the small pail on the ground beside her and retrieved another worm. Mirella stared askance at the squirming brown creature. Only by exercising fortitude was she able to keep from shuddering as she reached out to pluck it from Pandora's fingers.

Taking a deep breath, she frowned in concentration, holding the earthworm in one hand and the hook in her other. Valiantly she attempted to imitate Pandora's demonstration, but the slippery creature began to slide out of her fingers. As she made a wild grab for it, she dropped the worm into her gaping shirtfront.

Letting out a screech, Mirella leaped to her feet, the hook falling to the ground as she frantically tugged her shirt out of the waistband of her breeches. Violently she shook the white homespun material until the worm fell out. With a heartfelt sigh of relief, she closed her eyes, only then becoming aware of the shrieks of laughter emanating from her companion.

She opened her eyes to see Pandora leaning against the trunk of a willow tree, convulsed with mirth. The girl's straw hat was tilted askew on her blond hair, and tears of merriment trickled down her cheeks.

"You wouldn't think it so amusing if it'd happened to you," Mirella grumbled. She shuddered, still feeling that clammy, writhing sensation between her bare breasts.

"I'm . . . sorry," Pandora managed between giggles, " 'Twas just . . . the look on your face. . . ."

" 'Tis all your fault for making me wear this silly garb." But, on beginning to see the humor in the situation, Mirella was sorely pressed to keep from smiling. To hide her budding laughter, she glared down at the male clothing she wore, which Pandora had "borrowed" from the laundry building. "This shirt is so big and baggy," she complained, "it must belong to Lucas Colby! If the front didn't gape so, I'd never have dropped that wretched worm down it."

"You know we can't fish properly in petticoats and silk gowns," Pandora said, her giggles subsiding. "And as for the size of that shirt, well, I just grabbed whatever I could without being caught."

Mirella heaved a dramatic sigh. "All right, all right. Let us get on with the lesson, then. I vow I'll master this sport if it takes until doomsday."

She sat down beside Pandora and located the wiggly worm on the ground. After several tries, luckily none as disastrous as the first, she finally managed to bait her hook. Then they stepped over to the nearby stream, where Pandora showed her the proper way to cast her line into the water.

"Now you must keep very still, else the fish may be frightened away," the girl informed her after they'd seated themselves on the grassy bank.

Mirella soon found that she was enjoying herself more than she'd thought possible when she had first promised to go fishing. There was something soothing in the sound of the flowing stream and the feel of the dappled sunlight warming her back. Occasionally, she heard the cawing of a crow overhead, the chattering of a squirrel, or a deep croak which Pandora told her was made by a bullfrog.

Idly she surveyed their peaceful, wooded surroundings. It was difficult to believe that Jason's house was less than a mile away. The forest was thick with pine, cypress and sweet gum trees. Tangles of wild strawberries and huckleberries abounded with fruit ripe for the picking. The wilderness, she realized in pleasant surprise, was not the unsavory place she had imagined. Now that she was here, she felt a rush of gladness that she had made this pact with Pandora.

And Pandora had more than fulfilled her end of the bargain. She had behaved with ladylike decorum these past few weeks, and was even beginning to assume her responsibilities as mistress of the manor. After some minor protests, she was learning under Mirella's guidance how to direct the growing and preparation of food for the household, everything from overseeing the dairy and the kitchen garden to approving the menus for the meals. Granted, there was still a mountain of duties for her to master, but at least the girl was trying.

Surreptitiously, Mirella stole a glance at her. Jason's sister was quite pretty even with that rough straw hat covering her honey hair. A light tan enhanced her silver-green eyes, and her boy's clothing outlined the slim beauty of her figure. Mirella suspected that Pandora's rebellious nature hid an awkward insecurity. Everyone either indulged her or scolded her rather than taking the time to get to know her. Her brothers were too busy running their plantations to bother much with her, and she disdained other girls her age. Mirella was glad she'd had the sense to approach Pandora on her own level.

Since Jason had spent a good deal of time in the

plantation office over the past weeks, today had been their first opportunity to escape into the woods. Last evening at supper, he had mentioned that he planned to ride out into the fields. So early this morning, after ascertaining that he was gone, they'd snuck out, changing into their male clothing once they were safely away from the house.

And if Jason were to catch them? He'd probably send us both to bed without our suppers, Mirella thought, smiling to herself. Though, of course, he might not notice *me* at all.

Her amusement faded. Why did it bother her so that Jason had lost interest in her? Despite her fears that she would give in if he should touch her again, he continued to ignore her. She should be glad his passion for her had faded, and thrilled that he showered his attention on Samantha, who had visited often of late. Daily, she expected him to make an announcement of his impending betrothal to that red-haired tart. Those two deserved one another, Mirella sniffed in silent disdain. So why did she feel a vague sense of distress?

Her thoughts jumped to the previous afternoon, when she had gone for a walk and had stumbled, unexpectedly, upon Jason outside the small church which served the local families. Instinct made her hang back in the trees, watching as he stood in the cemetery, gazing down at one of the tombs. After he mounted his horse and cantered off, curiosity compelled her to enter the graveyard. It was no surprise when she saw the stone he had been looking at. The inscription was a memorial to his dead wife and son.

The incident had strengthened Mirella's suspicion

245

that Jason might still harbor feelings for Elizabeth. And now, after nine years, was he finally ready to remarry?

Her fishing pole suddenly jerked, drawing her mind back the present. Mirella glanced at Pandora in excitement.

"I've caught something! What do I do now?"

While hanging onto her own pole, Pandora told Mirella how to pull in the line. Scrambling to her feet, Mirella did as she was instructed. To her glee, she soon found a moderate-size fish flopping on the ground beside her.

" 'Tis a bit small," Pandora pronounced, eyeing the catch critically. "Perhaps we should toss it back."

"Don't you dare!" Mirella squeaked. "I worked hard for that slimy creature, and I'm not about to give it up!"

Pandora grinned. "I was only teasing. Of course, you can keep your fish."

Over the next few hours, they managed between the two of them to catch a full stringer of trout and bass, though Mirella never quite got used to baiting her hook. Finally, she glanced up at the sky and noted by the position of the sun that it was well past noon.

" 'Tis time we started back," she announced.

"Must we?" Pandora pleaded wistfully. "Jason won't return until supper, so couldn't we spend the whole day out here?"

"I'm afraid not. Don't forget, the dancing master is due to arrive later this afternoon."

"Oh, all right," Pandora grumbled as she got up from the bank and brushed off the seat of her pants.

A few days earlier, Troy had stopped by to tell them

that he was planning a party at his home near the end of July, several weeks hence. Obtaining Jason's approval, Mirella had arranged for a dancing instructor from Williamsburg to come stay with them for a short time, knowing that Pandora needed the training. She herself planned to take advantage of the lessons, too, for though she had learned some basic dance steps as a young girl, she realized that it would be prudent to brush up on her skill.

After gathering their fishing gear, Mirella and Pandora headed for the clump of bushes where they had concealed their feminine attire. There, they cast aside their male shirts and breeches, chattering to each other as they slowly dressed.

The cream-colored stallion cantered past a field of green tobacco, guided by its master toward a stretch of uncleared land bordering the James River. With the midday sun beating down on him, the wooded setting seemed to beckon to Jason. By damn, it was hot today, he thought, wiping his brow with the back of his hand.

Trickles of sweat were soaking into his white shirt as he finally reached the forest. He slowed the stallion to a walk, knowing that the animal must be feeling the heat as much as he. Already a cool breeze was sweeping across his face. Cutting through the stand of timber might have taken him out of his way but the more tolerable temperature made it well worth his while.

Mockingbirds trilled in the trees, and he saw a flash of scarlet as a cardinal flew by. Yet the beauty of the scene failed to ease his vague sense of irritation.

Why the devil was he returning home anyway? Jason wondered. Earlier he had decided that since he was in the vicinity, he might as well head back to the house for dinner, served punctually at two o'clock each afternoon. But he knew deep down that was only an excuse. The lure that drew him back home was Mirella.

As they passed a stream, the stallion jerked the reins.

"Thirsty, Pegasus?" he asked the animal.

He dismounted, his boots lithely landing on the grassy bank. As the horse drank its fill, Jason paced restlessly through the surrounding trees.

His lips twisted with annoyance as he thought of Mirella. Though in front of her he maintained a façade of cold indifference, he was still obsessed with her. Instead of going out to the fields, as he knew he should, he had stuck close to the house these past weeks on the pretext of working in the plantation office. Yet his true motivation was that he hated the prospect of long hours without catching even a glimpse of Mirella's swaying hips or sweet smile. This morning, he'd had to force himself to get onto his horse and ride away.

Why the hell was he so bewitched by that woman?

With a start, Jason realized that he had wandered a good distance from the stream where he'd left Pegasus. He was about to retrace his steps when the faint sound of laughter drifted to his ears. Mirella, he thought instantly.

It couldn't be, he scoffed. Yet somehow his feet were carrying him in the direction of the noise.

Jason stopped short as he caught sight of Mirella

248

and his sister. They were standing with their backs to him, laughing and talking to one another. Neither of them noticed as he moved quietly to a clump of bushes, just behind them, where again he paused, his stunned gaze riveted to Mirella.

She was stark naked.

Jason felt his blood flame in instant response. As he watched, she half-turned to don her chemise, stretching her arms high as she pulled the lacy garment over her tumbled ebony hair. Her bare breasts were revealed in their full glory. The lush swells were the color of magnolia blossoms, the tips a deep honey-brown hue. His eyes descended to her rounded derrière and well-shaped thighs just before the chemise fluttered down to cover her.

By damn, how he wanted to feel that silken skin beneath his fingers! His muscles were tensing to propel him forward when a movement beyond Mirella reminded him of Pandora's presence.

Jason glanced at his sister in confusion, wondering what she was doing out here in the woods. For that matter, what were both women doing here? He looked at what lay on the ground beside them: two fishing poles, a stringer of fish, and a pile of what was unmistakably men's clothing.

Fury welled inside of him as he realized the truth. The moment he'd left, they'd snuck off to go fishing! Incredible though it might seem, Mirella had accompanied Pandora on this hoydenish excursion. To think he had trusted her to teach his sister how to act like a lady! It appeared that all she had done was to encourage Pandora's wild ways. By God, she would pay for having duped him so!

Jason strode out from behind the bushes. A twig snapped beneath his foot, and the two women whipped around. Pandora gasped in horror. In speedy unison, both of them reached for their gowns to hide their partial nudity.

To his grim satisfaction, he saw a flicker of fear in Mirella's widened, dusky blue eyes. Yet he couldn't help but feel a reluctant admiration for her, because an instant later, her chin tilted upward in bold courage. Whatever her faults, she was no coward.

She stepped between brother and sister. "Jason, this is not Pandora's fault. I take full responsibil—

"Save your explanations," he ordered curtly. "I'll expect to see you in my office in half an hour."

Pivoting, he marched off, his relentless stride reflecting the outrage that burned inside of him.

A short while later, Mirella left the house, the hem of her silver-gray gown skimming the path of crushed shells that led to the plantation office, a one-story brick building some fifty yards away. Pandora had been so upset by Jason's discovery that she had tearfully begged to go along and help explain matters. But Mirella had refused the girl's offer. With his temper at a fever pitch, there would only be a shouting match which would widen the breach between brother and sister. And she couldn't allow Pandora to take the blame when the situation had not been her fault.

On reaching the office door, Mirella hesitated, letting her brave façade drop for a moment. Jason had been so very angry. When he had stepped into the clearing and caught them red-handed, his face had been dark with fury. Never had she seen him look so harsh and uncompromising.

Calling forth every shred of her willpower, Mirella stilled her fears. What could he possibly do to her? Give her twenty lashes? Throw her off this plantation, when leaving was what she dearly wanted to do anyway?

She stiffened her spine, raising her hand to rap firmly on the oak panel before her. Loud footsteps sounded within, then Jason whipped open the door. Without speaking a word of greeting, he moved aside to allow her space to walk in.

The plantation office was decorated with the same impeccable taste as the main house, though here there was an air of businesslike efficiency. A large cherrywood desk dominated the center of the room. On it, ledgers lay open and papers were strewn about. Three of the four walls were lined with bookshelves, and against the one remaining wall were a couch, and a sideboard holding crystal decanters of wine and brandy. The drapes had been drawn back so that bright shafts of sunlight streamed through the long, multipaned windows.

Mirella turned to face Jason, who stood watching her, hands poised arrogantly on his hips. His golden eyes were grim and unyielding, but she refused to let that deter her. If he wished to release his wrath on someone, then let it be on her, rather than Pandora.

Taking a deep breath, she said, "Jason, I want you to know from the start that I take full blame for what happened. Your sister is not at fault. I'll explain why if you'll listen."

He gave a cold laugh. "Go ahead, tell me the tale you've concocted. It should prove to be entertaining

251

if naught else."

Rounding the desk, Jason sat down and leaned back, perching his boots atop the polished surface in front of him. He was the picture of ease, yet there was a relentlessness emanating from him that made Mirella swallow hard before speaking.

"The fact of the matter is," she said, "going fishing was my idea, not Pandora's. These past weeks, your sister has worked diligently at learning how to run your household. 'Twas only fair that for once she be allowed to do something which gives her great enjoyment. There was no harm intended."

"No harm," Jason repeated with deceptive quietness. Suddenly his feet crashed to the floor as he surged out of his chair. "You call it *no harm* when my sister runs about the countryside dressed like a man?" he roared. *"No harm* when the woman who is supposed to set a good example for her encourages her wild ways? By God, Mirella, what made you agree to such a damn-fool scheme?"

"There was nothing foolish about it," she argued heatedly. "Pandora has as much right to enjoy herself as you do."

Jason slammed his fist down on the desk. "Not if it means she'll behave like a hoyden! By damn, Mirella, you're supposed to be teaching her the ways of a lady! Yet no sooner do I turn my back than I find you acting as much like a hellion as my sister. I fail to understand how this came about!"

"If you would cease your yelling and listen, perhaps you might understand my reasoning."

"There is naught you can say that could justify your behavior. Don't you realize how dangerous the

252

woods can be? Any number of creatures could have injured or even killed the both of you! Bears, rattlesnakes, wolves, panthers, not to mention renegade Indians! How could you have acted so irresponsibly?"

Mirella let him finish ranting, meeting his gaze unflinchingly. "I promised to go fishing with Pandora in order to gain her trust. Don't you see? She's trapped between her desire to please you and her need to let out her high spirits. She loves you, Jason, and she's been trying so hard these past weeks to make you proud of her. Don't you think she deserves a reward every once in a while so long as she behaves properly the rest of the time?"

"She is a lady, and I wish her to act accordingly."

"And are you always the perfect gentleman?" Mirella retorted.

Jason stared at her without expression, then unexpectedly he burst out laughing. "I never thought I'd admit it, but I suppose there is something to what you say." His face grew serious again. " 'Tis simply that I am concerned about my sister's safety as well as her reputation. She must learn to curb her wild ways."

"She will, Jason, I promise you. Just give her a little time." Mirella hesitated, then added, "And will you forbid her to fish, then?" She held her breath, waiting for his answer.

"I suppose 'twill be all right so long as you two stay close to the house," he said grudgingly after a moment of reflection. "You have my permission to handle matters as you see fit. But be discreet. I'll not have the entire colony gossiping about the tomboy my sister has become."

Relief washed over her. "Thank you. If that's al[l] I'll excuse myself." She whirled, eager to relay th[e] good news to Pandora.

"Wait." Jason's crisp voice stopped her befor[e] she'd taken a step. He rounded the desk to stand i[n] front of her. "You've a smudge on your cheek."

Before she could wipe it off herself, he was gentl[y] rubbing the spot away. His fingertips felt slight[ly] calloused against her soft skin, and his breat[h] feathered her forehead. Her heart suddenly wa[s] throbbing at twice its normal pace. His scent was a[ll] around her, a heady combination of sweat an[d] horses and pure male. She had to restrain an im[-] pulse to press her mouth against the glistenin[g] golden brown hairs revealed by the open collar of h[is] shirt.

"You and my sister must be two of a kin[d] running about and getting dirty," he tease[d.] "There, you're all clean now."

His hand remained on her cheek a mome[nt] longer, as if he were reluctant to break the contac[t.] He gazed down into her eyes, and for the first tim[e] in weeks, his expression held a warmth that melte[d] her insides. More than anything else in the worl[d] she yearned for him to bend his head and take he[r] lips.

Abruptly the brief tenderness vanished from hi[s] face and was replaced by that familiar cold forma[l-] ity. Jason dropped his hand, taking a step back[-] ward.

"Good day to you, madam."

Mirella mumbled a good-bye and fled out th[e]

door. The cool breeze off the river quickly restored her senses but not her peace of mind. Berating herself for her weakness, she thanked the heavens above that Jason appeared to have lost all desire for her.

Had he not, she might be tempted to forego her scruples and become his mistress.

Chapter Fourteen

"Emma, do you think my freckles are too prominent?" Mirella frowned at her image in the looking glass. The dusting of specks across the creamy skin of her cheekbones and her nose had deepened over the past few weeks due to the hours she and Pandora had spent outside.

" 'Tisn't anything to worry yourself about," her friend assured her, reaching over to adjust the ribbon holding Mirella's bodice together. "Why, I've no doubt you'll be the belle of the ball tonight."

"Miz Colby ain't lyin'," Clea put in. "You sure gonna have the menfolk fightin' over you."

"Now stop it, you two," Mirella said, giving them a mock glare. "You're embarrassing me."

Turning her attention back to the oak-framed oval mirror in a corner of her bedchamber, she surveyed herself with critical eyes. She had to admit that she could find no fault with her appearance.

Her gown was an exquisite concoction of amethyst tabby silk with an underskirt of a lavender so pale it was almost white. The low neckline revealed an

257

alluring expanse of milky skin. She had attached her mother's cameo to a violet ribbon and fastened it around her neck, so that the delicate piece hung just above the enticing valley between her breasts. The gown's wide-hooped skirt accentuated the slenderness of her waist, and Venetian lace flounces edged the three-quarter-length sleeves.

At first she had been reluctant to accept such an extravagant garment from Jason, but he had told her in no uncertain terms that he would not have the friends and neighbors who would be at Troy's party thinking him too stingy to provide his "cousin" with the proper attire. And, after all, Mirella reasoned, the gown was only fair payment for the work she had done these past weeks.

She swirled around, her petticoats rustling. "Well, if I attract the slightest attention tonight, I owe it all to the both of you. Emma, you've outdone yourself with the sewing of this gown, and Clea, you've worked wonders with my hair."

The black woman had fussed for nearly an hour, crimping Mirella's long, ebony tresses into curls which cascaded down to the nape of her neck. Tucked into the side of the creation was a cluster of miniature white roses tied with a long, violet ribbon. A tiny vial of water kept the blooms fresh. Mirella had chosen not to powder her hair as was the current rage, preferring this simple, elegant style.

Clea beamed at Mirella's compliment. "Be there anythin' more Ah can do for you, ma'am?"

"No, and thank you again, Clea."

After the black woman had left the bedchamber, Mirella took a deep breath, her insides a vortex of excitement and apprehension. Back in England, after her father had gambled away the family fortune, she had shunned society in favor of a quiet country life. Hence, this would be the first party she had attended as a grown woman.

"Oh, Emma, I wish you were going with us tonight! 'Twould be far easier to face meeting all those new people if I had a friend at my side."

A smile lit Emma's elfin face. "You don't need me. You have Pandora—and Mr. Fletcher, don't forget."

Mirella's restless feet carried her to the opened balcony doors, where she pivoted to retort, "Jason will be too busy with Samantha to pay any mind to me."

"That woman? Why, she couldn't hold a candle to you. And anyway, I've seen the way Mr. Fletcher looks at you. He doesn't feel a speck for her what he does for you."

Mirella gave a noncommittal shrug, sure that her friend's words sprang from loyalty to the owner of her paper of indenture. In Emma's eyes, Jason could do no wrong. If only Emma knew the truth, Mirella thought in bitter anger. Were he to notice her at all— and she was certain he didn't—his attention would be due solely to lust. Hadn't he himself told her that he had no wish to be encumbered with a wife?

"Never mind all that," she said, impatient for a change of subject. "I still wish you were accompanying us tonight. 'Tisn't too late for me to ask Jason about it. You could borrow one of my gowns, and I'm sure we could find something for Lucas to wear."

Emma smiled again, though she shook her head. "Thank you for thinking of us, but 'twouldn't be right for indentured servants to attend. And anyway, I

259

rather doubt Lucas would allow me to dance or drink spirits in my condition."

"Your condition?" Mirella repeated sharply. "You're ill, then? Had I known, I would never have allowed you to work those long hours on this gown!"

Emma laughed, her topaz eyes twinkling. " 'Tis no ailment but a perfectly natural occurrence. I'm to have a baby in six months' time."

For an instant, Mirella was stunned. Then she flew across the carpet to embrace her friend. "Oh, Emma, that's wonderful news! Why didn't you tell me earlier?"

"I suspected the truth while we were still aboard the ship, but before I announced it to the world, I wanted to be sure that my monthly flow hadn't ceased due to the strains of traveling."

"So late next January will herald the babe's arrival, hmm? As soon as I return from Troy's, we shall have to begin sewing the child's clothing."

Yet, despite her cheerful words, Mirella couldn't suppress a twinge of envy at her friend's happiness. Would she herself ever know the good fortune of having a husband who loved her and the sweet sensation of carrying the fruit of his seed in her belly? Or was she destined to live forever on the periphery, experiencing such joys only through others?

When Emma departed, Mirella went in search of Pandora. She rapped softly on the door to the girl's bedchamber, entering when she heard a muffled "Come in."

Mirella stopped short at the scene that met her eyes. Ophelia stood in the middle of the room, hands roosting on her ample hips. Across from her, Pandora was perched on the bed, clad only in lace chemise and drawers. Her face was set in a mutinous expression, and her long blond hair spilled over her shoulders in turbulent disarray.

"What's wrong, Pandora?" Mirella asked, walking inside. " 'Tis nearly half past three, and you know that Jason wishes to leave at four o'clock. Why are you not readying yourself?"

"Because I don't want to go to that silly old party," Pandora pouted.

Mirella was baffled by the girl's attitude. Custom here in the colonies dictated that the younger folk be allowed to join in on the festivities until their bedtime. Though Pandora had been a bit quiet of late whenever Troy's party had been mentioned, she had given no indication of this reluctance to attend it.

"My poor honey child been a-carryin' on like this all day," Ophelia told Mirella, a helpless look on her broad black face. "Ah thinks you should just let her stay home with her mammy tonight."

But Mirella was determined to find out what was behind the girl's reluctance. "Ophelia, I'd like to speak to Pandora alone, if you don't mind."

The black woman sent her a suspicious frown. "Only if you swears you won't make my baby do nothin' she don't want to do."

"I give you my word of honor."

Ophelia pursed her lips, tilting her turbaned head in distrust. "All right, then," she said finally. Mumbling under her breath, she waddled out of the chamber, slamming the door behind her.

Mirella sat down on the edge of the bed, being careful not to wrinkle her gown. "Now, why don't you

261

tell me what this is all about? I presumed you were going with us since you hadn't said otherwise."

Pandora gave an uncooperative shrug. "I was, but I changed my mind, that's all."

"But I thought you were looking forward to seeing Troy."

"That doesn't mean I want to go to his *party*." She spat out the last word as though it were a worm. "And if you try to force me to go, I swear I'll run away and never come back." Lifting her chin in obstinate rebellion, she glared at Mirella.

"I won't force you to do anything," Mirella assured her. "I'm merely trying to understand your reasoning. Don't you want to visit with all the other young people your age?"

"I don't want to talk to anyone. I'd rather stay home."

"But what about the friends you haven't seen in a while? They'll all miss you if you don't go."

"No one will notice if I'm not there," Pandora muttered, averting her silver-green eyes to stare stonily out the window. Her long fingers dug into the fragile lace of her shift, betraying her inner tension.

Mirella sensed an emotion other than stubborn defiance in Pandora. Could it be that the girl was afraid to attend the party for some reason? Afraid somehow that she wouldn't fit in?

She reached out and gently touched the girl's clenched hands. "Pandora, how can you say such a thing? Of course you'll be missed. Why, all the boys will be desolate if they're deprived of the chance to dance with the prettiest girl in Virginia."

"No, they won't be!" Unruly blond hair swirled

about her shoulders as Pandora swung her head back toward Mirella. "They'd just laugh at me if I were to flutter my fan like some simpering female. And it's not fair! I can climb a tree faster than any of them, but if I try to act like a lady, they won't like me anymore! I hate them all!"

Her mutinous expression dissolved into tears, and she flung herself over onto her stomach, her sobs muffled by a pillow. Mirella's heart twisted at Pandora's anguish. It was far more difficult for Pandora to accept her approaching womanhood than it was for most girls; she was certain that the boys who had once accepted her as an equal would reject her now. Little did she know that as they grew to manhood their attitude toward her was ripe for change. Pandora soon would discover that her feminine charms would incite far greater interest than any tomboyish feats.

Mirella placed a hand on the girl's shoulder. "Pandora, no one will ridicule you," she said gently.

"All the boys will." Pandora turned her head slightly, so that her miserable, tear-stained face was half visible. "I used to be their friend, and now they'll think I'm just another dumb girl. They'll laugh when they see me trying to act like a lady."

"You won't lose their esteem simply because you're becoming a woman. They'll admire you all the more for it."

"But how can they like me if I'm no longer allowed to prove that I'm as good as they are?"

Mirella smiled. "Because the respect between a grown man and woman isn't based on trivial physical tests like being able to run faster or shoot with greater accuracy. It springs from your strength of character.

Just be proud of yourself, and don't allow the antics of a few immature boys to bother you. Once they see their teasing doesn't affect you, they'll grow to respect you even more than they did before."

Pandora wiggled into a half-sitting position, supporting herself with an elbow. "Do you really think so?"

The vulnerability in her eyes touched Mirella's heart. "I'm certain of it," she reassured her. "You're a lovely young lady, and no one could help but like you."

"But I'm not as pretty as you are." The flicker of optimism vanished, and Pandora's face became despondent again. "I'm too tall and ungainly. Men like dainty women."

"You have a natural grace," Mirella countered. "The dancing master told me so himself. And besides that, you have a pleasing figure and beautiful hair and eyes that would invite the envy of many a woman."

"Truly?"

"Truly," Mirella said firmly. "Now what do you say about dressing for the party?" She slid off the coverlet, extending a hand to Pandora.

The girl still hesitated. "But . . . but what if things don't happen the way you say? What if I make a fool of myself in front of all those people?"

"Everything will be fine. Just remember to hold your head up high and take pride in who you are. If you believe in yourself, then you'll soon find that everyone else will too."

But as she helped Pandora don a gown of peach-colored silk, Mirella wished that life could be as rosy as the picture she had painted. Certainly she herself

264

had a strong self-respect, yet Jason had failed to honor her, for he had seduced her in spite of his awareness of her principles. He hadn't afforded her any esteem, and of late she might have been a stick of furniture for all the recognition he gave her. Much as logic told her that was for the best, the knowledge continued to rankle her. She had no wish to be his mistress, yet she didn't want to be ignored either. What was it about him, she wondered, that made her yearn so for his admiration?

Mirella had arrived at no answer to that question when, a short while later, she and Pandora settled themselves aboard the small sailboat that would carry them upriver to Troy's plantation. Since they would be staying the night, a servant stowed at their feet a trunk containing a change of clothing. With Jason at the helm, and a middle-aged black man expertly unfurling the canvas sails, the craft was soon slicing through the gently rolling waters of the James.

Today Jason wore a pristine white shirt with a ruffled stock, and tan breeches. His waistcoat and frockcoat, both fashioned of a rich burgundy fabric embroidered with gold thread, lay carelessly draped over the cushioned seat beside Mirella.

She tightened her fingers around her folded fan of mother-of-pearl and painted vellum, trying to erase his virile image from her mind. The late July afternoon was warm and humid, but a gentle breeze cooled her cheeks and stirred her hair. A whippoorwill warbled somewhere on shore. The winding river carried them in a northwesterly direction, past alternating stretches of wilderness and cleared land. Countless freshwater streams emptied into the salty sea tide which now flowed inland to aid their progress.

Jason pointed out to Mirella the estates of a few of his neighbors, the Harrisons, the Byrds, the Carters. But beyond that, he said nothing to her, directing what little conversation he did make at his sister. His expression was aloof, and though once she caught him studying her, his brooding eyes were like chips of dark gold, metallic and cold. It was clear that in terms of their relationship, tonight would be no different from any other. Why, she fretted, did that bother her so?

Oblivious to the strain between Mirella and Jason, Pandora chattered without respite. The girl had bounced back from her attack of nerves, and was now her usual bubbly self.

"Richmond lies up the river, some twenty miles distant," she told Mirella. " 'Tis little more than a trading post, but mayhap Troy will take us there sometime. Don't you think 'twould be great fun to trek through the woods—"

"Pandora," Jason interrupted brusquely, "put that idea out of your head. The wilderness is dangerous, and no place for ladies on pleasure jaunts."

Pandora's face took on a familiar stubbornness. "Why is it that men get to go wherever they want, but ladies never do?" she grumbled.

Sensing an impending argument between brother and sister, Mirella swiftly intervened to change the topic of conversation. Of late, Jason had exhibited little tact, she thought. He had been in a foul mood, and impatient with everyone. Mayhap his ill humor was due to the strain of running such a large plantation, she concluded, dismissing it with a shrug.

The bow of the small craft sliced cleanly through

the water, its sails snapping in the breeze. The river grew more narrow and twisting as they neared their destination. It was almost dusk when they docked at Troy's home.

The final rays of the setting sun streaked through the trees to illuminate the beauty of the stately brick mansion at the top of a steep hill. A series of terraces covered the slope. As they approached the portal, the door opened. Troy strode down the steps to greet them, his tanned face wreathed in a smile.

"Hello, everyone." He shook his brother's hand, hugged Pandora, and planted a chaste, cousinly kiss on Mirella's cheek. "Come on in. You're my first arrivals."

In the spacious hall bisecting the house, a broom-stick-thin white woman wearing a mobcap over her gray hair was arranging roses in a vase situated on a table against one wall.

Troy put an arm around Mirella's waist, leading her away from the others and toward the woman. "Mirella, you haven't met my housekeeper, Mrs. MacGuire. Mac, this is my dear cousin from England, Mirella Weston."

As he spoke the nickname, Mrs. MacGuire sent him a disapproving glare, then turned a respectful smile on Mirella. "Pleased to meet you, Miss Weston."

"I'm sure I don't have to tell y'all that Mac is responsible for supervising the preparations for the party. Why, I don't know what I'd have done without her."

Troy leaned over and kissed her bony cheek. Mirella was amused to see a blush creep over the older

267

woman's face. It seemed that not even the house-keeper was immune to her employer's charm.

"If you will excuse me," Mrs. MacGuire mumbled, "I have tasks which require my attention." Recovering her dignity, she sailed out of the hall, her spine straight as a ship's mast.

Troy swung Mirella around to face his brother and sister. "And now, Cousin Mirella," he said, tightening his arm about her waist, "the only thing I lack to ensure tonight's success is a hostess. Would you be so kind as to help me greet my guests as they arrive?" There was a wicked twinkle in his green eyes as Troy looked at his brother. "You won't mind relinquishing her company for a short while, will you, Jase?"

Jason regarded him with an almost bored expression. "Of course not," he said curtly. "Why should I?"

Mirella suspected that Troy was trying again to make his older brother jealous. Although she knew his task was futile, she saw no reason to refuse his request.

" 'Twould be an honor to help you out," she told Troy.

A knock on the door heralded the first of a steady stream of friends and neighbors. Jason drew his sister into the drawing room, leaving Troy and Mirella in the hall. Soon guests were arriving in droves, some in carriages and on horseback, and others by boat. Standing at Troy's side, Mirella met members of the finest families in Virginia. To her relief, no one questioned her blood relation to the Fletchers.

Candles in wall sconces and chandeliers were lit to brighten the darkness, and the doors and windows were opened wide to entice inside the cool evening breeze from the river. Mirella found her foot tapping in rhythm with the tune being played by a fiddler perched on the stair landing. Pleasure bubbled up inside her as she watched dancers begin to crowd the spacious hall.

"May I have the honor of this dance, m'lady?" Troy asked, capping his request with a sweeping bow.

She sank into a deep curtsey. "Why, 'twould be a pleasure, m'lord!"

Mirella took his outstretched hand as the fiddler began to play a fast-paced reel. This was a dance indigenous to the colonies, and the steps were new to her, for she had just learned them. When the lively music finally ended, she was flushed from exertion.

"You Virginians have more vigor than I," she gasped, putting a hand on her heaving bosom.

Troy grinned. "Nonsense. A short break and a spot of refreshment should restore you in no time at all." He towed her into the drawing room, heading toward the silver punch bowl set on a table placed against the wall.

With eagerness, Mirella accepted the goblet he handed her. The cool liquid tasted of brandy and honey, and soothed her parched throat. To escape the heat of the crowd, she and Troy stationed themselves near one of the opened windows.

"You've worked wonders with my sister," he remarked. "She's looking lovely tonight. So grown up."

He nodded toward the other side of the large room, where Pandora stood, surrounded by a bevy of youthful swains. The girl shyly grasped the hand of one as he led her into the hall to dance.

"I've enjoyed getting to know her," Mirella said.

"She's needed a friend like you. 'Twas a lucky day when Jason found you and brought you here from England."

"Mmm-hmm," she murmured, distracted by the mention of his brother's name. Where had Jason disappeared to? Absently sipping on her silver goblet of punch, Mirella searched the throng of elegantly clad men and ladies for his familiar visage. Then a group of guests shifted, and she caught sight of him, engrossed in conversation with a lanky, periwigged man.

Jason was facing her, a lighted taper in the wall sconce above him casting a golden sheen on his hair. The deep burgundy hue of his coat emphasized the broadness of his shoulders. The two men were clearly talking business matters, for Jason's handsome features were drawn into a frown. How she yearned to place her fingers on his brow and smooth away those lines of worry. . . .

The sound of Troy's voice broke into her reverie. ". . . do you not agree?"

Mirella whipped her gaze back to her companion, a flush bathing her cheeks. She opened the fan that dangled on a violet ribbon from her wrist and waved it over her hot face, hiding her expression. "I'm sorry. What did you say?"

" 'Tis of little consequence." He gave a theatrical sigh. "Ah, if only I had met you first, and had the power to put such a light in those lovely eyes of yours."

"I . . . I don't know what you mean," Mirella stammered. Oh, dear, he must have seen her watching Jason!

"Mirella, I'm no fool," Troy said, his voice lowered to avoid being heard by anyone else. "I've seen the way you and my brother look at one another. Yet there is an animosity betwixt the two of you, and I cannot help but wonder at its source."

Her fan fluttered furiously, and she averted her eyes, gazing at the forest green waistcoat that covered his chest. "Sir, you are mistaken. Jason and I treat one another with simple cousinly courtesy."

"There's no need to pretend around me, Mirella. You're no more related to the Fletchers than King George is." Strong fingers firmly pushed away her fan, then lifted her chin until she was forced to meet his sympathetic eyes. "Tell me now, is that not the truth?"

Mirella caught her lip between small white teeth. He was right. It was no use trying to bluff him, for he had seen through her masquerade. For a moment, she wished that she could have met this brother first. Troy would have treated her with kindness and respect. Yet despite his charm and attractiveness, he failed to stir her desires the way Jason did.

"How did you guess?" she whispered, oddly relieved to erase the lie between them at last.

Troy shrugged as he released her chin. " 'Twas simple. My grandparents were from England, but they were merely poor farmers who came to Virginia and managed to pull themselves up in society. You, though, were born a lady, and could be no relation of theirs." He smiled rather grimly. "And besides, the very fact of your beauty makes me suspect my brother's motivation. So tell me, what is the quarrel between you and Jase? Has he made unchaste advances

271

toward you?"

"Oh, nay, 'tis nothing like that . . . really it isn't," Mirella hastened to say. Under no circumstances could she reveal to Troy the details of her first meeting with Jason, or her subsequent loss of virtue. And heaven forbid that anyone should guess that she longed for him still!

"Are you certain?"

"Truly."

Troy's brow was furrowed with suspicion, though he finally gave a resigned nod. "I must take you at your word, then. But will you at least promise to come to me if I can help you in any way?"

"Of course, though there's no need for concern." Mirella touched him on the arm, her lips curved in a reassuring smile. "And thank you, Troy. You're a good friend."

Watching them from across the room, Jason clenched his teeth in rage. Though he managed to maintain a cool exterior and to continue discussing politics with a neighboring planter, inside he was seething with frustration.

Damn this obsession he had for Mirella! It was ridiculous to feel a surge of jealousy every time he saw her with Troy. She was only a schemer, like so many women. Ever since she'd found out how wealthy the Fletchers were, she had lost no time in showering her attentions on Troy. Doubtless she thought Troy was the more gullible of the two brothers, and therefore a more likely marital prospect.

He trained his eyes on the spindly man standing in front of him, trying to keep his mind on their conversation. Yet Mirella's image continued to float through his consciousness. His bewitchment made little sense, he argued to himself. Certainly she was comely, but then so were many of the other unmarried women here. What quality was there in Mirella which caused him to yearn for her alone?

Glancing at her through the milling crowd, he noted that Troy was no longer with her. Now she was flirting and laughing with another man. By damn, you're acting like a lovesick calf! Jason railed at himself in disgust.

He had to get out of here before he made a fool of himself. Muttering a polite excuse to his companion, he pivoted sharply and shouldered his way through the assemblage to exit the drawing room.

Unbeknownst to Jason, his departure had been observed by a pair of almond-shaped eyes. Samantha was standing against the white wall, her pink mouth frozen into a smile as the fat man in front of her droned on about the workings of his vast estate. She cast a disparaging look at his massive body, at his protruding belly which threatened to pop the gold buttons of his waistcoat. Were it not for the need to hedge her bets, she would have sneered in the pig's face.

'Tisn't fair! she wailed silently. Why should she have to pretend an interest in a boring, pear-shaped excuse for a man when she really wanted Jason Fletcher?

If only her father had had the initiative and intelligence to build his land into a profitable holding, like the other men in this room, she wouldn't be in her present dilemma! But William Hyatt was lazy, following the tradition set by his father before him. Hence, his plantation gradually had become more and more run-down over the course of time, and it was now barely large enough to qualify his only child for entry into this elite segment of Virginia society.

Impatiently, Samantha tapped a slippered foot on the plush Turkish rug, murmuring an absent-minded comment to her companion. Mayhap she shouldn't have wasted so many years chasing after Jason. But if it were only wealth and social acceptance for which she was searching, she could have gotten that from a number of men, including the overblown swine standing before her, a man who was enthralled because a beautiful woman was paying him some attention.

But, oh, how she wanted Jason!

Her loins began to throb with excitement as she recalled that night many weeks earlier when they had made love. They hadn't shared a bed since, though she had made a point of visiting him often, using all of her wiles to entice him.

Samantha felt a flicker of fear. She was twenty-seven already, and with the meagerness of her dowry, her marital prospects diminished with each passing year. Daily she bathed her face in a concoction of barley water and balm of Gilead, yet that precaution thus far had failed to prevent a network of fine wrinkles from developing. Once she lost her looks, there would be nothing left. She concealed a shudder of disgust at the possibility of being forced to wed a man like the dreary creature beside her . . . to feel his pudgy hands kneading her breasts and his fat lips kissing her. . . .

Unaware of her thoughts her companion reached into his pocket for a silver snuffbox, then inhaled a pinch of the pulverized tobacco, sneezing into a lacy handkerchief until his nose turned red.

It simply isn't fair, Samantha thought again, watching his actions in disgust.

Turning ice-blue eyes across the crowded drawing room, she threw an angry glance at the black-haired woman who had become such a thorn in her side. Jason's cousin, indeed! It was likely that this prim and proper miss had concocted a blood connection in order to worm her way into his household, and now she was trying to entice him into marriage by playing the demure virgin.

Samantha had seen the coy way Mirella pretended not to notice the hungry looks Jason sent her. Oh yes, time and time again she had observed him mooning over that sugar-sweet girl—this very evening in fact! Whatever did he see in Mirella?. Why, she didn't even have the fashion sense to powder her hair!

A wave of intense jealousy and hatred washed over Samantha. If it weren't for Mirella, she would have a better chance at attracting Jason. The desperate straits she was in stemmed from the sly scheming of that coal-haired witch! Mirella was leading Jason down the garden path, as easily as if he'd had a tether tied around his neck.

Well, that wouldn't last much longer, Samantha vowed. Somehow she would have to devise a way to get rid of her competition.

And she would have to do something soon, before it was too late.

* * *

Mirella thanked the blushing youth who had been her partner for the minuet. Politely extracting her fingers from his sweaty grasp, she excused herself and slipped away through the throng of guests. She waved her fan over her hot face. The slight breeze she created helped to relieve the humid discomfort of the night.

These Virginians were friendly people, she mused, strolling to the open front doors for a breath of fresh air. Over the past few hours, she had experienced no lack of dance partners, though Jason hadn't been among them. She stifled a ripple of longing, staring fiercely into the darkness outside. Now why was she wasting time thinking of him?

Mirella pivoted, intending to rejoin the party, but the prospect of returning to the crowded drawing room held little appeal. Instead she headed for the library, hoping that it might be a bit quieter and cooler there.

On entering the book-lined room, she saw that an oak desk had been pushed back against the wall to create space for several small tables. Here, men and women alike were gathered around playing whist, the cards in their hands illuminated by the tapers which flickered at each corner of the tables.

Mirella grimaced as she saw the piles of coins glinting in the candlelight. What induced these otherwise upstanding people to gamble? Women as well as men lost prodigious sums this way. It was like a fever, this urge to wager one's fortune on the luck of the draw. If she'd had but a fraction of the wealth her father had lost at that worthless pursuit, she wouldn't have been forced to abandon her homeland and live on Jason's charity.

But as she turned to leave, her heart missed a beat. That golden brown hair and those broad shoulders were achingly familiar. It was Jason, sitting with his back to her at a table in the corner. He had discarded his burgundy coat, and when he shifted position, she could see the play of his muscles through his fine white shirt.

Suddenly he tossed down his cards, and leaned forward to rake in a pile of coins stacked in the center of the table. It was then that Mirella noticed the woman sitting at his right, for Samantha threw her arms around him, planting a congratulatory kiss on his cheek. Its natural flame color hidden beneath a liberal dousing of powder, her hair was wound in white strands atop her head. Her elaborate coiffure was adorned by wagging peacock feathers which matched the iridescent blue of her low-cut gown. A tiny black beauty patch was pasted at the corner of her mouth.

After releasing Jason, Samantha turned her head and looked straight at Mirella, a glow of satisfaction suffusing her artfully painted face.

Mirella felt as though she'd been bitten by a viper, for jealousy surged through her veins like venom. Clenching her fingers into fists, she wheeled sharply and hurried out of the library.

For the next hour, she threw herself into the gaiety of the party, dancing with one young swain after another. Mirella told herself that she didn't care whether Jason discarded her for a cheap tart, or not. Those two were meant for one another! And, after all, *she* didn't need a man to make her happy. Men couldn't be trusted, for deep down, they were only concerned with drinking, gambling, and lusting.

Yet no matter how hard she tried, she couldn't purge Jason's image from her mind. Finally, after one more dance, she slipped out the back door.

After the stifling warmth inside, the fresh air felt wonderful. Overhead, the leaves of an oak tree whispered in the breeze. A three-quarter moon shed a silver sheen over a stand of blooming crape myrtles.

Close to the house, there were a few guests walking about. Spurred by a desire to be alone, Mirella roamed farther and farther away, until hers were the only feet crunching on the narrow path of crushed shells.

Her restless slippers carried her to the formal gardens. She strolled aimlessly along the deserted walks, breathing in the sweet fragrance of roses. In the distance, the sounds of music and laughter drifted to her ears. Concentrating on the beauty of the night, she felt the tension inside her slowly begin to ease.

At the far end of the garden was a maze of well-clipped boxwoods, their smell strong in the air. Intrigued, Mirella wandered inside it, the dark walls of the hedges rising high around her. The shadowed path twisted and turned, enticing her deeper and deeper into its web. Finally she arrived at the center of the maze, where a small hexagonal summerhouse sat, surrounded by neat beds of marigolds and daylilies. Its white latticed sides gleamed in the moonlight and the cool darkness within seemed to beckon her. Strangely drawn, Mirella stepped toward the structure.

She was about to mount the short stairs leading inside when a sudden, almost imperceptible movement caught her eye. Her head shot up, her startled gaze riveting to the man now filling the doorway of the gazebo, his rugged features bathed in the pearlescent glow of the moon as he stared down at her without speaking.

She gasped, the tiny sound breaking the stillness. It was Jason.

Chapter Fifteen

"Don't run away."

Jason's deep voice froze Mirella in midturn. Her head jerked around as she stared up at him warily, fighting the instinct which urged her to flee as fast as her feet could carry her.

A sleepy bird in a nearby tree chirped once. Then all Mirella could hear was the blood pounding in her ears. Should she humiliate herself by fleeing or stand her ground and show Jason how little he meant to her? Pride won. She had no desire to reveal just how much she feared being alone with him.

She squared her shoulders and swung back to face him. "I wasn't running. I merely didn't wish to intrude."

"You weren't intruding. As a matter of fact, I've been wanting to speak to you, and now is as good a time as any." His expression giving no hint of his thoughts, Jason extended a hand to her. "Will you come inside and sit with me for a moment?"

Mirella hesitated. Enter that shadowed bower with the man whose touch she craved? Madness! But

Jason no longer wanted her, she reminded herself, so there was no need to worry about disgracing herself again.

Nibbling on her lower lip, she reached up and slipped her hand into his. The fingers grasping hers were strong and warm, and drew her up the steps with gentle pressure.

The air inside was perfumed with the scent of some vine flower which trailed over the outside of the lattice. A wooden bench circled the perimeter of the gazebo, and Mirella sat down on it, her petticoats rustling as she nervously arranged her skirts. For the first time, it occurred to her to wonder what it was Jason had to say. Suddenly her blood ran cold. Perhaps he had decided that since she refused to become his mistress, it was time she left his house for good. Or worse, maybe he wished to announce his impending betrothal to Samantha. She wasn't certain which alternative was the more distressing.

She glanced at him, fidgeting with the fan loosely looped to her wrist by a violet ribbon. Jason had seated himself a few feet away, and was staring into the gloom in front of him, his elbows resting on his knees, his hands clasped before him. Though most of the interior lay deep in shadow, the angle of the moonlight falling through the lattice behind him cast a checkerboard of ebony and alabaster over his face.

Jason turned his head toward her. "I've been wanting to tell you what a fine job you've done with my sister," he said, his voice somewhat gruff. "At first I was skeptical of your methods, but now I can see that you were right. I owe you a great deal for what you've accomplished."

Mirella relaxed, his praise igniting a tiny glow of pleasure inside her. "Pandora and I have become friends. 'Tis a pleasure, not a hardship, to teach her the skills she needs to learn."

He gave a self-derisive laugh. " 'Twould seem that after just a few short weeks, you've grown closer to her than I, her own brother. It's become a habit for me to treat her harshly, and I cannot blame her if she hates me for it."

"She loves you, Jason, I've told you so before." She leaned toward him, touched by the vulnerability in his face. "All you need do is to be a little more patient with her. And don't be afraid to show her how much you care."

He ran a restless hand through his hair. "Yes, yes, you're right. 'Tis just that I've been moody of late. . . ." His words trailed off, and Mirella became aware of a sudden, strange tension emanating from him.

"Have you had business problems, then?"

Jason stared at her, his golden eyes gilded by the moonlight. "Is that what you believe?" he asked softly. "Did it never occur to you that my frustrations might arise from a different source entirely?"

The intensity of his gaze made her heart jump inside her breast. She wasn't quite certain what he meant; all she knew was that her nerves sensed danger, and she again felt an impulse to flee. It was foolhardy to remain here alone with Jason, with the sweet scent of flowers in the air, and the gazebo enclosing them in a cocoon of enchanting darkness.

"I really should be returning to the party." Abruptly Mirella rose, heading toward the silent maze

283

beyond the shadowed doorway.

"Wait."

In a flash, Jason was standing beside her, his fingers curling around her upper arm. Through the thin silk of her gown, the heat of his hand burned into her flesh. Their eyes locked, and she couldn't seem to move. The faintly musky smell of him tantalized her. She was certain that the throbbing of her heart must be audible in the quiet air.

"I've not yet danced with you tonight," he murmured. "May I?"

Mirella exhaled the breath she hadn't realized she'd been holding. "Yes . . . of course."

Again, she made a move toward the doorway, expecting him to release her so they could return to the house. But his hand held her firmly in place.

"I meant here," Jason said.

She stared at him blankly. "Dance . . . *here*? But . . . there's no music."

"Yes, there is. Listen."

Mirella turned her ear toward the house. At first she heard only the wind sighing through the trees, and a cricket rasping somewhere nearby. Then suddenly the soft strains of a minuet floated through the midnight air.

"You're right, there *is* music!" Her lips tilted in delight.

Jason smiled back. "Then shall we?"

Without waiting for her assent, he released her arm and took her hand in his. And so they began the ritual of the dance. Jason bowed as Mirella dipped into a graceful curtsey. The small floor of the gazebo limited the usual stately promenade of the minuet, but he led her in a modified version which she managed to follow without missing a step. With only their fingers touching, they executed the elegant, precise movements of the dance, guided by the sound of distant notes played in three-quarter time.

In and out of the dappled moonlight they glided, their eyes on each other. The soft tread of their feet mingled with the rustling of her gown. Mirella felt herself being drawn into the web of some magic spell from which there was no escape. Yet she had lost the desire to flee. With a faint shock, she realized that all evening she had longed for a chance to dance with Jason, to be in sole possession of his attention. A sense of danger stirred deep inside of her, but she ignored its warning. What harm could there be in indulging just this small whim?

It was a moment before she realized that the melody had ceased. They faced each other across the width of the summerhouse, and Jason's fingers remained firmly over hers. The dark, deserted garden was silent except for the rise and fall of their breathing. They might have been the only two people alive. Her heart began to pound madly. She knew it wasn't so much the contact of their hands that caused the hot throbbing in the pit of her stomach. It was his expression that held her enthralled.

At the gentle tug of his fingers, she let him draw her to him until scarcely an inch separated their bodies. Releasing her hand, Jason cradled her jaw in his warm palms, gazing deeply into her eyes. Yet he made no move to kiss her.

He hesitates because he doesn't really want you, a little voice inside her whispered. You should be glad of that. After all, by being here alone with him you take great risk.

But Mirella was helpless to stop the yearnings that washed through her. She wanted to taste his mouth once more and feel his strong arms embracing her. Her sensitive skin registered the slight roughness of his fingertips. The male scent of him enticed her further into the spell. There was something magic about the night, something that stripped her of her willpower and banished her inhibitions.

Jason stared down at Mirella, wrestling with an intense urge to tear off her clothes and make passionate love to her. He reminded himself that this was the woman who now plotted to snare his brother in the trap of holy matrimony, all because she wanted a rich husband. Why had he invited her here, knowing the hypnotic effect she had on him? Hadn't he warned her that before they next lay together, she would have to come begging on her hands and knees? Yet all he could think of was her soft female shape. Where was his strength of will?

Fool, Jason chastised himself. You know what a temptress she is. So why do you continue to stand here, wanting her as you have wanted no other woman?

But still, he couldn't bring himself to let her go. His fingers wandered over the smoothness of her cheeks. How well their bodies complemented each other! He remembered how exciting it had been to feel her writhing beneath him in passion, her lips tasting sweet, her low sounds of pleasure driving him wild. In his imagination, he saw her skin bared to his gaze . . . her moonlit breasts the milky hue of magnolia blossoms, her indigo eyes slumberous with desire as he stroked her to a frenzy of delight. . . .

God help him, he had to at least kiss her!

As Jason's head descended, Mirella found herself straining upward to meet him halfway. Her fan slipped from her wrist and fell to the floor unnoticed as she raised her hands to the white linen shirt covering his muscled chest. Their mouths met tentatively at first, then with burgeoning hunger. Her lips parted to let him taste her more deeply. When she touched her tongue to his, she felt his body tremble with need.

He did want her! The knowledge made her melt against him, her moan muffled by the demanding pressure of his mouth. In wanton desire, she pressed herself to him, threading her fingers into the thickness of his hair. She was conscious of nothing but the scent and taste and feel of him. Her blood was a pulsing river of lava that ran hottest at the joining of her thighs.

Jason traced her jawline with his mouth, trailing kisses down to her throat. Eyes closed, Mirella leaned her head back, reveling in the sensation of his warm breath on her skin. A shiver of arousal gripped her as he played with the ripe swells of her breasts exposed by her low décolletage. One calloused fingertip dipped briefly inside her gown, probing the hidden secrets within. Then abruptly he withdrew his hand.

Mirella opened her eyes, her mind drowsy with desire. Why had he stopped? Jason's face was shadowed, preventing her from reading his expression. There was a tension emanating from him that baffled her.

"I want to see all of you," he murmured, his deep voice taut with urgency.

His hand hovered over the violet ribbon lacing her bodice, yet he made no move to undo the fastening. It was almost as if he were awaiting her permission. Dear God, couldn't he *see* how much she wanted him?

"Please, Jason . . . "

"Please what?" he returned hoarsely.

Mirella swallowed hard as a glimmer of reality penetrated the fog in her brain. Why was she panting for his caresses like some cheap trollop? He sought only to use her! Yet even as she chastised herself, she was tormented by her need for him. After so many weeks of fasting, she couldn't suppress the hunger that burned deep inside of her.

"Please . . . touch me." The low, imploring whisper sounded as if it had been wrenched from her throat.

Immediately she felt his impatient fingers plucking at the confining ribbon until her bodice lay open. Brushing aside her chemise, Jason bared her breasts to his gaze. He cradled one ripe mound in his palm as his thumb gently rubbed across the taut, honeyed-rosetip.

The last feeble prickling of her conscience was buried beneath an avalanche of sensation. Jason bent and put his mouth to her nipple, suckling her and stroking her until her whole being trembled with pleasure. Her fingers wove into his hair, pressing him closer.

"Mirella . . . Mirella . . . I can't get you out of my mind . . . I want you . . . I'm burning for you. . . ."

His mouth sought hers again, his tongue parting her lips. Mirella gloried in the feel of his body, the touch of his hands. The night cloaked them in deep shadow. They kissed and caressed while slowly divesting themselves of their clothing. At last, all she wore was her cameo on a ribbon around her neck. The pile of their discarded garments cushioned her back as Jason urged her down onto the floor of the gazebo, his muscled length sprawling over her nakedness.

"You taste so sweet . . . your skin is beautiful . . . like satin." He nibbled at her earlobe, his breath hot against her flesh. "Tell me, Mirella . . . tell me again that you want me."

Her spine arched as he kissed the throbbing pulse in her throat, his chest hairs rasping against her sensitive nipples.

"Jason . . . oh, yes, Jason . . . yes . . . yes."

His face was barely visible in the faint moonglow, but Mirella imagined she saw a tenderness there which made her throat tighten. His heart beat swiftly against her breasts. In the grip of some strange emotion, she embraced him, her hands stroking the broadness of his shoulders. When he slipped his fingers between her thighs, she parted her legs in a mindless rush of desire. His caresses spiraled her higher and higher until her whole body shattered with ecstasy.

Even as the last tremor faded, he entered her, and incredibly, the rapturous sensations began to build once more. Burying her face in the moist warmth of his neck, she felt him fan the embers of her need until the fire again raged hotly through her veins, erupting in a final blaze of pulsating pleasure.

Afterward, reality was the dampness of their flesh and the musky scent of their love making. Mirella was suspended in a cobweb of contentment, floating in a fantasy of euphoria.

But this illusion was doomed to destruction.

"Jason!" a woman called from far off. "Jason, are you out here?" Distant footsteps scraped on the shell path.

Recognizing the voice, Mirella stiffened in horror. Samantha!

Muttering a succinct curse under his breath, Jason rolled off her and stood up. Mirella wriggled into a sitting position, staying out of the patch of dappled moonlight, even though she knew the maze of boxwoods hid the gazebo. Dear God, what had she done? While Jason donned his clothing with quiet haste, she grabbed her chemise with shaking fingers and covered her naked breasts.

He got down on his haunches and tenderly stroked her tousled hair. "Keep still," he murmured in her ear, so low that she had to strain to hear him. "I'll get rid of her."

After branding her mouth with a swift kiss, he surged to his feet, his movements as lithe as a panther's. The next instant he was out the door, his footsteps crunching over the path as he strode through the maze.

"So there you are, darling." Samantha's pouting words floated across the night air. "What were you doing, hiding from me?"

Jason's reply was muffled; all Mirella could make out was the deep rumble of his voice. Then his companion replied sulkily, "I know I'm a little early, but I just couldn't wait any longer. . . ." The sound of her voice trailed off as the two of them moved in the direction of the house.

Humiliation washed over Mirella in waves as the full

impact of Samantha's words hit her. So the reason Jason was out here in the first place was because he'd arranged an assignation with that . . . that trollop! And now he had gone off with her, calm as could be, as if his recent love-making had never even occurred.

Mirella groaned, mortified by the memory of what had just happened. Compared to the ecstasy that had flamed through her flesh, her body now felt as though it had turned to ice. How could she have been so foolhardy? She had begged Jason to take her! By surrendering, she had stooped to satisfy the base desires of a man who believed women were naught but amusing playthings.

Appalled, she rose to don her clothing with shaking hands. Her gown was wrinkled badly, but she was so filled with bitter shame that she scarcely noticed.

Yet Jason *had* wanted her. An unexpected yearning spurted through her veins as she recalled the endearments he had whispered to her in the heat of passion. Firmly, she repressed that renegade longing. She should have known better. All men lusted, and Jason Fletcher was no different from the rest. He only wanted to use her to indulge his own selfish pleasures.

Her mind churned relentlessly as she tugged on her amethyst dancing slippers. Only one thought stood out with crystal clarity. It was dangerous to stay around him any longer.

She had to get as far away as possible . . . and tonight, while he was preoccupied with Samantha.

Chapter Sixteen

Once the decision had been made, Mirella wasted little time questioning it. She would leave while the party was still going strong, and no one would notice her absence.

Hastening through the deserted garden, she planned feverishly. It was out of the question that she depart in the boat in which they'd arrived, for she had no knowledge of how to work the sails. Taking a carriage would be equally foolish. Not only did she lack the skill to harness the horses, but the use of such a vehicle could impede her progress when it was necessary to move as fast as possible. After all, what if she had to hurry off the road and hide? No, it was best that she make her escape on horseback.

Mirella's first impulse was to go directly to the stables and find a suitable mount. The humiliation clawing at her insides nearly made her forget all but the driving need to escape Jason. However, a flash of logic reminded her that no matter how much her churning stomach rejected the notion of eating at the moment, she would require food for her journey.

Changing direction, she veered back toward the house, where a lively tune being played by the fiddler mingled with the sounds of conversation and merriment. Pale light shed by hundreds of candles spilled out the open windows, enabling Mirella to see that the festivities were still in full progress even though it was past midnight.

Her slippers scurried over the moonlit path. It wasn't difficult to determine which of the nearby brick buildings was the kitchen, for lights flickered there, also, and as she watched, several black servants emerged from the doorway, laden with trays of food for the party.

Mirella paused in the shadows outside the structure, smoothing her wrinkled gown and tumbled hair. Assuming an expression of what she hoped was nonchalance, she stepped into the kitchen. The big room was bustling with activity as a crew of women busily prepared a late-night buffet supper. The temperature here was even hotter than it was inside the house, for the fire blazed in the massive brick hearth, and the smells of cooking meat and baking biscuits filled the air.

Mrs. MacGuire stood in the middle of the kitchen with her back to the door, directing the preparations. Preferring not to be seen by the housekeeper, Mirella quickly scanned the contents of the silver platters sitting on a nearby table. The crabmeat and oysters she rejected, for shellfish would spoil rapidly. Bypassing other equally unsuitable items, she opted for cheese, a few slices of beef, and bread still warm from the oven. Several of the servants eyed her quizzically as she snatched as much food as she could carry. But her fine clothing must have caused them to hold their tongues, for no one questioned her as she slipped back outside.

Creeping around the corner of the building, Mirella sought the deepest shadows. There, she squatted down, piling the provisions in her lap without any regard for protecting the amethyst silk of her gown. After several unsuccessful tries, she managed to tear off a hunk of her petticoat, using the stiff, lacy material as a makeshift knapsack in which to wrap the food.

Then she straightened up again and scurried through the darkness toward what she hoped was the stables, the bundle swinging from one hand. And now to take a horse without being caught by the stable-boys. Somehow, she'd have to figure out how to saddle her mount. . . .

Abruptly, she halted in dismay beneath the gently swaying branches of an oak tree. Was she to ride demurely through the wilderness on a sidesaddle, clothed in a dainty gown as if she were on her way to a tea party? That would be absurd! Jason would catch up to her in no time!

So she would have to get rid of these long skirts, but where would she get her hands on more suitable garments? Suddenly Mirella smiled, remembering where Pandora had gotten her male garb. Why, the laundry, of course! The question was, where was it located?

Silent as a wraith, she slipped from shadow to shadow, making her way past the well-lit house. A few guests strolled the lawn there, and she had no desire to be seen by them. Up ahead through the darkness loomed a one-story brick building. Mirella tried the door, but the knob rattled uselessly in her hand. Peering into a window, she discerned the murky shapes of a desk, chairs, and bookshelves. The plantation office. It was a shame the place was locked, for she might have found money there with which to buy passage to somewhere far away. Troy, she knew, would not begrudge her a few coins.

For a moment, she longed to ask Troy for help. But she feared that in doing so, she would turn brother against brother. It was best that she simply vanish from their lives.

Resolutely, Mirella wheeled around and continued down the path. A hundred yards ahead was another building, and this time, when she rotated the knob, the door glided open on well-oiled hinges. Quietly, she stole inside, seeing her way with eyes already adjusted to the darkness. Success! she thought, looking around the room. Moonlight streamed in the uncurtained windows, onto piles of clothing and the other accouterments of the plantation laundry.

After tossing her package of food onto a nearby table, she located a stack of freshly washed male garments. She tore off her gown and petticoats, hesitating over her chemise and drawers. The loose undergarments would bunch uncomfortably, she decided, sliding them off. Swiftly, she donned a homespun shirt and a pair of breeches which looked her size. Though the garb was a bit snug, she was too anxious to be particular. Snatching up her sack, she headed out the door, pausing first to make certain no one was about.

A soft melody from the direction of the house

drifted through the warm night air. As Mirella neared the stables, the faint fiddle music competed with a thin, lively tune played on a reed flute. There were people close by! Heart pounding, her bundle of food clutched to her breasts, she crept toward the source of the sound, careful to keep within the safety of the shadows.

When she reached the barn, she stopped, hiding behind a large rain barrel that stood at the corner of the building. Slowly she raised her head to peer over the top of the keg, expecting at any moment that someone would challenge her presence.

Some twenty feet away, in the flickering light of several scattered lanterns, was a group of black stable-boys and drivers. A few were perched on a fence, smoking their corncob pipes, while others were engaged in some sort of game involving the tossing of stones. A boy sitting at the back of the gathering played the tune that sweetened the air.

Nibbling on her lower lip, Mirella gauged the distance to the open stable doors. How was she to sneak inside without being seen, not to mention lead out a saddled horse? To make matters worse, a lighted lantern hung over the entryway, destroying any chance of slipping inside under the cover of darkness. There was no tale she could think of that would explain her male garb, or her desire to ride out alone in the middle of the night.

Mirella felt a brief rush of despair, then the answer that struck her was so obvious that she almost laughed aloud. *Fool!* she scolded herself. Of course, there had to be a back entrance.

Reversing direction, she hugged the wall of the barn

as she tiptoed away from the group of men. When she reached the fence, she bent to slip between the horizontal slats. Feeling something catch at her breeches, she stifled a yelp and whipped her head around, expecting to see a human shape looming over her. But she had only caught her clothing on a nail sticking out from the fencepost. Chiding herself for her nervousness, Mirella extricated her breeches and stepped into the grassy pasture behind the barn.

The double doors at the back of the stables were shut, though the latch was unlocked. Stealthily, she eased one side open. The hinges suddenly gave a loud squeak which resounded like a gunshot in her ears. She froze in fear, certain that someone would come running, crying out, *Thief, thief!*

But the reed flute continued without pause, and the hum of distant conversation still rose and fell.

Taking a deep breath to calm her racing heart, Mirella carefully pushed the door wide open. The barn was dim inside, the air ripe with the scents of horse droppings and hay. Only the lantern swinging from a hook over the front entrance far ahead cast light sufficient for her to make her way without stumbling.

Her fingers clenching the small bundle of food, she began searching the row of stalls for a likely mount. She found what she was looking for almost immediately, as a stallion stuck his dark head out to nuzzle her hand, his brown velvet eyes blinking in sleepy curiosity. He exhibited no signs of nervousness as she cautiously unlatched the stall door.

Crooning to him softly, Mirella slipped inside to examine him more closely. She ran a hand over his

298

well-groomed coat, smiling at the way he nudged her with his head for attention. Obligingly, she stroked his neck. He possessed precisely the qualities she was seeking: calm and friendly, yet with long legs and a powerful body which would be useful in making good her escape.

Now all she needed was a saddle and bridle. Quietly relatching the half-door, Mirella left her sack of food on the floor outside the stall and went to find the tack room. To her dismay, it was located at the front of the stables, just to the right of the flickering lantern. Through the open barn doors she could see the group of servants sitting outside.

Taking a deep breath for courage, Mirella inched her way forward, staying as deeply in shadow as possible. She kept her eyes trained on the gathering of men, and prepared herself to run if any of them spotted her. Finally, she slipped safely into the tack room. Heaving a sigh of relief, she inhaled the rich fragrance of fine-tooled leather.

Mirella strained her eyes to peer through the gloomy interior until she spied a row of saddles against one wall. Carefully stepping across the dark room, she bent to pick one up. It weighed far more than she'd expected. As she struggled to heft it up, she felt something scurry across her feet. A mouse!

Mirella let out a half-choked screech of surprise, and dropped the saddle, which landed on the dirt floor with a thump.

Outside, the reed flute stopped abruptly as a man called out, "Hey, y'all hear that?"

Another voice accused grimly, "Somebody messin' around in the tack room. If it be that scamp Ezra again, he gonna get a thrashing he won't never forget."

Mirella looked wildly about for a hiding place as the sound of heavy footsteps approached the stable. She dove beneath a table in the corner near the door, and tried to make herself as small as possible. Heart thudding in frantic fear, she crouched on petrified limbs.

The glow of a lantern preceded the entrance of male legs encased in dark homespun pants as a man walked through the doorway. "You come out here, boy, 'cause if you don't, Ah'm gonna tan your hide."

The light shifted, and Mirella sensed that he was lifting the lamp high as he peered around the cluttered room. She held her breath, praying that he wouldn't turn and look beneath the table behind him.

But she realized her hopes were doomed to be dashed, for his feet were slowly inching around in her direction as he searched the shadowed recesses.

Suddenly, there was a brief scuffle in the far corner, and then a gray cat leaped into the circle of light, a wriggling mouse clenched in his jaws. Paying no heed to the servant, he marched out of the room, his striped tail lifted in pride at the success of his hunt.

The man gave a deep chuckle. "Well, Ezra, you sure lucky it weren't you." Still laughing, he strode back outside, his booming voice relating the tale to his comrades.

Mirella relaxed her tensed muscles. By the heavens, that had been a close call! She could well imagine Jason's fury were he to discover her attempt at flight. What had happened between them this evening had renewed her conviction that he wanted her as his

300

mistress. And judging by his behavior in England, he would keep her under lock and key if she failed to comply with his wishes.

Yet she knew deep down that he wouldn't have to use force to make her yield to him again. A wave of shame washed over her as she recalled her wanton response to his love-making. Precisely why she must leave, she told herself in fierce anger. She would not be branded a scarlet woman!

Waiting until the thin notes of the reed flute again began to play, Mirella crept out from her hiding place beneath the table. She couldn't take any more chances of being discovered, she decided. Another unexplained noise, and the men outside would realize that the cat wasn't the cause. Therefore, it was too great a risk to lug a saddle out of here. Besides, she had a sneaking suspicion that it would be well nigh impossible for her to heave the heavy saddle onto the stallion's back. So she would have to make do without, and hope that riding bareback wasn't too difficult a skill to master.

Grabbing a bridle that hung from a nail on the wall, Mirella stole out of the tack room, being careful to stay within the shadows. She tiptoed down to the back of the stables, breathing easily only when she entered the stallion's stall. He nickered softly in greeting, nudging her hand.

"Hello, old boy," she whispered, stroking his neck. "You and I are going for a ride. Would you like that?"

He took the bit easily between his teeth, eying her with a placid expression as she slipped the leather harness over his head and ears. Now what was she forgetting? Her bundle of food, she remembered. Fetching it from outside the stall, Mirella managed to tie the sack to her shirttail, leaving her hands free.

Then she led the horse out into the open air, moving slowly to muffle the sound of his hooves. Beside the door was a water trough, on which she climbed, balancing on the edge as she threw her leg over the stallion's back. Clutching the reins tightly in her sweating palms, she gave a light slap of the leather strips to urge him forward. Obediently, he began picking his way across the moonlit pasture behind the barn.

A soft breeze tossed a strand of hair across her face. She brushed it aside impatiently, resisting the urge to break into a gallop and quickly reach the sanctuary of trees in the distance. Though she felt vulnerable out here in the open, she couldn't risk someone hearing the thunder of hoofbeats.

At least riding bareback wasn't going to be as difficult as she had anticipated, Mirella thought in relief. The horse responded easily to the guidance of the reins and the pressure of her legs. It felt odd to wear breeches, she mused, but odder still to ride astride like this. Though she had ridden often back home in England, she had always used a sidesaddle, her long, heavy skirts arranged in a ladylike fashion. Now she realized what she had been missing. The sense of freedom she felt was exhilarating.

Finally she reached the fringes of the forest. The shadows were deep here, with only an occasional moonbeam thrusting through the whispering leaves. An owl hooted somewhere nearby. Mirella felt a shiver of apprehension as she peered into the darkened woods. What manner of wild creatures lurked here? Wolves, panthers, and bears, Jason had told her, and of course, savage Indians. What could be easier prey than a lone woman without even a knife with which to defend herself?

Slapping at a mosquito, she forced herself to get a firm grip on her fears. It would accomplish little to work herself into a state of panic. And, after all, she assured herself, it was likely that Jason had exaggerated in order to keep her and Pandora close to home. It might be dangerous to travel alone through the wilderness much farther to the west, but certainly not in this civilized portion of Virginia, where large plantations abounded.

Keeping that brave thought uppermost in her mind, Mirella guided her mount onward. Her plan was to skirt the edge of the trees, looping around the plantation outbuildings while aiming for the road that would carry her southwest toward Williamsburg. Her progress was slow, for she was afraid the stallion might trip in the darkness on an exposed root.

Finally, she emerged onto the long drive that led from the house and bisected the road. Pulling on the reins to halt the horse, Mirella stared toward the mansion which was barely visible in the distance, its windows glowing with faint candlelight. A pang of sadness seized her. No more would she laugh with Pandora and Troy . . . nor would she see Emma's baby born . . . and never again would she and Jason make love. Her heart suddenly felt as if it had been wrenched in two. Was it possible that she was beginning to care for him?

Never! Mirella told herself fiercely. She was glad to

be ridding herself of that accursed devil! Her fingers lifted to surround the cameo hanging above her breasts on its narrow ribbon. She had all that mattered in the world right here with her. And there was no one she could depend on but herself.

Swallowing the lump in her throat, she slapped the reins, at the same time applying a light pressure with her knee to turn her mount away from the house. He cantered down the dirt-packed drive, carrying her onto the narrow road that led to Williamsburg.

With studied determination, Mirella focused her thoughts on the long journey ahead. It was a good forty or more miles to the city, a distance she should be able to cover by the following afternoon. Then she would have to find a ferry to carry her across the James, since Williamsburg lay on the other side of the river. Once she arrived, she hoped to find a job of some sort and earn the fare she would need to travel to a distant colony. It was unthinkable that she return to England, not since the law might be searching for her in connection with the stabbing of Sir Harry.

Her worst fear was that Jason would track down her easily. After all, wouldn't he expect her to head straight for the largest center of population in Virginia? It was distressing that she knew of nowhere else to hide.

Mirella was a quarter-mile down the road when she abruptly reined the horse to a halt. Perhaps there was another option, one that had slipped her mind until now. Hadn't Pandora made mention of a nearby trading post by the name of Richmond? The girl had said it was but twenty miles away, and that was much closer than the capital city.

She smiled into the darkness. Going to Richmond, farther into the wilderness, would be the last thing Jason would expect of her. Especially if she made doubly certain of convincing him that she had fled to Williamsburg. By the time he realized she hadn't, her tracks would be too cold for him to follow.

With one hand, she reached up to untie the violet ribbon that trailed down the back of her tangled hair. The white miniature roses which had graced her curls had long since vanished, likely having fallen out back in the gazebo.

Yanking the ribbon free, Mirella urged the stallion over to the side of the road and looped the slender satin strand through the branches of a bush, where it would be seen easily by any passing rider. Then she turned the horse in the opposite direction. Urging him into a canter, she quickly retraced her route, deciding that since Richmond lay upriver, she would take this road which, she presumed, paralleled the James.

Mirella rode as fast as she dared on the dirt surface. The only illumination came from the winking fireflies and the pale moonlight sifting through the trees. She passed fields of tobacco interspersed with wide stretches of virgin forest, where crude wooden bridges provided passage over the numerous creeks. It wasn't long before the adrenaline spurring her onward began to wear off, and a bone-deep exhaustion gripped her body. But she refused to stop and rest, reminding herself that she needed to put as much distance as possible between herself and Jason.

She saw no one during the long, dark hours. Her eyelids grew heavier and heavier, the rocking motion of the horse lulling her senses.

Something skittered through the underbrush. Mirella jerked upright, aware that she had been dozing. Behind her, the first light of dawn was beginning to filter through the trees. To her dismay, she realized that over the course of the night, the road had become little more than a bridle path. She frowned, trying to gauge how far she had come. Perhaps this wasn't the way to Richmond after all. Her weary mind had trouble sorting through the problem, and she decided to take a quick break to refresh herself.

No sooner had Mirella guided her mount onto a barely visible track leading deep into the trees than the sound of approaching hoofbeats banished her sleepiness. From behind the shelter of a clump of bushes, she watched as a rough-looking man on horseback rode by. He was dressed in buckskins.

It was dangerous to remain on the road in plain view of any passing stranger. Not only was there the threat of someone challenging her, but if she were seen, Jason might discover where she was headed. So now what?

Her stomach grumbled a protest as she tried to decide what to do. Dismounting beside a small stream, she sat down on a log and opened her knapsack to nibble on a piece of meat and bread, pondering her situation as she ate. Perhaps she should head northwest through the woods. Eventually, she ought to hit the James, which she could then follow to

Richmond. It was the only plan she could think of.

Mirella rose and brushed off her breeches, walking to the stream to quench her thirst. Her hair tumbled over her shoulders, dipping into the water and making her aware of its disheveled state. Quickly she twisted the black strands into a long braid down her back and tied the end with a strip torn from her knapsack. Looking down at herself, she couldn't help grinning. What a sight she was, in her tight boy's clothing and fancy amethyst dancing slippers!

The stallion was cropping the sweet grasses along the bank. He was quite a beauty, she noted, admiring the way the early morning sun shone on his mahogany coat. She was no expert in judging horseflesh, but surely he was worth a good deal of money. Perhaps she could get a good price for him in Richmond.

Feeling considerably more cheerful, Mirella guided him over to a fallen log and clambered onto his back. Then she headed the horse onto the path that led northwest.

The trail twisted and turned through the trees, the terrain becoming hilly in places. For hours, her horse plodded along the narrow track as weariness again slowly settled into Mirella's body. More than once, she found herself dozing off. She took only a short break for the noon meal, finishing the last of her meager rations. Perspiration dampened her shirt as the day grew hotter. The sun burned down through the leaves, steadily dipping lower and lower in the western sky.

Mirella began to feel apprehensive. How many miles had she covered since she had last seen signs of civilization? And shouldn't she have reached the river by now? Perhaps Pandora had been mistaken about the distance to Richmond.

She felt a sudden, prickling sensation along her spine, as if she were being watched. Turning, she scanned the forest, but saw nothing unusual. Don't be so silly, she scolded herself. 'Tis just your overactive imagination.

But the feeling of being stalked persisted over the next hour. Dusk was falling when she reluctantly decided that she was going to have to find a suitable spot to stop for the night.

Up ahead, she spied a stream running through a dense thicket of trees. That would be a good place. She slapped the reins, impatient to rest her aching muscles.

The stallion grew skittish as they neared the water. Mirella had but an instant to wonder at the cause when a loud, inhuman scream rent the air. Her mount reared and plunged, throwing her to the hard ground as he tore off into the underbrush.

Stunned, she started to pull herself into a sitting position . . . only to find herself staring into a pair of yellow eyes near a bush a few yards away. She gasped in horror. The huge, catlike beast must be a panther!

In her petrified state, everything seemed to happen in slow motion. She saw his tawny brown tail swish lazily, as if he considered her but little challenge. Then his powerful muscles bunched in preparation to spring.

A cry of pure terror tore from Mirella's mouth. The panther leaped. Then abruptly he contorted in mid-air, and his body thumped to the earth and lay still, so close to her that she could faintly sense the heat of his flesh.

The realization that the animal was dead did not penetrate her raw shock for a moment. An arrow quivered in its throat, dark blood trickling from the fatal wound to stain the grass beneath the beast.

Mirella's hands trembled as she raised them to her face, scarcely able to believe that she was alive. Dear God, she had almost been ripped to bits! If someone hadn't come along . . .

Her heart catapulted in her breast as she focused on the feathered shaft protruding from the animal's body. That was not the weapon of a white man.

A new surge of horror choked her, and she twisted around.

Behind her towered a dark-skinned savage, clad in a loincloth and moccasins, his face daubed with red and yellow paint. She screamed as he clamped his hands on her arms and hauled her roughly to her feet so that she stared straight into his alien black eyes.

Chapter Seventeen

"Pandora!" Seeing his sister in front of the house chatting with one of the departing guests, Jason stuck his head out the open window. "Will you please come in here when you're through?"

The girl nodded and waved, then swung back around to continue her conversation. Jason peered into the midmorning sunshine, leaning a white-shirted shoulder against the window frame as he idly watched the congestion of carriages and horses lining the drive. Most of the guests who'd attended the party last night were just now leaving, having slept at Troy's rather than travel many miles through the darkness to their homes.

He felt a restless urge to get back to his own plantation, where he and Mirella could be alone together without the eagle eyes of society watching them. A sense of satisfaction glowed deep within him as he recalled her passionate response to his love-making. By damn, she had been eager for him! This time, she couldn't argue that he had taken advantage of her. She had begged him to touch her.

And it meant that she had given up on Troy. Undoubtedly she had enjoyed the power of pitting brother against brother, but finally had tired of the game. Now she would be more agreeable to becoming his mistress.

The problem was, where had Mirella disappeared to this morning? It was odd that he hadn't been able to find her anywhere. Come to think of it, he hadn't seen her since the previous night. When he had returned to the gazebo later, after getting rid of Samantha, Mirella had been gone. Jason shrugged off a twinge of worry. Likely, she had gone up to bed early, then this morning had wandered away on a walk. Pandora would know where to find her.

Damn it, what was taking his sister so long? he wondered impatiently. But even as he watched, the girl waved good-bye to her friend and ran into the house. A few moments later, she entered the library, self-consciously smoothing back a strand of honey-colored hair that had slipped out of her chignon.

"Good morning, Jason," she said, a little shyly. "Did you want me for something?"

Jason bit back his eagerness to find out where Mirella was. Thoughtfully he studied the uncertainty in his sister's posture as she hovered in the doorway. Mirella might be right. Perhaps Pandora avoided him not because she hated him but because she was afraid of displeasing him.

Jason left the window to approach her. "Yes, but first, I neglected to mention last night how lovely you looked at the party. You put all the other girls to shame."

A wistful expression softened her silver-green eyes.

312

"Do you really think so?"

"Of course, I do." Smiling, he reached out and touched her cheek. "I'm proud to have a sister like you."

Pandora glowed with pleasure. "Oh, Jason, I'm so glad to hear you say that." She hesitated, then threw her arms around him.

He hugged her back, aware of the depth of his feelings for her. He was ashamed that he so seldom took the time to show her how much he cared. When she let him go, the happiness on her face was reflected on his own.

"Don't you ever forget that I love you," he warned with a grin, "no matter how gruff I am sometimes."

"Sometimes!" Pandora scoffed, wrinkling her nose. "Of late, you've been grumpy all the time!"

Jason winced inwardly, though he knew his sister only meant to tease him. "Then I promise to improve in the future," he said briskly, "Now 'tis time we headed home. That's why I called you in here, to see if you knew where Mirella had disappeared to."

"I have no idea. I haven't seen her since the party last night."

He frowned. "Not even when you went to bed?"

Pandora shook her head in denial. "Nay, but then she might have slept in one of the other bedchambers. Would you like me to go upstairs and check?"

"If you wouldn't mind."

"Of course not." The girl pivoted and left to do his bidding.

The sensation of apprehension which Jason had felt earlier returned to plague him. He stood in the center of the library, hands on his hips. Was it possible

313

something had happened to Mirella? She might have wandered off into the woods and been attacked by a wild animal, or perhaps fallen and broken an ankle. His anxiety grew the more he thought about it. At this very moment, she could be praying that someone would discover her absence and come looking for her.

He couldn't just stand around here and twiddle his thumbs, not if there was even the remotest chance that Mirella might be hurt . . . or worse. Refusing to let himself contemplate the most gruesome possibilities, he strode out of the room, intending to search the grounds for her.

But as he rounded the doorframe, he ran smack into Troy.

"Whoa, hold up," his brother said, his face worried. "I need to talk to you, Jase."

"I'm sorry, but it'll have to wait."

Impatiently he attempted to shoulder past, but Troy restrained him. "This is important, Jase. Trojan's been stolen."

"What?"

Taking advantage of Jason's surprise, Troy prodded him inside the library and closed the double doors. "I just came from the stables. Plato said that when he went to feed the horses this morning, he found Trojan's stall door unlatched and one of the back barn doors wide open. Somebody snuck in last night and took my most valuable racehorse!"

Jason's attention was riveted to his brother. He didn't want to believe the startling suspicion that had just occurred to him. "Are you certain Plato isn't just covering up for his own carelessness? Maybe he left the doors open, and is afraid to admit it."

314

"Hell, no," Troy replied, his expression morose as he sank into a leather wingback chair. "I'd trust Plato with my life. And besides, he and the other slaves heard somebody rustling around in the tack room sometime after midnight. They saw a cat, and assumed the noise was just a cat going after a mouse."

"Was anything missing there?"

"Yes, a bridle."

"And you're certain one of the guests didn't mistake Trojan for his own mount, and ride him home early this morning?"

"Be realistic, Jase. There isn't a horse as fine as Trojan anywhere in this colony. No one would be fool enough to do a thing like that."

Jason knew his brother spoke the truth, yet he had to pursue every possibility before he faced the probable cause of Trojan's disappearance. Mirella. It was too much of a coincidence that both of them had vanished at the same time. But why would Mirella steal away in the middle of the night? A sinking feeling seized him. Had he been wrong once again about her willingness to become his mistress? So wrong that she had fled rather than admit to her desire for him?

"Jase, I can tell you've thought of something," Troy observed sharply. "Do you have a suspicion as to who stole my horse?"

Restlessly Jason paced the Turkish rug. He knew he owed his brother an explanation, yet he felt a childish reluctance to speak, as if not uttering his theory aloud would render it false.

"Well?" Troy prompted.

Jason took a deep breath, then looked at his brother

315

and growled, "Mirella is missing."

Troy stared, his head tilted in puzzlement. "What do you mean, missing? She spent the night upstairs with the other women, didn't she?"

"I don't—"

The library doors suddenly burst open, and Pandora rushed inside. "Jason, no one remembers seeing Mirella upstairs last night or this morning! Where do you suppose she could be?"

Troy looked from his sister to his brother, then he surged out of his chair. "What the hell is going on here, Jase? First Trojan's missing, and now Mirella! Don't try to tell me *she* took my horse!"

The combination of worry and guilt he felt made Jason lose his temper. "That's precisely what I do think," he snapped. "But don't get yourself all worked up because I intend to find her. You'll get your precious stallion back!"

Jason pivoted to stride out of the room, but Troy seized him by the shoulders. "Hold it, brother. First I want to know what you did to that poor girl to make her leave here in the middle of the night!"

"Mirella ran away?" Pandora asked in bewilderment.

"Get out of here, Pandora," Jason barked.

"But I just want to know—"

"Sir?" All eyes turned to the doorway, where Mrs. MacGuire hovered. "May I have a moment of your time?"

"Later, Mac," Troy said impatiently.

The housekeeper pursed her thin lips at the nickname but stood her ground. "Sir, I need to speak to you before all the guests leave."

"All right, all right, but this had better be important."

Mrs. MacGuire stepped into the library, reaching into the pocket of her apron. "One of the gardeners just brought this to me. I thought you might wish to find its owner before everyone departs." She handed Troy a folded fan of mother-of-pearl and painted vellum, which Jason recognized as belonging to Mirella.

Troy's eyes narrowed. "Where was it found?" he demanded sharply.

"In the gazebo, I believe."

"Thank you, Mac. You've been more help than you could ever imagine."

"You're welcome, sir." Her spine erect, the housekeeper walked out of the room.

"That's Mirella's fan," Pandora said. "What was it doing in the gazebo?"

"Out, little sister," Troy ordered grimly. "I want to talk to Jason alone."

"But I—"

"No more arguments." Her brother propelled her into the hall, shutting the double doors. Then he wheeled toward Jason, his expression tight with fury. "So Mirella was in the gazebo last night. I'll wager you were out there with her, weren't you?"

"That's none of your damned business!"

"Don't tell me her disappearance isn't my concern." Troy flung the fan onto a nearby table, where it skidded across the slick surface and fell to the floor. "By God, what did you do? Force yourself on her? Is that why she ran off?"

"I don't owe you any explanations. Just get out of

317

my way so I can go after her!"

"How could you treat a decent woman so cavalierly?" Troy demanded, not budging from his stance in front of the doors.

"Don't play the saint with me, Troy. You've had your share of dalliances, probably many more so than I."

"With a bored married woman or a whore, yes. But never with an innocent girl!"

"You're jealous because you want her for yourself," Jason accused, wracked by guilt that he had, indeed, caused Mirella to flee. And if something happened to her, he would never forgive himself. . . .

"Don't be absurd," his brother scoffed. "Mirella and I are only friends."

"Pardon me if I fail to believe you," Jason sneered. "Now, for God's sake, move aside so I can find her!"

Angrily he shoved his brother away and banged open the doors. Troy strode down the hall after him. "Jase, I'm coming with you."

"Suit yourself," Jason growled as he headed outside to order a horse saddled.

Mirella stumbled helplessly through the rapidly darkening forest, hauled after her captor by means of a sturdy, deerskin thong. The toe of her slipper caught on an exposed root, and she fell to her knees. Weary despair wrenched a cry from her lips as the Indian jerked on the long strip connecting their bodies, relentlessly dragging her to her feet again to resume the swift journey through the wilderness.

She shuddered, recalling her first glimpse of his savage, painted face. As the Indian had hauled her up

318

against his naked torso, she had screamed, earning herself a head-stunning slap on the cheek. With quick movements he had tied her wrists tight with one end of a cord, and had secured the other end to the loincloth string at his waist. Then he'd yanked her over to a small pack hidden behind a tree trunk. Petrified with horror, she had watched him draw forth a long, wicked-looking knife.

Certain that he was going to use the weapon on her, Mirella closed her eyes, praying for a swift, merciful death. But a tug on the thong made her eyelids snap open again. Uttering a few guttural words, the savage gestured for her to follow him. Heart pounding, too terrified to disobey, she let him tow her over to the dead panther. There, he plunged the blade into the carcass and sliced off several generous hunks of meat dripping with blood. These he wrapped in a piece of deerskin and shoved into his pack. Mirella averted her eyes as he wrenched out the arrow and then swiftly skinned the beast, tying the fur into a bloody bundle.

After slipping the bundle over one chestnut brown shoulder and his pack over the other, he sprang to his feet, picking up his longbow from the grass, and again gesturing that she was to come with him. The relentless pull of the thong on her wrists gave her little choice but to comply.

Now, as they hurried through the hilly forest, Mirella dreaded to think of what lay ahead. Where was the Indian taking her? Would he rape her? The prospect made bile rise bitterly in her throat. She tried to calm herself with the thought that at least he couldn't want her dead, else he surely would have murdered her already.

Suddenly an owl hooted somewhere nearby, and she saw her captor raise both hands to his lips, returning the haunting call. As they rounded a small outcrop, an Indian brave on horseback materialized out of the deeply shadowed trees. With a shock, Mirella realized that he rode the stallion she had stolen from Troy's stable.

The horse snorted nervously as he caught the scent of the panther skin. His rider quieted the animal with soothing words. The men softly greeted one another in their strange tongue, then they continued their trek, single file, through the woods, the horseman leading the way.

Night slowly settled over them like a black shroud. The moon had not yet risen and Mirella tripped more than once, too weary to concentrate on the darkened path before her. She was forced to maintain a swift pace, her cameo thudding against her breasts.

Finally, when she was about to drop with exhaustion, they rounded a bend in the trail to see a fire glowing in a small clearing just ahead. Two young Indian women and a copper-skinned boy of about five stood near the flames, staring at Mirella as the party approached.

Mirella couldn't help gaping back in shock at the scantiness of the women's garb. Each wore only a deerskin skirt extending to midthigh, their naked breasts displayed openly. Strings of shell beads adorned their arms and necks.

The small boy snuck forward, curiosity evident in his wide, coal-dark eyes. Mirella gasped as he suddenly reached up and jabbed a finger into her soft breast, as if reassuring himself that she was female

320

despite her male attire.

A sharp word from one of the men sent the child scurrying as the women returned to their task of preparing supper. The brave on horseback dismounted and led the stallion a short distance away, fastening the reins to a bush. Meanwhile, Mirella's captor untied the thong from his loincloth and attached it to a stake, which he pounded securely into the ground so that she was tethered like a dog.

Too weak to protest, Mirella sagged to the grass, her body aching with fatigue. Her feet throbbed, her dainty slippers having provided scant protection against the hard trail. The length of the cord enabled her to ease her tired back against a nearby tree trunk. Half-dazed, she watched the activities around the campfire.

The smell of barbecuing meat soon filled the air. Shortly thereafter, the men squatted near the flames to eat, dipping their spoonlike utensils into the cooking vessels, and spearing hunks of meat with their knives. Mirella's mouth watered as she realized how long it had been since her noon meal.

When the men were through, one of the women approached Mirella, smiling tentatively. She set down two small clay dishes and proceeded to untie Mirella's wrists. Then she returned to the fire.

Mirella flexed her numb fingers and eagerly reached for the food. The charred meat in the first container tasted wonderful, though it was a little tough and stringy, and she tried not to dwell on the irony that it came from the panther who had nearly had *her* for *his* dinner. Lifting the other vessel, she found a mushy corn cereal the consistency of cooked oatmeal, which she ate with a large, ladlelike spoon.

No sooner had she finished than the woman scurried back to collect the empty dishes, and the tall brave who had captured her came striding over. Mirella stared up in alarm at his near-naked body, the fear that had been lulled by her meal rushing back in full force. She swallowed hard. Was she to finally discover the reason he had abducted her?

Clamping his hands on her arms, the Indian hoisted her to her feet. Then he gave her a push in the direction of the dark woods beyond the light of the fire.

Mirella stumbled ahead of him, her feet scuffling through the underbrush. Her captor made no sound as he walked, though she could feel his presence behind her.

A short distance from the campsite, his fingers squeezed her shoulder to bring her to an abrupt halt. Heart pounding with dread, she pivoted slowly, realizing that she was free to run. But common sense told her that in her weakened condition, there was no chance of escaping the hard, muscled savage who stood before her. And perhaps it was cowardly, but she didn't want to die. Wasn't it better to endure this rape in the hopes of later being rescued?

The man said something in his unfamiliar language, then to her astonishment, instead of ripping off her clothing, he turned on his heel and walked to a nearby tree, casually leaning a shoulder against it. Mirella stood stupefied as he waved at her impatiently. What did he want her to do? Surely not leave, after he had taken the trouble to hold her prisoner!

Suddenly he levered away from the tree and dipped

into a squatting position, speaking to her and gesturing.

Her face flamed as she finally caught his meaning. He wanted her to relieve herself!

Though comforted by the realization that he meant her no harm, Mirella was tense with embarrassment. She couldn't obey his request in front of him! Yet the thought of the long hours of night ahead gave her little choice. Mortified, she hid behind a leafy bush and hastily attended to her needs.

When she was finished, the man prodded her back to camp, where he retied her hands behind her back and then to the tether, this time also binding her feet. Then, as Mirella sat against a tree trunk, he suddenly drew forth his knife.

Her eyes widened in fear. Now what did he intend?

Firelight glinted on the long, sharp weapon as he brought it closer to her throat. Her heart pumped frantically. She felt the heat of his body, smelled his musty male scent as he leaned over her, his painted face and glittering dark eyes looking more savage than ever before.

There was an abrupt *snick* as the blade sliced the violet ribbon around her neck. His fingers nimbly seized her cameo before it could drop inside her shirt. Clutching the prize in his hand, he strode away to rejoin the others.

Mirella's relief at being spared her life was swiftly replaced by a helpless anger. He had stolen her most precious possession, the last thing she had that had belonged to her mother! And there was nothing she could do about it!

A short while later, one of the women brought her a

thin grass mat, indicating that Mirella was to sleep on it. Bound so uncomfortably, Mirella was certain that she wouldn't be able to rest at all. She lay still, listening as the small band of Indians settled themselves for the night. Bullfrogs croaked in the distance and a cricket sang for a moment, then fell silent.

She wriggled her bonds in the faint hope that she might be able to free herself while the others were asleep. But she was tied securely. Even were she to escape, she thought in despair, the Indians would track her down like an animal.

Oh, dear God, why had she ever run away from Jason? Her reasons seemed trivial in comparison to the predicament she was now in. She admitted in her heart that she longed to see him again, to feel his protective arms around her. But what if he never bothered to come looking for her?

Slowly her churning thoughts subsided, and her eyelids grew heavy. Her lack of sleep the previous night coupled with the exhausting events of the day gradually eased her into a dreamless slumber.

Mirella spent the next few days adjusting to her captivity. During the day, her feet were untied, though she was forced to stay within the area dictated by the length of her tether. The men spent the long hours hunting, bringing back meat which the women dried by placing it on sticks above a banked fire.

Mirella was thankful that except for the binding of her hands, the Indians treated her with a measure of respect. And though she was alert for a chance to escape, none came. To alleviate her boredom, she tried to keep her mind occupied by observing the women as they gathered wood, ground corn into a powder to make the mushy cereal they ate with every meal, and stretched out the panther skin before scraping it clean. The small boy stalked squirrels and birds at the edge of the camp, pretending to be a great hunter.

But it was difficult for Mirella to stop worrying. Bitterly she chastised herself. Why had she been so brilliant as to leave her ribbon alongside the road to Williamsburg? Of course, Jason would assume she had headed east. He would never think of looking west . . . until it was too late.

Still, hour after hour she watched and waited.

And then her hopes were dashed when, at dawn on the third day of her imprisonment, the band packed up their meager belongings and headed west. They traveled single file, her captor in the lead pulling Mirella by her tether, two women and the child following, and finally, the brave on horseback.

Mirella trudged along the narrow path, her mind wracked with despair. The deeper into the wilderness they traveled, the less chance there would be of rescue. She forced herself to admit that even if Jason realized she might have gone to Richmond, no one had seen her, and by now her trail was so cold that he'd never track her down.

She swallowed hard, wondering what the Indians intended for her. They surely wouldn't keep her tied up forever. Where were they taking her? Was she to be a slave once they reached wherever they were headed?

The terrain became hillier, and they passed through stands of oak, hickory, and walnut trees. It was sundown when they finally stopped beside a stream to set up camp for the night. Mirella's tether was staked to the ground, and the stallion was let loose to crop the wild grasses.

Dusk deepened into full darkness. Suddenly the two braves rose, so silently that Mirella only caught a glimpse of them as they melted into the gloom at the edge of the encampment. The women calmly sat cross-legged, though one now held a knife in her hand and the other pulled the small boy to her side.

Mirella's heart beat faster. She jumped when the horse gave a soft whinny. Why had the men disappeared? Clouds scudded across the moon, making it impossible for her to see beyond the circle of light cast by the fire.

The minutes dragged by. Then abruptly the Indians returned, a third man walking between them.

She gasped, her eyes widening as she identified the newcomer.

Chapter Eighteen

For an instant, Mirella thought her eyes were playing cruel tricks on her. But as he strode into the firelight, there was no mistaking that tall, muscled body encased in the fringed buckskins of a frontiersman.

With a joyful cry, she struggled to her feet. "Jason!"

He glanced sharply at her, his intent golden eyes glowing like dark amber. Then, to her bewilderment, he turned away without saying a word. One of the women scurried forward to take Pegasus, leading away the cream-colored horse by its reins. The three men seated themselves near the flames, the Indian women and child squatting nearby. Jason said something to the men in their strange tongue, then one of the braves reached into a pouch dangling from his loincloth and drew forth a large clay pipe.

His expression grave, he stuffed the bowl with dried tobacco while the other warrior reached into the fire and brought forth a burning faggot to light the pipe. The first Indian took three puffs, then handed the pipe to Jason, who did likewise. The pungent smell of smoke drifted through the night air.

Mirella watched the ceremony in growing confusion. Why was Jason ignoring her? He had managed to track her down, yet he seemed indifferent to her welfare. Why had he bothered to travel so far and through such rugged territory if he didn't care what happened to her?

Her question was answered as the men rose and walked over to the horses. Jason stroked the neck of the mahogany stallion she had stolen from Troy's stable. As he crouched to examine the animal's long legs, the reason for his coming struck Mirella with the force of an earthquake.

All he wanted was to get his brother's horse back!

Rage bubbled like hot lava through her insides. That despicable cur! How dare he value an animal above her! Mirella's fingers balled into fists as she sank back down on the hard ground. She had never dreamed that any civilized human being, even a man, could be so contemptible!

In helpless anger, she jerked at the thong binding her wrists. It only went to prove how foolish it was to depend on a man. By all that was holy, she would escape the Indians herself, and then pay Jason back for his cruelty if it took the rest of her life!

Fuming in silence, Mirella watched as the men returned to the fire. For a long time, they sat talking, passing around a flask which Jason had produced from his saddlebag.

Her mouth tightened with repressed fury. Jason must be haggling over the amount of the stallion's ransom. The cold-hearted bastard! He hadn't even had the courtesy to greet her, let alone determine if she'd been treated well!

Yet, as the evening wore on, she became aware of an ache deep inside which nipped at the edge of her wrath. Mirella stared fiercely into the fire. She couldn't be hurt by Jason's callousness, she assured herself. After all, he meant less than nothing to her. No, this odd feeling of pain was simply the result of her acute disappointment at losing a prime chance at freedom.

The exhaustion of the day's trek began to catch up with her, and her eyelids grew heavy. One of the women silently brought her a mat, and retied Mirella's hands behind her back. Mirella lay down, intending to stay awake in the hope that she'd have a chance to vent her anger on Jason. But even her churning emotions couldn't keep her eyes from closing.

Something tugged her from the depths of slumber. Mirella woke abruptly, experiencing an instant of confusion before reorienting herself to her surroundings. She was lying on her side, staring into the glowing embers of the fire. The camp was quiet, only the night sounds of insects and bullfrogs disturbing the stillness.

Then, behind her back, she felt someone's fingers pluck at the thong lashing her wrists together. With a choked cry, she twisted to see who was there.

"You!" she sputtered. Bitter resentment welled in her throat as she discerned Jason's features through the gloom.

"Stop wriggling," he whispered. "You're making it difficult for me to see what I'm doing."

"I don't need your help!" In blind fury, she tried to jerk away from him, but he caught her easily.

"Hush," he hissed back. "I'm only untying you. You'll sleep easier without these bonds."

"Don't pretend to care about my comfort," she snapped. Yet despite the humiliation of accepting his help, she realized it was almost worth anything to have her hands freed. Swallowing the bile in her throat, she lay unmoving until she felt the deerskin thong drop away from her wrists.

Mirella sat up, flexing her stiff fingers. It must have been a belated sense of guilt that had made him unbind her, she reflected bitterly. Jason was crouched on one knee in front of her. His face was shadowed, the last light of the dying embers too dim to reveal his expression. The heady male scent of him wafted across the inches separating them, and desire suddenly throbbed deep within her belly. In violent vexation, she crushed this traitorous reaction.

"You've done your good Samaritan deed," she spat sarcastically. "I'll thank you now to leave me in peace."

"Sssh," he murmured. "Keep your voice down, else you'll have the Indians slitting our throats for disturbing their rest." He jerked his head to the small group sleeping at the opposite edge of the camp.

"Go away!" she hissed.

"So that you can try to escape?" He gave a low chuckle. "Nay, Mirella. The terms of your release include me sleeping right here beside you."

For the first time, she noticed the opened bedroll that lay next to her mat. Her temper seethed. Did the cad think to seduce her again before he abandoned her for good?

"Oh, no, you're not!" Her tone was subdued but forceful.

"And how do you plan on stopping me?"

Mirella glared, all too aware of his superior strength. "I'll sleep by the Indians rather than stay here with you." She sprang up, bending to grab her mat.

Suddenly his hands circled her waist, bringing her down onto her knees with a jolt. "Listen, Mirella, and listen good," he growled in a voice no louder than a whisper. "The Indians expect me to claim what's mine, and by damn, that's precisely what I intend to do!"

She fought his grip without success. "You don't own me!"

"In their eyes, I do. I told them you were my runaway wife."

"You *what*!" Astonishment overcame her rage, and she ceased struggling.

"The Indians respect the fact that a wife belongs with her husband. Even so, I had to pay a hefty price in copper and silver beads to get you back." His hands tightened briefly about her waist, then he let her go. "By God, you're lucky I don't beat you, as they would a disobedient woman."

Mirella stared, too awash with relief to take offense. "You mean you're taking me home with you?"

He gave a short laugh. "Of course. Why else would I have come all this way?"

"But I thought . . . the horse . . ."

"You thought I only came for Troy's stallion?" Wry amusement laced his voice. "Mirella, when I walked into camp I had to act as if I were disinterested in you. The Indians would have lost respect for me had I shown any emotion."

"Oh," she said lamely. Jason made it all sound so logical that Mirella felt foolish for having misconstrued the situation. He might have his faults, but at least he wasn't so cruel as to leave her here.

She couldn't help wondering what emotion he had felt on finding her. A joyous, heart-soaring relief? With deliberate cynicism, she crushed that unexpectedly wistful thought. Jason believed that he owned her, and therefore he had felt only satisfaction at retrieving his property.

"Lie down and get some sleep," he ordered softly. "We leave here at dawn."

Mirella obeyed, lowering herself to the mat and onto her side, her back to Jason. There was a slight rustling as he settled himself on the bedroll beside her, then all was silent except for the sounds of the night. Her heart beat fast as she waited for him to reach for her. She didn't want him to . . . and yet she did. But nothing happened.

Frowning, she gazed into the crimson ashes of the fire. She knew she ought to despise Jason for thinking of her as a possession, but instead she felt a peculiar warmth. Thank God he had found her! Though the Indians hadn't harmed her, she shuddered to contemplate spending the remainder of her life in their captivity. The comforting knowledge that Jason was near gave her a feeling of security. Slowly her tense muscles relaxed, and for the first time since she had left Troy's, she slept the untroubled slumber of a babe.

Jason awoke to see a faint lifting of the darkness in the eastern sky. He felt more rested than he had in a long while. The fear, the worry, the guilt that had crowded his thoughts since that morning five endless days ago, when he had discovered Mirella's disappearance, had finally eased.

He recalled his frantic ride with Troy toward Williamsburg, after they had found her ribbon entangled in a bush alongside the road. But by the time they had ridden as far as his plantation, nearly halfway to the capital city, it had occurred to him that she might have deliberately misled them. That suspicion had grown stronger the more he'd pondered it. Troy had argued that a woman would never go into the wilderness, but Jason had been unable to shake the nagging feeling that Mirella had tricked them. Experience had told him that when she was determined, she had the courage to dare just about anything. Leaving his brother to press on to Williamsburg, he'd stopped at his plantation for a fresh mount and then retraced his route.

For three grueling days he'd systematically explored every trail leading off the main road west of Troy's land, looking for some sign of Mirella's passage. He'd begun to doubt his intuition, yet he'd refused to give up. And then, on the afternoon of the third day, he was elated to find a scrap of a woman's petticoat alongside a stream, a few crumbs of bread still clinging to it. A short distance away, he spied a horse's hoofprint alongside the trail.

Following the tracks, at dusk he came upon another stream, where he discovered the remains of a panther, its bones half-picked clean by scavengers.

His heart jumped, and he dismounted to examine the scene. *Dear Lord, had Mirella encountered that wildcat?*

There were deep hoofprints nearby which led off into the trampled underbrush, sure signs of a horse bolting. Jason's first impulse was to pursue the animal in the hope that Mirella had managed to stay on him. But closer scrutiny of the panther's carcass deepened his feeling of dread. The bits of hide which still clung to the bones appeared to have been cut by a knife. Someone had skinned the beast. Indians?

Checking the surrounding area, he found a flattened spot of grass which might be where Mirella had fallen off Trojan. Fear clutched his chest. If she had been unseated when the stallion had reared and there were Indians nearby, she might well have been captured.

Worry made him press on, though the light was fading and he was dead tired. Leading Pegasus by the reins, Jason followed a barely visible path through the forest. Finally he found what he was looking for, a half-blurred woman's footprint. Mirella had come this way; he knew it in his heart.

With renewed determination, he continued to track her until full darkness forced him to stop for the night. He was hard on her trail again at the first light of dawn. Several hours later, he came upon the remains of an Indian camp. The ashes of the fire, still warm to his touch, told him that she was not far ahead of him.

Jason hurried westward along the trail, praying that her captors were of a friendly tribe. If she had fallen into the wrong hands . . . He tried not to imagine the possibilities.

Night fell before he finally saw the glimmer of a fire just ahead. Dismounting, he debated what to do. Wait and try to rescue Mirella while the Indians slept? Or walk peaceably into their camp and risk being taken prisoner himself? He decided to make his way closer, to better gauge the situation.

Jason had been turning to tie his horse's reins to a bush when two Indian braves had suddenly materialized out of the shadowed trees. The arrows in their longbows had pointed directly at him.

He'd frozen, cursing his carelessness. Though he had taken pains to be quiet, he must have made some noise that had alerted them to his presence. His eyes flashed to the musket that was fastened to his bedroll. No help there. An arrow would pierce his heart before he could take half a step toward the firearm.

He wracked his brain for the words of Algonquian dialect which he had learned several years before, when he and Troy had traveled through western Virginia in search of land to purchase. Slowly he dropped the reins to hold out his empty hands, palms up.

"Greetings," he said in the language he hoped they understood. "I come to you in peace."

For a long moment, he held his breath as the braves stared menacingly at him through the darkness. If they were of an Iroquois tribe, he knew he was doomed to a slow death by torture.

Then the older-looking of the two Indians lowered his bow and replied in the same tongue, "Why do you come here?"

Jason felt a rush of relief. The Algonquians were more likely to be friendly than other tribes. Quickly he explained that he was searching for his runaway wife and the horse she had stolen from him.

Without expression, the Indian told him to accompany them. Leading his mount, Jason walked between the two of them toward the camp. As they approached, he could discern by the glow of the fire Mirella's dejected figure sitting at the edge of the clearing, her hands tied and tethered to a stake in the ground. She appeared to be unharmed. A tidal wave of emotion threatened to overpower his self-restraint, but he fought the urge to rush over and draw her into a fierce embrace. He couldn't jeopardize her safety, he reminded himself. It would be a delicate enough problem to negotiate her release, one which he would have to handle with great care.

Now, in the growing light of the dawn, Jason turned and propped himself on his elbow as he studied the woman lying beside him. Mirella was curled up in a ball, on her side, facing away from him. Tenderness washed through him, and he smiled. In her boy's clothing, she looked like an urchin. But beneath her dirty breeches, her hips had a delectably feminine curve, and her bottom a delightful roundness. Her silky black hair was wound into a long, disheveled braid.

By damn, he should be furious at her for running away! But despite her bedraggled condition, all he could think of was that he wanted her more than he had ever wanted any other woman. Dare he hope that this encounter with the Indians had given her time to think, to realize how foolish she was for leaving him?

Across the camp, he saw the Indians stirring. He reached out and gently shook Mirella's shoulder. "Wake up, love," he murmured.

She rolled over onto her back and murmured a protest. Her indigo eyes focused on him with a sleepy sensuality that made Jason catch his breath. Unable to resist, he touched her soft cheek, and she pressed her face against his fingers like greedy kitten. Emotion welled deep inside of him. It was an odd, giddy sensation, something more than mere desire, something akin to affection and admiration. . . .

Abruptly Mirella stiffened, the warmth vanishing from her expression as she sat up. Averting her eyes, she smoothed back the sides of her hair.

"Jason . . . good morning."

There was a distance in her voice that made the tender feeling inside him curdle and die. Well, that answered his question. How could he have ever hoped she might be ready to admit that she wanted him?

" 'Tis time for us to go," Jason announced coolly.

Gathering up his bedroll, he strode away without giving her another glance. Yet even as he saddled his horse, he was conscious of her petite figure moving about the campsite, helping the women prepare the morning meal. By damn, why was he acting like such a besotted fool?

Exercising rigorous control over his wayward thoughts, he steadfastly refused to even look at her as they partook of the food offered to them by the Indians. It wasn't until they were about to depart that he glanced at her. She was standing rather hesitantly beside Trojan, fidgeting with the reins as she watched the Indians gather their belongings.

337

Thinking that she needed aid in mounting, Jason impatiently walked over to her. "Come, Mirella, I'll give you a hand up."

But she didn't move, biting her lip as she continued to stare at the Indians.

"Mirella?" he prompted in a sharper tone.

"Hmm?" This time her head jerked around in surprise.

Her eyes were shiny with tears, deep gray-blue pools like the sea at dusk. With her lips parted and the wild ebony wisps of hair floating about her face, she might have been a faerie startled in the forest.

His heart melted. Her obvious distress was disconcerting, and all he knew was that he wanted to ease her hurt. "What's wrong?" he inquired gruffly.

Sable lashes fluttered down to conceal her tears. Mirella pivoted and began to stroke Trojan's neck, so that her expression was hidden. " 'Tis nothing."

Jason hesitated, then stepped forward to turn her chin toward him. "But you're weeping," he said gently. "Will you not tell me why?"

Uncertainty flickered across her features. Finally she sighed and said, " 'Tis just that . . . the Indian who captured me took away my cameo. 'Twas the only thing I had left of my mother's."

"You should have told me so earlier. I'll get it back for you."

But her fingers curled around his arm before he could walk away. "Jason, no. You've already done enough for me. I couldn't ask you to do more."

He touched her face, wanting to say that he would give her the sun and the moon and the stars if only he could. Yet such a rash declaration would reveal the

338

power she had over him, and any woman would use that knowledge to twist a man around her little finger.

"Don't argue," he said firmly.

Before she could object further, he spun on his heel and headed across the clearing. It took a bit of bargaining, but the brave finally exchanged the cameo for another string of the copper beads which Jason knew the Indians prized highly. The numerous strands which he had traded for Mirella's release already adorned the man's neck and arms.

Mirella gratefully accepted the cameo, tying the violet ribbon around her neck. Then Jason helped her up on Trojan, and they headed east down the trail in the opposite direction from the Indians. They rode all morning, making only a brief stop for the noon meal.

The day was fair and warm, but in late afternoon, ominous black thunderclouds began to roll over the sky. Jason reined Pegasus to a halt.

"We'd best find shelter," he told Mirella. "There's a storm brewing."

He located a hillock with an outcrop that would provide a modicum of protection. Amidst flashes of lightning and the first fat raindrops, they settled themselves with their backs to the low rocky wall, huddled inside his bedroll to keep the worst of the shower off their heads. Mirella was perched crossways on his saddle, while Jason sat on a flat stone beside her.

He silently cursed the weather that had forced them into such intimate quarters. Her nearness was enough to test the willpower of a saint. The tight shirt and breeches she wore outlined every delicious curve of her body. If he didn't distract himself, he was going to pull her into his arms and kiss her, despite her protests.

"Why in God's holy name did you run blindly into the wilderness?"

Mirella's eyes narrowed at his clipped words. " 'Twas hardly blind," she said defensively. "I was heading for Richmond."

"Richmond!" He couldn't resist a hoot of mocking laughter. "By damn, woman, you were some forty miles west of there when I found you."

The look on her face told him that she failed to appreciate his mirth. "The Indians captured me, else I would arrived there just fine." She tightened her lips, staring out into the pouring rain.

Jason decided it was politic to withhold the comment that obviously she had already been lost when she had encountered the panther. The old Indian trail she had been following led more west than north. It was plain to see that she had misjudged the direction, bypassing the small settlement at the headwater of the James by many miles. Yet he wasn't about to let her off lightly. She had given him the scare of his life, and he didn't particularly enjoy recalling the gut-wrenching emotions he had felt during that long search.

"You know, you're damned fortunate I found you when I did. The Indians were planning to sell you as a whore to the chief of a tribe west of the mountains."

He'd wanted to shock her, and by her widened eyes, it was clear that he had succeeded. "I . . . I'd wondered. . . ," she stammered.

"I hope your captivity gave you plenty of time to ponder your foolishness," he added ruthlessly. " 'Tis sheer luck you were abducted by a band which was

340

reasonably friendly. If they'd been Iroquois they might have raped you, then scalped you and left you for dead."

He saw her swallow hard. "Scalped?"

In no-nonsense terms, he described the process by which certain tribes removed the hair and skin from the skull of an enemy—often while the victim was still alive. Mirella's horrified expression told him that his words had had the desired effect.

Scowling, he turned away to stare out into the storm. Lightning cut a jagged path across the black sky. The horses stood stoically under the pelting rain, only the trees overhead lending them any protection from the elements.

After a while, Jason glanced back at Mirella. She was hugging her knees, gazing out, as he had been, at the drenched landscape. Seeing her shiver, he felt a sudden surge of remorse. She looked like a forlorn waif who had just been soundly chastised. Yet he'd had to scare her, to make absolutely certain that she never took such an awful risk again.

In an effort at peacemaking, Jason rummaged in his saddlebag and pulled forth a flask. Uncorking it, he thrust the vessel into her hand.

"Here, drink some of this," he growled.

She looked askance at the bottle. "What is it?"

"Brandy. 'Twill warm your insides."

Mirella put the flask to her mouth and took a swallow. Instantly she coughed, her hand on her heaving bosom. "What sort of rotgut . . . is this?" she choked out.

"Madam, you offend me!" he teased, rubbing her back until the spasm passed. "Why, 'tis the finest

341

peach brandy distilled on my plantation. You'll get used to it if you take smaller sips."

Cautiously, she uptilted the flask again. This time, the liquor appeared to go down more easily. She passed the vessel back to Jason and he took a healthy swig, fancying that he could taste her lips on the rim. A warmth that had nothing to do with the effect of the spirits washed through him.

Trying to divert his attention, Jason concentrated on the rumble of thunder and the patter of drops on the sodden bedroll. The storm was lessening in severity, and if they were lucky, the sun would come out just long enough to dry off the worst of the wetness before they camped for the night.

Yet he couldn't tear his mind away from the slender woman at his side. Brandy burned down his throat as he took another drink. Dammit, why was Mirella so mule-headed about becoming his mistress? If that night in the gazebo was any indication, her passion ran as deep as his. Didn't she realize that he would shower her with gifts and fulfill all of her physical needs? What more could a woman want?

The more he drank, the more illogical her behavior seemed. Why had she run from all he had to offer her? Glancing at her, he saw that she was gazing pensively into the drizzle, oblivious to his scrutiny. They were so close that he could feel the warmth of her rose-petal skin. His loins filled with heat as he recalled her wild response to his love-making. His fingers itched to touch her, to rouse her to the driving desire he knew lurked beneath that cool beauty.

Rather unsteadily, he set down the flask, placing his hand over the small fist resting on the pommel of the saddle and lacing his fingers through hers.

Mirella stared first at their entwined hands, then at his face. A flash of lightning illuminated her eyes, big and smoky with a delicate fringe of black lashes—and so utterly lovely. Slowly his fingers slid up her sleeve, hesitated, then touched her breast. When he cupped the ripe swell, he heard her catch her breath, yet it was not a sound of protest. Emboldened, Jason stroked the tight bud which was clearly visible through the rain-dampened cloth. He bent toward her, his heart pounding.

"Sweet . . . Mirella," he whispered. He felt the soft sigh of her breath an instant before their mouths met. Folding her in his arms, he drank in her brandy taste. His gut throbbed with emotion, and his bloodstream was a pulsing river of passion. Oh, God, how he wanted this woman! No one else could satisfy the ache in him. Beneath his hands he felt her yielding flesh . . . and then suddenly she was stiffening.

"Nay, Jason . . . we cannot do this!" The saddle leather creaked as Mirella wrenched herself from his embrace, crossing her arms protectively over her breasts.

Jason was stunned by a lash of angry frustration. A moment earlier, she had been as eager as he! How could she deny that?

"Dammit, Mirella, I'm tired of these games! Why can you not admit to your desire for me?"

"But I do," she moaned softly.

A disbelieving laugh tore from his throat. "Then why? Why did you stop me? Why do you refuse yourself the pleasures we can give one another?"

"Because 'tis wrong." Her voice was low but full of

343

conviction. "Oh, perhaps not for you. You are a man, and people would look the other way should you take a lover. But what of me? What if our union results in a babe? I would be forced to hang my head in shame, branded a scarlet woman."

"I would support you—"

"Money!" she scorned. "Could you buy back my honor? Or remove the stigma of bastard from our child?"

Jason scowled, fighting the guilt that was destroying the mellow influence of the brandy. "We would be discreet. And why concern yourself with things that may never happen anyway?"

Mirella surged to her feet. "That is the difference betwixt man and woman. A woman thinks ahead to the consequences of her action, and to the child who would suffer for her imprudence, while a *man*"—she spat out the word like a curse—"a man thinks only of his own selfish pleasures." Turning on her heel, she stalked off through the drizzle.

Jason stared moodily at Mirella as she headed over to the horses. By damn, if she were trying to goad him into making her an offer of marriage, she could wait until doomsday! After Elizabeth, he'd had his fill of ill-tempered, peevish wives. If ever he remarried—and that day was a long way off—he'd choose a young girl who was sweet and biddable, someone he could mold as he pleased.

Still, he couldn't help feeling as if he'd been kicked in the gut. Much as it pained him to admit it, he craved Mirella's esteem. She had worked wonders with Pandora, and she had also helped with the smooth running of his household. And what had he

344

given her in return? Not even enough courtesy to consider her viewpoint. If nothing else, he owed it to her to respect her wishes.

So, if a life without love-making was what she wanted, then he would never touch her again. Never.

Morosely he searched out her petite figure. She was standing by Trojan, stroking his wet coat. Her damp, close-fitting garments clung to every feminine curve.

Well, he'd try his damnedest not to, anyway.

Chapter Nineteen

Mirella knelt before the rose bed alongside the house, inhaling the rich scent of soil. Digging her fingers into the dark earth, she hummed along with the harpsichord music that was drifting out the drawing-room window just above her. The music master was here, and Pandora was hard at her weekly lesson.

As she tugged out a weed, Mirella was aware of a deep sense of contentment. More than a month had passed since she and Jason had returned to his plantation. Home. It was odd that she now felt as if she belonged here at Elysian Fields. Her life in England and that terrifying encounter with Sir Harry seemed merely bad dreams. What was even more disturbing was that she had lost all heart for running away.

It would be so easy to stop fighting what her body craved, to surrender herself to Jason, to exist, however briefly, in a world of physical rapture. . . .

And to relinquish her pride and self-respect? Never!

The clashing needs made her heart feel like a

battleground. It was both torture and relief that Jason had ceased pressuring her to become his mistress. Ever since their confrontation the day they'd left the Indians, he had again treated her with polite remoteness, as he had before Troy's party. And so she had locked her desire for him beneath a veneer of formality. Yet, encountering him in the hall unexpectedly, seeing him laugh with Pandora at the dinner table, catching a glimpse of him in the stableyard astride Pegasus . . . those were the moments when a sharply sweet ache of regret wrenched her insides.

She sighed, recalling the nights they had camped out in the forest on their way home. For long, sleepless hours she had lain on the hard ground, knowing that Jason was near enough to touch. More than once, she had come close to bending her rigid pride. Then common sense would prevail, and she would stiffen her body against his appeal.

Oh, why could he not care for her in the way he clearly still yearned for Elizabeth?

Mirella stifled the wayward thought. So what if Jason occasionally visited his wife's grave, and hung her portrait in the hall where he would see it every day? What difference should that make?

With the back of a hand, she brushed away a strand of hair that had slipped into her eyes. Humidity hung in the afternoon air, and black thunderclouds hovered on the horizon. She prayed that the rain which had threatened for several days would hold off until the tobacco harvest was completed.

For the past week, Jason had been supervising the work in the fields from dawn until dusk, returning to the house each evening sweat-stained and weary. It was clear that he saw no disgrace in honest toil, unlike the nose-in-the-air gentlemen of England who scoffed at manual labor. More and more, she was learning that while these Virginia planters might emulate the British aristocracy in dress and manners, when it came to business matters, they brooked no idleness.

Coach wheels suddenly clattered on the drive out front. Leaning back on her knees, Mirella peered around the corner of the house. Her lips compressed in irritation as she identified the unexpected visitor. Samantha. The woman had an annoying habit of dropping by on the most flimsy of excuses, clinging to Jason like a leech, and cooing syrupy compliments into his ears. And if he objected, he kept his feelings well masked. It was enough to make a person ill!

Usually Mirella tried to fade into the background whenever Samantha was around, but today Jason was out in the fields and Pandora was in the middle of a harpsichord lesson. A deeply ingrained politeness told Mirella that she ought to at least greet their guest.

With a resigned sigh, she slapped the loose dirt off her hands and got to her feet. What a time to have to act as hostess! The humid air pasted damp, wispy curls to her nape, and the white apron covering her simple gray gown was smudged with soil and grass stains.

Walking to the front porch steps, she balefully eyed the vision in wisteria blue silk that wafted daintily out of the coach. Today Samantha wore her rich red hair unpowdered and piled high atop her head, adorned with a froth of blue and white ribbons. A cloud of cloying perfume preceded her as she minced toward the house, her wide-hooped skirts swaying over the shell path.

"Hello, Samantha," Mirella said civilly as the redhead drew nearer.

"Well, if it isn't Jason's little cousin." Frosty, almond-shaped eyes scanned Mirella's dirty apron dismissingly. "Were you making mud pies? Pray, don't let me keep you from your amusement."

"I was gardening."

"Indeed? Why, if I were in your shoes, I'd be ashamed to show my face outside. Imagine, being captured and raped by savages!" Samantha gave a delicate shudder.

Mirella held onto her temper only by exercising every ounce of her willpower. To explain her disappearance, Jason had quietly spread the tale that she'd gone for an early morning ride and had gotten lost, wandering deeper and deeper into the wilderness until she'd stumbled upon a small band of friendly Indians. Mirella appreciated his effort to protect her reputation. But Samantha refused to let the topic die, dropping a snide comment whenever possible.

Feeling it best to ignore the redhead's remark, Mirella counted to ten before speaking. "If you're looking for Jason, I'm afraid he's out in the fields. You're welcome to wait in the library, though I doubt he'll return until after sundown."

"My, don't you sound like the mistress of the house," Samantha mocked. "I fear you're suffering from delusions of grandeur, little girl. Jason may have rescued you from those dirty savages, but don't forget that you're just another piece of property to him. He'd have gone after a runaway slave the same way."

The blood drained from Mirella's cheeks. It was

350

one thing to suspect privately that Jason thought he owned her, and quite another to hear someone else flaunt it in her face. But she'd rot in hell before she showed this . . . this latter-day Lilith one iota of the humiliation she felt!

"Why, Samantha," she replied sweetly, "I do believe you're jealous! Hasn't Jason been paying you enough attention of late?" Smiling at the astonished rage on Samantha's face, Mirella turned her back and started up the porch steps.

"Don't get any foolish ideas about marrying above your station," the redhead lashed out from behind. "I'm an heiress, but what have you to offer a man of Jason's stature?"

Mirella kept walking, her pace unhurried as if Samantha's jeering words meant nothing, but pain clawed at her heart, and she was bewildered by its origin. Why should she feel torn asunder by the thought of Jason wedding someone else? After all, she had no desire to be shackled to the man for the rest of her life.

Of only one thing was she certain. Jason lusted for her body, and she must never, ever make the mistake of believing his interest in her stemmed from any other cause.

Thunder growled in the distance as Samantha watched her rival enter the house. That black-haired bitch must be trying to entice Jason to the altar with sweet smiles and a demure disposition. The question was, would he succumb? Despite the heat of the day, Samantha felt a cold prickle of fear. It wasn't common, but a wealthy man sometimes did marry a woman with little or no dowry. She herself had been hoping that the rundown state of her father's plantation wouldn't deter Jason from offering for her.

Desperation clutched at her insides, making it difficult for her to catch her breath. She couldn't lose him. She just couldn't! She wanted his money, his social position, but most of all, his body in her bed. There was no man who satisfied her as Jason did. Oh, God, if only she were younger! This morning, she'd found a gray hair amongst the red, and there was already a webbing of fine wrinkles at the corners of her eyes. It wasn't fair!

Suddenly, overcome with envy of Mirella's youth, her misery blossomed into an ugly hatred. Somehow, she had to come up with a plan to keep that coy girl from stealing the most eligible bachelor in the colony!

Samantha gnawed on her lower lip. But was it already too late for her? Were Mirella and Jason lovers?

No, they couldn't be. Though he might look at Mirella with desire, she had noticed none of the seemingly accidental touches or exchanged heartfelt glances of secret lovers. Maybe his little "cousin" was playing for broke, withholding her body as an enticement to marriage.

The corners of Samantha's mouth twisted in a sly gesture that bore only a surface resemblance to a smile. If the uppity wench were fool enough to refuse her master's advances, it was but a matter of time before Jason lost interest. And then he would return to the woman who had pleasured him for so many years.

Samantha's belly began to throb with desire. If Jason were here, she might have teased him into his bedroom, for surely he was growing bored with Mirella. She toyed with the idea of searching for him out in the fields, but rejected the notion. Away from the breezes of the river, it would be hotter, and she was loath to ruin her makeup in what might be a fruitless hunt.

She pivoted and roamed down the path toward the outbuildings with a vague destination in mind. There was a restlessness in her, a nagging dissatisfaction which she knew from experience was a result of unslaked passion. She wanted a man betwixt her thighs, to feel that rush of excitement and power as she aroused his carnal appetite.

Bypassing the laundry, Samantha peered into a brick barn, blinking as her eyes adjusted to the dimness within. To her irritation, the cavernous interior was deserted. She scowled, resting her hands on the wide panniers at her hips. She'd half-hoped to find a young buck to lure into a discreet corner, but it seemed all the able-bodied men were out working in the fields. On her father's plantation, she could relieve this fever inside her by seducing an overseer or a slave.

Luckily, she knew she needn't worry that her lovemaking would bear fruit, not since that time so long ago when she had gone to an old black woman to rid herself of the babe that had threatened to distort her figure. For an instant, Samantha was back in that dark cabin, swallowing a bitter draught from a hollowed-out gourd, hearing the chant of some primitive spell, feeling a searing pain lance her insides. But she had never regretted the experience, for it now left her free to fulfill her needs without the threat of any disgusting aftereffects.

She walked out of the barn, her skirts swishing impatiently about her sensitized thighs. Turning the corner, Samantha prowled like a she-panther searching for her next meal. The sounds of activity emanating from a small brick structure caught her attention.

She swept down the path to the building, which stood beneath the snakelike fronds of a willow tree. A blanket of heat hit her as she paused in the wide doorway. This was the smithy, and as she watched, a hulking, dark-haired white man thrust tongs holding a bit of metal into a blazing charcoal fire while a small black boy furiously worked the bellows. When the metal glowed yellow-hot, the man turned and placed it on an anvil and began striking it with a hammer, the sound of each blow ringing through the air.

Samantha stared with sharpened interest. The blacksmith wore a leather apron over his bare torso, and his back muscles bulged and gleamed with sweat. His shoulders were massive, befitting the mountain of a man that he was. Her blood heated as she wondered if unbuttoning his breeches would reveal a sex as prodigious as the rest of him.

He threw aside his hammer and plunged the tongs into a bucket of water on the dirt floor, the piece of metal hissing and steaming. Then he removed the newly formed nail from the tongs and added it to a pile on a nearby table. Stripping off his apron, he knelt to wash his face and hands.

Samantha watched in fascination as he rose, rivulets of water running down his colossal naked chest. He looked vaguely familiar. Wasn't this the indentured servant Jason had brought from England, the husband of that plain seamstress woman with whom

Mirella was friendly? Luther? No, Lucas was his name.

Eyes glittering, Samantha strolled inside as he was wiping himself with a towel. "Hello, Lucas."

The blacksmith looked up, his broad features reflecting a slow-witted astonishment at seeing a woman in his shop. "Ma'am? Be there somethin' I can do for you?"

"I would like to speak to you alone for a moment. Outside, if you please."

"Why, surely, ma'am." He took a step toward her, then stopped awkwardly and glanced down at his bare chest. "I'll be out soon's I get fixed up properlike."

"Please, don't bother." She put a hand on his arm to stop him, tipping her chin up to flash him a sultry smile. "This won't take long."

Lucas hesitated, his expression still slightly baffled. Then he nodded. "Yes, ma'am, whatever you say." He looked at his small black helper. "Be back soon, Moses."

Samantha strolled through the doorway, hearing Lucas's heavy footsteps following in her wake. Without stopping, she headed straight for the barn, aware of a hot throbbing dampness between her thighs. Lord, she could scarcely wait to feel him inside her.

They entered the big brick structure, and she tugged the doors shut behind them. The air here was cool and dim after the heat of the afternoon, and smelled of fresh-mown hay.

"What can I do for you, ma'am?" Lucas asked.

She uttered a throaty laugh. "Why, Lucas, don't you know?"

"No, ma'am," he replied, his voice mystified, his

355

head tilted in bewilderment.

What a dolt, Samantha thought impatiently. Was he so dense that he had no inkling of what she wanted? Still, what matter was his intelligence level so long as what lay within his breeches was huge and stiff?

She sauntered up to him, laying a hand on his magnificent torso. His musky man-odor was as dizzying as a whiff of opium. Her fingers threaded into the thick, wiry hairs on his chest, and began stroking his broad male nipples.

He sprang back in horror. "Ma'am! What . . . what are you doing?"

"What do you think I'm doing?"

"I . . . I don't rightly know."

He backed up, and Samantha followed, stalking him with the lazy assurance of a female beast of prey who plays with her quarry before devouring him. "Come, come, now, Lucas. Don't you want to touch me?"

She loosened the white ribbon at her bodice, pulling apart the wisteria blue fabric of her gown so that her breasts were exposed. Lucas froze, drawing in his breath with an audible gasp as his wide eyes stared at the small, creamy mounds of flesh. Then abruptly he wheeled around and ran blindly into the shadowed depths of the barn.

With a wicked smile, Samantha lifted her gown clear of her feet as she pursued him. This little game of chase was new to her, and she found it whetted her appetite.

Just ahead, she saw Lucas reach a wall piled high with hay bales, then he whirled, glancing around wildly. Swiftly, Samantha blocked off his path of escape, stopping in front of him so that he was backed into the corner. For all his size, he looked like a frightened child.

"Go away," he said, a thread of desperation in his voice.

She laughed, reaching out to stroke the thick muscles of his arm. "Why? Don't you want me?" Her hand danced down to his hard stomach, where she coyly inserted a fingertip into the waistband of his breeches.

He sucked in his breath, straining back against the wall. "Stop that . . . I'm married!"

"So? I won't tell if you won't."

Samantha leaned forward, rubbing her naked breasts against his chest. Darts of pleasure shot through her at the feel of his rough hairs on her tender skin. Her fingers began to unbutton his breeches.

"No!" He knocked her hand away, but she put it right back.

"If you don't do as I say, Lucas, I'll be forced to tell your master that you tore open my gown and tried to rape me. Why, he'll be so angry he'll throw you and your wife off his plantation."

"You're lyin'," Lucas choked out. His big hands closed tightly on her shoulders but he didn't push her away.

"Can you afford to take that chance?"

"I . . . I . . .," he stammered.

Listening to him, Samantha smiled. She had known others like him, dim-witted country yokels who were unable to think for themselves. Just a few more moments, and she would have him mindless with carnal desire, throwing her onto a nearby bed of hay and thrusting deep within her.

Her fingers slipped inside his breeches and closed around his shaft. Hot blood seared her veins as she began stroking him. With a moan, she sank to her knees in a whisper of silk, seized by a fierce lust to take him into her mouth.

"Lucas!"

A shocked female voice rang through the air. More vexed than mortified, Samantha whipped her head around to focus passion-glazed eyes on the plain-faced woman standing a few yards to the rear.

"Emma?" Lucas whispered stupidly, as if his slow brain couldn't quite sort out what was happening.

His wife uttered a chokèd cry, then she whirled and ran away, the swift patter of her footsteps fading as she disappeared out the barn door. Samantha looked up to see Lucas staring after Emma with horrified eyes.

A deep groan of animal pain tore from his lips. He shoved Samantha aside and stumbled after his wife, buttoning his breeches as he went.

"Come back here, you addlepated oaf!" Samantha surged to her feet, glaring at his departing figure, her insides seething with angry frustration.

Emma fled down the sloping lawn toward the river, scarcely able to see for the tears blinding her eyes. Her overworked lungs were seared by every breath but she failed to slow her pace, for she could think of nothing but putting as much distance as possible from the agonizing scene she had just witnessed.

Only minutes earlier, she had been hard at work in

the laundry's sewing room, humming happily as she snipped through a bolt of cotton for the baby gown she was making. By chance, she'd happened to glance through the window at the same moment Lucas was following Samantha into the barn. Emma had continued to cut out the tiny pattern on the table before her until curiosity got the better of her. When the two didn't come back out, she had lain down her shears and gone to find out what was going on.

Emma reached the riverbank and pivoted to plunge recklessly into the thick foliage that bordered the lawn. Twigs tore at her gown, but she paid them little heed. Finally, exhaustion forced her to stop in a small clearing, and she sank to her knees, panting and sobbing.

She felt as if a vital organ had been ripped from her insides, leaving a gaping hole out of which her life was seeping into the hard earth beneath her. Slumping against a tree trunk, she stared unseeing past the tangle of vines and timber to the wide expanse of river beyond.

Abruptly, shock struck her anew. Lucas with another woman! Why, *why?* Was he repelled by the tiny child that grew inside her belly? Had his love for her died?

Grief gripped her heart. God in heaven, how could she lose the man who meant more to her than anyone else in the world, her own dear baby included?

With a crashing of heavy footsteps, her husband ran into the clearing and came to an abrupt halt, his broad features twisted with worry, his dark hair in wild disarray.

"Emma, Emma . . . ," he gasped. He started

toward her, bending as if to pull her into his arms.

Anger gushed into the void of her despair. "Don't touch me!" she snapped.

He reared back as though he'd been struck. "But I made you cry, Emma! I hurt you. . . ."

"Go away," she said brutally. "I don't ever want to see you again." Averting her head, she focused on the river, though a wetness in her eyes blurred the scene.

Lucas dropped to his knees in front of her. "Don't say that! I'll die without you!"

Emma bit her lip, unable to keep from turning her gaze back to him. Despite the pain of his betrayal, she felt a sudden wrench of pity for her husband. His head was bowed, and his slumped shoulders reflected his inner agony. But it was the tears running unchecked down his cheeks that struck a chord deep inside her. Never before, not even when he'd lost all their savings at the gaming table, had she ever seen him weep.

She reached out and touched his wet face. Lucas seized her hand and planted a fervent kiss in her palm, staring at her in misery. "Don't send me away from you, Emma. Please say you won't."

But all she could force out was a stiff, "Tell me what happened."

With a ragged sigh, Lucas ran a hand through his rumpled hair. "The lady said how she needed to talk to me 'bout somethin'. But then she . . . she undid the front of her gown like a lewd woman, an' started touchin' me. Even when I ran away she come after me. I . . . I tried to stop her, but she said how she'd tell Mr. Fletcher I made her do it. I was a-feared I'd lose my place here an' wouldn't be able to feed you an' the babe, an' . . . an' so I let her . . . do what she wanted."

His tormented eyes squeezed shut for an instant. "I hurt you, Emma. I'm sorry . . . so sorry."

A surge of love banished the bleakness in Emma's soul. Though that horrifying scene was still vivid in her mind, she saw that her husband spoke the truth. She had almost forgotten how easily people took advantage of Lucas; he had been well treated and respected since their arrival in Virginia. And he'd only meant to protect her. Later, when he was not so distraught, she would have to explain to him about Samantha. Emma tightened her lips. That deceitful, selfish woman! Samantha had been well aware that her threat was a lie. It made no sense that Jason Fletcher would send them away after he'd paid for their articles of indenture.

"Oh, Lucas," she sighed, putting a hand on his bare shoulder. " 'Twasn't your fault."

"But I made you weep." His eyes were dark and wretched with shame. "Oh, Emma, I'm so slow and stupid. You should've wed somebody else. I ain't good enough for you."

Her heart melted. "You're a kind, gentle man," she said softly. "I've never wanted anyone else."

"Then . . . you won't send me away?"

She slipped her arms around his waist, laying her head on his broad chest. "Of course not. I should never have said that. 'Twas only the anger in me speaking."

Lucas gave her a fierce hug. "I never meant to hurt you . . . never." His deep voice trembled with emotion, his hand sliding between them to rest gently on the slight rounding of her stomach. "I love you and our babe."

Emma's eyes were misty with happiness. "I love you, too, Lucas, so very, very much."

Their lips met in an ardent kiss that reavowed the special closeness that had been theirs from the first moment of their meeting, so long ago. Breathing in his male scent, tasting the slight saltiness of his lips, Emma felt awash with emotion. This was her man, and no other woman could claim him! Passion tingled in her, a rich feeling of warmth that made her head spin and her heart swell with joy.

He pressed her down on the grass, his strong body positioned carefully over her delicate frame so as not to crush her. Exchanging soft words of love, they were swept up in waves of enchanting sensation, spiraling to a sweet promise of heaven on earth.

Chapter Twenty

"What do you mean, the tobacco is rotting? I thought it was all harvested."

Looking at Jason, Mirella frowned in perplexity. His dark gold hair was coated with raindrops that shimmered like crystal in the pale light shed by the candles in the entrance hall sconces. Outside, water dripped from the eaves in monotonous plops. For the past week, the weather had been damp and dreary. The storm that had threatened for so long had struck five days ago with great bursts of lightning and thunder before settling into this unceasing drizzle.

Jason stripped off his sodden cloak and handed it to Pandora. "The crop may have been cut but the leaves still need to cure. This infernal weather is preventing them from drying."

"I wish there was something we could do to help," his sister sympathized.

" 'Tis kind of you to offer," he said, walking into the hall. "But I—"

"Don't move another step in them muddy boots, y'hear?" Ophelia's scolding voice rang out as she came waddling from the back of the house as fast as her plump legs would carry her. "You just set down there and let me pull 'em off of you."

Mirella and Pandora stood to one side as Jason obediently sank onto a nearby bench and let the black woman tug off his footgear. Then Ophelia bent and began wiping away the mud that smeared the fine wooden floor, tut-tutting to herself as she shook her turbaned head.

Watching Jason, Mirella felt an unexpected wave of tenderness. His head was tipped back against the wall, and his eyes were closed. The soft glow of candlelight threw his profile into rugged relief, illuminating the lines of exhaustion etched across his face. His arms were stretched along the back of the bench so that his shirt was pulled taut over his muscled chest.

"Of all the bloody luck," he muttered, opening his eyes to stare into the shadows. "Who would have thought it would rain for five days straight? And my careless overseers failed to thin the bunches of leaves hung to dry in the barns. Now every blasted leaf has to be rehung, and quickly before the whole crop rots. The trouble is, I trust no one but myself to make certain the task is done properly."

"So you'll have to supervise all six barns?" Pandora asked. "Why, that'll take days!"

"I know," her brother said gloomily. Abruptly, his fist slammed down on his thigh. "By damn, if this rain keeps up, I'll likely lose most of the crop!"

An idea flashed into Mirella's mind. Pondering it, she paced the hall, her coral gown swishing about her feet. Then, decisively, she swiveled toward Jason.

"Why don't Pandora and I help you? With each of us taking a barn, you could be done three times as swiftly."

"Of course!" Pandora clapped her hands in excitement. "Whyever didn't I think of that?"

Jason let out a snort of impatience. "Don't be absurd. Not only do you two know naught of tobacco, but the men would never take orders from women."

"You can show us what needs to be done," Mirella argued. "And the overseers will do as you say."

But Jason looked skeptical. "You two don't realize how uncomfortable it can be to stand out there in the cold rain, your feet sinking into muck, and the stink of rotting tobacco in the air." He shook his head. " 'Tis no place for a lady."

"We're not made of sugar that a few drops of water will melt us," Pandora scoffed.

"Will you not at least try us out?" Mirella asked. "What have you to lose?"

She knew she had a point, but would Jason admit it? Scarcely breathing, she watched as he glared first at her, then at his sister. The male hands that gripped the back of the bench clenched and unclenched. Suddenly the corners of his mouth relaxed into a rueful grin.

"I must be going mad to even consider such a harebrained scheme. All right, then, you can help but only under two conditions: that the both of you work together as a team, and that you vow to dress and act like ladies."

The countryside was wreathed in tendrils of fog as they rode away from the house at dawn the next day.

The fields were ghostly pools of gray; the woods still sheltered the last lingering shadows of night. A damp chill pervaded the air and crept into Mirella's bones. She shivered, drawing her cloak tighter and her hood more securely over her hair for protection against the relentless drizzle. For an instant, she wished she were riding bareback. That brief taste of freedom when she'd escaped into the wilderness made it difficult to return to the discomfort of a sidesaddle and heavy skirts.

Yet she and Pandora had agreed to Jason's terms, and if wearing a gown instead of breeches was part of the bargain, then so be it. Looking ahead to the blond girl who rode at Jason's side, Mirella smiled. Had it not been for Pandora, she would never have known that it was sometimes expedient to dress in male garb.

A short while later they arrived at the first tobacco barn. The structure was some seventy feet in length, and constructed of rough-hewn timber. It looked much like the log cabins Mirella had seen along the river, except for the walls, which consisted of horizontal beams alternating with open slats so that air could circulate freely inside. A crew of field hands trudged single file toward the barn.

Jason swung down from Pegasus, then turned unexpectedly to Mirella. His hands slipped beneath her cloak to lift her effortlessly from the saddle. Yet when her feet touched ground, he didn't let go, but stood gazing down into her indigo eyes with an expression of naked longing. Her insides throbbed in instant response. She knew only the heat of his touch, the male scent that filled her senses, the hammering of her heart. Her knees felt like jelly. Without conscious intent, her gaze strayed to his lips, the memory of his taste as real and potent as a swallow of brandy.

But even as she began to sway toward him, the softness drained from Jason's face. Flames couldn't have induced him to jerk his hands away more abruptly than he did. Turning on his heel, he strode over to join Pandora, who was peering curiously into the barn.

You should thank God he walked away, Mirella told herself. You very nearly made a fool of yourself.

Her legs were still wobbly as she followed in his wake. The barn was crammed from floor to ceiling with tiers of tightly bunched leaves hanging upside down. A strong, putrid odor hung in the damp air. Jason pulled a bundle of tobacco from the scaffolding, untying the twine that held the stems together.

"See the moisture beaded on the surface of the plant?" He held out a broad leaf for their inspection. "That sweat is what makes the tobacco turn black and smell of rot. 'Tis my theory that if we thin the bunches, the leaves will stand a better chance of drying." Jason hesitated, looking at the women. "Are you two certain you won't return to the house and spend the day in comfort?"

"This is ever so much more interesting than being cooped up inside," Pandora vowed. Silver-green eyes twinkling, she added, "And besides, I know how you can demonstrate your gratitude for our help. You can take us along when you go to Williamsburg next month for the Assembly meeting. Don't you think 'twould be a just reward, Cousin Mirella?"

"Oh, indeed, 'twould be most generous of your brother."

"You drive a hard bargain," Jason grumbled, though the corners of his mouth twitched in amusement. "If a visit to Williamsburg pleases the both of you, then so be it."

After giving them a demonstration on how to re-hang the leaves, he remounted Pegasus to head for a barn on another part of the plantation. Mirella and Pandora joined in side by side with the field hands to begin the task of untying the bunches and thinning them.

Over the long days it took to complete the project, Mirella grew accustomed to the pungent stink that pervaded the air. A slimy rot coated her hands until they looked as putrid as the brown-black leaves of tobacco. Her back ached, and the damp weather chilled every inch of her body.

It was with great jubilation that she awoke at dawn on the fourth day to see the sun filtering through the magnolia tree outside her window. The cessation of rain meant that the tobacco would dry, and Jason wouldn't lose his crop. For a moment, it struck her as odd that the joyous relief surging inside of her went far beyond that of a mere employee. It was simply, Mirella reasoned, the hard work she had put in these past days which made the victory seem a personal one.

After all, what concern was it of hers whether or not Jason suffered financial ruin?

When Mirella first saw its graceful, tree-lined streets, Williamsburg had existed for more than half a century. Jason had told her of the town's history. In the late sixteen hundreds, two buildings, the College of William and Mary and the Bruton Parish church, had been erected on land carved out of the forest, forming the cornerstones of what was to become the capital of Britain's largest and wealthiest colony in America. Now Williamsburg had grown into a bustling town which teemed with life, especially in the fall and spring during what was known as the Public Times, when the House of Burgesses convened.

Whole families left their plantations along the James and York Rivers to stream into the small city, giving rise to a seemingly endless parade of balls, dinners, theatricals, fairs, and assemblies as everyone celebrated the end of a long season's toil. Every day, men gathered in the open Exchange behind the Capitol to conduct business and to discuss prices and politics. And for the women, it was a chance to refurbish both wardrobe and household by patronizing the milliners, wigmakers, silversmiths, shoemakers, and jewelers.

Today the mood was festive, for a steeplechase was to be held that afternoon. The open Fletcher carriage joined the throng of vehicles rattling down the sandy, rutted Duke of Gloucester Street to the race course on the outskirts of town, past the stately brick Capitol Building.

Mirella's senses delighted in the passing view. In the week since they had arrived here, she had been charmed by Williamsburg. White picket fences framed neat brick houses and gardens ablaze with fall color. Golden maple leaves blended with scarlet oak and dogwood, and red berries on the holly bushes glowed like ripe stars. Overhead, a flock of geese honked as they flew south for the winter.

Since he planned to enter Pegasus in the race, Jason had left earlier to inspect the course. In her mind's eye Mirella could still see him, sitting erect on the horse's back, his tawny hair gleaming in the sunshine. Their relationship had remained cool since he'd rescued her from the Indians, and she knew she ought to be glad of that. But the emotion that warmed her whenever she saw him continued to perplex her. She drew in a deep breath, then slowly let it out. Would she ever get over this foolish infatuation?

"That was a profound sigh. Is something bothering you, cousin?"

The deep, drawling voice that sounded so like Jason's came from the other side of the carriage. Startled, Mirella turned her gaze on Troy. She had very nearly forgotten that he and Pandora were sitting there.

Fumbling for words, she matched his friendly smile. "In truth, I was merely drawing in the crisp smell of autumn. 'Tis a fine afternoon to spend outdoors."

"Is that so?" Troy's green eyes twinkled, and Mirella had to discipline an urge to shift uncomfortably against the leather seat.

"Troy, what would you wager are Jason's chances of winning today?" Pandora asked.

Mirella was grateful for the diversion as brother and sister embarked upon a lively discussion of the contenders in the race. Their arguments were still going strong when the carriage arrived at the course and they got out to wend their way through the crush of vehicles and people.

It looked as if all of Williamsburg was there, from

silk-bedecked ladies strolling on the arms of dapper gentlemen in tricornered hats, to dirty urchins who darted in and out of the throng, engaged in a lively game of tag. The fragrances of a myriad of perfumes mingled with the scents of sweat and horses and falling leaves. Many wagers were being cast, if the snatches of conversation Mirella caught were any indication.

The weather was cool though the sun shone brightly, and she was glad for the woolen shawl that covered the shoulders of her burgundy gown. Pandora saw a friend and excused herself, slipping away. Mirella trailed along with Troy until they stopped for a moment to join the people surrounding a family of acrobatic tumblers, who performed for coins thrown into a hat. One, a boy of no more than six or seven, nimbly executed a sword dance, twirling the sharp blade so fast that Mirella's heart lodged in her throat.

When the show was over, she and Troy moved on to the oval-shaped course set up with fences and hedges over which the horses would have to jump in order to reach the finish line.

"The contenders must make the circuit thrice," he told her. "Say, there's Jase! Let's go join him."

Mirella had little choice but to follow, for Troy grabbed her hand and towed her along after him. Near the starting line, a bevy of saddled horses were tended by black grooms. Some of the animals nervously pawed the ground, while others placidly waited for the race to begin.

The sight of Jason made her quiver. Tall and handsome, his hair ruffled by the cool breeze, he might have been his mythical namesake preparing to embark upon a journey of bold adventure. She could not remember having seen such a carefree expression on his face.

She shifted her attention to his companion. The stranger was a rather large, affable-looking man in his early twenties, garbed in the finery of a wealthy planter. He wore his powdered hair tied neatly at his nape. When he saw them approach, his face broke into an engaging grin.

"Ho there, Troy! Where did you manage to snag yourself such a lovely lady?"

"This is my cousin, Mirella Weston. Mirella, meet Ben Harrison, the man who plans to give Jase a run for his money."

"Pleased to make your acquaintance, m'dear." Harrison gallantly kissed the back of Mirella's hand. Then he added, his eyes twinkling, "And I *am* going to win today."

Jason grinned. "Twenty-five pounds says you're wrong. Against Pegasus, that chestnut of yours doesn't stand a devil's chance in heaven."

Harrison gave a merry laugh. "My friend, to prove you wrong, I'll up the ante to fifty—unless of course you think it too risky to agree."

"Now how could I refuse a chance to reap such an easy profit?" Jason said, chuckling. "You have yourself a wager." The two men shook hands to seal the deal.

"If Trojan hadn't gone lame yesterday morn, I'd have bet a hundred I could beat you both by a furlong," Troy put in.

"And you'd have wasted your money," Harrison

averred. "Why, everyone knows I own the finest stallion in all of Virginia."

Mirella observed the men from a short distance away as they launched into a friendly argument of the relative merits of their mounts. Bending, she picked up a catalpa pod from the ground, and began to shred its long, slender shape. Somehow she couldn't help feeling a little sick listening to them wagering such large sums of money as unconcernedly as if they spoke of pence instead of pounds. Her father had squandered a fortune that way, and were it not for his weakness, she never would have been plunged into the desperate straits that had forced her to seek work on the waterfront of Bristol. Couldn't they see the danger in what they did?

"Why so solemn?"

Mirella looked up to see Jason beside her. The hint of concern on his face sent her senses reeling. She swallowed hard, searching for a reply amidst the turbulence in her brain. "I . . . I was just thinking," was all she could come up with.

"About your father?"

His insight was disconcerting. With a show of nonchalance, she let the remains of the catalpa pod flutter out of her fingers. "How did you guess?"

"There was something in your expression when Harrison and I were making our wager." He added, softly, so that no one around them could hear, "It made me recall what you'd told me about your father."

Mirella bit her lip, remembering her galling disappointment on discovering that the parent she had worshiped had feet of clay. Bitterly she said, "Yes, he

373

lost everything we owned, until there was naught left but the entailed estate."

"And so you now abhor all gambling. 'Tis understandable, and yet you should also realize that an occasional wager among friends can do no harm."

"Until it becomes a fever," she insisted bluntly. "And once the sickness is caught, 'tis but a short ride to total ruin."

Jason shook his head, a peculiar blend of concern and gentleness softening his sun-lit features. "Mirella, your father may have succumbed to the lure of the dice, but not everyone does. 'Tis simply a sport to most, no different from dancing or attending the theater or playing a game of whist. If done within reason, 'tis no more addicting than any other pastime. Can you not see that?"

His hand came up to stroke her cheek reassuringly. There was an almost loving quality to the gesture which made her heart ache. Belatedly Mirella recalled the folly of indulging her yearning for him, and recoiled.

"Don't touch me."

The words came out more harshly than she'd intended, but it was too late to call them back. As if struck by an arctic storm, the warmth vanished from Jason's expression and his golden eyes froze to hard chips of metal.

"As you wish."

Pivoting, he strode over to Pegasus. A few moments later, she felt Troy take hold of her arm and lead her off the turf to a place where they would have a good view of the race. Through a numb haze, she heard him chatting to her, and was aware of her own

374

distracted replies. Why did it hurt so to destroy the tenderness in Jason when it was best to keep their relationship cool? She came out of her stupor to realize that Troy was posing a question.

"What say you to a private wager between the two of us? I think Harrison has the edge, and something tells me you'd bet on Jase. So how about it?"

"I . . . I have no money."

Troy dug into his pocket and withdrew a handful of silver. "Now you do," he announced cheerfully, pouring the coins into her palm and closing her fingers around them. "We'll each bet five pounds."

"I can't accept this," Mirella protested.

She tried to return the money, but he drew back, grinning. "Oh, yes, you can. 'Tis no fun to watch the race if you haven't wagered on the outcome. Besides, when I win, you can repay me the silver, plus grant me the pleasure of a dance at the governor's ball tomorrow night."

"And if *I* should win?" she asked dryly, tempted by his teasing words.

His green eyes twinkled. "Then *I* owe *you* five pounds plus a dance. So have we a bargain?"

His good humor was infectious. Was Jason right about gambling? Was she too harsh in her condemnation of what was to most people simply a harmless game? Recklessly, she found herself nodding her agreement to Troy's wager.

Eight sleek and powerful horses edged the starting line. Mirella's eyes riveted to Jason. From astride Pegasus' back, he held the reins as the cream-colored stallion snorted and danced impatiently.

Then came the sharp retort of a pistol shot, and the

375

horses were off, hooves pounding the earth, clods of turf flying. Shading her eyes against the bright afternoon sun, Mirella saw Pegasus soar over the first fence with a beauty and an economy of movement that was unmistakable.

The horses thundered around the top bend in the track, leaping the hedges and walls that obstructed their path. It was difficult to tell who was in the lead, for running neck and neck were Jason, Harrison on his chestnut, and a black. Then suddenly, the black misjudged a fence and stumbled, his rider swiftly rolling free of the plunging hooves that followed.

Mingled groans and gasps from the spectators greeted the unfortunate competitor. Mirella's heart jumped absurdly as she picked out Jason, bent low over Pegasus' neck as he continued down the track, leading the remaining six horses and clearing the hurdles with effortless grace. The thud of galloping hooves shook the ground as the contenders streamed past the crowd for a second, then a third time to begin the final circuit that would determine the winner of the race.

Jason was ahead until the chestnut inched forward to seize the lead. The throng of spectators surged against the ribbon strung to mark the edge of the course, and Mirella found herself cheering along with them as they urged on their favorite.

Then disaster struck again.

As the bunched-up horses rounded the last oval bend before the home stretch, leaping the final hurdle, one went down in a flurry of milky legs. The sun dazzled her eyes, and for a heart-stopping instant, Mirella thought it was Pegasus. Then she blinked,

376

realizing with intense relief that a trick of light had paled the bay coat of the fallen horse to a rich cream.

On the straightaway Jason spurted into the forefront again, passing Harrison on the chestnut to shoot by the winning post with half a length to spare.

Troy seized Mirella by the waist and twirled her around. "So how does it feel to win five pounds and a dance with a handsome bachelor?"

"Wonderful!" Yet, breathless with glee, she knew it wasn't the money that caused this exuberant feeling, as if a weight had been lifted from her shoulders. In a flash of insight, she realized that deep down she had wondered whether or not she might have inherited her father's weakness. Glad as she was to see Jason win, she had no burning desire to gamble ever again.

Grabbing Troy's hand, she laughed her relief as she pulled him through the milling crowd toward the finish line. They were just in time to see Jason swing out of the saddle, his face alight with jubilation, people congratulating him and slapping him on the back.

As they approached, Jason wheeled around, his eyes finding Mirella's. Triumph was written over his features, and his tawny gold hair was tousled rakishly. His expression held an invitation that made her heart soar. Right or wrong, there was nowhere else in the world she wanted to be at this moment but in his arms, with her cheek pressed against his sweat-dampened shirt.

He took a step toward her. Then he stopped, looking beyond her to the hand which was still entwined with Troy's.

His face lost its luster, and his eyes narrowed. At the

same moment, a woman in a multicolored flowered silk gown forced her way out of the throng.

Mirella watched, stricken, as Jason drew Samantha into his embrace. Seeing them, Troy put a comforting arm over Mirella's shoulders, but she scarcely noticed. The joy had gone out of the day, and she felt deflated, like champagne that had lost its fizz.

Unbeknownst to her, Mirella herself was under scrutiny.

Sharp male eyes peered through the shifting crowd, studying her glossy ebony chignon, the slender waist beneath her shawl. Ah, yes, it was her, beyond a shadow of a doubt.

The watcher smiled to himself; a look of pleasure to the casual eye, yet on closer inspection, its evilness became apparent. The brain beneath the powdered wig plotted lazily. Now that his quarry was in sight, there was no need to rush. He would spend long hours formulating his plan and best of all, savoring the moment when he would come face to face with her.

Yes, he could well afford to bide his time. Then, when he had his chance, he would strike.

The man straightened his black cloak around his shoulders as he melted into the horde of people returning to their carriages. Excitement gripped him. He could hardly wait to see the fear that would leap into those extraordinary gray-blue eyes.

Chapter Twenty-one

Against a charcoal sky pricked with stars, the white
moon tangled in the half-bare branches of a mulberry
tree. Candles winked in windows along the street, and
the sounds of distant merrymaking floated through
the evening air as the residents of Williamsburg
continued the revelry begun at the steeplechase earlier
that day.

Broodingly, Jason propped a bare shoulder against
the window frame and peered out into the night. As
victor of the race, he knew he ought to join in the
festivities but at the moment he had little stomach for
celebration.

Abruptly he grasped the narrow cord that dangled
beside him, closing the wooden Venetian blind with a
vicious snap. But he couldn't shut out the thoughts
that had plagued him since that afternoon. Over and
over again he remembered how Mirella had coldly
ordered him not to touch her, how later he had seen
her clinging to Troy's hand. Jealousy reared up in
Jason like a writhing, outraged beast. After he'd fairly
groveled for a crumb of her attention, she had re-

served her sweet smiles for his brother! By damn, that was the last time he'd ever let down his guard in front of a woman!

Pivoting sharply, Jason strode across the bedchamber, his naked body gleaming like gold in the firelight. He snatched up a crystal decanter from atop the mahogany dressing table and uncorked it, splashing brandy into a silver tumbler. The liquor burned down his throat, leaving a smooth taste in his mouth. But the draught failed to relieve his inner turmoil. Though his senses were dulled from drinking steadily these past hours, he could still feel a relentless ache deep inside him. Why the devil should it matter so much to him what Mirella said or did?

There was a sudden rustle of linen from the direction of the bed, then a female voice purred seductively, "Are you not cold, Jason? Come back here and let me warm you."

With a flash of irritation, Jason turned his eyes to the woman who lay nestled against the pillows, the pink tips of her small breasts peeping out alluringly from beneath the quilt. He had been so wrapped up in his own dark meditations that he had forgotten where he was. After the race, in a fit of smoldering rancor, he had let Samantha entice him here, to her rented rooms, hoping to erase Mirella's image from his brain once and for all. But it had been to no avail.

He drew in a deep breath to clear his head. The air was ripe with the pungent aroma of wood smoke from the fire crackling in the hearth. Another equally strong smell assailed his nostrils and gave him a faint feeling of sickness. It was the reek of Samantha's perfume, cloyingly heavy in contrast to the pure, feminine essence he associated with Mirella.

"Come here, darling," Samantha repeated, a hint of petulance in her voice. Her lower lip pouted as she beckoned to him with open arms. "And don't scowl so. If you'll let me help you relax, you'll soon regain your manliness."

As she wriggled to a sitting position, the covers fell away to reveal her nakedness down to the tuft of red hair at the juncture of her thighs. But rather than firing his blood, the sight made Jason feel like a lump of cold stone.

Disgust rose in his throat like bile. Damn it all, this was humiliating! For months, he had toyed with Samantha, acting on the theory that doing so would make Mirella jealous. Until tonight, he had avoided the intimacy the redhead offered freely, confident that he could use her to release his sexual frustrations if his need were strong enough.

But he had been wrong.

He reached for the decanter, glowering at the liquid inside which glowed amber against the backdrop of the fire. For the first time in his life, he had been unable to perform. It was downright mortifying to face the fact that he wanted no woman but one, an ebony-haired enchantress who had woven a spell around him so binding that any other female body left him limp and soft as an undeveloped boy. Why the bloody hell did Mirella have so much power over him? She had stolen his virility, rendered him impotent with any woman but herself! And then after she had him hooked like a damn-fool fish, she had turned her wiles on his brother!

Bitter rage erupted in him. "By damn, I won't

stand for it!" Jason muttered.

His fingers tightened around the neck of the decanter, and his arm reared back to hurl the fragile vessel into the fire. On the brick hearth, it shattered into a thousand glistening shards, the spilled brandy blazing high in hissing, spitting blue flames.

Wheeling around, he grabbed his breeches from where they lay on the threadbare Eastern carpet. As he stepped into them, he swayed from the effects of the liquor, but a quick shake of his tawny gold hair cleared the haze in his head.

The sheets whispered a protest as Samantha crawled out of bed. "Jason, why are you dressing? Surely you're not leaving, are you?"

"Yes."

"But why? You haven't yet made love to me."

Her plaintive tone fed Jason's black mood. God in heaven, he didn't need this whining female! Since he obviously had failed in his campaign to make Mirella jealous, there was no sense in continuing this farce of a relationship with Samantha.

Her arms were clutching at him like tentacles. With a growl of disgust, Jason thrust her away so that she stumbled backward, her bare bottom striking the bed with a tiny thump.

"Samantha, you and I are finished." He reached down for his shirt and yanked it on.

"I . . . I don't understand."

"Then allow me to make myself clearer," he replied curtly. "I don't ever want to see you again."

As Jason sank onto a rush-bottomed chair to tug on his boots, Samantha scrambled forward to kneel beside him, hands grasping at him in supplication.

"Jason, please, darling, you can't really mean that! Why, we've been together for so long. . . ."

Flashing her a sardonic smile, he slapped her naked rump. "And 'twas enjoyable while it lasted."

"But . . . but I thought you and I would wed."

Samantha stared up at him with such pathetic bewilderment that for a moment Jason almost felt sorry for her. Almost. Then contempt washed over him. He had made her no promises. Whatever sly schemes she had concocted had been of her own dreaming. She was just another cunning female who sought to use her body to trap him into marriage.

"Darling," he mocked softly, "I'd sooner wed Medusa."

Surging out of the chair, Jason snatched his coat from the bedpost and dug into one of the pockets. As Samantha watched open-mouthed, he pulled forth a handful of gold and flung it at her feet, the coins shimmering and clinking as they fell. "There you are," he said in contempt. "That should amply settle my account. 'Tis far more than any whore is worth."

Then he strode out of the chamber, banging the door shut behind him.

Samantha gazed after Jason in stunned disbelief, the cold finality of his words permeating her body like a draught of bitter medicine. She felt numb, nauseated. Unconsciously, she folded her arms over her naked breasts, rubbing her chilled skin. He really meant it this time. He had spurned her for good.

Self-pity enveloped her. Now what was she to do? The years had crept up without warning and, at twenty-seven, she could no longer afford to dally. She *had* to marry. Yet with so many heiresses available, no virile young man would want her, knowing the meagerness of her father's wealth. Like it or not, she would be forced to wed an old man with foul breath and a sagging belly, someone who could be enticed with her only remaining asset, her sultry beauty.

It was either that or spend the rest of her days in poverty, for her father had informed her recently that since the September rains had destroyed his crop, he was cutting off her funds.

How could Jason have left her at a time like this? she wailed inside. He had shattered her plans with as much willful disregard as he had the crystal decanter.

Samantha bent and picked up a sliver of glass that twinkled amidst the glinting gold coins covering the rug. The needle-sharp shard pricked her fingertip. She stared down, mesmerized, as a fat drop of blood welled atop her alabaster skin.

Somehow the tiny stab of pain pierced her despair. It aroused in her a fierce desire for revenge, and suddenly fury spun within her. Her obsessive passion for Jason was submerged by a tidal wave of rage. It wasn't fair! No man could treat her so harshly without suffering the consequences.

And if it hadn't been for that coal-haired witch, Mirella, none of this would have happened! That coy girl had deliberately set out to woo Jason away. And like a glassy-eyed sheep, he had succumbed to the lure.

The bastard! Samantha seethed. He had tossed her aside as if she were dirt, as if the long years of their relationship had never existed. Hadn't she given him her body, sacrificed her reputation?

Viciously she kicked a bare toe at the coins strewn over the rug, sending the shiny circles rolling to all four corners of the chamber. To think Jason expected her to be placated by a few pieces of gold!

By the heavens, she would ruin both him and Mirella if it was the last thing she ever did!

But much later, when her fury finally subsided to a cold, consuming hatred, Samantha scrabbled on all fours, greedily scavenging the coins she had scattered so carelessly.

After all, she rationalized, she at least deserved his money.

Mirella woke from a restless sleep. The faint recollection of a strange dream teased her consciousness before fading into oblivion. Staring into the darkness, it took a moment for her to realize where she was. This was Jason's house in Williamsburg. Pandora and Troy occupied bedchambers down the hall, while Jason's was directly across from hers.

That is, she corrected, he was *supposed* to be across from her. When he hadn't returned home after the race, it had been clear that he was spending the night in Samantha's bed.

Resolutely, Mirella closed her eyes. But a churning jealousy refused to loosen its grip on her mind. Why couldn't she overcome this absurd resentment of Samantha? What did it matter with whom Jason made love?

As she tried to sleep, a distant church bell chimed twice. Sighing, Mirella acknowledged that she was wide awake though it was two o'clock in the morning. She was accomplishing little by lying here tossing and turning. Perhaps a dull tome from the library would distract her from her roiling thoughts.

The rug was cold beneath her bare feet as she slipped out of bed. Shivering, she drew a robe over her thin gown, then went to the fireplace to light a candle from the last tiny flames that licked at the red embers.

Opening her door, she crept out, careful lest she awaken Pandora and Troy. The taper in her hand cast a flickering halo of gold around her and pooled deep shadows in the corners of the hall. She was lifting the hem of her robe to descend the dark staircase when a small clinking sound from the direction of Jason's chamber broke the night's stillness.

Startled, she whipped around. His door was cracked open, as it had been when she'd gone to bed. If perchance he had returned home since then, wouldn't his door be shut?

Then what had caused that noise? A thief perhaps? Should she go waken Troy before investigating?

Of course not, she scolded herself. It was merely the eerie gloom of the night that caused her nervousness. The sound she'd heard was likely an innocent shifting of timbers.

To calm her quickened pulse, she would march across the hall and prove to herself that she had nothing to fear.

Taking a deep breath, she raised her candle high, bravely tiptoing across the chilly bare floor. Slowly she pushed open the door to Jason's chamber and stepped inside the black, silent room.

She froze as something moved in the shadows.

Heart pounding, she sucked in her breath to scream. At the same instant, an irritated male voice

386

spoke.

"Wha' th' devil are you doing in here?"

The cry died in her throat. The fingers that held her candle trembled with aftershock as the pale circle of light revealed Jason, rising from a wingback chair in the murkiness of the corner ahead of her. His hair was mussed and his shirt was unbuttoned but she thought she had never seen a more welcome sight.

"Oh, 'tis only you," she sighed in relief.

"Who else? Unless you intended t'enter m'brother's chamber and stumbled into here by mistake."

His insinuation about Troy was so ridiculous that she dismissed it, concentrating instead on the slight slur in his voice. His glass clinked against the bottle he held as he poured himself a brandy. That was the sound she had heard in the hall, Mirella realized. With growing disgust, she watched as he downed the liquor in one gulp.

"You're drunk," she pronounced contemptuously.

"Pard'me," he mocked loudly, with a sweeping bow that threatened to spill the contents of the bottle. "I didn't mean t'offend m'lady's purity with m' decadent behavior."

"Hush, or you'll waken the whole house." Annoyed, Mirella turned and quietly shut the door. She set down her candle on the nightstand and then swung toward Jason, holding out her hand. "Give me that bottle and glass, and hie yourself to bed to sleep this off."

A lascivious smile crossed his face. " 'Tis an intriguing proposal you make, m' lovely Mirella. An' will you join me on yon sheets?"

He nodded meaningfully toward the bed, and

Mirella's eyes followed the path of his, coming to rest on the wide mattress. A rich, brocaded cream fabric hung from the fourposter, creating an intimate bower which was lit by the soft glow of a single taper. Her brain conjured up a fantasy of their naked bodies entwined there in ecstasy. She had to tear her gaze away, and suppress the leaping of her heart with a rigorous exercise of willpower.

"I fear I must disappoint you," she said, striving for a note of disdain. "Now, put aside those spirits before you become so besotted that you fall to the floor and rouse everyone with your noise."

"Why d' you deny me? D' you think a few drinks would hinder me from pleasuring you? Never fear, m' love, I'll make your sweet flesh quiver wi' delight."

Jason thunked down his bottle and glass on a table. Pivoting toward her, with only a slight sway to betray his inebriation, he began to strip off his shirt. Mirella stood transfixed as his broad, bare shoulders emerged into the dim light. Although the air was chilly, she felt flushed with heat. Unbidden desire warmed her body, and she was gripped by a sudden yearning to press her breasts against the hardness of his chest. Her hand reached up to clutch together the edges of her robe as if that would protect her from such foolishness. Dear God, she had to get out of here before she betrayed herself!

"I've no wish to lie with you, drunk or not," she stated firmly. "And since you clearly refuse to listen to me, then you may sleep on the cold floor for all I care. Good night to you."

Chin held high, Mirella marched toward the door, a single thick braid of ebony streaming down her back.

But Jason stepped into her path before she could reach her goal. When she made a move to brush past him, he seized her shoulders.

In vain she tried to wrench herself free. But though he might be a bit unsteady on his feet, his superior strength was unimpaired.

"Methinks th' lady doth protest too much," he murmured.

Dipping his head, he put his mouth to her cheek. His warm, brandied breath heated her flesh as he sowed tiny kisses over her softness. His hands glided down over her spine to draw her closer to him. Through the barrier of her robe and his breeches, she felt his full arousal. The knowledge caused her loins to throb with an answering hunger.

In desperation, she arched away. Uttering a low chuckle, Jason buried his face in her neck, nibbling her skin with relentless tenderness. Too late, she saw the folly of entering his bedchamber. She ought to have left the moment she knew he was in here. Why hadn't she?

"Jason . . . please!" she gasped. "I demand that you release me!"

"Nay, m' love, no more games. You're mine." His hands parted her robe and, as his kisses roamed below her throat, his voice was so muffled she had to strain to hear him. "Mine alone . . . no other man shall have you!"

The fierce declaration robbed her of resistance. Mirella clung to his words, wishing with all her heart that he belonged to her as completely as she did to him. Was this the way he felt about Elizabeth?

With sudden, blinding insight, she realized that her

feelings for him had grown much deeper and richer than she'd ever imagined possible. She loved him.

The acknowledgement left her weak and shaky. How could she have fallen for a man who viewed her as his property? One who only sought to use her callously for his own satisfaction? Yet her conscience leaped in to defend him. Despite his faults, he could be warm and kind, teasing and tender. How could she fight the intensity of her emotions?

Her arms looped around his neck as she offered him her surrender. Her senses greedily absorbed his every nuance, her fingers reveling in the silky texture of his hair. With each quickened breath, she inhaled his scent, a heady combination of man and brandy. There was another essence clinging to his skin, an oddly familiar odor that teased her memory, but before she could determine what it was, his lips closed over the peak of her breast.

The gentle suckling made her belly flare with hot excitement. She melted against him as sweet sensations coursed through her body. So long deprived of this beguiling magic, she could scarce keep from crying out her need for him. The dim chamber grew dreamlike; reality was his encircling embrace and the wonders wrought by his mouth.

She felt herself dizzily tilting. Then an awareness of something soft beneath her made her realize that Jason had pushed her against the sheets, his muscled form straddling her completely. Running her hands over his naked back, she returned his caresses with an ardor that threatened to betray her love for him.

"Do I please m'lady?" Jason asked in a raspy whisper.

Her robe was spread wide, the low neckline of her nightgown brushed downward so that the full swells of her breasts were bared to his gaze. As his fingers played with one taut nipple, dark honey in the candle-light, Mirella moaned her acquiescence. He shifted so that the hardness at his loins rubbed against her soft thigh.

"An' tell me, m' sweet love," he commanded, showering fervent kisses over her trembling mouth, "d'you yearn for any other man but me?"

He had called her his love. Mirella focused on those words as she stared up at him, wanting desperately to believe that the intensity on his face was an indication of the depth of his feelings. Had he finally forsaken his affection for his dead wife? Was it possible he was afraid to express his true feelings, to take the risk of again suffering the pain of loving?

Her lips parted to reassure him; then the elusive smell she had noticed earlier distracted her. What was that oddly familiar essence adhering to Jason's flesh? It was faint but cloying, like a woman's perfume. . . .

Sickness seized her stomach as she identified the source of the odor, and shock drove the desire from her body. Dear God, she had forgotten where Jason had been earlier that evening. That was Samantha's scent.

Her dream world came crashing down around her. Jason felt only lust for her, she realized, bitterly hurt. In the heat of passion, he undoubtedly spoke words of love to Samantha, too. His sole goal was the fulfill-ment of his own selfish pleasures.

"M' love, I await your reply," he murmured, his large hand cradling the side of her face.

His tenderness now seemed a parody. Anger sprang from the wreckage of her heart. He had come from that witch's bed, half-drunk, and now he blithely sought to seduce her. Did he think her a fool?

She flung her arms up and thrust at his chest with all her might. Jason shied backward in surprise long enough for her to wriggle out from under him.

"You scoundrel!" she hissed. "Don't you ever touch me again!"

Befuddled by drink, Jason watched in bewilderment as Mirella scrambled to her feet, tugging the edges of her robe together to conceal her naked breasts. For a fleeting instant, he thought she had never looked more beautiful, her indigo eyes flashing fire and wisps of ebony hair tumbling wildly about her face. Then the ache in his loins reminded him of his unsated passion. Sprawled on his back across the mattress, he frowned up at her in puzzlement. What had caused this abrupt change in her?

"Wha's wrong?" he slurred. "Thought you liked me t' touch you."

"I'd sooner bed the devil himself. You lack the morals of . . . of a snake!"

Her scathing tone irritated Jason. He leaped to his feet, regretting the impulse as his head reeled sickeningly. Steadying himself by grabbing hold of the bedpost, he growled, "Wha's that supposed t' mean? We each desire th' other. Where's th' wrong in that?"

"The wrong is that I am no more to you than another whore to bed." Taking a deep breath, Mirella bit back the hurt that threatened to bubble forth. He must never guess that she loved him, for he would only use the knowledge to wind her around his little finger.

Carefully, she made her words icy. "I can smell the stench of Samantha on you. Surely you cannot expect me to lie with you when you have just now come from her bed. I won't be treated like secondhand goods."

Was Mirella jealous? Jason wondered hazily. Yet her cool, haughty tone belied that notion. Then what? His tipsy brain slowly searched for a reason. She must be trying to manipulate him, to tell him what to do! Outrage washed through him. Was this his reward for long months of physical frustration? For suffering the torture of knowing she slept under the same roof? If it killed him, he would never admit to her that he had broken off his relationship with Samantha. That would only give Mirella more power over him. By damn, it didn't pay to consort with females. They caused a man more grief than pleasure!

"An' so what if I was with Samantha?" he jeered. "Women! Always wanting t' put a collar on a man's neck and lead him around like a pet dog." Swaying slightly, he jabbed his hand at Mirella. "You need t' be taught who's master around here."

"You're not my master!" she snapped back. "And if you dare lay so much as a finger on me again, I'll leave your household for good!"

The prospect wrenched her heart, but her pride refused to let her retract the threat.

"An' go where?" he mocked. "Face it, m' love. You need me. C'm 'ere an' I'll show you how much."

He made a lunge for her but she stepped easily out of his reach, watching with outward frostiness as he grabbed the bedpost for support. Hurt by his callous treatment of her, she said coldly, "Troy will take me in."

Jason's eyes flashed like storm clouds. "Tha's what this is all about, isn't it?" he demanded. " 'Tis m' brother you really want! You're using this as an excuse t' warm his bed!"

Mirella had had enough of his drunken accusations. All she wanted was to return to her chamber and nurse in solitude the pain of her new-found love.

"Who I do or do not want is none of your concern," she said wearily. "But heed me well, Jason. You're setting a bad example for Pandora with your drinking and whoring, and if you continue to tread that same path, I vow we both will go live with Troy."

Hastening past him, she headed for the door. But she had taken no more than three steps when his hands closed around her arms and spun her back toward him. Swaying slightly, he glared down at her.

"Don't you dare go to m' brother!" he thundered. "I've seen th' way you lust for him, and by damn, I'll not stand for it!"

Mirella refused to be intimidated, yet his irrationality made her bite back an outraged reply. It wasn't so much that she feared he meant her physical harm, but rather that he might try to make love to her again. And that could only cause her more emotional anguish.

"Jason, calm yourself," she ordered quietly. "I seek only to return to my own chamber."

"First vow you'll never go t' Troy. You belong t' me, Mirella."

She pursed her lips, hating the way he asserted his ownership of her. A piece of property, she reflected bitterly, that was all she was to him. Despite her good

394

intentions, she felt a painful anger clutch her heart. "I'm sorry, Jason, but—"

"Promise me, dammit!"

His fingers tightened around her arms. She gasped as he hauled her against him, so that only a few scant inches separated their faces. His features were etched in rough relief by the glimmer of candlelight. Against her breasts, Mirella felt the rapid rise and fall of his chest.

His gaze moved to her lips, and his eyes softened, a familiar thrilling warmth entering those dark golden depths. Her heart began to throb at a pace that had nothing to do with fear. Dear God, if she didn't do something, he would kiss her!

"I'll make you no promises," she spat wildly. "If I choose to go to Troy, then you cannot stop me!"

His expression hardened again as he gave her shoulders a shake. "Bitch! You'll not—"

The abrupt click of the door interrupted him. Mirella whipped her head around to see Troy enter the chamber. His hair was disheveled, and his legs were bare below the heavy silk robe that extended to his knees.

"Here, now!" he exclaimed. "What's the trouble? I vow your voices will awaken all of Williamsburg."

"Get out!" Jason roared. "Else I'll be forced t' throw you out m'self!"

Mirella felt a twinge of embarrassment that Troy had caught her in such a compromising situation. Here she was, in his brother's chamber in the middle of the night, the both of them clad scantily. It was mortifying! But Troy appeared to accept the scene with amazing aplomb.

"Jase, unhand Mirella," he ordered calmly. "You're drunk, and unfit to be in any lady's company."

He walked toward them as if to add weight to his words.

"Keep away from her," Jason snarled. "She's mine, and you'll not have her!"

As he spoke, he moved backward, dragging Mirella along with him. Suddenly he stepped on the hem of her robe and lost his balance, staggering against the bed, his head striking the post with a dull thunk.

He crumpled onto the mattress like a limp rag doll. Pulled forward by his momentum, Mirella collapsed atop him, feeling his grip slacken as he sank into unconsciousness.

Stunned, she lay there for an instant, arms and legs splayed over his large body. Then Troy's hands were on her shoulders.

"Are you all right?"

But Mirella's only concern was for the man beneath her. Ignoring Troy's anxious inquiry, she scrambled off Jason and frantically probed the back of his head to find a lump already swelling there.

"Oh, no!" She turned worried eyes on Troy. "Shouldn't we get a physician?"

Troy shook his head. "He would do naught but apply a few leeches. 'Twould do Jase no good."

"Are you certain?" Mirella asked, doubtfully eying his brother's sprawled form.

"Absolutely. He'll survive just fine, though I've no doubt he'll have a monstrous headache come morning— and from more than just that tap on his skull." He held out a hand. "Come, the best thing we can do is leave him to sleep off the effects of his liquor."

"Shouldn't we at least cover him, so he doesn't catch a chill?"

"My dear Mirella, you are entirely too kind to my big brute of a brother."

But he obediently rounded the bed and gripped Jason under the armpits, straightening him on the mattress as Mirella tugged the quilt out from beneath him and draped it over his senseless form.

She tucked a pillow under Jason's head, then gazed down at him for a moment, brushing back a lock of tawny hair that had fallen onto his forehead. Emotion washed through her as she studied the classic male beauty of his face. With those dark lashes veiling his eyes he looked as innocent as a babe. Yes, it was love, she thought. What else would explain this sentimental feeling for a man who smelled like a brewery?

She very nearly bent and kissed him, until the faint brush of a foot on the carpet drew her attention. She glanced up to see Troy watching her steadily. To cover her confusion, she turned her back and reached blindly for the candle on the nightstand.

"Shall we go, then?" she asked abruptly.

He nodded, and they went out into the shadowed hall. At the door to her chamber, she stopped to say good night.

Troy smiled as he touched her cheek. "Don't worry so," he said softly. "Jase will be fine. He's quite hard-headed, you know."

As he left her, she thought she heard him add under his breath, "In more ways than one."

Chapter Twenty-two

Softly falling snow draped the forest in a mantle of white. Only a few brown tufts of last summer's grass stuck bravely out of the frigid blanket. The gray afternoon sky foretold an early dusk, and the woods were shadowed and silent. The only sound shattering the hush was the rhythmic clopping of horse hooves on the snow-packed dirt road.

Bored with the dreary January scenery outside, Samantha let the curtain swing back over the coach window. She longed for an end to this interminable journey. A raw bite in the air made her nestle her gloved fingers into the warmth of her squirrel muff. The flannel-wrapped bricks on which she rested her slippered feet already had lost most of their heat. And there was still some distance yet to travel.

To distract herself, she studied her companion. The interior of the swaying vehicle was dim, but not so much so that it prevented her from discerning the man occupying the seat across from her. He sat dozing, his chin sunk into his stocky chest.

A black cloak enveloped his stout form, and Samantha knew that the frockcoat, waistcoat, and breeches beneath were a brilliant ruby brocade adorned with large gold buttons. Personally she thought his ensemble a bit garish, but then what matter so long as he'd paid for the fashionable turquoise velvet gown she wore?

His balding pate was concealed by a white-powdered periwig that curled to beneath his shoulders. How well she had come to know those dark, feral eyes and beefy hands these past weeks! Despite his oxlike body, in bed he was surprisingly adept, delighting in a slow torturing of the senses. Even now, out here in this wintry weather, the memory sparked a throbbing warmth in her belly. Granted, he did not match Jason's performances, but at least he assuaged a portion of her lust.

Jason! Samantha's lip curled into a sneer. Tonight that bastard would finally get the first taste of what was coming to him. He would watch helplessly as his precious Mirella quaked with fear.

And she owed the sweet pleasure of her revenge to the man sitting opposite her, the man who had become her constant companion these past few months.

Samantha closed her eyes, remembering their first meeting. It had been the night after Jason had broken off with her, at a masquerade held at the Governor's Palace in Williamsburg.

Nursing her hatred, she had lurked in the doorway to the front parlor, watching in bitter jealousy as a throng of young swains had vied for the attentions of a lady sitting on a couch near the fireplace. Though a jeweled mask concealed the woman's face, there was no mistaking her identity, for her coal-hued hair stood out like a beacon in the crowded chamber. Only Mirella lacked the fashion sense to powder her curls like all the other females present.

Hostility threatened to choke Samantha's throat as she stared at the scene. What did Jason see in that whey-faced chit? He stood with an elbow propped on the mantelpiece, gazing broodingly at Mirella like a lovesick calf.

It just wasn't fair! If only she could think of some plan to wreak vengeance on the both of them!

"Such a grimace is scarcely suitable for this merry occasion!" a male voice had suddenly chided from behind. "Is there someone within against whom you bear a grudge?"

Samantha had whipped around to see a short, barrel-chested man standing nearby, a black mask hiding his features. He wore the sort of inconspicuous clothing that made it difficult to guess if he were a planter, a merchant, or both. As his words sank in, she realized that she had let her mask slip, baring her expression to his gaze. Flushing, she raised the silver domino over her face.

"Sir, I fear you are mistaken," she denied stiffly. "I harbor no enmity for any guest."

The stranger went on as if she hadn't spoken. "Might I venture to say you despise the black-haired woman occupying yon couch?" He nodded in Mirella's direction. "Do not attempt to deny it, for your look betrayed the truth."

"And indeed if 'tis so, what concern would it be of yours?" she challenged.

The man chuckled. "More than you could imagine,

madam." He offered her his arm. "If you would care to listen, I have a business proposition for you. Allow me to escort you outside for a moment—what I have to say requires a quiet place away from listening ears."

Samantha hesitated. To be seen leaving with a total stranger would only increase the talk she knew circulated about her, yet this man had piqued her interest. Curiosity got the better of her, and she let him lead her into the dark, autumn-chilled garden. When he finally unmasked and introduced himself, revealing the reasons behind his own animosity toward Mirella, she knew she had been right to follow her instincts.

Now Samantha smiled and leaned her head back, eyes closed, as the coach swayed, carrying her and her cohort to the first stage in their plan for retribution. Ah, yes, the fates had been kind in granting her this well-deserved revenge. . . .

Her companion's voice interrupted her reverie.

"Care to share the jest?"

Samantha opened her eyes to see that he had awakened from his nap. "I was imagining Mirella's face when she realizes that you're still alive."

Sir Harry Weston gave an evil laugh, savoring the anticipation as he had done nothing else before. When Mirella had run away from his estate, he had sworn he'd get her back if it was the last thing he ever did. His resolve became a grim, burning intent after she stabbed him and left him for dead along the filthy waterfront of Bristol.

A twinge of pain in the healed chest wound made Sir Harry wince as he twisted into a more comfortable position on the leather seat of the coach. Damn that troublesome bitch! After her attack, he had lain for weeks in a fevered coma, fighting for his life. By the time he'd recovered, her trail was cold. Finally, traveling incognito, he had tracked her here to the colonies. And now the time had come for her to pay.

It was fortuitous that he had met Samantha Hyatt. She bore her own grudge against Mirella and Jason, and that suited Sir Harry just fine. Because he was posing as a lowly merchant, one Mr. Harold Wesley from London, he needed an introduction to the first families of Virginia society, where he would be likely to encounter Mirella. Samantha had provided him with that entry. Besides, he thought, eyeing her critically, she had been a lusty wench in bed, satisfying his physical desires until he would finally be able to force Mirella to become his wife.

" 'Twill be an interesting evening, indeed," he muttered aloud.

Samantha's smile broadened. "Well, I for one can scarcely wait to see the both of them destroyed. 'Tisn't a moment too soon for my tastes."

"Patience, my lovely, patience," Sir Harry chastised. "Remember, you cannot enjoy the sweetness of this reprisal to its fullest if you act impulsively."

Samantha pursed her lips, shifting restlessly against the cold leather seat. She and Sir Harry had argued much these past weeks on this business of holding off. Her eagerness to act had been almost uncontrollable, and she had badgered him relentlessly to make his move, while he had been content to wait until the right moment presented itself. Thank heavens that moment finally arrived in the form of an invitation to a Twelfth Night party at Berkeley, Ben Harrison's plantation home. Hearing through the grapevine that Mirella and Jason planned to attend, Sir Harry decided at last to set their plot into motion.

Not only did Samantha crave revenge, she could scarcely wait for the monetary reward it would bring.

"Sir Harry?"

"Harold, my love. Pray, do not forget that tonight I am plain Mr. Wesley, a merchant visiting from London."

"Harold, then," Samantha revised with an impatient flutter of her hand. She leaned forward, her face gleaming with the greed of a child demanding another bedtime story. "Tell me again about all the money we're going to steal from Mirella."

Sir Harry smiled indulgently. "A small fortune, my dear. Not a king's ransom, but enough to allow us to live in prosperity for quite a good while." Abruptly his features darkened. "That wily bitch, Caroline! Had I not intercepted the letter the bank sent to Mirella, I might never have known the jewels existed. That inheritance is mine, as the rightful heir to the Weston estate!"

"Of course it is, darling," Samantha soothed. "We'll get it back from that sweet-faced slut."

But her sympathy failed to quell Sir Harry's ire. Moodily, he thought of Mirella's late mother, Caroline, who had watched her husband, Andrew, gamble away the family fortune. Wanting to ensure a comfortable future for her only daughter, Caroline began hiding her jewels bit by bit, apparently telling Andrew Weston that the pieces had been sold to help pay off their monumental debts. Over the years the jewelry accumulated, and Caroline arranged to have it secretly stored in a vault at the Bank of England so that

404

when Mirella came of age she would have a dowry that would snare her a rich husband. On her eighteenth birthday, the bank was to notify Mirella of her inheritance.

Sir Harry smiled grimly. When the letter, along with a copy of Caroline's will, arrived at Weston Manor, he had stolen them before Mirella could learn of their existence. And so she still knew nothing of the wealth her mother had left her.

To gain control of the jewels he would force Mirella to marry him. That plan had certain added benefits, he reflected with an evil smirk. For too long now, he had wanted to feel Mirella's body writhing defenselessly beneath his.

Excitement quivered in his loins. But first, before he bedded her, he would toy with her, as a cat plays with a mouse, rousing her fears so that she wondered when next he would strike. There was nothing more thrilling than to savor helplessness in another. As a boy, he had enjoyed pinning live butterflies to a board and watching them squirm and flutter.

And, like the butterflies, after he'd wed Mirella and had his fill of her, then she would die.

Sir Harry laughed to himself. Ah, yes, this had been well worth the wait.

Just a few more miles, and the sport finally would begin.

Snug within the thick brick walls of Berkeley mansion, Mirella stood before the yule log in the south parlor and tossed a sprig of holly into the flames to burn up her troubles of the past year. It was a custom she recalled from her childhood, but this was the first time she had ever wished it would really work.

With a sigh, she turned from the marble fireplace to scan the crowded room. The assemblage of well-dressed guests had been invited by Ben Harrison to celebrate Epiphany, the Twelfth Night of Christmas. Here were representatives of the foremost names in Virginia: Byrd, Carter, Lee, Randolph, Burwell, and of course Fletcher, for Jason and Troy were part of a small circle of men across the chamber, engrossed in a discussion of tobacco prices and politics. Pandora was around somewhere; upon their arrival an hour ago, she had gone off with a friend.

Pretending to listen as a group of ladies exchanged news of the latest London styles, Mirella stole a glance at Jason. His good looks surpassed those of every other man present, with the close exception, she amended, of his brother. But though Troy might be handsome, Jason was . . . well, special. To her prejudiced eyes, those intelligent features and that hard, muscled physique in the form-fitting charcoal frock-coat had no match anywhere.

The weeks since they had left Williamsburg to return to Elysian Fields had passed with monotonous slowness. It was somewhat of a relief that Jason appeared to have cooled his relationship with Samantha. Yet he had avoided Mirella like the plague. Their estrangement had been reforged by their last confrontation in his bedchamber.

And luckily so, Mirella told herself fiercely. Had he so much as beckoned with one little finger, her pride would have dissolved, and she'd have melted into his arms in total surrender. It was degrading, this control he wielded over her. How could she be so weak when she despised the sort of man he was, disrespectful and grasping, wanting only her body and not her mind or her heart?

Still, a rush of wistful love enveloped her as she saw his lips form a rare smile. How long had it been since he had looked so relaxed, since he had last bantered with and teased her? Oh, why couldn't he love her with the devotion Lucas showered on Emma? Or with the affection she was certain he still bore for his dead wife?

Abruptly Mirella excused herself from the ladies and wandered to the window. Her mood was beginning to border on the maudlin! She must remember that it was an unusual man indeed who didn't exploit women for his own selfish purposes.

She sighed, breathing in the scents of bayberry candles and burning wood. Rubbing the heel of her hand over the chilly window pane, she made a peephole in the misted glass. Outside, dusk was falling. Snow flurries swirled in a frenzied dance of freedom before settling into the frosting of white on the ground. In the distance, past the pearly mounds of boxwoods in the gardens, she caught a glimpse of the James. The recent cold spell had frozen the river nearly half a mile out from shore, and she had heard that on rare occasions the ice extended all the way across, so that a person could walk to the other side.

Mirella's eyes were drawn back irresistibly to the other end of the parlor. Idly she fingered the cameo which hung around her neck on a smoke blue ribbon that matched her taffeta gown. Yes, she must always keep in mind that men were users. After all, hadn't her father squandered her mother's fortune?

"He cares for you far more than he'll admit."

Troy's soft voice startled her. He added, so low that no one around them could hear, "If Jase would but swallow his stubborn pride, no doubt he would realize that the two of you belong together as man and wife."

Inexplicably, her earlier yearning exploded into anger. "And why should *I* wish to wed *him*? There isn't a man alive who's worth the bother." No sooner than the spiteful words were out, Mirella regretted them. "I'm sorry, Troy. I didn't mean for you to bear the brunt of my ill humor."

"Forgiven," he said, his green eyes twinkling. "Here's something to distract you from your gloomy mood." He reached into his pocket and then dropped a hot roasted chestnut into her palm. Automatically she blew on the nut to cool it, and began stripping away the softened shell to reach the fragrant, steaming meat inside.

As he peeled his own chestnut, Troy's face was serious. "The truth now, Mirella. Hows goes it between you and Jase? I vow you've hardly spoken a word to one another in weeks, at least not when I've been around."

She shrugged, weary of hiding her hurt. "He has no interest in me," she admitted bitterly. "I've no money or land, and as I refuse to become his mistress, why should he wish to bother with me?"

"Don't underestimate yourself," Troy said softly. "Because whether Jase realizes it or not, for the first time in his life he's in love."

His casual statement shook Mirella. It couldn't be true. Or could it? She looked across the room, and at

408

the same moment, Jason's eyes lifted to meet hers. There was no affection in that cold, golden stare. Her heart squeezed painfully as the brief hope sank into oblivion. Biting her lip, she wrenched her gaze away. No, it was obvious that Troy was mistaken.

"And what of his late wife?" she forced out, remembering the angelic blonde in the portrait hanging in the entrance hall at Jason's house. "He loved her . . . he likely still loves her."

"Elizabeth?" Troy gave a scoffing laugh. "You've far more to offer Jase than she ever had, and the more fool he if he's too pigheaded to see that."

She had no time to ponder his words, for her attention was suddenly riveted to the parlor doorway. Two new arrivals stood there, a man and a woman. The blood drained from Mirella's face, and bits of chestnut shell slipped unnoticed from her trembling fingers to scatter on the Turkish rug.

It was *him*. It was impossible.

She closed her eyes in disbelief, but when she opened them, Sir Harry was still there, as large as life, a ruby coat embroidered in gold thread covering his familiar stocky chest. And he was staring at her, his mouth twisted into a leering grin which confirmed once and for all that he was the same man she had stabbed and left for dead in Bristol.

Sir Harry Weston was alive!

Fear gushed through her veins. She wanted to run but her feet were incapable of movement. Swallowing hard, she noted dazedly that Samantha was at his side, fashionably attired in a hooped gown of voluminous proportions, her hair a mountain of crimped, white-powdered curls. Ben Harrison went up to the two of them and began to introduce them to the other guests.

"Mirella, is something the matter?" Troy asked, concerned. "You look as though you've seen a ghost."

I have, she wanted to scream. "I . . . I feel a bit faint," she managed calmly. " 'Tis the closeness in here. I . . . I believe I'll go get a breath of fresh air."

"I'll accompany you."

"Nay . . . nay, I'll be fine." She stayed him with a touch of her hand. " 'Tis nothing serious, and I'd really rather you not bother yourself."

Fighting panic, Mirella plunged into the crowd. Her heart pulsed in great, hurting throbs of shock. Blindly she hurried across the wide hall and into the first doorway she saw.

It was the dining room. A centerpiece of greenery topped by fruit and brilliant red nandina berries adorned the long mahogany table. The scent of fresh-cut pine mingled with the aroma of food as a bevy of slave women busily set out a buffet supper that consisted of roast goose, honey-glazed ham, wild turkey, acorn squash, scalloped oysters, roast beef, sweet potatoes, mince and pecan pies, spoon bread, plum pudding, marzipan, and the traditional Twelfth Night cake.

Ordinarily the feast would have set Mirella's mouth to watering, but at the moment she was too agitated to think of her empty stomach. Walking unsteadily to the fireplace, she put her cold hands over the flames. She knew instinctively that Sir Harry would follow; no matter where she fled, there would be no escaping him. She might as well gird herself and get this confrontation over with.

410

Their meeting was not long in coming.

A flash of red caught the corner of her eye, and she turned to see Sir Harry ambling toward her. With maddening unconcern, he paused to snatch a slice of gingerbread from a silver tray a servant was placing on the table. He took a huge bite out of the spiced cake before continuing toward Mirella. She watched in disgust as he licked the crumbs off his thick lips. Now that the initial shock was over, she felt strangely calm, her spine erect as she prepared herself to face whatever was to come.

"Well, my dear cousin Mirella, fancy meeting you here, of all places. When we last parted, I venture to guess you never thought to see me again. So tell me, how have you fared in the interim?"

"I've no wish to bandy polite phrases with you. Say what it is you want from me and be done with it."

Sir Harry's dark eyes narrowed. "Still the same outspoken bitch you always were. Hasn't your new master been able to crush the defiance in you after all these months?"

"I belong to no man," she said through gritted teeth. "Now out with it. Tell me why you're here."

"Can you not guess the reason?" he sneered. "We have unfinished business to discuss, the matter of our nuptials to begin with."

He seized her arm and hauled her over to a Chinese screen in the corner of the dining room, away from the servants' listening ears. Through the flounce of lace at her elbow, she felt the heat of his beefy palm. She jerked out of his grasp.

"Your touch makes my skin crawl. I would no more wed you than I would the devil himself."

"And if the alternative is to spend the remainder of your life languishing in prison? Mayhap you'd enjoy a whipping first . . . to be stripped to the waist, your flesh bared for everyone to see, your back shredded and bleeding." Sir Harry let out a low chuckle that sent a shiver down her spine. "Nay, my sweet, you are in no position to refuse me."

"Then turn me in," she challenged, praying that her surface defiance hid her growing inner dread.

"All in good time, my pet." He patted her on the cheek, and the hot dampness of his palm made her recoil. "I'll grant you a few weeks to ponder the matter. Betrothal or retribution, 'tis your choice." With a brief, mocking bow, he strolled over to the dining table and began to cram tidbits of food into his mouth.

Mirella stared after him, trying to rein in the fear that clawed her insides. For an instant she saw a vivid picture of herself being whipped, then thrown into a dirty cell, sleeping on a lice-infested pallet for the rest of her life. After all, what judge would believe the word of a penniless woman against that of a supposed gentleman?

Yet was she to wed Sir Harry, and let his greedy paws rove over her intimately? Never! Dear heavens, what was she to do?

Pivoting, she picked up her skirts and swept blindly out of the room. Scurrying into the spacious hall, she ran smack into a solid body.

It was Jason. He caught her by the shoulders, frowning down at her in concern.

"You're trembling! Is something wrong?"

Mirella felt dizzy with relief. The warm familiarity

412

of him enveloped her. There was nowhere else she wanted to be but in the protective circle of his arms. Dare she hope for help from him? She took a deep breath to steady her voice.

"Jason, I . . . I must tell you—"

But before she could continue, she felt him tense suddenly. He was staring over her head, his fingers digging painfully into her shoulders. Twisting, she saw that Sir Harry stood leering at them. At the same moment, Samantha exited the parlor and linked her arm through Sir Harry's.

"Ah, Jason," she purred, "how pleasant to see you again. And Mirella, how lovely you look tonight."

Jason's gaze was riveted to the portly man beside her. "What the devil—" he exclaimed.

"Allow me to introduce Sir Harry Weston." Samantha's ice-blue eyes gleamed with enjoyment. "Sir Harry, this is Jason Fletcher."

"So we finally meet," her companion said. "I've waited many months to make the acquaintance of the man who helped my dear cousin flee from her only living relative in exchange for certain, shall we say, services rendered."

"Mirella is my sister's companion," Jason said, his voice clipped. "That is the only service she has ever provided either me or my family."

A lecherous smile crossed Sir Harry's face. "Companion? Or your mistress?"

"Aye," Samantha put in maliciously, "the entire colony is whispering about the relationship you two share."

"Whilst I offer the wench the respect of holy wedlock," Sir Harry added.

413

Jason's hands circled Mirella's waist. "If that's not what she wants," he said grimly, "then you'll not touch her."

Sir Harry tilted his periwigged head in mock distress. "My good man, I do hope you realize you're aiding and abetting a common criminal. I could turn you in to the authorities along with her."

"But you won't," Jason returned with menacing softness. "Not if you value your life."

"You won't always be around to champion her," Sir Harry sneered. "Now, pray excuse us." Putting his arm around Samantha, he led her away, but not before she sent Mirella a final look of triumph.

Worriedly, Mirella gazed up at Jason, rubbing her cold hands over her sleeves. "He really means it. He'll have the both of us thrown into prison if I don't marry him."

"Not if I have any say in the matter."

"But Sir Harry has a point. You can't protect me forever."

"Mirella." Jason's hands framed the sides of her face, and the intensity in his eyes made her heart skip a beat. "I pledge to you on my life that I will never allow that man to harm you. Don't forget, I'm the only witness to the stabbing. If he tries to prosecute you, I'll testify that you acted in self-defense."

"But . . . would the judge believe you? If he'd heard the rumors about us . . ."

"You think I'd be deemed a liar because of a few malicious gossipers?" he scoffed. "Don't fret so, Mirella. 'Tis my guess Sir Harry is only bluffing. Now come, let us rejoin the party and prove to him that you don't frighten easily."

Mirella let him lead her into the crowded parlor, though her thoughts were still troubled. She hadn't wanted to admit it to Jason, but she was as anxious about his welfare as her own. If she were convicted, then he could be accused of hiding a criminal. Could she risk dragging him down with her?

But perhaps he was right. For now, the best plan of action was to keep her spirits up and show Sir Harry that she wasn't intimidated.

And with Jason close at her side, her fears gradually receded. It was a rare treat to be the subject of his attentions, and the warm feeling that glowed within her failed to be diminished when she saw a few matrons raise haughty eyebrows at them while whispering behind their fans.

Yet later, as Pandora and her friends gathered to sing yuletide carols to the guests, Mirella couldn't help but wonder at Jason's unexpected protectiveness. Had he leaped to her defense because of some deep, emotional reason?

Or had he sought only to safeguard what he believed was his?

Chapter Twenty-three

Darkness shrouded the entrance hall at Elysian Fields. Only a small circle of light shed by a single taper pierced the blackness. Shuddering and swaying in the chilly draft, the tiny flame threw its dim illumination onto the holiday greenery still decorating the walnut balustrade as Mirella made her way down the stairs.

The house was silent until suddenly the slow, sonorous tones of the clock in the drawing room chimed the hour of midnight. Moving quietly, she headed across the shadowed hall. The door to the first floor bedchamber was open, the room empty. After supper Jason had been called away by the news that one of his mares, whose foal had been sired by Pegasus, was about to give birth. Jason must still be at the stables.

Mirella snuffed out her candle and set it on a table. Clutching her mantle tightly around her, she went out into the frosty night.

The ebony sky was speckled with stars, and a sliver of moon cast light sufficient for her to see the path before her. An icy wind blew, whipping back and forth the thick black braid that hung to her waist. Cold seeped through her dainty slippers as she crunched over the thin crust of snow deposited by yesterday's storm.

But the shiver that seized her stemmed from more than just the wintry weather. Slightly more than twenty-four hours had passed since she again had come face to face with Sir Harry, and in that time she had examined his threats over and over. Her intellect told her it was wrong to stay here under Jason's protection so long as there was the slightest risk of endangering him, too. But her heart balked at the prospect of leaving him.

The events that had occurred on the previous night at Berkeley had caused more than one complication, she admitted. Rather than satisfying her starved needs, Jason's unaccustomed attentiveness had awakened an even greater craving inside her. More than anything else in the world, she wanted to see him, to talk to him again, to reassure herself that something really *had* changed between them, that there would be no return to their uncomfortable, stilted relationship of the past months. And so, unable to sleep, she had left the warmth of her bed to seek him out.

Nearing the stables, Mirella spied a glimmer of light beneath the closed doors. Silently she slipped inside the structure. The interior was reasonably warm after the biting wind, and the air smelled of hay and horses. Halfway down the corridor, a hanging lantern cast a soft sheen over Jason and a stable hand, both standing just outside a stall looking in.

Jason glanced up as she joined them and flashed

her a preoccupied smile; then his attention returned to the chestnut mare lying on the straw within, her swollen side straining with effort. In the lamplight, her coat was glossed with sweat.

"This be it," murmured the big black man.

As they watched, the mare grunted, her body heaving to expel its burden. Mirella held her breath as one perfectly formed hoof suddenly appeared, followed by another; and then the foal's long slim head, protected by a pale, glistening membrane, emerged into the world.

Abruptly the contractions ceased. Minutes stretched by without further progress. The half-born foal lay on the straw, silent and motionless.

"You think it be dead?" the stable man muttered.

His face grave, Jason didn't reply, entering the stall to crouch beside the mare. Gently grasping the foal's shoulders, he gave it a slight twist and tug. Within moments, nature took over again, and the rest of the colt flopped out onto the straw. Its eyes blinked open, its head stirring feebly with the first breaths of air. Then the stable hand was kneeling beside Jason, peeling away the birth sac.

Jason returned to Mirella's side, and they watched the newborn, cream-colored as its sire, struggle to its feet and begin to totter drunkenly around the stall. The colt bumped against the water trough, then finally found its now-standing mother, and nuzzled her hungrily.

"A fine colt, sir, big and strong."

Jason smiled at the black man. "Thank you for waiting up with me, Jeremiah. You may return to your cabin now; there's no more here for us to do."

419

The slave left, his soft whistling fading as he strode out the stable door. Jason turned and squatted before a bucket, dunking his hands into the water and scrubbing them. Though the barn was chilly, he wore no coat over his white shirt. The sleeves were rolled up to his elbows, revealing the strong sinews of his lightly tanned forearms. When he moved, the play of muscles across his back was evident through the fine fabric of his shirt.

Love washed through Mirella, pure and unfathomable. What had sparked this deep emotion she felt for him, when she had sworn never again to fall under the control of any man? Somehow he had become a part of her, as necessary as breathing. It was a vulnerable sensation which both exhilarated and frightened her.

"You're up late this night," Jason commented as he dried his hands on a bit of cloth.

She clutched the stall's half-door, fumbling for an excuse. "I . . . couldn't sleep."

There was a pause, then he inquired softly, "Why?"

He was watching her intently, wary and waiting, and she had the impression that he was more than casually interested in her reply. She had wanted to talk to him, to be with him. But was that the only reason she had tossed and turned in her bed? Confused, she ran the tip of her tongue over her lower lip, and saw his eyes follow the movement. Desire swept her body. It struck her then that she had been deluding herself. What had really lured her out here was a thirst for the feel of his hands on her breasts, his warm breath in her hair. Yet self-respect restrained her from revealing that.

420

"I wondered if the foal had been born yet," she said lamely.

"I see." His words were clipped, his voice assuming that familiar, chilly stiffness.

But as he pivoted to hang the towel on a nail, Mirella saw a flicker of something in his eyes, a raw look holding a trace of both hurt and disappointment. Was it possible, then, that he had hoped, as she had, that last night might mark the beginning of a closer relationship between them? Jason wished only to use her, she tried to assure herself. But what if she were wrong? What if his feelings for her had deepened over these past months? And if there were even a faint chance of that, was she to let her silly pride get in the way of their happiness?

She took an uncertain step forward and curled her fingers around his forearm. His flesh was hard, and gave off a heat that traveled straight through her veins and into her heart.

"Jason, the foal was only an excuse." His golden eyes seemed to peer into her very soul, and her courage faltered, so that she had to lower her gaze to his shirt front in order to continue. "What I'm trying to say is that . . . I needed to see you, to find out if you still . . . wanted me."

For a long moment, he didn't move or speak. Fearing rejection, Mirella stared miserably at the white fabric before her. Then his hands were framing her face, tilting her head up so that she was forced to meet his eyes, eyes which held a warmth she thought she might have dreamed, so badly did she want to trust in it.

He laughed softly, a sound both exultant and

disbelieving. "God, yes, I want you!" Yet the urgent huskiness of his avowal belied the tension she sensed in him, the source of which became clear when he added, "But what of Williamsburg? By damn, Mirella, in a drunken fit I tried to force myself on you! I thought you despised me for that."

She reached up and stroked the pads of her fingers over the rough stubble of his cheek. "Jason, what I feel for you bears little relation to hatred."

He stared down at her. "By God," he uttered in a hoarse whisper, "if you've any doubts, speak them quickly."

She only smiled, sliding her hands around his neck.

Suddenly his arms were enfolding her, drawing her cloaked form against him as his lips took possession of hers. Her lashes fluttered down, and she opened her mouth to him, dissolving under the seduction of his tongue, tasting his faint brandied sweetness. A primitive urge to increase their closeness compelled her hands to flatten over his back as she pressed herself against the latent power of his body. Fire melted her bones. A delirious pleasure originated deep within the pit of her stomach, and radiated outward through every pulsing vein. A need to feel his touch upon her bare skin burned inside her.

"Come," he muttered.

On shaky legs she followed him into the shadows of an empty stall, where the floor was covered with sweet, fresh straw. There he pulled her into his arms again, resting her head for a moment against his chest. The stable was hushed; the only sounds were an occasional muffled scrape of a horse's hoof and the quickened rasp of their breathing. Then the fastening of her mantle loosened under the deft manipulations of his fingers, and the garment slipped to the ground. Jason bent and placed his lips against her throat, his tongue caressing its fluttering pulsepoint.

His arms circled her as he undid the hooks down her back, his mouth searching the softness of her face all the while. Her gown fell away, exposing her shoulders to his hot kisses. Mirella was acutely aware of the thrum of his heart beneath her palm, the abrasion of his shirt against her tender breasts as she writhed against him, wanton and willing. Her perceptions were heightened; each stroke of his fingers, each lungful of his masculine scent was a sensual delight, a taste in an Epicurean feast.

The remainder of her clothing disappeared under the guidance of his hands. Then he loosened her braid so that her hair spilled around her face in an ebony cloud. Spreading her mantle over the bed of straw, Jason pressed her down, pausing to deposit a lingering kiss on the peak of a breast before standing to discard his own apparel.

Without his warmth, the air was chill, so Mirella pulled the edges of the cloak over her. She lay waiting in anticipation as his broad chest and narrow hips emerged into the dusky light. His hard muscles were the badge of a man who spent his hours at honest toil, a man who had no room for idleness in his life. She caught her breath at the sight of his virility, and her body ached to absorb his male beauty.

"Please," she implored, holding out her arms to him.

And then he was lying atop her, driving away the wintry night with the heat of his passion.

"For so long I've wanted this," he murmured, his breath feathering her skin. "I've needed you . . . dreamed about you. . . ."

Her senses reeled as his mouth closed over her breast. Excitement shivered over her skin, cascading through her veins in heavy pulses of enchantment. Caught up in blissful ecstasy, she threaded her fingers into the crispness of his hair, feeling her stomach muscles tighten deliciously as he spread his palm over the silken softness of her belly. His hand strayed over her hip and down along her slender leg, then up again to seek the most sensitive part of her body, stroking until she moaned and twisted with need.

Emotion flooded her, as sharp and real as the physical sensations coursing over her flesh. The words rose, not from conscious intent, but from the depths of her being: "Jason . . . Jason . . . I love you so much."

The words surrounded Jason like warm molasses. Sweet and soft, they flowed into his soul, seeped into each pore of his body, every corner of his mind. Their enormous appeal was not something he could have explained, even if his brain hadn't been hazed with passion. All he knew was an indefinable joy that she cared so deeply for him.

"Mirella, you're everything I've ever wanted . . . I love to hold you . . . to feel you beneath me. . . ."

He hadn't returned her words, Mirella realized in a flash of sanity. But at the moment it didn't seem to matter. Pleasure spread through every nerve as he plunged into her. With an impatient cry, she moved against him, needing him as she had never before needed any man. Their mouths clung as their bodies surged, fused, strained with mounting urgency. The

424

wonder of their union filled her spirit with a blinding radiance. Limbs entwined, they soared together in an erotic, primal rhythm to a realm of overwhelming rapture.

Her senses were the first to recover. Gradually she became aware of the pleasant scent of his skin, the salty-sweet taste of him lingering on her tongue, the sound of his slowing heartbeat. A chilly draft whispered against a narrow strip at her side where his warmth failed to cover her.

Then she remembered. Jason, too, had spoken of love but only for her body, without the deeper, mystical meaning she craved to hear. Yet . . . there was something different in his attitude toward her tonight, a depth of feeling that she'd never sensed in him before. Perhaps it was difficult for him to express his emotions. Had the shock and pain of losing his first wife erected a barrier within him that kept him from loving again so easily?

Feeling him move, she lifted her lashes, her indigo eyes meeting his golden gaze. She was conscious of how very vulnerable she was. He held her heart in his hands, and if he chose to spurn her now . . .

"I've missed you," he murmured, smiling down at her with a tenderness that wrenched her insides.

The last of her misgivings melted. "And I, you," she replied softly.

Jason propped himself up on an elbow. "I'd love to stay here all night, lying with you like this, touching you, kissing you. . . ." He slid his hand down the silken slimness of her side, dipping his head to nuzzle her throat.

She marveled at how easily he aroused her. "Then

why don't we?" she asked breathlessly.

He chuckled. "Easily spoken when you're not the one with your bare backside to the cold air. However . . . I've an idea."

Without warning, he sprang up, magnificent in his nudity as he strode away, leaving her chilled and sputtering protests. In a moment he returned with two blankets. One he rolled up and placed beneath her head, and the other he pulled over the both of them, cuddling her against his side.

"There now, how's that?" he announced with lazy satisfaction.

"Prickly," Mirella grumbled, wriggling, her skin sensitive to the rough wool.

A lascivious glint entered his eyes. "Tell me where you itch," he teased, "and I'll be happy to ease your torment."

His fingers playfully roamed over her breasts, her waist, and down to her thighs, exploring far beyond what the blanket touched. She laughed and tried to push his hands away, but he seemed to have sprouted as many arms as an octopus. No matter how much she squirmed, his strong body held her trapped.

Warmth began to pulse through every fiber of her. Though the tussle had started as pure sport, it swiftly took on an element of sensuality. Rather than fighting, she lay fluid and willing in his embrace. The tickling of his fingers had altered to a slow, erotic stroking that encouraged her to press herself against his nakedness. . . .

Abruptly he grinned and slapped her bare bottom. "Have you any more complaints, m'lady?"

"Ouch! And yes," she added, miffed that he had

ceased his bewitching caresses, "now that you mention it, 'twould appear there is another matter. This blanket reeks of horses." She wrinkled her nose in disgust.

"My abject apologies, for 'tis all this paltry establishment had to offer." A more serious expression replaced his amusement, and his arms tightened around her. "Ah, my love, would that I didn't have to leave for Williamsburg on the morrow!"

She had known, for she had heard him speak of it the previous night. But she had put it out of her mind, not wanting to contemplate a week apart from him. "You promised the governor, did you not?" she asked, her voice subdued.

"Yes, and besides, I've business matters to attend to." A pause, then he kissed her forehead. "There is naught else I want but to have you with me always, Mirella, yet I must leave you behind, else I would get little work accomplished."

Through the shadows, his golden eyes studied her. She felt a sudden breathlessness. He spoke as if their destinies were to be entwined from this moment forward. Was it possible, then, that he would ask her to wed him?

"I dislike leaving you for another reason," Jason went on, his face grim. "If Sir Harry finds out I'm away he might come here in my absence and try to badger you. You're to stay close to home, do you hear?"

"I'll be fine."

"Before I leave, I'll tell Ophelia not to admit that snake should he be so bold as to set foot on this plantation."

"He'd be a fool if he did," Mirella said, trying to convince herself that there was nothing to worry about. "Naught will happen, you'll see."

"I hope you're right." His hands slid down the smooth skin of her back, pressing her to his hard length. "Because by God, I can't bear to think of another man touching you like this."

He rolled atop her, his mouth claiming hers in a kiss both violent and tender, sparking anew the embers of passion. They came together in a fury of need that dissolved the fears and uncertainties of reality. She sensed another dimension, too, beyond a mere merging of the physical. Though fragile and tenuous, there was no denying its presence.

It was a melding of the minds, a sharing of their spirits.

Chapter Twenty-four

"Miss Mirella?"

With both hands full of silver forks, Mirella looked up to see Ophelia lumbering into the dining room. The woman wore a woolen cape over her broad figure, and as usual a white turban concealed all but a few wisps of her kinky, graying hair.

"Ah'm goin' over to the kitchen to make sure them lazy, good-for-nothin's ain't settin' on their tails instead of fixin' supper. Ah'll bring you back some hot tea water if you wants me to."

"Thank you, Ophelia, I would appreciate that."

The housekeeper waddled toward the far wall, going outside through a door which was situated there so that food could be brought directly from the kitchen to the table. Mirella let the silver utensils clatter back into the drawer of the mahogany sideboard before wandering to the window to watch Ophelia carefully pick her way across the icy, brown landscape. The weather had warmed the day after Jason had left for Williamsburg but the balmy temperature had lasted only long enough to melt the thin crust of snow before another cold spell had swept over the countryside, freezing the puddles and necessitating the fires that blazed in every hearth.

But even the dreary day failed to dampen Mirella's spirits. Jason was due to return on the morrow, and the prospect made her heart sing. The memory of that night in the stable glowed inside her. Though he hadn't uttered the words of love she longed to hear, his affection and esteem for her had been unmistakable. Over the past week she had done little else but dream of the moment when he would ask her to share the rest of her life with him.

The beliefs which had ruled her judgment for so long were now tempered by her deepening emotions. Yes, there were men who were interested in nothing but gambling, drinking, and whoring, but it didn't mean Jason should be lumped into that category. If she really loved him, then she would have to take the risk of believing in his integrity, and allow him the freedom to be human, to make an occasional mistake.

Mirella returned to the sideboard to complete her inventory of the silver, checking off the number of utensils against a master list. But her mind was only half on the task. Just a little over a fortnight would herald the last day of January, Jason's twenty-ninth birthday, and she was planning a surprise party to celebrate. She mentally examined the guest list as she worked, adding and discarding names.

She was locking the drawers after finishing with the silver when there was a banging on the front door. Mirella hurried from the dining room to answer the summons. With Ophelia out in the kitchen, there was no one else in the house; earlier she had seen Pandora stealing away in the direction of the stable when the girl was supposed to be in her chamber studying her French lesson.

The impatient knocking again echoed through the entrance hall. She shook her head in amused exasperation as her slippered feet scuffed over the wooden floor. Reaching the door, she pulled it open.

The smile died on her lips. For one disbelieving instant she stared in paralyzed silence at Sir Harry's grinning visage, then reality returned, and she made a move to shut him out.

But he was too swift for her. Shoving his way into the house, he stripped off his crimson cloak, revealing a dark green frockcoat lavishly embroidered in gold, with matching waistcoat and yellow velvet breeches. The dandified ensemble looked absurd on his rotund figure.

"I'm so glad you invited me in, dear cousin. 'Tis cold as a witch's tit out there."

Mirella stood beside the open portal, heedless of the gusts of icy wind rippling her skirts. "You're not welcome here. I'll thank you to leave quietly, unless of course you'd rather I call someone and have you thrown out."

"Polite as ever, I see," Sir Harry mocked, rubbing his reddened hands. "Tell me, where might I find a spot of sherry to warm my insides?"

Without waiting for a reply, he strolled away. Mirella hesitated, then closed the door. It couldn't hurt to be alone with him for a few moments. There was little he could do to her with servants just outside the house, close enough for her to reach if she needed help.

431

She followed him into the drawing room, where he stood before a table, filling a glass with amber liquid from a crystal decanter. He took a large gulp of the wine, then belched in appreciation.

" 'Tis a fine house you live in," Sir Harry commented, picking up a porcelain figurine and examining it with sharp eyes. "What a pity you're mistress of only one room—the master's bedchamber." Between chortles, he drained his sherry, then poured himself another.

Mirella itched to argue that he was wrong about her relationship with Jason, but caution held her back. What if the snake found a way to use the information to his advantage? She couldn't risk that merely to salvage her pride.

"Pray, do not make yourself comfortable," she snapped as he slouched into a chair near the fire. "Jason will have your head if he finds you here."

Sir Harry calmly settled his bulk against the cushions, his lips curling upward slightly. "Then how fortuitous it is that I saw your lover last evening in the capital of this dreary colony. His absence should give us ample time alone to talk."

"We've naught to say to one another."

"Why, I beg to differ. There is the matter of our coming nuptials, for one."

Mirella's stomach twisted with revulsion, her mind reeling at a sudden image of herself lying beneath him as he pawed the most intimate places of her body. It seemed sacrilege after what she and Jason had shared. She couldn't stop herself from blurting, "There will be no wedding between us!"

Sir Harry was silent, merely staring at her with the

lazy intensity of a viper eying its next meal. There was a quality of lustful appreciation in his gaze that reminded her she was alone in the house with him. Instinctively she stepped behind a Windsor chair, as if that fragile barrier could shield her from his treachery. She immediately regretted her action, for that subtle admission of fear brought a gloating smile to his fleshy face.

"You speak as though you've already made your decision," he said, his taunting tone implying another message: *We'll see about that.*

"And if I have?" she challenged bravely.

"Then you must have forgotten the alternative— spending the remainder of your days moldering in a cell, not to mention dooming your lover to the same hell. Many die in prison, they say. How long do you wager you'd last?"

Clinging to the notion that he was bluffing, that Jason would testify she had stabbed Sir Harry in self-defense, Mirella was goaded to retort, " 'Tis the lesser of the two evils when given the choice of marrying you."

"Indeed? And what makes you so certain you wouldn't enjoy being my wife?"

With slow deliberation, Sir Harry finished his wine, setting the glass on a table. Then he rose, closing the short space between them at a leisurely pace. His dark eyes hinted at his lewd thoughts, and as he drew nearer, she swallowed hard, winding her fingers around the wooden back of the chair, refusing to succumb to a cowardly urge to flee. She searched wildly for a way to distract him.

"Where is Samantha?" she stalled. "You two

seemed to share a cozy relationship at Ben Harrison's party."

Sir Harry chuckled lazily, pausing almost within touching distance. "She was furious at missing out on the sport today. 'Twould seem she derives great satisfaction from watching you squirm. But you see, my dear,"—he took a step closer—"I thought she might be a hindrance. After all, a man doesn't bring his mistress along when he goes courting a wife."

"If you dare come any nearer, I'll call one of the servants to throw you out."

"You're bluffing, my pet. You can't afford to anger me."

Before she could react, his arms snaked out with a swiftness that belied his stocky build. His fingers bit viciously into her shoulders as he slammed her against his bulk. She tried to wrench herself free, but he was squeezing her too tightly. His breath stank of soured sherry as he surveyed with satisfaction her frustrated fury. He was so close that she could detect each red, broken vein on his bulbous nose.

"Now," he grunted, " 'tis time I had a taste of what awaits me in our marriage bed."

Repulsed, Mirella jerked her head aside so that his moist lips landed on her cheek rather than her mouth. Again she twisted, panting, intent on wriggling out of his loathsome grasp. His brutal fingers closed around her breast to pinch her tender flesh, and through her skirts, she felt the hard bulge of his lust.

In desperation, she raised her foot and with all her strength jabbed the wooden heel of her slipper downward onto his instep. The ploy worked. He howled with pain, and his grip slackened. Taking full advantage of the opportunity, she propelled herself backward and out of his arms, snatching up a pewter candlestick with which to defend herself.

A sudden clatter behind her made her whip around. Relief spread through her as she saw Ophelia depositing a tray on a table. The big woman advanced on Sir Harry, brandishing a silver teapot in her hand.

"Touch her again, you devil, and Ah'll dump this hot water on you, and then bust you over the head!"

"Insolent bitch!" Sir Harry was hopping on one foot, looking like a clumsy, overstuffed pigeon, his cheeks crimson with anger. "You dare threaten me, a white man? I'll have your black hide whipped for that!"

"Lay a finger on her," Mirella snapped, "and you'll have both Jason and myself to answer to. Now I would advise you to leave here before you embroil yourself in worse trouble than you already have." Adding weight to her words, she raised the candlestick menacingly.

Sir Harry glared at her, the harsh sound of his breathing mingling with the soft crackle of the fire. "You'll regret having spoken to me in that tone," he blustered. Straightening his lacy jabot, he edged past the two women, favoring his injured foot while watching their makeshift weapons with mistrustful eyes.

At the doorway, he paused and said coldly, "You have until the first of February, cousin. If you fail to do as I say, a warrant will be issued for the arrest of you and your lover. I shall enjoy seeing the both of you shackled and carted off like dogs. And don't get any foolish notions about running. No matter where you go, I'll track you down." Pivoting, he limped out of the room, the front door slamming behind him a moment later.

"That man is no good," Ophelia pronounced as she placed the silver teapot on a table. "The massah, he gonna be mad as a hornet when he hears 'bout this."

"That's precisely why you're not to breathe a word to him of what happened."

The housekeeper stared. "You crazy? That man, he was pawing you like you was some loose woman! The massah, he ain't gonna stand for that, not for one minute he ain't!"

Mirella's fingers tightened around the base of the candlestick. Ophelia was right, but the problem, she feared, was that Jason wouldn't be content until he had spilled Sir Harry's blood. And at this point, injuring the villain would only bring the law down on their heads all the sooner.

" 'Tis for Jason's own welfare that I ask you not to tell him. Wreaking vengeance could result in his imprisonment, and to what purpose? No real harm was done me, and 'tis unlikely Sir Harry will return to bother me again." At least, she amended silently, not until the deadline.

The black woman shook her turbaned head in doubt. "Ah don't know. That man, he deserves a whuppin'."

"Please, Ophelia, trust me," she begged. "We must let this incident die here and now. Everything will turn out best that way, you'll see."

Finally the housekeeper agreed to hold her tongue. Grumbling her disapproval, she departed, leaving Mirella sitting before the fireplace, sipping lukewarm tea.

436

For all her brave front, Mirella felt a surge of uneasiness as she pondered Sir Harry's threats. She feared his retribution, not only for herself but for Jason. His visit today brought her dilemma into sharper focus. As she saw it, she had three choices. First, she could run away in the hopes that Sir Harry would be so busy tracking her that he would forget about Jason. Yet he might still prosecute Jason later, so what good would that accomplish?

However, if she stayed, there was a slim chance that she might be cleared of the crime. With Jason the only witness, perhaps they could prove that she had acted in self-defense. If nothing else, that fact might gain her a lighter sentence. But what if the judge chose to believe the word of a titled English gentleman over that of two commoners?

Then again, she could wed Sir Harry.

Mirella grimaced, the thin porcelain cup rattling as she set it down on the silver tray that sat atop the japanned tea table. The thought of submitting to his beastly, carnal demands made bile rise bitterly in her throat. Yet if she were to marry him, she would save Jason from the ignominy of being dragged through a public trial and possibly sentenced to prison for sheltering a criminal. Did she have the courage to make that sacrifice?

At least she had until the first of February to decide, she reflected, the day after Jason's birthday, a little over a fortnight away.

Mirella had just stepped from her bath the next morning when she happened to glance out the window

437

and into the pale, wintry sunshine. The tide had washed away much of yesterday's ice, leaving only a frozen edge along the embankment of the river. A small sailboat was approaching the dock with Jason at the helm.

She caught her breath, staring in disbelief. He must have left Williamsburg at the crack of dawn! Not expecting him to arrive until midafternoon at the earliest, she had dawdled in the steamy tub in front of a blazing fire. Now he was here, and she was far from ready!

Hastily she dried herself, then wound the towel around her dripping hair. Darting to the door, she poked her head out and called Clea.

Without waiting for the maid's arrival, Mirella scurried over to the bed where her undergarments lay neatly arranged. Frantically she donned chemise, drawers, and hooped petticoat, the laces and starched linens rustling. Merciful heavens, she had planned to be waiting sedately for him in the drawing room, all perfumed and polished, the very image of a lady. Instead she was rushing about like a madwoman!

There was a knock at the door, then Clea entered the bedchamber. "The massah's home, ma'am."

"Yes, I know! Make haste, and help me into my gown."

She stepped into the shimmering folds of a lilac sacque, adjusting the full skirt with trembling fingers as Clea nimbly fastened the back. The low, embroidered bodice revealed the shadowed valley between her breasts, and the sleeves were close fitting to the elbow, ending in deep, treble ruffles.

She perched on a stool before the fire, fidgeting in

restless excitement as Clea first toweled her hair, then began combing the long, ebony tresses. Not two minutes later, the door burst open without warning, and Jason strode into the bedchamber. Mirella sprang up with a gasp, her hair damp and rippling down her back.

"Out," he softly ordered, flicking a glance at Clea. The black girl smiled and bobbed a curtsey as she left the room.

Watching him, Mirella felt her blood beat a swift tempo. As always, his appearance was a blend of gentlemanly elegance and blunt masculinity. His clothing was in the latest style, yet simply executed, without the frills and furbelows of a dandy. Jason's inscrutable gaze moved slowly over her. What was he thinking? Had he missed her with the same aching intensity as she had him?

Her doubts were swept away when suddenly he uttered a low, hoarse sound and surged forward to enfold her in his embrace. His mouth came down on hers, his fingers sliding into the moist mass of her hair, fingers which still held a trace of cold from the outdoors. Her lips parted to the tender demand of his tongue. Wreathing her arms around his neck, she melted into his hard body, the staccato throb of her pulse pounding in her ears. Against her breasts, she could feel the answering thud of his heart, swift and heavy.

"I'm so glad," Jason murmured, his warm breath on her lips, "glad to be home and back in your arms."

She laughed, a sound breathless with delight and desire. "I didn't expect you so early. I've not yet finished dressing—I must be a sight—"

"For sore eyes," he finished, smiling down at her with such softness that she wondered how it could possibly have taken her so many months to realize that she loved him.

"And anyway," he went on, " 'tis a shame you bothered donning all these garments"—his finger slipped inside her bodice, boldly caressing a nipple—"when I'm only going to take them off again."

"Now . . . here . . . in the middle of the day?" She was aghast, yet aroused despite herself. "What will people think? You shouldn't be in my bedchamber alone with me to begin with!"

"You worry overmuch, my love. But while I'm distracted, I may as well give you a present I bought you in Williamsburg."

Laughing in response to his light-hearted mood, Mirella let him haul her over to the looking glass, where he twirled her around so that she was standing in front of him, facing her reflection. In the mirror, she saw him reach into the pocket of his coat. Then his arms were encircling her, his hands burrowing beneath her heavy mass of damp hair to fasten a piece of jewelry around her neck.

It was a fragile webwork of sapphires and diamonds which glinted in the watery sunshine streaming in the window. Her smile slowly dissolved as she reached up to touch the stones with her fingertips. The gems felt cold against her flesh, and she was conscious of a peculiar, icy prickling deep within her.

"Does the necklace please you?" Jason asked with a touch of anxiety, caressing her cheek with the back of his hand. "I thought the sapphires would go well with your eyes."

She stared at his reflection in the mirror. "Why?" The word was a mere whisper, a sigh in the stillness, punctuated by the snap of a burning log.

"What do you mean, why? You have lovely blue-gray eyes, and I—"

"No," she broke in. "Why do you give this to me?"

A slight tilt of his head indicated puzzlement. "Because it enhances your beauty . . . because I want to give you pretty things." He turned her to face him, smiling down at her, his hands warm on her shoulders.

"By damn, Mirella, I thought you *expected* me to bring you a trinket. Don't you know that a mistress isn't supposed to question a gift from her lover?"

Chapter Twenty-five

Shock drained the blood from Mirella's face. Though the first sight of the gemstones had caused a faint stirring of suspicion in her, she was unprepared for the devastation that ripped through her on hearing her premonition confirmed.

Mistress. That was all he intended to offer her, all he had ever intended. How could she have been fool enough to think he'd changed? That he had fallen in love as deeply as she had? That he would want to marry her?

"I see," she said, her voice stiff and bitter with disillusionment. Again, she fingered the necklace, a part of her still resisting its significance. "And do I presume correctly, then, that this . . . this *trinket* is payment for services rendered?"

Jason gave a wary laugh. "No, of course it isn't meant that way. I merely wanted to give you something that would make you happy."

All I wanted was your love! she longed to cry out. That yearning was smothered beneath an emotion which boiled up inside her, a seething, savage fury that was directed with equal force at both his callousness and her own stupidity. With a violent twist, she spun out of his arms.

"How dare you!" she spat coldly. "How dare you presume to buy me like a common trollop!"

Her fingers closed around the stones, and with a vicious jerk, she broke the delicate clasp, heedless of the stab of pain as the metal scratched her neck. She flung the necklace at him, and he caught it against his chest.

Every trace of amusement vanished from his face, like a slate wiped clean. "What the devil's wrong with you? You're misinterpreting a simple gift—"

"A gift? Why not call it a reward, like a bone thrown to a dog? Or do you mean it as a bribe to ensure I'll continue to warm your bed? Well, you've failed, because I'm not for sale."

Resentment flashed over his features. "I should have known better," he said with a harsh chuckle. "You'd think I'd have learned by now not to trust a woman's word. Do you derive some perverse enjoyment out of leading a man on?"

"I never said I would be your mistress!"

"Not in so many words. But what else was I to presume when you gave yourself to me that night in the stables?" His voice softened. "My God, Mirella, you said you loved me!"

The blatant reminder of her foolishness brought a choking lump to her throat. She stared at him, her mind frozen. In self-protection, she knew she should laugh and say she had lied to him, but words failed her. Helplessly she watched the stunned expression steal over his face. . . .

"By damn," he swore quietly, "did you expect a proposal of marriage from me?"

It was the final humiliation. She had bared her soul to him only to suffer a crushing rejection. With jerky movements, she turned away, feeling the force of pain in every fiber of her body. Through blurring eyes, she gazed out the window, seeing nothing, intent on controlling the tears that threatened to spill forth at any moment.

His hand settled tentatively on her shoulder. "Mirella, what can I say? I thought you understood I've no interest in marrying."

There was an odd note in his voice, something akin to both bewilderment and wistful regret. For the space of a heartbeat, she felt herself softening, beset by a peculiar urge to put her arms around him and comfort him. Then wrath flared inside her again. Damn him for attempting to play on her sympathies as if *he* were the wronged party, not she! Keeping her gaze trained on the window, she shook off his fingers.

"Get out of here!" she hissed through gritted teeth.

"Mirella, believe me, I never meant to hurt—"

"I said, *get out*! And don't ever come near me again!"

Behind her, he was silent for a moment, then in a voice that was heavy and stiff, he said, "As you wish."

She heard the muffled tread of his steps crossing the carpet, and the click of the door as he left. Only then did her spine lose its rigidity, and she slumped to the floor, weeping.

By the following evening, her raw agony had subsided to a dull ache. Mirella stood at the drawing-room window, the fluttering flames in the hearth behind her reflected on the night-darkened glass. Today the memory of Jason's rebuff was at least bearable. After her initial, cathartic outburst of tears, a blessed numbness had settled over her battered emotions. Since then, she had been able to function with a modicum of normality, hiding her inner trauma from the rest of the household.

Beyond that, she had been unable to decide what to do.

On impulse she turned and left the drawing room, stopping before the gilt-framed portrait of Elizabeth Stirling Fletcher which hung in the entrance hall. Elizabeth was the daughter of an earl, and her aristocratic heritage was evident in the classic elegance of her face. Mirella recalled that Ophelia had told her Jason had married Elizabeth in London and then brought her here, only to watch her die in childbirth a year later.

Mirella studied the painting. In the soft glow of light from the wall sconces, Jason's wife looked like an angel. She was standing in a pastoral setting, gazing into the distance as if she dreamed of her lover. Hair the color and texture of spun gold formed curls that cascaded down one pearly shoulder. A gauzy, orchid purple gown draped her slim figure, hinting at the feminine curves beneath.

How could any man fail to be mesmerized by a woman of such glorious beauty? Mirella wondered wistfully. It was likely that Jason's bitterness toward marriage stemmed from the pain he'd suffered upon Elizabeth's death nine years ago. He undoubtedly was still in love with her. Why else would he have left her portrait hanging here, where he would see it every time he walked into the house?

Was there any chance of exorcising Elizabeth's ghost from Jason's heart, of freeing him to love once again?

Absently Mirella played with the cameo pinned to the bodice of her dove gray gown. On a rational level, she tried to tell herself that there was no future with him, that she should leave Elysian Fields and make a life for herself elsewhere. Yet hope lingered in her like a guttering candle flame that valiantly refuses to die. How could she give him up when she loved him so?

Soon, though, her hand would be forced, if Sir Harry had his way. She had two weeks in which to make a decision. Marry him, or risk his vengeance on both Jason and herself. Was it not best to do as Sir Harry wished, and thereby at least save Jason from suffering the consequences of her deed?

The clock on the drawing-room mantelpiece chimed softly as the front door opened. Mirella turned to see Jason stride into the entrance hall just ahead of his brother. Ever since Troy had arrived early that afternoon, they had been in the plantation office discussing business matters.

She fought a cowardly impulse to run. Until this moment, she had managed to avoid coming face to face with Jason. But now pride compelled her feet forward, and she greeted the two men with her lips curved into a smile which she hoped wasn't as stiff as it felt.

Supper was an ordeal. She wished Pandora were there, filling the air with her chatter, but the girl was visiting a friend overnight. Though Mirella did her best to engage the men in conversation, she feared her speech sounded stilted. Jason was silent for the most part, his manner polite but pensive, giving little hint of the thoughts churning behind those brooding gold eyes. By the time the meal was over, all she wanted was to escape to her chamber, where she could drop the mask of enforced gaiety.

She was about to excuse herself when Noah appeared in the doorway of the dining room. "Sir," he addressed Jason, "Ah come to tell you Ah found the missing ledger."

"Good. We can look at it in the office." Jason threw down his damask napkin and got up. He frowned as his brother made no move to follow. "Troy, aren't you coming?"

"You go on without me, Jase. I've had enough of numbers for one day."

Jason hesitated, then glancing at Mirella with an almost indiscernible tightening of his lips, he left the room.

As soon as he was gone, she rose. "If you'll excuse me, I believe I'll retire for the night."

"Whoa," Troy said, leaping up to catch her arm before she could advance more than two steps. "Why so early? With Jase gone, we can't pass up this opportunity to discuss his surprise birthday party."

Despite her eagerness to be alone, Mirella reluctantly accompanied him into the drawing room, settling herself on a brocaded couch. Troy closed the doors, then poured two glasses of Madeira, handing her one as he sat down beside her.

"Are the invitations ready for me to deliver?" he asked.

"Almost. If I don't have them completed by the time you leave tomorrow, I'll think up a pretext to send them to you without arousing Jason's suspicions."

"And what of the other preparations? Is there any way I can help you there?"

"Thank you, but Pandora, Ophelia, and I should be able to handle the rest."

Mirella took a large swallow of the pale wine, intending to finish it quickly and retreat to her bedchamber. Much as she liked Troy, it was a strain to keep up this cheery façade.

"So tell me, what's happened between you and Jase?"

The blunt question disconcerted her. "I don't know what you mean," she stalled.

"Come now," Troy scoffed gently. "This afternoon, he was as ornery as a bear with a sore paw, and when I mentioned your name, he nearly bit my head off." He reached out to squeeze her hand reassuringly. "I've no right to pry, but I thought you might need someone to talk to."

The sympathetic understanding on his face pierced the bulwark protecting her emotions, and Mirella found herself pouring out the painful story of how Jason wanted her as his mistress. Troy listened gravely, his support a balm to her battered feelings.

"I'd always known Jase was mule-headed, but this is beyond belief," he said grimly when she was through. "How could a brother of mine treat you with such deplorable insensitivity? I've a good mind to go knock some sense into his thick skull."

Mirella observed his balled fist with alarm.

449

"Please, I didn't mean to cause trouble between the two of you. I should never have spoken of this to you. Promise you won't come to blows with Jason over me!"

Troy's dark frown faded, and a crooked smile lightened his face. "Would that I could convince myself your concern was for my welfare, but alas, I know 'tis only my brother who could wrench such a passionate plea from your lips."

"I would not want to be the cause of either of you being harmed," she disagreed.

He heaved a dramatic sigh. "Such are the crumbs I must settle for. All right, then, if it pleases you, you have my pledge that I won't fight with Jase." In a more serious vein, he added, "What are your plans now, Mirella? Remember, if you need a home, you're welcome to stay with me for as long as you like."

"Thank you, but I must decline." She set her wine glass aside, attempting a smile. "You see, this incident has taught me a bitter lesson—that I'm weak. I simply cannot bring myself to leave Jason, not just yet."

Troy slipped an arm around her shoulder. "Don't torture yourself so," he murmured. " 'Tis no weakness, but a natural desire to be near the one you love."

"Then you don't think me a coward?"

"Heaven forbid, no. A man could never ask for a finer sister-in-law."

She managed a laugh. "Aren't you being a mite premature?"

"Here now, you must show more optimism," he chided gently. "Jase simply needs time to recognize what a treasure he has in you. He'll come around,

450

you'll see."

Putting down his glass, he pulled her against him in a reassuring embrace, and Mirella drew comfort from both his words and the friendship he offered without restrictions. His hands stroked her back in a way that was more supportive than sensual. For the first time since her confrontation with Jason the previous morning, she felt her spirits lift. It was a relief to spill her troubles to someone; keeping them bottled up only sapped her energy.

The sound of a door opening shattered the fragile peace. Hearing the swift tread of footsteps across the carpet, Mirella lifted her head from Troy's chest—and froze, seeing Jason's angry face. His large hands seized her shoulders and thrust her aside.

He hauled his brother up from the couch and, in one fluid motion, buried his fist in Troy's midsection.

Troy staggered backward from the force of the blow. As he stumbled against a small table, a porcelain figurine slid off the slick surface to shatter on the floor. Jason lunged forward, and with a muted crack, his fist connected with his brother's jaw.

The realization that Troy intended to keep his vow of not fighting his brother galvanized Mirella. She leaped up from the couch to wedge herself between the two men before Jason could inflict any more damage.

"Jason, stop! Have you gone mad?"

"Get out of my way!" he snarled.

She dug her fingers into the smooth linen of his shirt, conscious of the coiled tension in his muscles. In desperation, she pleaded, "Haven't you done enough damage already? Dear God, he's your *brother*!"

"He has a fine way of demonstrating his brotherly love. No sooner do I walk out of the room than he's trying to seduce my woman!"

"You have this all wrong, Jase," his brother said, gingerly wiping away the blood that trickled from a corner of his mouth.

"I don't want to hear any of your lies," Jason sneered. "You've overstepped the bounds of my hospitality, so get out of my house!"

Troy made no move to obey. "Mirella, would you rather I stayed?" he asked quietly, turning his green eyes on her.

Though touched that he would protect her at the risk of enduring his brother's wrath, she hastened to reassure him. "Thank you, but I'll be all right."

Troy threw his brother a grim look. "If you harm so much as one hair on her head, you'll be sorry."

"Wouldn't you just love an excuse to take her from me," Jason mocked. "Well, think again, brother, because I'll never let you have her."

Troy merely gave him a level stare, then turned on his heel and strode out of the drawing room, past Ophelia and two wide-eyed serving girls who stood in the doorway. Seeing them, Jason scowled.

"Get back to your work," he ordered.

The girls immediately scuttled into the dining room, where they had been clearing the supper dishes. But Ophelia waddled into the drawing room, hands straddling her wide waist.

"How you expect a body to get anythin' done 'round here with all this fightin' and shoutin' like crazy folk? Your mama'd be ashamed of you!"

"I'm in no mood for your backtalk," Jason said

testily. "You have duties to attend to."

"Yes, *suh*!" The black woman bent her substantial body and, muttering to herself, began picking up the pieces of the porcelain figurine which scattered the floor.

"I meant now, Ophelia."

"I'm workin'," she said in stubborn defiance, her displeasure with him radiating like a tangible presence in the air.

"Oh, for God's sake!" he snapped.

Snatching Mirella's hand, Jason hauled her out of the drawing room, slamming the door behind them; then he pulled her into his bedchamber, banging shut that door also. He pivoted to face her, hands on his hips, his face cold and uncompromising in the soft light of the fire blazing in the hearth.

"Are you having an affair with Troy?"

The blunt demand made Mirella burn with an anger born of pain. Though well aware of his superior physical strength, she responded with reckless disregard.

"How can you believe such a thing of me—or of your own brother? Just because you lack scruples, don't assume the rest of the world does, too."

"Mirella, I want the truth," he warned, his voice dangerously low.

"You wouldn't recognize the truth if it reached out and slapped you in the face!"

In two long steps, he closed the distance between them, his hands tightening around her shoulders. "Answer me, damn you! I want to know . . . I *have* to know what's between you and my brother!"

There was something haunted, something deeply

tortured in his expression. It penetrated her defenses, draining away that brief surge of fury until she felt only an overwhelming desire to sooth him. "Nothing," she found herself reassuring him. "Troy and I share only friendship."

For a long moment Jason stared at her, his golden eyes troubled. Then he sighed, and she felt the tension seeping out of his muscles. "Fool or not," he whispered, lifting a hand to touch her cheek, "I believe you."

He bent his head and, in the split second before he kissed her, Mirella knew she ought to pull away for the sake of self-preservation. But instead her lips parted in wanton invitation. His mouth tasted sweet; his familiar scent enveloped her. Excitement pulsed through her bloodstream. She felt her bones dissolving, and she had to lean against his hard frame for support, her fingers creeping around his neck to thread into the thick silk of his hair.

A wave of love washed away her common sense. No matter what the cost, she craved the joy of their physical intimacy, a mindless state where she could pretend that he cherished her as much as she did him. Soon she might be forced to leave here, and that made this moment of closeness all the more precious.

The gentle sensuality of his hands caused her to tremble with need. Eyes closed, she arched her neck as his mouth roamed down to her throat to kiss the spot where her pulse beat rapidly. Without lifting his lips, he reached around to unfasten her gown. Her bodice and chemise pooled at her waist, and his warm breath feathered the ripe swell of her breast, his tongue playing with a taut nipple.

Desire poured through her veins, compelling her shaky fingers to undo the buttons of his shirt. Sliding her hands inside the garment, she pressed her palms against the muscles of his chest, reveling in the strength of him, feeling the swift throb of his heart.

Then somehow they were both undressed, and he was lying atop her beneath the bedcovers, his long legs entwined with hers. He combed his fingers through her tangled ebony hair, the fire painting his face with a golden glow.

"Mirella . . . what you do to me . . . what you make me feel. . . ."

He looked slightly baffled, as if he couldn't quite fathom the nature of her hold on him. She lifted a hand to stroke his cheek, helpless to keep from voicing the emotion that surged from the depths of her soul.

"I love you, Jason."

He exhaled—a strange sigh that bore a trace of both relief and bewilderment. Then his lips came down on hers in a kiss of such fierce tenderness that it sapped her remaining strength. Reality receded until she knew only the thrust of their bodies, the salt taste of his skin, the mounting need that pulsed in her belly. And in a rush of overwhelming sensation, her world exploded with ecstasy.

Afterward, they lay with limbs intertwined, two parts of a whole, lungs and pulsebeats slowing to normal rhythms. Mirella drifted in a haze of euphoria, his warmth enveloping her like a protective blanket.

Yet an intruding thought began to nip at her contentment. When they made love, did he ever wish she were Elizabeth? In his heart, did he rail against the fate that had stolen from him the one woman he cherished more than any other?

Jason propped his head on his hand, gently stroking away a strand of hair from her cheek as he gazed down at her with a hint of apology. "Mirella, I want you to know that I never meant to make love to you tonight. I had every intention of respecting your wish not to be my mistress."

She was touched by his sincerity, yet she also felt a twinge of misery. Why couldn't he love her? Was there no hope of him ever wanting more of her than just her body?

"Is it because of Elizabeth?" she blurted.

"Elizabeth?" he repeated blankly. "You mean my wife? Whatever has she to do with us?"

Mirella already regretted her impulsive question. Though perhaps, she told herself reluctantly, it would be good to hear from Jason's lips how much he cared for his dead wife. It would make it easier for her to leave when the time came.

She swallowed hard. "You still love her, don't you? 'Tis understandable," Mirella rushed on, delaying the moment when she would have to face the inevitable. "In her portrait she looks sweet and pure and lovely, like an angel. I don't really blame you for being reluctant to marry again. It must be difficult enough for you to accept the fact that she's gone, let alone to find a woman who could replace her in your affections."

Jason was staring at her with a peculiar expression. "Whatever in God's holy name gave you the notion that I pine for Elizabeth?"

" 'Tis plain enough. Why else would you leave her

portrait hanging in the hall so that you should see it whenever—"

"I wanted to remind myself of my folly," he finished coldly. "As far as Elizabeth being sweet, you couldn't be further from the truth. She was a sulky, vain, ill-tempered bitch who got whatever she wanted by whining and manipulating. I'll grant you she was lovely—that was what lured me into her snare in the first place—but she had the sinuous beauty of a serpent. And pure?" He let out a harsh laugh. "On our wedding night, I found out that I hadn't been the first to experience her charms. You see, it seems Elizabeth had a yen for stable boys and lords alike; rank mattered little to her so long as her target was male and willing to unbutton his breeches for her. And I was an idealistic fool who insisted on waiting to bed her until we were properly united."

Mirella gaped at him in astonishment. "Then you never loved her?"

"At the time, I thought it was love, but in retrospect I can see 'twas pure infatuation," Jason said, his voice filled with self-disgust. "I'd gone to London on business right after my parents' death, and being at the impressionable age of eighteen, I was easy prey for Elizabeth. It seems her father feared a scandal over her sexual indiscretions, so he gave her an ultimatum—choose a husband or he'd find one for her himself. She set her sights on me, a wealthy colonial who knew naught of the gossip whispered about her. I was fool enough to believe she was wildly in love with me."

"Oh, Jason," Mirella murmured in sympathy.

"Idiot that I was," he continued, "I was willing to

457

forgive and forget, especially when Elizabeth swore very prettily that though she'd made a few mistakes they would never be repeated. And so I brought her here to Virginia—and discovered exactly what my benevolence had accomplished. Some months later, I came home early one afternoon and found her in bed with the local dancing master. Needless to say, that destroyed what little remained of our marriage."

His voice was emotionless as he went on, "When Elizabeth learned to her disgust that she was pregnant, I had no idea if she carried the fruit of my seed or some other man's bastard. Yet so long as there was a chance that the child was mine, I was determined to raise him or her as my own; at least I'd have salvaged an heir from the wreckage of my marriage. Elizabeth hated the way her body swelled as the baby grew, and she made life hell for everyone around her. It was a difficult birth, and the child—a boy—lived only a few hours. Elizabeth succumbed to a fever several days later."

He rolled over on his back to stare at the pale canopy overhead. "The worst of it," he added heavily, "is that to this day I've no idea whether or not the infant buried in the family cemetery is my son."

"Jason, I'm so sorry."

Laying her head on his shoulder, Mirella strove to comfort him, sensing that his pain and bitterness went far deeper than he would admit. So she had been wrong about Elizabeth. That time when she had seen him at the Fletcher family gravesite he must have been mourning not his dead wife but the child who might be his son. Though Elizabeth was the reason he disdained marriage, it was not because he still loved her, but because she had betrayed him. And now Mirella could understand why, when he'd found her in Troy's arms, he had reacted with such violence. After Elizabeth's treachery, who could blame Jason for his mistrust of women?

He tipped her chin up so that their eyes met. "Will you sleep beside me tonight?" he asked. "I'll awaken you before the first light, so you can return to your own bed without anyone seeing you."

"Of course," she said softly.

The invitation was too tempting to refuse, even if she hadn't heard the raw thread of need in his voice. Though she suspected the true nature of their relationship had long been evident to the servants, she was glad that he cared enough to want to make the gesture of protecting her reputation.

She cuddled against his warm length, feeling the security of his arms enfolding her. A deep contentment stole over her; perhaps, she hoped dimly as her eyes grew heavy, her love would someday be sufficient to erase the torment of his past.

Long after Mirella was asleep, Jason lay awake, staring at the shadows that danced on the dark paneled walls. The fire was burning low, and he knew he ought to throw another log onto it to chase away the chill of the night, but he was loath to leave, even for a moment, the woman who was curled against his side.

He bent his head and dropped a gentle kiss on her forehead, winding his fingers into her tousled hair. He was in love with her; that much he had admitted to himself earlier this evening. What else but his intense feelings for her could have induced him to strike his own brother?

For many months, he had been avoiding examining his emotions. Now he realized why he had so stubbornly insisted she be his mistress. By relegating her to a position lower than wife he could continue to deny his feelings for her. He had sought only a physical relationship, one that would protect him from the pain that commitment could bring.

And now that he had acknowledged the truth, where would he go from here?

Longing warred with a deep sense of vulnerability. By damn, he wanted to bind her to him with the vows of holy matrimony, to keep her by his side all day and in his bed each night! But his one marriage had been a tragic mistake. Hadn't he learned not to put his faith in a woman?

It wasn't that he equated Mirella and Elizabeth; the two were as different as black and white. Yet this time he risked being hurt far worse; this time his emotions were involved to a degree that caused a cold knot of fear in his gut.

Could he trust Mirella's love? A fact he had long ago accepted was that a woman's first priority in choosing a husband was the extent of his wealth. What if Mirella's affection for him sprang in part from the life of luxury he could provide her? And even though he believed her avowal that she and Troy were only friends, would he ever overcome this helpless dread that she might someday betray him for another man?

She stirred, snuggling more closely to him. The feel of her silky skin against his body heated his blood, but Jason made no move to waken her. He was content to lie beside her, holding her in his arms, knowing that at least for this moment she belonged to him alone.

For the first time in his life, he discovered there could be as much pleasure in simply being with a woman as there was in the physical act of love itself.

Chapter Twenty-six

"Oh, Emma, he's such a darling," Mirella sighed, gazing down at the baby in her arms. "Lucas must be so proud."

The infant was sleeping peacefully, wrapped in a swaddling blanket with only his face and tiny clenched fists peeping out. He had been born the previous evening after long hours of labor, with both Mirella and a midwife in attendance. Lucas had hovered over them anxiously, adamantly refusing to leave the small cabin until finally they had allowed him to sit beside the bed and hold his wife's hand.

"We're both pleased to have a healthy son." Emma was propped against the pillows, looking tired but serene.

"If this little boy had delayed a few more minutes, he'd have shared a birthday with Jason."

Her friend smiled with delight. "Oh, in all the excitement, I'd forgotten! You're planning a surprise party tonight for Mr. Fletcher, aren't you? Heavens, you must be terribly busy with the preparations."

"Yes, but I couldn't resist stopping by again to see

you and your son."

Mirella gently stroked the newborn's velvety cheek, imagining the joy of holding her own baby. Before the year was out, she would have that chance, for she was carrying Jason's child.

Though her monthly time was only a little over a week late, the certainty of her pregnancy burned deep within her heart. Their child had been conceived that night in the stables when she had first told Jason she loved him.

Over the past few days, she had devoted a great deal of thought to the future. Tomorrow she would have to give Sir Harry her answer. If she married him immediately, she might be able to convince him the child was his, and her baby would at least escape the ignominy of being born out of wedlock. But even if by some stroke of luck Sir Harry didn't guess the truth, could she subject a helpless infant to that man's villainy?

Never. So, then, she could either remain here or leave. If she stayed, she had enough faith in Jason to trust that he would be more than generous with financial support. But knowing the way he felt about marriage, he wouldn't wed her, and that meant her baby would be branded a bastard. She would do anything to prevent that from happening.

That left her no choice but to leave. If all went well, she could lose herself in one of the colonies' large cities, Boston or Philadelphia perhaps. To legitimize her pregnancy, she would pose as a widow who had suffered the recent loss of her husband. The problem was she had no money, not until she could find a job to support herself. For that reason, she regretted having refused the necklace Jason had wanted to give her. Now, for her baby's sake, she would have swallowed her pride and accepted it, then sold it to obtain the funds she so desperately needed.

And if Sir Harry fulfilled his promise of prosecuting Jason in her stead? She couldn't consider that possibility; she had to think first of the tiny life growing within her. Nor could she dwell on what would happen if Sir Harry tracked her down and turned her in to the authorities. According to the law, a woman was immune from punishment so long as she was pregnant, but afterward, who would take care of her child?

"Someday you'll have one of your own."

Emma's gentle voice brought Mirella back to the present.

"I hope that when I do, he's as sweet as yours," Mirella replied, careful to keep her tone light, for no one but herself knew just how soon that blessed event was to occur.

She handed the baby back to his mother. On impulse, she leaned down and hugged Emma, knowing that this likely would be the last time she would ever see her friend. Repressing tears, she quietly left the tiny bedroom, careful not to disturb Lucas, who was stretched out asleep in front of the fire in the main room of the cabin, exhausted from having stayed up most of the night.

The midmorning sun shone brightly over the brown landscape, though the air betrayed the chill of late January. On the horizon, dark clouds hovered. Would it snow before the day was over? wondered Mirella, drawing her mantle close to ward off the icy wind.

That might hinder her, for late tonight, after the party was over, she planned to slip away to make a life for herself and her child elsewhere.

Her throat tightened at the thought of leaving Jason. For the past two weeks, she had been helpless to resist him. Over and over, whenever they could seize a stolen moment, they had made love, and each time, their coupling was tinged with a bittersweet urgency, as if they were both storing up memories for the lonely years ahead.

There was no mistaking the tenderness and esteem he felt for her. But though she often told him she loved him, never once did he voice his own emotions. She had decided finally that she was living in a fool's paradise. Their child's welfare had to come before her own dreams of Jason someday changing his mind about marriage.

There was only tonight's party left to endure, and then she would part from him forever.

"Hush now, they're coming," Pandora whispered, racing back into the drawing room from her post at one of the entrance-hall windows.

The buzz of conversation died down. Mirella surveyed the darkened chamber, only the fire in the hearth illuminating the sea of faces, all friends of Jason's who were gathered here to celebrate his twenty-ninth birthday. Complying with her instructions, they had arrived early, concealing their carriages and horses in the barn. Troy had connived to get his brother to visit him that day and had promised to keep Jason occupied until well after the scheduled arrival of the guests.

466

Two sets of boots tramped up the porch steps. Mirella heard the deep rumbling annoyance in Jason's voice as the door swung open and the men entered the house.

"I still don't see why it was necessary for you to come back here—"

"Surprise!" The word was exclaimed in unison by a tumult of male and female voices, and a bevy of servants began scurrying about the drawing room lighting candles.

Jason stood in the doorway staring at the crowd with a startled expression, melting snowflakes glinting on his coat and hair. "What the devil—"

" 'Tis your birthday, big brother," Troy said, clapping him on the shoulder.

A slow grin touched the corners of Jason's mouth. "So that's why you simply *had* to have my advice today on which of your fields to plant come spring."

There were a few stifled laughs from the guests as Troy gave a modest shrug. "I had to get you out of the house, else Mirella would have murdered me."

"Ah, *Mirella*. I might have known she was involved in this." Jason's eyes searched the throng for her. "Come here," he said, holding out his hand.

Smiling, she stepped toward him, her blue-gray silk moire skirt swishing softly. When she drew near, he slid his arm around her waist, pulling her close against the hard length of his side.

"So I have you to thank for all of this." Bending, he dropped a chaste kiss on her cheek.

"Can't you do better than that?" someone called out from the back of the drawing room, a voice which Mirella identified as belonging to Ben Harrison.

"Here, here!" several others seconded.

Jason flashed a wicked grin at the crowd. "I'm certainly willing to try."

He looked at Mirella, his smile softening, the molten gold of his eyes darkening with desire. His palms, still cold from the outdoors, framed her face as his mouth lowered to hers.

For an instant, she was aghast that he would kiss her with such intimacy in front of so many people. Then she forgot all her scruples, the world fading until only the two of them existed. She parted her lips to the seductive temptation of his tongue. Her fingers curled around the lapels of his coat, the wool broadcloth smooth to her touch. A rapid pulse beat in her ears. She was awash in sensation, rejoicing in the brandied taste of his mouth and the masculine scent of his body.

His lips left hers with a slowness that told Mirella he was as reluctant as she was to end the kiss. Her eyelids fluttered open, and she looked up at him. The tenderness on his rugged features made her heart twist with longing. Oh, if only she didn't have to leave him!

A smattering of applause reminded her they were not alone. She turned her head to gaze at the crowd in mortification, her cheeks flushing pink though most of the guests wore smiles of understanding.

Jason glanced at her distressed expression, then he took a step forward to address the milling people. "Well, what is everyone waiting for? Let's begin the party."

Conversation and laughter swelled the room, and in one corner, a fiddler started to play a merry tune.

* * *

Samantha stood at the back of the drawing room, the exotic beauty of her face distorted by hatred as she watched Mirella and Jason. God, how she despised those two, especially that simpering girl, Mirella! There was nothing she wanted more than to see their budding romance destroyed.

Sir Harry had warned her not to attend this party, that little would be accomplished by angering Jason and suffering the embarrassment of being thrown out. But she had been unable to resist coming here on her own, uninvited, to take advantage of this opportunity to gloat over what would happen on the morrow. If Mirella didn't agree to wed Sir Harry, then he planned to have her arrested. Either way the bitch wouldn't have long to live. Then, once Mirella was dead, they would have the jewels her mother had left her.

Samantha's scowl deepened as she saw Jason fetch Mirella a glass of punch and bend over her solicitously. It just wasn't fair! He should belong to *her*, not to that whey-faced chit!

Impatience swept Samantha. By God, she couldn't wait another day to get her revenge! Suddenly her lips curled into a crafty smile. Why was she standing here like a helpless ninny when she could be having a little fun stirring up trouble between those two? Ah, yes, how amusing it would be to tell Jason a pack of lies, and then stand back and watch the fireworks!

Restlessly she minced back and forth across the rear of the drawing room, awaiting her chance. To her delight, it came within a matter of minutes.

When Jason happened to spot her through the

crush of guests, she batted her lashes at him in blatant flirtation. The good humor vanished from his face, and his eyes narrowed, his mouth tightening. He said something to Mirella, who shook her head in response, turning to stare in the redhead's direction. Then he left Mirella to thrust his way through the crowd until he reached Samantha's side.

"I understand you weren't invited," Jason said, his tone menacing but low, so that no one around them could hear. "I suggest you leave before I'm forced to throw you out."

Samantha arched her eyebrows. "Why, I'm doing you a favor by being here tonight. I have some information that should be of interest to you."

He gave a scornful laugh. "Is that so? Too bad, for I've little stomach for gossip. Come along, 'tis time I saw your backside heading out the door."

He grasped her elbow and propelled her into the entrance hall. Samantha felt anger churn inside her. Who was he to treat her with such obvious distaste, as if she were a darky trying to hobnob with her superiors? She was just as good as he was, and she certainly was better than that low-class Mirella!

"Let me go!" Samantha hissed, jerking her arm free. Seeing several guests stare at them curiously, she lowered her voice to a conspiratorial whisper. "I think you'll want to hear me out. You see, what I have to say concerns your dear *cousin* Mirella."

"What the hell is that supposed to mean?"

"Find us a private spot to talk, and I'll tell you."

He frowned, clearly torn between evicting her and listening to her. "I'll give you five minutes," he growled, turning on his heel and stalking toward the library.

She followed, a victorious smile curving her lips. So far, so good. She had gambled successfully that the mention of that slut's name would pique his interest. Now to spin a lie that would have the two lovers at each other's throats. . . .

As she strolled into the quiet, book-lined room, Jason closed the double doors behind her. He was annoyed that Samantha had dared come here tonight. She was a vindictive woman, and the fact that she had taken up with Sir Harry Weston only illustrated how low she had fallen. That was precisely why he wanted her out of his house; he suspected she was up to no good, and he wouldn't abide anyone hurting Mirella.

Mirella. Jason felt a rush of tenderness as he thought of her. Over the past weeks his love had grown, intensifying his need for her until he felt on the brink of making a commitment. Yet the fear of betrayal was still there. It prevented him from speaking his feelings; it kept him from trusting her enough to ask her to share the rest of her life with him.

He perched an elbow on the mantelpiece, watching as Samantha prowled around the library, touching a book here, a silver inkwell there, as if she lusted for his possessions. Again, he felt a flash of irritation. All he wanted was to return to Mirella, and instead he had to deal with this bitch.

"Out with it, Samantha," he ordered. "What exactly is this nonsense you feel you must tell me about Mirella?"

"Nonsense?" She raised her eyebrows. "I'd hardly call it that. Why, don't you remember what tomorrow is?"

"I'm in no mood for guessing games, so say what's on your mind and be done with it."

She sent him a look of genuine surprise. "You really don't know? Didn't Mirella tell you who visited her while you were away in Williamsburg?"

"No."

"How very interesting," Samantha drawled. " 'Twas Sir Harry who came to see her—to give her an ultimatum."

Jason's eyes narrowed. "What ultimatum?"

"He said she'd have until tomorrow, the first of February, to decide between marriage to him or punishment for attempted murder. And this morning she sent him a note with her answer." Her lips formed a gloating smile. "I just couldn't wait to see your face when you found out she's decided to leave you and marry him."

"Don't be absurd," Jason scoffed. "Even you ought to be able to dream up a more convincing lie than that one." Yet he couldn't help feeling the faintest prickling of unease.

"What makes you so sure it isn't the truth?" Samantha said.

"Because Mirella hates him—enough to have used a knife on him. And she knows he can't have her imprisoned, not so long as I stand as witness that she acted in self-defense."

"Mayhap 'twas the money, then, that attracted her."

"What money?"

"Well, you see, when Mirella spurned him before, Sir Harry lacked wealth. But in the meantime, he's had a few successful business deals which have made

472

him a rich man." Samantha flipped idly through the pages of a leather-bound volume before setting it down. "Ah, yes," she sighed, " 'tis strange how a little gold can make a woman change her mind. *You've* exhibited no intention of marrying her, so who can blame her for grabbing at this opportunity? And don't forget, Sir Harry also is offering her a chance to return to England."

It wasn't true, Jason assured himself. It *couldn't* be, not considering their closeness these past two weeks. Yet why had Mirella kept silent about Sir Harry's visit? Because Sir Harry's new-found wealth made him more attractive than he'd been in the past? Jason's blood ran cold. Now that Mirella understood why he himself had no interest in marriage, it made sense that she would deem him a lost cause. Yet if she were bent on acquiring a husband, why hadn't she turned her attentions on Troy or another wealthy planter? Unless maybe she really *was* homesick. Now that he thought on it, hadn't there been times in the past few days when she had seemed preoccupied, dreamy and yet sad, as if she pondered some secret prospect? When he had questioned her about it, she had offered him vague excuses which at the time he had dismissed with a shrug. Now, though, he wondered. Could it be she had been longing to return to the home she had grown up in back in England, the home Sir Harry owned?

But still Jason resisted believing Samantha spoke the truth. Mirella loved him, for God's sake! She wouldn't leave him! Yet Elizabeth, too, had spoken false words of love. . . .

"If Sir Harry is so rich, why don't you want to

marry him yourself?" he demanded skeptically.

Samantha sent him a look of pure hatred. "Because I derive great pleasure out of seeing you spurned. 'Tis worth any price to watch you get a taste of your own medicine."

A sudden fury swept through Jason, and he surged forward to seize her by the shoulders. "You goddamned bitch!" he snarled, giving her a violent shake. "You're lying to me! Admit it!"

"If you don't believe me, then why don't you ask Mirella yourself?" she sneered.

"By damn," he swore through gritted teeth, "I don't want to hear any more of your vicious falsehoods!"

"Then just ask Mirella," she taunted again.

He fought an urge to wring her neck as an ancient Greek would slay the bearer of bad tidings. Flinging her from him, he turned on his heel and strode across the room to wrench open the double doors. His entire being was focused on escaping the confines of the library, as if that action somehow would mend his shaken faith in Mirella.

He emerged into the entrance hall and took a deep breath to calm himself. Only dimly did he understand that it wasn't really Samantha he was angry at; his rage stemmed from the frustration he felt at doubting Mirella when he had just begun to learn to trust her.

A flash of blue-gray silk at the top of the stairs caught his eye. Mirella. By damn, he had to reassure himself—now.

Oblivious to the merriment emanating from the drawing room, Jason veered toward the staircase, his impatient strides taking the steps two at a time.

* * *

Mirella entered her bedchamber, relieved to have escaped the crowd for at least a few moments. When she had dressed earlier, she had been so distracted that she had forgotten to pin on her cameo.

At least that was the excuse she had given Troy for slipping upstairs. The real reason was that it was difficult to maintain a pretense of cheer when all she could think of was her impending departure.

Mirella walked to her dressing table against the far wall, wondering where Jason had disappeared to. He had insisted on expelling Samantha when the woman had shown up uninvited. But then he hadn't returned to the party.

Suddenly the bedchamber door burst open. Mirella whirled around to see Jason walk inside. He stopped in the middle of the room, hands astraddle his hips.

A soft smile of greeting lit her face. "Why, Jason, there you are! I'd wondered—"

"Are you leaving me?" he demanded abruptly.

The warmth drained from her body. For the first time, she noticed his challenging stance and grim expression. Her mind spun in shock. How had he discovered her plans? She had confided in no one! Or was he just guessing?

"Why,"—she had to swallow to ease the dryness in her throat—"why would you think I'd do a thing like that?"

"Just answer the question. Are you or are you not planning to leave here?"

Mirella stared at him, her brain racing frantically. If she said "yes," he would try to stop her, and she couldn't risk having him guess she was pregnant.

Though he would not marry her, she had little doubt he would want to claim his bastard heir. But no child of hers would go through life bearing the stigma of illegitimacy, not if she could help it!

"No, you are mistaken," she said firmly.

"Then why did you hesitate?" A mixture of disbelief and pain cracked the coldness of his expression. "You *are* intending to leave me, aren't you?"

Mirella gripped the dressing table behind her, feeling the edge bite through her heavy skirts into the backs of her thighs. " 'Tisn't true," she said in as calm a voice as she could manage. "I don't know how you've gotten such a notion into your head, but you're wrong. Why should I leave when I have no money, no prospects?"

"But you do have a rich man wanting to take you to wife," Jason said bitterly. "So Samantha was right. You do intend to wed Sir Harry. I can understand a woman coveting a wealthy husband, but why that bastard? The opportunity to return to your home in England cannot possibly be worth that kind of sacrifice."

She gaped at him, bewildered logic resisting the impact of his words. He believed she was spurning him in favor of Sir Harry! It was plain what had happened. That witch Samantha was trying to stir up trouble, and by chance had told a lie which partially coincided with Mirella's plans. Yes, she was leaving but not for the purpose Jason thought!

Resentment gushed through her veins. He was certainly quick to accept Samantha's tale! Except for the baby, she had been completely honest with him these past two weeks. Was it too much to ask him to trust her in return? After she had bared her soul, how could he even think she'd marry another man, let alone Sir Harry?

It infuriated her to see him standing there in the middle of her chamber, so haughty and knowing, like a judge condemning her without regard for her testimony.

Seized by an overwhelming need to vent the volcanic rage burning inside her, Mirella groped the dressing table behind her. Her fingers closed around an object, and without thinking, she hurled it at his accusing face.

Jason ducked in swift reaction. The missile sailed past him and struck the heavy wooden armoire with a sharp *crack*.

"You little witch," he snarled.

But Mirella wasn't listening. She was staring, wide-eyed, at the article lying in pieces on the carpet. Some capricious twist of fate had caused her to throw her mother's cameo, and now she had ruined it!

The realization distracted her from her anger. Uttering a cry of distress, she brushed past Jason, sinking to her knees beside the damaged brooch. To her relief, she saw that the onyx face was unblemished, the classically beautiful profile as perfect as ever.

But the back had fallen off, and beside it on the rug was a tiny square of paper. Picking up the yellowed scrap, Mirella unfolded it to discover a woman's cramped handwriting which, even in the dim light, took only a moment to identify.

All this time, the cameo had concealed a note written by her mother!

Mirella's eyes returned to the broken halves as a faint memory washed over her. She was a child of eight or nine, standing in her mother's bedchamber, enthralled by the winking strands of rubies and diamonds and sapphires Caroline Weston searched through, trying to decide which jewels to wear to a party that evening. It was then that her mother had dug deep into the casket of gems, bringing forth the cameo. And she had shown her daughter how to open the back to find the secret compartment within. . . .

Until this moment, Mirella had completely forgotten about the hidden niche.

"Dammit, Mirella! Have you nothing to say? Or is a piece of jewelry more important to you than our relationship?"

Jason's bitter voice intruded, but Mirella was too anxious to read the note to reply. Rising, she carried the paper to the mantel, where a candle cast light sufficient for her to make out the small spidery script.

My dearest Mirella, I am hoping you will remember the night I showed you the secret back to this cameo. Would that I could trust my husband and not have to resort to this ugly subterfuge!

With the aid of a family friend, I have secreted my jewels in a vault at the Bank of England to be held in trust as your dowry. Andrew, poor dear, knows naught of what I have done; to avoid a confrontation, I have let him think the gems were sold to help pay our mounting debts. The jewels were my personal property, bought and paid for by my father, who saw Andrew's shortcoming at the time of our betrothal and tried to warn me against marrying him. Upon failing to change my mind, my father was wise enough to require Andrew to sign a paper relinquishing all claim to the jewels.

'Tis for your sake I do this, Mirella. But please, do not be overly harsh in judging your father. He is not a bad man; he is merely weak, finding it impossible to resist the lure of the gaming tables.

When—if—you discover this letter, I beg you, do not show it to your father, else he may try to convince you to give him the jewels. I understand now, as I never did in my youth, the difficulty in curing a man of this hunger for gambling.

In the event you do not find my letter, the bank will notify you of your inheritance on your eighteenth birthday. I would tell you of it now, but you are yet too young to understand and accept the failings of your father.

Remember that despite all else, he loves you, as do I.

The letter was signed by her mother and dated March 2, 1741, the day Mirella had celebrated her tenth birthday. It had been only a few months later that Caroline Weston had fallen from a horse and broken her neck.

"What is that you're reading?"

At the sound of Jason's voice, Mirella looked up from the yellowed paper. "A note from my mother," she replied, her voice faint from shock. " 'Twas hidden inside the cameo."

Automatically she handed it to him, turning to stare into the writhing flames of the fire. A deep sense of disbelief gripped her. She was an heiress! No longer did she need worry about how she would support her child! The revelation was like a dream come true.

Yet why hadn't she been contacted by the bank? Had her father somehow discovered her inheritance and then gambled it away? There was another possibility, one which she thought more plausible. What if the bank had sent a letter and Sir Harry had intercepted it? That would explain his interest in marrying her which, suspiciously enough, had begun not long after her eighteenth birthday.

Eagerly she turned to Jason to tell him her theory, but he spoke before she could, his voice distant and cold.

"So 'twould appear you're a wealthy woman, Mirella. Does this mean that you'll now jilt Sir Harry as you've already done me?"

His words pierced her like a spear. In her excitement at finding the letter, she had forgotten their earlier argument, and now she felt her resentment flooding back.

"I'll not jilt him because I was never intending to wed him in the first place," she snapped. " 'Twas all a lie dreamed up by Samantha—and you were fool enough to believe her."

"Is that so? Methinks 'tis *you* who alters the truth to suit your purpose." Jason gave a harsh laugh. "And if I was a fool in believing anything 'twas in thinking you were no mercenary. But all your talk of love was only meant to snare you a rich husband, wasn't it,

Mirella? Now that you have a fortune, you have no need for a man. I only pray your jewels will be sufficient to keep you warm at night."

The letter left his fingers, fluttering dangerously close to the fire. With a small cry, Mirella bent to snatch the precious scrap of paper, snuffing with her bare hand the tiny flames that licked the edge. Didn't Jason understand that the note itself was as important to her as the message it contained—that this was the last link she had to her mother?

She looked up, bitter words forming on her tongue, but he was already striding out the open door. The futility of going after him struck her in full force. He wouldn't believe a word she said, so what good would arguing do? Since she was preparing to leave anyway, did it really matter what he thought of her? At least if he hated her, he wouldn't follow and try to bring her back here.

Yet though logic reassured her, her heart felt as if it had been torn in two.

Samantha shrank into the shadows outside the door, watching as Jason disappeared down the stairs. She had crept up here to listen to him and Mirella, and the ensuing quarrel had been highly entertaining.

What luck that she had thought up that tale about Mirella abandoning him for Sir Harry! Apparently the chit had some secret scheme to leave here, and when Jason had caught on to the fact that she was hiding something, it had only served to assure him of Mirella's guilt.

Suddenly Samantha's smirk was replaced by a scowl. Mirella now knew of the jewels her mother had

481

left her, and that could only mean trouble. Of all times for that bitch to discover the truth!

Like it or not, Samantha concluded, she would have to return to her father's plantation immediately and notify Sir Harry of this new development so that he could decide whether or not to change their plans for tomorrow.

She snuck around the open door, heading for the stairs and hoping that the party sounds from the drawing room would mask any rustling of her gown. Sir Harry wouldn't be pleased to hear the news. That was precisely why Samantha had no intention of telling him she had been responsible for instigating the argument which had led to Mirella breaking the cameo and thus finding the letter. What the man didn't know couldn't hurt him . . . or her.

Mirella mounted the stairs with slow, tired steps. The candle in her hand made shadows snake in strange patterns over the walls, but she paid little heed to her surroundings. All she could think of was that the party was finally over, and so were her last moments with Jason, filled with chilly indifference though they had been.

She should be glad to leave, she told herself fiercely. If she had any doubts over parting with him, their quarrel should have put them to rest. Granted, Jason had had an unpleasant experience with marriage, but still she couldn't help feeling the pain of his rejection. If more than his pride had been hurt when he'd thought she'd meant to wed another man, he would have countered the offer with one of his own. Yet all he had done was rant at her and then storm out of the room.

Mirella had reached her bedchamber door when she heard a light patter of footsteps racing up the stairs. Turning, she saw a small black boy, whose face she didn't recognize, coming toward her.

"Ma'am?" he queried breathlessly. "You be Miss Mirella?"

At her nod, he thrust a piece of paper into her hand and then sped back down the staircase. Shrugging at his odd behavior, she raised the note to the light of her candle.

It was a man's handwriting, bold and dark, and it read:

Mirella, I must speak to you away from prying eyes. Can you come meet me down by the river immediately? 'Tis a matter of grave importance.
Troy

What could Troy have to tell her that was so vital it couldn't wait until morning? Mirella wondered. He certainly had given no hint at the party that he harbored any secret. Yet there was no doubt that she would respond to the summons. Earlier, she had been so wrapped up in maintaining a happy façade that she hadn't taken him aside to tell him she was leaving. And considering the friend he had been, she at least owed him that much. She might also prevail upon him to loan her enough to tide her over until she could claim her inheritance.

She slipped into her bedchamber to exchange her silk gown for one of wool, moving quietly so as not to waken Pandora. The girl had relinquished her own room to several ladies who were staying overnight.

Though common sense told Mirella she should stay until morning since Jason knew she was leaving anyway, she did not wish to see him again. Therefore, she would depart directly after speaking to Troy.

Into her pocket went the pieces of the cameo along with her mother's letter. Then she donned a warm mantle and tiptoed over to the bed to gaze down at the girl whose golden hair tumbled over the pillow. Sadness squeezed Mirella's heart. She would miss Pandora, and all the other people here who had become so very dear to her.

She took one last look at the familiar surroundings, then left the room. Creeping downstairs, she blew out her candle and left it on a table in the darkened drawing room.

Outside, a light snow was falling. She drew her hood over her hair and headed down the slope to the river beyond, resisting the impulse to look back, to give in to the tears that pricked her eyes. It was better to concentrate instead on the frosty bite of the wind and the squeak of her shoes on the snow.

The embankment was empty and silent, and a thin coating of white covered the ice, which ended several hundred yards out into the river.

"Troy?" Mirella called softly, peering into the gloom in either direction. When there was no reply, she stepped toward the tangle of black forest, keeping to the narrow path that edged the water. Against the inky murk, she could see nothing but the faint outline of trees and bushes.

The trail was slippery beneath her feet. What if Troy had fallen? She had a sudden vision of him lying out there, hurt or unconscious, and concern induced her to venture deeper into the woods.

"Troy?" she said again. "Are you there?"

Suddenly she heard a faint scratch, and then a dim light bloomed a few feet ahead. A lantern lifted to illuminate a man's face.

Her brief smile of relief vanished.

It wasn't Troy who awaited her. It was Sir Harry. And beside him, smirking in triumph, was Samantha.

Chapter Twenty-seven

Jason paced the length of his bedchamber, brooding on the thoughts that had plagued him since his quarrel with Mirella. Now that his bitter fury had cooled, he couldn't escape the nagging feeling that he had misjudged her. He was uncomfortably aware that he had been willing to accept Samantha's tale without even listening to Mirella's side. Had he been looking for a way to prove to himself that Mirella was as untrustworthy as other women? Had he wanted an excuse to avoid taking the risk of committing his life to her?

Yet he hadn't misinterpreted her hesitation when he'd asked her if she was leaving him. If he could believe her statement that she wasn't wedding Sir Harry, then did she plan to run away for some other reason? Perhaps because she had decided there was no future to their relationship?

Abruptly Jason wrenched open the door and strode across the entrance hall to the portrait of Elizabeth. The house was silent as a tomb. A lone candle flickered in a wall sconce, casting a pale light on the painting before him.

He saw a woman who was beautiful on the surface yet an empty shell within. Mirella had thought he was still obsessed with Elizabeth, and in a twisted way, she was right. He was obsessed in the sense that his wife had taught him never to have faith in a woman.

With sudden, blinding insight, he realized that even from the grave Elizabeth had been manipulating him. She would have loved knowing she had wielded such power over him for so many years.

But no longer. It was time to bury the ghosts of the past, and turn his mind to the future . . . a future in which he desperately wanted Mirella to play a part.

Reaching up, Jason lifted the portrait from its nail and then set it in a corner, facing the wall. Tomorrow he would have it stored in the attic where it belonged. He no longer needed a reminder of his youthful folly.

Too anxious to speak to Mirella to wait until morning, he lit a taper and then mounted the stairs. The callous way he'd treated her had probably strengthened her resolve to leave him. He only hoped it wasn't too late to convince her to change her mind.

In the upstairs hall he heard the muffled rumble of snoring emanating from one of the guest rooms. Quietly he eased open the door to Mirella's chamber and stepped inside to let the circle of candlelight shine on the bed. But only Pandora slept there.

Apprehension clenched his gut. Where was Mirella? Had she already left? Had he made her despise him so much that she couldn't bear another moment in his house?

Suddenly Jason saw a slip of paper lying on the rug. He picked it up and scanned the three lines on it, staring at the name 'Troy' scrawled across the bottom.

His expression grew grimmer. Dropping the note, he strode out the door, so swiftly that his candle sputtered and died.

Mirella blinked away the icy flakes that clung to her lashes. Before her on the snowy path stood not the man she had expected to meet but Sir Harry and Samantha. It took only an instant for her to realize why. That note had been forged. Having never seen Troy's handwriting before, she'd had no reason to doubt its authenticity.

Warily she watched Sir Harry take a step toward her, steeling herself to run if he came too close. Whatever game he played could only spell trouble.

"How pleasant to see you again, dear cousin," he said, sweeping back his dark cloak with a flourish as he gave her a mocking bow.

"What do you want?"

"What I've always wanted—your hand in marriage."

His blunt declaration made anger stir in her, though she resisted a rash impulse to blurt out that she knew the truth. Yes, it was greed that made him so persistent in his suit. But telling him so would only infuriate him, and she couldn't take that risk.

"You gave me until the first of February to make up my mind," she stalled.

He smiled in a way that made her flesh crawl. "If I may point out, my dear, 'tis after midnight, and therefore already the date in question."

"You'll have my decision with the light of day, and not a moment earlier."

"Why quibble over such trivial matters?" Samantha broke in, rubbing her gloved hands impatiently. "Mirella, he knows about you finding your mother's letter. Why else do you suppose we saw a need to lure you out here in the middle of such a dreary night?"

Mirella stared, trying to make sense of the woman's words. Then realization struck, and wrath rose within her. "You were listening at my bedchamber door, weren't you?" she said accusingly. "I should have known you'd want to witness the fruit of your meddling. Yet perhaps I owe you a debt of gratitude. Were it not for the lie you told Jason, I would never have thrown the cameo at him and thereby discovered the letter."

Sir Harry's expression of sardonic amusement evaporated as he turned to Samantha. "What is this about a lie? You never mentioned that part to me."

"She's making it all up," Samantha blustered. "She cannot hold me to blame for her quarrels with Jason."

He set down the lantern on the snow and advanced on her, his face menacing. "You bitch! 'Tis *your* fault she knows about the jewels, is it not?" Samantha backed up but he easily seized the front of her mantle. "Tell me the truth!" he growled.

Mirella began to edge away from them, taking advantage of this timely distraction. Giving them one last look, she pivoted, lifting her skirts as she scurried down the path, intent on reaching safety. The ground was slippery, and she had to concentrate to keep from falling. She hadn't gone more than a few steps when she heard Samantha cry out, "She's getting away, you fool! After her!"

Feet pounded through the woods behind Mirella.

Feeling a surge of fear, she recklessly increased her pace. Her hood flew back to expose her head to the frosty wind. Snowflakes blinded her eyes, and frigid spears pierced her chest with every breath she took.

Yet she managed to maintain her lead. Ahead, she glimpsed an almost imperceptible lightening of the black night. It was a break in the trees, the sloping lawn that led to Jason's house.

Hope soared within her. Then abruptly, fate intervened with a vengeance.

Her heel hit an icy patch, and she lost her balance, tumbling onto her posterior with a painful thump. Her palms spread over the snow to propel her up again, but her advantage was gone. No sooner did she scramble to her feet than Sir Harry caught up to her, Samantha trailing in his wake, carrying the lantern.

He grasped Mirella with vicious strength and thrust her against the trunk of a tree. "Bitch!" he grunted, breathing heavily. "You'll pay for that!"

Crack! His bare hand struck her cheek.

The stinging slap ignited rage in Mirella. "I'll never marry you, do you hear?" she blazed, fighting against his grip. "You'll not steal my inheritance!"

"Those jewels are mine!" he snarled. "They're a rightful part of my estate, and I'll have them back if it's the last thing I ever do."

"You can't force me to take my vows with you!"

"We'll see about that," he said grimly. " 'Tis regretful you had to discover the truth but it merely presents minor complications. It so happens I know of a clergyman who is inordinately fond of gold. He can be persuaded to look the other way if the bride be unwilling."

Mirella felt a sinking sensation in the pit of her stomach, but she refused to let him see her fear. "If you dare try such a scheme, you'll have Jason to answer to."

"Ah, your champion," Samantha jeered. "Have you so quickly forgotten his quarrel with you? When he discovers you gone, he will only think you've left to lay claim to your fortune."

"Yes, this time there will be no escaping me," Sir Harry said with an evil chuckle. "Before a score of hours have passed, you will be my wife."

His mouth twisting into a lecherous leer, he ground his lower body against hers. Revulsion bubbled up in Mirella, emerging from her lips in a scream.

That earned her another slap. "Shut up, bitch!" Sir Harry snapped.

Whipping out a handkerchief, he stuffed it between her teeth, knotting it tightly behind her head. Tears sprang to her eyes as his action wrenched a few hairs from her scalp. Then he seized her arm and jerked her down the path.

Mirella stumbled along beside him, feeling as if the jaws of a trap were closing about her. In the light of Samantha's lantern snowflakes glistened, still falling softly, obliterating their tracks. Even if Jason were to discover her absence and come after her, Mirella thought miserably, by morning there would be no trace left of their passing. And after their bitter parting it was unlikely he would search for her. He would only think she had gone to recover her jewels.

Despair gripped her heart, as dark and cold as the surrounding woods. Through the trees to her left, she could see a pale glimmer which was the frozen edge of the James. There was no escape that way. Her only sanctuary was the house behind them, and they were moving farther away from there the deeper they walked into the forest.

Sir Harry's hands bit cruelly into her arm as he yanked her along the slippery trail. The night was silent except for the scuffling of their feet and the rasp of their breathing. Finally they arrived at a small clearing alongside the river, where two horses awaited them.

"You'll ride with me," Sir Harry grunted, hauling her over to a piebald mare.

Suddenly a twig snapped behind them, and a familiar voice rang through the air. "Halt right where you are," Jason ordered. "You're not going anywhere."

Her captor spun to face him, his cloak flapping about his legs. Abruptly he snatched Mirella by the waist to heave her astride the horse. Realizing his intent, she raked her nails down his cheeks.

As Sir Henry screamed a curse at her, Jason tackled him. Mirella stumbled backward, tearing off her gag as she watched the two men grapple on the snow. Though Jason was the taller and more muscular of the two, Sir Harry had the strength of a bull. But slowly Jason was getting the better of him.

Then, to her alarm, she saw Samantha creeping up from behind them, gripping the lantern as a weapon, raising it high with both hands to strike Jason over the head. . . .

Mirella sprang forward to knock the woman aside. The lamp tumbled to the ground. There was a tinkling sound as the glass chimney broke, and suddenly flames shot upward.

She saw to her horror that hot oil had spattered Sir Harry, causing his cloak to catch fire. Jason leaped back in time to escape all but a few sparks.

Uttering a howl of animal pain, Sir Harry tore unsuccessfully at the fastening of the blazing garment. Then he whirled to run blindly toward the river, slipping and sliding down the embankment, a screaming pillar of flame.

Jason raced after him, and Mirella was close on his heels. Ahead of them, Sir Harry dashed across the snow-covered ice, his shrieks of agony echoing through the air.

Then there was an ominous crack, and his burning body plunged from sight, into the frigid waters.

Jason stopped short, and when Mirella caught up to him, she panted, "Dear God, Jason, we must pull him out!"

"There is naught we can do to save him," he said gently. " 'Twas merciful he fell into the river."

She realized he spoke the truth. Yet the horror of what had happened still sickened her. Pressing her face against his chest, she tried to forget those hideous cries of suffering. It was not a way she would have wanted even her worst enemy to die.

"Come," Jason murmured, "we must return to shore before the ice gives way again."

Numbly Mirella let him lead her toward land. When they reached the clearing, only one horse remained of the two that had been there earlier.

"Samantha is gone," she stated.

"And good riddance," Jason said. "I would venture to guess she's learned her lesson about seeking revenge." His hands cradled Mirella's face as he added softly, "And about never again conspiring to drive us apart."

She caught her breath, trying to read his expression through the darkness. "Then you realize she lied about me wanting to wed Sir Harry?"

"Yes, I arrived at that conclusion after my anger had cooled. But when I went upstairs to offer you my apology I found that note, and knowing the handwriting wasn't Troy's, I came after you. Thank God I got here in time!"

Jason drew her into a tight embrace, dipping his head to brush his mouth against hers. Their cold lips swiftly warmed under the influence of the kiss. Desire drove away the chill of the night. She felt weak and shaky from what had happened, the disaster intensifying her feelings. Desperate with need, she clung to him, losing herself in his familiar taste and scent.

"Mirella . . . Mirella . . ." he groaned, burying his face in her hair. "Don't ever leave me . . . promise you won't."

His request brought her crashing back to earth. She yearned to comply, but how could she make such a vow when she had their baby's future to consider?

Snowflakes struck her cheeks like icy pinpricks. "Nay . . . I cannot," she moaned, wrenching herself from him, her heart twisting in anguish.

He was silent for a moment. Then he said quietly, "And if I told you I love you, that I want to marry you?"

She had so longed to hear him say those words that for an instant she was afraid she had dreamed them. "You really love me?" she whispered.

"Yes." The avowal was deep with yearning, yet contained an undercurrent of something taut and troubled, as if he feared she might reject him.

Tenderness flowed through her. Did he think she might still leave him, even knowing what he felt for her? Awash with emotion, Mirella ran to him. "Oh, Jason, I love you so very much!"

His arms tightened around her, and their lips fused in a kiss that was ripe with the passion of mutual surrender, both of them trembling with the need to express the depth of their feelings.

Later she would tell him about the child that grew in her, but for now, Jason was her only reality. She had found her destiny.